THE RAVEN WARRIOR

Lugh reeled groggily, his temple hot with pain. He saw his attacker, the woman warrior Morrigan, standing over him, arms raised, black cloak furled about her like great wings. Her head was forward, the blue glass beads of her eyes fixed on him greedily.

He tried to get his weapons up in defense, but she struck too swiftly. With a hoarse cry that was both hiss and shriek at once, she threw herself upon him. Her weight drove him back against the hearth. But as he fell, he realized with horror that it was now no human being who was upon him, but a giant raven, bigger than a hawk, black as a moonless sea.

The bird was maddened by bloodlust, fighting to strike at his bleeding wound, raking at his chest with its great claws, beating him about the head with heavy wings that raised a deafening thunder in his ears. . . .

THE RIDERS OF
THE
SIDHE

Kenneth C. Flint

BANTAM BOOKS

TORONTO • NEW YORK • LONDON • SYDNEY • AUCKLAND

THE RIDERS OF THE SIDHE
A Bantam Book / June 1984

ISBN 0-553-24175-3

Published simultaneously in the United States and Canada

Bantam Books are published by Bantam Books, Inc. Its trade-
mark, consisting of the words "Bantam Books" and the por-
trayal of a rooster, is Registered in U.S. Patent and Trademark
Office and in other countries. Marca Registrada. Bantam
Books, Inc., 666 Fifth Avenue, New York, New York 10103.

PRINTED IN THE UNITED STATES OF AMERICA

H   0 9 8 7 6 5 4

THE RIDERS OF
THE
SIDHE

BOOK I

THE SEA GOD

I

THE ATTACK

THE SHIPS SWEPT in suddenly from the silver mists which clung to the edge of the northern sea.

They were beautiful ships, their soft, glowing sails extended like great wings, swooping gracefully toward the island's rocky coast. But it was the hard, bright edge of death that they carried within them.

The grey-uniformed warriors who filled their decks looked up in cold disdain at the towering cliffs and the line of fortress walls along their top. Swiftly, skillfully, without a flicker of care in any of the hardened faces, they readied ropes and grapples and weapons for their attack.

High above them, the alarm had already been raised.

Warriors swarmed within the walls of the clifftop fortress. Defensive points were manned. Captains shouted orders to the companies who formed in the training grounds before the central keep.

From an upper window of the keep, a dark-haired woman watched the activities with concern. Her gaze often lifted to the sea beyond, where the sleek vessels soared in as unwaveringly as hawks descending upon prey.

Though a young woman yet, still slim and vigorous, grey showed in the billowing blackness of her hair, and lines aged the smooth, even-featured face. The days of Taillta's life had not been easy. But she knew, as she watched the ships come, that the hardest ones lay still ahead of her.

The commander of her companies entered the room behind her.

"My Queen, there are a score of large boats in the fleet," he announced. "We estimate at least a thousand men!"

She turned to him, regarding him with a calmly appraising eye as she asked bluntly:

"Can you withstand them, Cecht?"

She searched for any sign of uncertainty, any hint of weakness, but the commander only smiled grimly as he replied.

"My Queen, we've waited on this island for fifteen years, guarding this lonely fortress, watching, our weapons always ready. We've prayed to every god for a chance to fight again. There's not a band of fighting men who'd have a better chance of holding them than we!"

She nodded, satisfied.

"Who is it coming against us?" she demanded. "What is their look?"

"The ships and sails are like none I've seen before. The hulls are as shiny and black as the hardest bog-oak. The sails stay full and steady regardless of the winds."

"And the men?"

"Their appearance is just as strange to me. They're big-bodied, square, hard-looking men, dressed in like tunics and trousers of smooth grey."

"There's no doubt of it, then," she told him with a chill certainty. "We have been found by them at last!"

"How can that be?" asked Cecht in surprise. "I've never seen any warriors of theirs who looked or dressed as these do."

"You've seen only their garrison troops. The worst of them. These are the household troops of Balor himself. He must know!"

She thought a moment, deepening those lines which fear of this day had etched into her face. Then she spoke, harshly and without compromise:

"Cecht, they'll not be easy to stop," she said. In fact, she knew that these attackers could not be stopped at all. But she had no wish to wound her commander's pride. "You must make this as hard as you can for them. It may mean the death of every one of us—every warrior, woman, child—but we must hold them as long as we can!"

"We know, my Queen," he replied. "We've always known."

She smiled at him gently, sadly, placing a hand lightly upon his arm.

"Loyal Cecht," she said. "It's glad I've been to have you beside me until this day. And it's glad I am to have you with me now."

He nodded, understanding the depth of feeling behind the simple words. She dropped her hand and added in a brisk voice:

"Go now. See to the defense. And have the boy sent up to me."

He hurried from the room and she turned back to the window. The ships were already against the cliffs below, out of her sight. But she knew that their warriors were swarming up the treacherous cliff-face without fear or hesitation. It would be only moments before they would come against the walls.

"Taillta," said a voice behind her.

She turned to face a boy, tall for his fifteen years, fair-haired and slender, and with a fine, long nose and boldly jutting chin that age would chisel to clean, sharp handsomeness. He was breathless with his run to her and vibrating with an excitement he could not totally control.

"Taillta . . . those ships . . . who are they? What's happening?"

"They're coming to attack us, Lugh," she answered bluntly.

"Attack!" The idea startled him at first. Then a look of determination hardened his young face. "I've got to join the companies," he said firmly.

He moved swiftly to the weapons hung along the walls and seized a longsword, pulling it from its brackets. But Taillta moved up behind him, gripping his shoulder.

"Lugh, you can't join them. You've got to leave."

He whirled to her, his look confused.

"Leave? What do you mean? I've got to fight!"

He was aroused by the expectation of battle. The fire of it ruddied his pale skin, lit his grey eyes. His muscles were taut with the need to act, his legs set solidly, his sword gripped tight. She saw all of it and she felt a sudden stabbing of regret. She had hoped that the need for this would never come. He had been a poet, a craftsman, a lover of the peaceful ways taught him. A mild boy, safe here from the worries of the world.

Harshly she reminded herself that she knew this day would

come. She fought back the sorrow which had threatened to overwhelm her usual control.

She moved close to him and stroked his beardless cheek lightly. He realized that her eyes were full of tears.

"Taillta," he said, concerned now for her. "I didn't think of you. Are you afraid?"

"It's not fear that's made my sorrow. It's regret for you," she replied evenly, her rigid control re-established. "Lugh, you will not be fighting here. You must run... and quickly!"

"Run from this?" he asked, struggling to understand. "You'll need every man..."

She seized his shoulders in a tight grip.

"Listen! Listen to me! I know what we're facing here. There's nothing we can do to hold these men for long. You have to get away!"

"But, what about the rest of you?"

"The rest, all of us, are here only to protect you. All of these years, our only purpose has been to keep you safe!"

"Why?" he asked again, more urgently. Things were happening so fast he couldn't think. There were too many questions.

"I cannot tell you. And there is no more time for talk. You only need to know that we have one aim here... to keep you alive. You must believe me and you must leave! If you don't, our lives here have been meaningless."

A sudden, burning wind blasted through the open windows of the hall. The force of it rocked the entire building. The roar of it deafened them like the combined fury of a score of gales.

Taillta and Lugh recovered from the shock and ran to the windows whose shutters had been torn away by the power of the blast. Below them the thick outer wall of the fortress was torn open, gaping like a jagged wound. The rubble of the massive stones was scattered about the inner court. Half the men of the companies were scattered too, killed or wounded by debris, stunned by the blast, buried in piles of splintered rock. The rest were trying gallantly to reform before a stream of heavily armed warriors already pouring through the opening.

"How could they tear down the wall so quickly?" Lugh asked, astounded by the force evidenced below. "And who are those warriors?" There was something about them that stirred vague, unsettling memories in him.

But Taillta gave him no chance to think.

"There's no more time!" she cried, seizing his arm. "Come with me!"

She dragged him from the hall and then ran ahead, urging him on. Uncertainly he followed her out of the keep and onto the upper parapet of the walls. Below them the attackers were flooding into the fortress grounds. The two passed defenders who were hurling spears and fragments of broken wall down on the advancing grey-clad soldiers.

By one section of the outer wall Lugh and Taillta stopped. Not far ahead their warriors held a stairway against the enemy swarming upward from the breached section. They were determined, sacrificing themselves valiantly to keep back the overwhelming numbers below, but they couldn't hold long.

Taillta turned a rusted torch socket in the outer wall and pressed inward on a massive stone. It swung back, revealing a staircase spiraling down, through the thickness of the wall.

"This passage leads down to a sheltered cove beyond the point!" she shouted to him above the battle's din. "A boat is hidden there. Take it and sail away. You should be unseen. Go east to Manannan's Isle. You'll find help there!"

He listened to her words in disbelief.

"You really believe I can run away from this? Leave my friends? Leave you, my aunt? My only family?"

"Lugh, I am no aunt to you," she told him. "You are not one of us. I am the daughter of Mac-Erc, the last great High-King of our tribe. Long ago we vowed to protect you, and I have been your foster mother ever since."

He couldn't grasp what she was telling him. This last assault on his sense of reality had dazed him. He shook his head and held on doggedly to the only truth that he did know.

"No ties of blood could make you more a mother to me," he cried. "You're the only family I have. All I love. I won't leave you!"

In despair she searched for the words that would make him go. She could find none.

She moved close and looked sorrowfully into his eyes.

"I love you as well," she told him gently. "And as if you were my son. Remember that."

She swung back her arm and, with a skillfully placed uppercut, dropped Lugh where he stood.

She stooped to check him and nodded with satisfaction. He was unhurt and merely stunned by the blow. Briskly she went to work, calling a nearby warrior to her.

Together they lifted the unconscious boy and started down the narrow stairway. The sound of battle dimmed as they spiraled down, through the wall, into a fissure in the cliff-face below. As they descended, a growing sound of rhythmic thunder echoed up to them. It was the sea.

At the bottom of the stairs a rough-hewn passageway opened onto a tiny scrap of shore, sheltered by a cave worn in the rocks. She and the warrior readied the small boat hidden there, raised its sail and set its tiller to take it toward the east.

The whole cliff above them groaned, the solid rock of it fracturing from another powerful blast. Fine rock showered into the water beyond the cave's mouth. More fell from cracks that opened in the cave itself. The boat had to be gotten clear!

"Hurry!" she said. "Get him in!"

They lifted and rolled the boy into the boat. There was no time for ceremony here. Taillta breathed a silent prayer for his survival as she and the warrior heaved the boat out to sea with all their strength.

It floated out sluggishly, its little headway slowed by the incoming waves. As it hung there, drifting just beyond the cave's protecting overhang, another massive blow struck the cliff above. Larger rocks plunged from the riven face into the sea. Two boulders bracketed the tiny boat, rocking it like a shred of bark.

She drew her breath in fright. It would be caught there. Crushed. He would be killed after all!

"Manannan, help us!" she shouted to the sea. "He's all that's left to us!"

The boat, perhaps pushed by the waves raised by the fallen rocks, moved forward. It cleared the cliff and the sheltering rocks and a breeze caught at it, pulling it out.

Once more the force, like a giant hammer, slammed against the cliff. With protesting rumbles, it shifted in its ancient bed. The whole structure of the cliff-face was battered to a fragile point, ready to collapse. And, under its base, the little cave began to give way from the pressure above. Cracks seamed its water-smoothed sides like a crushed egg. They widened rapidly, broken rock falling from them in a continuous hail.

"My Queen, we must go back!" the warrior cried.

The boat was well away now, skimming out over the waves at an ever-increasing speed. There was no more that she could do.

Abruptly she turned away and ran to the stairway, the warrior close behind. But he didn't make it. With a roar the cave's roof gave way all at once. The avalanche of stone caught him, drove him down and buried him.

She hesitated and looked back, but he was gone. The delay nearly killed her too. For even the stairs began to give way as she started up. The tight spiral seemed to fold down into itself, almost to be sucked down, each step collapsing, crumbling away nearly under her feet.

She ran upward desperately, just ahead of the void which opened below and chewed upward at the stone, threatening to swallow her as well. Her legs ached with the climb, and if she slowed for an instant she knew she would be gone.

Perhaps that was the best way, she thought. To stop and be carried away rather than face the death awaiting her above.

Yet her instinctive need to fight for life pushed her on. She reached the top just ahead of the disintegrating stairs. The entrance to the stairs was still open, but it too was breaking away, slipping out and down. Leaping through it as it fell, she crossed a widening gap to the edge of the surviving parapet walk.

She struck the edge and slid back, hanging on with one hand gripping the ragged stone, the other tangled in a length of trailing cloth. Below her the whole outer curtain of cliff had slid away into the sea, taking the section of wall with it. She dangled above a sheer drop to the water.

With an effort she was able to pull herself up, hauling at the cloth, throwing her other arm forward over the edge. One great heave forward brought her body up onto the walk.

She found herself meeting the gaze of a dead warrior whose jaw gaped neck to nose from a sword cut. It was the cloak about his neck that had saved her.

She scrambled to her feet. The walk was empty save for the other bodies which littered it. But on the inner walls beyond the keep the fight still raged.

Scooping up a dead warrior's fallen sword, she ran toward

the keep, thinking to join the survivors. She reached its doors as one of her men staggered from it with a cry and fell, a spear piercing his back.

Behind him a large attacker clad in the strange, grey uniform emerged. With a tug he pulled his spear from the dead man's body. He looked about for other challengers and saw Taillta. A grim smile stretched the thin, tightly clenched lips. Several other grey-clad soldiers moved out behind him, drawing up on either side of him, bloodied weapons ready.

"Well, woman, I think you're one of them we've been lookin' for," the first one said with satisfaction. "You and the boy. Where's the boy?"

"I'll not be talking to the likes of you with anything but this!" she cried, waving her own sword defiantly.

"You lost your protection with your fortress," he told her. "What can you do?"

"I am the daughter of a High-King," she said, drawing herself up proudly.

He laughed. "And what do you think that'll save you from? Put down that sword and come along with us."

"Careful!" she warned, backing to a corner where none of them could come behind her. "I'm daughter to a king and a warrior as well. You'll not find me so easy to take."

The warrior laughed again. He nodded to one of his men who started toward her.

But he staggered back at once, pierced through the side by a lightning thrust of her slim blade.

Two more moved in, but her skill was a match for theirs and her slender body disguised a powerful strength. She parried the attack of both and wounded one. The other stepped back, his battle-hardened face showing fear.

"We've grown a bit tired of this," the leader said, no longer amused. "We need you to tell us where that boy is!"

"Come and ask me yourself, why don't you then?" she taunted, the sword flicking out at him.

"I will do that," he told her in a hard, chill voice.

He signaled the remaining men and they all moved in around her at once.

In the tiny boat that sailed toward the east, Lugh lay still unconscious.

It might have been his pain and the disturbance created in

his mind at seeing the strange warriors, but something made him dream.

He saw those warriors in another setting. They were moving slowly forward through the doorway of a room behind an immense, black figure that seemed to be something other than a man.

He realized that someone was holding him. Close above him the white, blurred oval of a woman's face seemed to hang, and he felt himself rocking gently.

She was shouting at the men across the room, but he couldn't understand her words. The men came on toward her and great, clutching hands stretched out to him. The glint of bright blades pained his eyes.

Then the men were swept from sight as he was whirled about. A bright square of light jerked into view, then swelled to fill his field of vision as he felt himself flying toward it.

There was a terrifying feeling of weightlessness. He sailed into the square of light and it swallowed him, and then there was light all about him, and he fell. There was a quick image of blue sky above running to sparkling sea below as he began to tumble. And then he rolled up again and a glowing shaft of white seemed to shoot up above him as a tiny square of blackness in its side shrank away to nothingness.

He felt an impact. A double shock as cold and darkness both engulfed him in one heartbeat. He choked as a strange, harsh liquid flooded his mouth and nose, cutting off his breath.

But immediately more hands clutched at him, gripped him, raised him up, and he was free of the clinging wet, emerging into the light again. Something warm enveloped him and he felt himself cradled, rocked, his panic easing. Now he sensed only the rocking and a swelling motion coupled with a rhythmic creaking noise.

Above him he glimpsed the blue sky again. And, as something turned him slowly about, he glimpsed for another instant the towering, glowing thing.

In the sunlight it was a rising pillar of ice, a sharply faceted mountain of glass so brilliant that it burned its image on his unprotected eyes.

Lugh jerked awake. He knew that he had dreamed this many times before. No wonder the grey soldiers had seemed familiar. But who were they? And what was that bright tower?

It suddenly came to him that the sensations of his dream still surrounded him—the swelling motion and the rhythmic creak. He sat upright, and the image from his dream seemed to confront him again!

There was the sparkling sea, the spread of sky. And there, hanging before his sleep-fogged eyes, was a rising column of light.

But this was a different light, warm red and undulating, not a frozen white. And, with that realization, the dream faded utterly and he saw what he was really facing now.

It was his fortress home, or its remains. The whole clifftop was ablaze, everything engulfed by the rising flames. The entire structure was shattered, its walls gaping open all along the cliffs. There was no question of its defeat or of the tremendous, ruthless force which had been thrown against it.

He sank back, stunned by this reality, while the boat swept him further from the wreckage of everything he'd ever known.

II

RESCUE IN THE FOG

THE FORTRESS ON the clifftop burned brightly in the dark-ness, like a beacon, casting a red, shifting light across the sea and ships below. Men were visible in the red glow, moving on rope ladders, crude paths and steps up and down the cliff-face. Most were returning now from their work, climbing down from the shattered fortress and boarding the waiting ships.

A grey-suited captain of the raiders, followed by a party of warriors, climbed onto the deck of the largest ship. He moved alone toward the stern where, masked by shadows, a figure waited.

It was not the figure of a man who waited there, and yet in some monstrous, vague way it was. Immense, motionless in the curtaining shadows which rippled and billowed with the firelight reflected by the waves, it was undefined and the

more terrible for that. The captain's eyes strained as he tried
to focus on it, wanting to see it, yet fearing to.

Finally, reluctantly, he addressed it.

"Balor?"

There was a long silence. Then, slowly, the figure moved.
It shifted with an irritated moan, like a great, ancient beast
prodded from its sleep. And somewhere in that upper mass
which might have been a head, there was a sharp click. A
light appeared in the blackness there, as if an eyelid had been
raised; it opened to a slit, a hairline crack, revealing a
glowing, ruby eye. But the intensity of that thin line of light
was enough to hint at the power shielded behind the lowered
lid. Many times more violent energy, more raging heat lay in
that blood-red glow than in the blazing fortress above.

Even in the coolness of the night, the captain felt the heat
of the eye upon him as its gaze turned slowly toward him, felt
the sweat start and crawl upon him.

"You have a report, Captain?" said a flat, sharp voice, like
iron spearheads rattled against a shield.

"Yes, Balor. We've searched the entire island and gathered
every family living there. We found no light-haired child
among them. We've searched the keep. It was empty, but
there were signs a boy had been living there."

"What signs?" the voice snapped.

"Some clothing, some old toys . . . and this!"

He held up a fine harp, intricately carved and inlaid with
ivory and gold. Red light flickered along its strings as he
extended it toward the dark figure.

"A harp!" The reply was a crash of sound. A great hand
swept forward from the shadow in a curve that ripped the
fragile instrument from the captain's hands and smashed it
against the ship's bulwark. With a plaintive shriek of rup-
tured notes it fell to the deck, a tangled pile of splinters and
curled strings.

The hand withdrew into the shadows. The voice, more
sharply edged, asked:

"And what about the woman?"

"We've captured her. We've brought her here."

"Let me see her."

The captain signaled to the group behind him. From their
midst the woman was drawn, now worn and covered with
blood from a bound cut in her shoulder, but still defiant,

shaking off the arms of the guards who tried to hold her, walking boldly forward to face the shadowed figure.

The ruby eye moved toward her, rested on her for a time before the voice came again.

"So, Taillta, you've made a harper of the boy. What else?"

"I don't know what boy it is you're speaking of," she answered flatly.

There was a movement of the head at that. It was faint, nearly imperceptible. But the slit that was an eye widened a fraction more, and the warriors drew back as the wave of heat and light bathed Taillta, making her wince involuntarily from the searing pain.

"For many years your father fought us," the voice crackled, "until we destroyed him and his power. He was as arrogant as you. Only he and you would have had the courage to hide the boy from me. It was you who vanished when the boy did. For all of these years I've sought to find that out and then to find you. Now . . . where is the boy?"

These last words rose into a shout that clanged against the cliff-face, echoing back out across the black water.

But neither its violence nor the stinging caress of the scorching red gaze could soften Taillta's cold disdain. She shook her head and answered him firmly, uncompromisingly.

"Balor, your time is wasted here. Search and question as you like, but you'll learn of no boy from any one of us."

The heat and light were like a white-hot iron blade, probing toward her, threatening to bore into her. She tried to keep from turning her head away.

Slowly, deliberately the voice replied to her.

"You and all those people you have here will pay for defying me."

"No more can we pay than we have already," she told her tormentor courageously.

During this exchange another soldier had climbed to the ship's deck. Now he moved toward the group in the stern.

"Commander," he called, timidly.

The slit narrowed again. The eye slowly shifted away to the newcomer. Taillta felt the heat subside and breathed deeply in relief, for the burning light had brought her near to collapse.

"Commander," the soldier went on, a bit hesitantly, "some

of our men have reported that they saw a small boat headed away from the island during the fight."

"During the fight?" Anger and indignation combined in the frigid voice. "And why wasn't it reported then?"

"The men were engaged in the battle in the fortress. The boat seemed unimportant . . ."

"Put them to death," the shadowed figure interrupted, condemning them in a mechanical tone. "What was the course of this small boat?"

"East, Commander."

Balor's attention and the eye swung back to Taillta.

"Tell us, where is your harper going now?"

"There is nothing more that I'll be telling you," she answered with finality.

"Then, woman, there is nothing more that we can do with you," he replied.

From behind her the warriors stepped forward, seizing her arms. And, from the shadows the figure moved toward her, bringing the darkness forward to cover her.

As darkness receded from the ocean, the first light of the rising sun made a glowing whiteness of the dense fog blanketing the waves.

It seemed to hang solidly, unmoving, like a wall that even the breezes could not stir. Then, deep within it, some movement became visible.

Something pushed forward through the grey-white shroud, driving it back and up in lazy spirals, furrowing through the fog like a sharp plow.

It was the small boat, still carrying its lone occupant steadily toward the east.

Within it, huddled against the sea-dawn cold, Lugh stared out dully at the encircling void. Inside the heavy bank of fog, which seemed to cut him off from everything and even smothered light and sound, he had little to keep him company. There were only tiny things: the creaking boat, the constant gurgle of sea under the prow, the throb on his sore jaw. And they were only irritants, reminders of how truly alone he was.

He'd tried at first to turn the boat and rejoin those in the fortress, if only to die with them. But the tiny vessel had somehow defeated his attempts. He'd battered at it until his hands had ached, screamed his frustration at it until he'd grown hoarse. It had ignored him, running placidly, stubbornly on before the constant western wind. Finally he'd given up and sunk down in exhaustion and defeat. Let the damned thing take him where it wanted. He didn't care. What was there left to him anymore?

Certainly everything he'd thought of as real and valuable was gone. Only a bewildering assortment of questions remained. They'd haunted him through the empty night.

But he had no answers. He had nothing, not even his own identity. It had all been lost in one, sudden, devastating attack. A despair magnified by his own sense of utter helplessness in this white void had crept upon him. He'd sat afraid to move, willing the fog to wrap him, conceal him, fill his mind, and make him part of it.

Then, with the growing daylight, other emotions began to stir in him, welling out from an inner self he didn't know. He felt anger and a surging, almost exhilarating desire to fight. He knew that he couldn't simply give up as long as his questions remained unanswered. And he knew something more: he couldn't rest as long as Taillta and the destruction of his home were unavenged.

He looked around him with a rueful smile. It was fine to make such bold decisions here, lost at sea, carried against his will by the arrogant breeze.

Still, he was headed eastward, at least so far as he could tell by the faint sun. And it was east, to the Isle of Manannan, that Taillta had told him he must go.

It was a strange place for her to send him, he thought. He remembered the tales of the island beyond the mists that he had heard in childhood.

The island's master, Manannan MacLir, had appeared in many guises in those tales. He was a wrathful god of the sea whose storms destroyed the ships of any mortals venturing into his domain. He was a sorcerer who could take the shape of a soaring bird or a great fish and could ride across the waves in a silver chariot. He was an obscene monster whose lush isle and beautiful women lured victims in to feed his insatiable maw.

None of the portrayals of the being were very comforting, thought Lugh. But he had little other choice. He had never even heard of any other lands beyond these constant mists.

Then his thoughts were interrupted.

Far out in the fog ahead, something broke the water with a brief, swooshing noise.

Lugh sat forward, peering intently ahead. The rising sun had lit the fog, but not torn through it. He might as well have been staring at a grey blanket hung before his eyes.

A dim shape, a streak of shadow, whisked through the fog far off to his right. He only caught the movement in the corner of his eye and jerked his gaze around toward it.

There was nothing there.

It was fish, he told himself. The fish were jumping out there, rising to the dawn light.

Behind him, and closer to the boat, a vague, dark mound rose upward from the sea. The faint splash of it reached Lugh and he jerked about again, but it sank swiftly as he moved, leaving only a ripple in the easy swells.

Lugh stared back at the spot for a long moment as the boat carried him steadily on. Then, very slowly, his eyes traveled about the encircling wall of fog, searching for any sign of movement. He held his breath, listening for any sound. But there was nothing. Nothing.

And yet, he knew with an uncomfortable certainty that he wasn't alone in the fog anymore.

A gurgling sound rose from the water beyond the stern and drew him there. He caught a glimpse of a smooth hump slipping away under the waves of the boat's faint wake. He moved about the boat, searching the waters close by for movements.

Then he stopped. He'd felt the hull vibrate very slightly as something brushed the keel. It was passing directly underneath!

He climbed quickly into the bow and looked down into the water there. He could see a shape, he thought. An undefined mass of shadow moving out from under the bow of the slowly cruising boat. A great salmon, perhaps? Or a dolphin investigating him? He leaned over further, peering down at the object, his head only an arm's length above the water.

The sea below his face suddenly exploded upward. A form shot from the water in an eruption of spray, throwing Lugh backward.

He fell heavily into the bottom of the boat, staring upward at the thing which rose from the water to loom over him.

It was a monstrous thing, much like a horse, with a barrel body, long legs and a flat head set on a long neck. But it was like a thing long drowned, its coat a slimy green-black, its mane like thick seaweed, washing about the muscled shoulders in wild, tangled waves. And it was webbed, clawed hands—not hooves—which pawed the air at the end of the thin legs.

It had reared up in the water as a horse would, towering over the tiny boat. From projecting bumps atop the large, horse's muzzle, lidless, yellow eyes were fixed on Lugh.

Momentarily paralyzed with terror, the boy watched the thing rise up until only its hindquarters were still submerged. Then it dove forward, striking at Lugh with both legs.

At that the boy came back to life. He threw himself sideways as the sharp claws of the forefeet drove deeply into the wood planks, tearing up splinters as they dragged back. The massive head swooped down, jaws dropping open to reveal rows of sharklike, pointed teeth. The ripping tools of a flesh-eater.

Lugh grasped one of the boat's light oars and swung out at the head. It darted back, but his blow struck one of the slender legs. The beast gave a shrill neigh of pain and slid back under the waves.

As Lugh climbed up, he was knocked forward by a sharp blow against his back. He rolled again, bringing up the oar in defense as another monstrous head darted in at him. He knocked it aside with a swipe of the oar, but this beast was more persistent. It struck again, the head moving swiftly, sinuously on the long neck, like a snake's. Lugh was barely able to avoid the lunges.

He managed to hit it solidly several times, finally forcing it to retreat. But even as it did, another attacked. Lugh was forced to swing about again.

The battle continued for long, agonizing moments. The beasts attacked one-by-one, each from different sides, keeping Lugh always off balance and never able to rest. He couldn't tell how many there were, but at least three, and all very good at this deadly game. He managed to keep them away, but their assaults became steadily more determined.

Then one beast managed to shatter Lugh's mast with a sweeping blow of the great head. The mast toppled, catching Lugh in a tangle of sail and ropes.

While he struggled to free himself, another of the beasts rose in a great spray of water and dropped half of its length

into the boat. Its weight heeled the tiny vessel over and
water began to spill over the side.

The head came down at Lugh, jaws snapping at him as he
rolled back and forth desperately. He swung out with the oar,
but the beast caught it and snapped the end off with its teeth.

The head lifted and then dove in on him again, jaws wide
to grasp the now-defenseless boy. Lugh thrust upward with
the stub of oar, thrusting it lengthwise into the open mouth.
It acted as a bit, jamming into the back of the jaws and
locking them open.

The enraged monster threw its head back and forth violently.
Unable to shake the stub free, it retreated, sliding out of the
boat.

The little vessel, now half-full of water, lifted sluggishly.
Lugh untangled himself and rose onto his knees. In the fog
three forms appeared, moving in on him from three sides. He
knew they were coming together to finish him this time.

The largest of them glided to the boat and lifted its head
above Lugh, ready to strike.

"Who are you to be wrecking my boat?" Lugh shouted
angrily. "I've done nothing to you! Now, clear off, you slimy
bastard!"

He lifted his fists, prepared to punch the thing in the
center of its wide, soft-looking nose.

The start of their uneven battle was interrupted by a loud
and rhythmic splashing sound arising in the fog.

Beyond the monster, Lugh saw a large shape rush in
toward them. Not another one of them, he thought!

But as his adversary turned its head toward the new
arrival, a slender line of light swept from the shadowy object
and whisked across the beast's neck in a blazing crescent.

The head, neatly severed by a single cut, plopped into the
boat at Lugh's feet, jaws working even in death. The headless
carcass, spewing a rancid, yellow ooze from severed neck
arteries, collapsed into the water.

The other animals wheeled away from the boat and charged
into the mists after their new enemy. There was a jungle of
shadowy movements, the flicker of that same, thin light as it
swept around in bright arcs here and there, screams of anger
and then pain from the monstrous beasts.

Then one of the animals rushed out of the clouds toward

the boat. But it didn't pause there. It surged on past Lugh, plunging away into the concealing fog and safety.

Silence fell again upon the fog-shrouded sea. The large, dim figure which had come to Lugh's aid now floated out there alone and motionless. He peered out at it in both hope and fear, wondering whether a friend or another, stronger beast had rescued him.

The silence was broken abruptly by a pleasant, almost cheerful inquiry:

"Are you all right, then?"

"Ah... well... yes, I think so," Lugh answered somewhat uncertainly.

"Good. That's very good!" the voice responded crisply. "I was hoping so. You had a bit of a hard time there. Those Each-Uisge can be somewhat bothersome."

"The what?" asked Lugh.

"The Each-Uisge. The Water-Horses. Nasty beasts. Seems I arrived just in time."

The casually amiable nature of the man in the fog had a bracing effect on Lugh. His sense of loneliness was replaced by the warmth of companionship.

"I thank you... whoever you are," he replied whole-heartedly.

"No trouble at all. Not at all!" the voice assured him. "I enjoyed it immensely. But what about you? Could you use any help?"

"My mast is gone," Lugh told him. "I'll need some help to get anywhere from here."

"Well, I can give you a tow easily enough! Where is it you're bound?"

"I think I was headed for a place called Manannan's Isle. At least, that's where I meant to go."

"Ah, of course! It's very near. Look here, just tie this on, will you? Near the bow somewhere would be fine."

A coil of rope arched through the intervening fog and fell into the boat. Lugh obediently tied it to a cleat at his bow.

"All ready!" he called back.

At once the shadowy vessel moved ahead, making a curious rhythmic, splashing noise, like the oars of rowers striking the water. The rope came taut and, with an initial jerk, the little boat began to cut briskly through the waves.

It wasn't long before the fog started to thin. The change

came abruptly, and they were suddenly out of it, pulling away from its last, clinging tendrils into an open sea.

As the fog disappeared, Lugh got his first, clear look at the man and the vessel which had come to his rescue.

The man was smiling pleasantly at him. He seemed all right. What set young Lugh somewhat aback was the fact that the man was standing in the back of a great chariot-of-war which a team of white horses was pulling across the surface of the sea at a brisk trot!

III

MANANNAN'S ISLE

THE MAN NOTED Lugh watching him and smiled broadly.

"Hello, there! Nice to see you at last. Sorry about the fog. Sometimes I wonder why I came up with it."

Lugh could only stare back at first, too awed by the peculiar sight to speak.

"How . . . how . . ." he finally stuttered out.

"How can I ride the waves so casually?" the charioteer supplied helpfully. "Well, that all has to do with one's viewpoint, you see. I mean, it seems only water to you, hardly a firm surface at all. But to me, it looks like a fine, open plain, as solid as any land."

Lugh examined his rescuer more closely. He was tall and long-limbed, clad in a simple woolen tunic and pants. His face was lean, with a casually matched set of features—small chin and eyes, long nose and broad forehead—which somehow managed to combine pleasantly. His most distinctive point was a head of silver hair in tight, unruly waves.

He seemed quite normal, not threatening in the least. And yet, with his chariot, he had to be . . .

"Manannan MacLir I certainly am," the man offered, as if he'd been reading Lugh's thoughts. "God of the Sea, Storm-Bringer, Ship-Crusher . . . and all the rest of that!" He waved it away as if bored by the idea of it. Then he nodded at the boy. "And you are Lugh."

"How did you know me?" the boy asked wonderingly.

"Oh, I know you quite well. In fact, I've been keeping watch on you since you entered my little fog. I wanted to be certain you'd reach my humble island safely. There's not far to go now."

He gestured ahead of them. On the dawn horizon an island was coming into view. The sun seemed to draw it up with it as it rose, haloing it briefly before detaching itself to drift up higher in the brilliant sky.

To this boy who'd known only the rocky island on which he'd lived, the land they approached was a pleasing one. His home had been a place of stark, grey cliffs, hard angles and rough stone scoured by winds. Here everything seemed soft, with green meadows rising gently inland to forested hills hung with a curtain of mist.

Manannan towed the little boat in, past a sheltering crooked arm of land. A wide beach came into view, and Lugh realized that a large crowd of people filled it. Their bright clothing made a shifting pattern against the grey-white sands. They were waving and calling greetings, and the sound of songs and instruments drifted out to Lugh.

"Who are those people?" Lugh asked.

"Oh, they're mine," Manannan answered. "That is, they live on the island with me. The welcome is for you."

"That's very nice," the boy said.

He found that the drifting music of the voices and the pipes was very relaxing. It lulled him like the sound of grasses rustled by a warm breeze or the evening call of settling birds. It called up images that shimmered before his weary eyes like sunlight on the sea. He saw pleasures offered by this land, the wealth, beauties and ease, the soothing caresses that washed away all pain.

He listened and his head sank down against the boat's side. His limp hand fell into the rushing water with a splash.

Manannan looked back and saw the boy's state. Abruptly he leaned down and scooped a handful of chill seawater into Lugh's face. As the boy sat up, sputtering, Manannan shouted irritably to those on shore:

"Look, could we do without the bloody singers and pipes?"

The music stopped abruptly, and Manannan turned to the now wide-awake Lugh in obvious embarrassment.

"I must apologize for this! They think that everyone who comes here has got to be enchanted into the state of a stunned sheep."

"Enchanted?" Lugh asked in bewilderment.

"Yes. You see, this is supposed to be an enchanted isle, and I am supposed to be a god, so it's helpful to keep visitors in a sort of sensual haze."

"I don't much think I'd care to be enchanted," Lugh told him emphatically.

"Of course not!" Manannan agreed. "And it doesn't apply to you at all. I want you to come only with a clear mind and by your own choice. That's very important."

"Well, I'm not certain about my mind anymore, and it doesn't seem as if I've much choice of where I'm to go."

"Still, you don't mind coming? I mean, you're not afraid?"

"Of course not!" Lugh said, trying to sound assured. He was afraid, of course. Things were too strange for any but a fool not to be. But he wasn't going to let his rescuer know that.

"Fine, then!" Manannan said heartily. "Let's go on in!"

Lugh tried to look relaxed while the team trotted on toward shore and ran the chariot right up onto the beach, drawing the boat up after it.

As soon as it was beached, the people moved in around it. Hands helped him to climb out, and he was instantly surrounded by the welcoming crowd.

His initial impression of them was somewhat confused. They moved about him so constantly. They were a handsome people, tall and slender and fine-featured, most with light eyes and glowing, pale skin. Lugh was particularly aware of the women. He could hardly help but be. They moved in very close about him, smiling boldly at him, caressing his cheek, teasing him with their perfumes.

They wove sensations around him like a living web, whirling about him in their flowing garments of bright hues, floating with the grace of frost-painted autumn leaves, swirling like a sun-gilded morning mist.

Or, thought Lugh, were they the mist itself, not really beings at all, but conjured and shaped by his sorcerer to beguile him in spite of all the assurances?

"Get back! Get back!" Manannan commanded impatiently.

He strode through the crowd to Lugh, and they fell back obediently.

"Can't you see the lad's worn out?" he said. "Someone, give him a drink!"

A flask was immediately passed to Lugh. Driven by a raging thirst, he lifted it at once and drank deeply. It was a pleasant surprise. The liquid wasn't water but something clearer and sweeter than anything he'd ever had. It washed through his entire system at once, carrying away the thirst, the aches, and the anxiety.

"Sorry again," Manannan murmured to him. "My people are very open and very spontaneous." He threw a critical look about at them. "But I think this lot's overdoing it just a bit."

"It's fine! It's marvelous!" Lugh assured him merrily. "I've never seen women so beautiful!" He grinned broadly at them and waved happily. He felt suddenly flushed and exhilarated and ready for anything.

Manannan beamed with satisfaction.

"So everything's fine, is it? Then come on with me!"

He moved to the chariot, Lugh following. He paused there to pull a sheathed longsword from a holder in the car. The sheath and hilt were bound with delicate and complex metal work set with many jewels, and Lugh eyed it with admiration.

"I don't want to neglect this," Manannan said. "It saved your life today."

"That's what I saw flashing in the fog!" said Lugh. "It must be a fine weapon for its blade to gleam in that faint light."

"It's a remarkable weapon. It's called 'The Answerer.'" He leaned close to Lugh and spoke in a more confidential way. "But, it's not really mine, you know. I suppose I shouldn't even be using it." He looked around guiltily as if someone were eavesdropping, then smiled. "But I like to sneak it out now and then for a bit of fun. I think it enjoys the action as much as I do. It can get dreadfully boring laying about here."

He pulled erect then and his voice briskly assumed its normal tones. "Now, let me show you where I live," he said, throwing a long arm about the boy.

He led Lugh along and the boy went willingly, looking about him with eager curiosity. The rest of the crowd followed them.

Beyond the beach and through a line of trees, the meadows opened up. They were thick with grass, so lush, so soft, Lugh thought. Smooth, gentle swells, and radiant and fragrant and soft, like the women. Everything was soft here. In fact, it was so soft that he seemed to be having growing difficulty in focusing on it.

He realized that there was a large structure ahead of them. It was difficult for him to define its exact form because it was difficult to separate what was building from what was part of the surrounding landscape. It grew out of a low hill as if it was a part of it. An immense dome, it was partially covered by earth, while its exposed portions were a mixture of timber and living trees, cut stone and natural rock formations. It filled all the middle of one vast plain and rose far above the meadows around.

The entrance was through an arch of yew trees forming a hallway that led to an inner space. As Lugh came into it, he stopped to look around him. In the simple, isolated life he had lived so far, there had been nothing to prepare him for the wonders of the room that now opened before him.

They had entered at a high point, and he could see far across the room. The space was enormous, encompassing meadows, groves of trees, streams, all encircling a central mound on whose top sat a rough circle of large stones. In some peculiar way that Lugh couldn't focus upon in his hazy state, the space seemed much larger inside than out. It was almost a separate world of its own. The place wasn't even a room so much as a piece of the outside loosely restricted by casually placed walls. Above the mound the dome arched up far above the tallest of the trees, its center seemingly open to the sky except for a spiderweb of light, supporting beams.

"Well, what do you think of my Sidhe?" Manannan asked.

"Sidhe?" Lugh repeated vaguely.

"That's what our home is called. It's nice enough, I suppose,"

"It's very much more than that!" Lugh exclaimed in awed tones.

They walked on, Lugh following Manannan along a path which meandered through the meadows toward the central mound. Behind them, the followers dispersed gradually, slipping off into the many side paths until it was only the two who mounted the gentle slope to the top of the mound.

The top was a smooth, flat circle of packed earth. The stones—each a rough-hewn block taller than Lugh—were set at equal distances about its outer edge, forming a large ring.

They stepped into the ring and Lugh stopped, still staring about him wide-eyed. It was all so much his senses couldn't encompass it. Manannan stood watching him carefully.

Lugh's wandering gaze came to rest on the objects that occupied the middle of the ring. At its exact center was another stone, smaller and more smooth with a rounded top. In a triangle about it the other objects were set. One seemed only a low, square block of stone with a flat top. Next was a vast cauldron of black iron that sat upon a fire. From the odor which drifted from it, Lugh decided that some marvelous food must be cooking there.

The last object was a second cauldron, smaller than the first, much cruder, and seeming much out of place. Whatever filled it was boiling angrily, the bubbling sound loud in the surrounding quiet.

But there was something very odd about it. Lugh stared, irritated that his mind had suddenly grown so muddled. Then, with a start of surprise, he realized what was wrong. The boiling cauldron had no fire beneath it!

Curious, he started forward, aware of a great weariness dragging at his legs.

"Not too close to that now, lad," Manannan said warningly.

Lugh stopped. Even at his considerable distance from the cauldron, he could feel the heat that radiated from it.

"How can it be boiling without any flame?" he asked.

"Do you see that pole?" Manannan asked.

Lugh did see it now. A slim length of dull, grey metal was suspended from a support above the cauldron, one end immersed in the liquid which foamed up whitely about it.

"Well, there's a spearhead fixed to that with an energy so great that the liquid in that cauldron barely manages to keep it cool enough for us to come this close. Its slightest touch is deadly, and only a warrior with the proper power can wield it."

He shook his head. "It's a most amazing thing," he said with a touch of awe. "But I've never really understood it myself."

"Never understood it?" Lugh said, surprised. "What do you mean? It's yours, isn't it?"

Seeing the boy's point, Manannan tried to explain.

"Well, it's not mine, you see. I mean, not really mine. It's only in my care, like the other things. Like this!" He held up the sword called Answerer, then walked to the low, square block, laying the weapon carefully on its top. He turned back to Lugh, gesturing at the other objects.

"All these things are really extraordinary. That large cauldron there, for instance, can never be emptied. Never! And its food can restore the power and energy to whomever eats, no matter how weak." His voice was filled with pride now as he described his charges, like a father with his children. He walked to the rounded stone and patted its top lovingly. "And this . . . this is the Lia Fail, the Stone of Truth! It never lies!"

"It talks?" said Lugh in a thick, bemused way.

"In a manner of speaking. To say it . . . well . . . moans would be more accurate."

He moved back to Lugh. "All of them are waiting here until the time comes when they'll be needed. Until then I'm their guardian."

"Do you know who'll use these things and when?"

"Certainly," Manannan answered casually. "It's a bit in the future yet."

"Then, your magic can give that kind of knowledge to you?"

"It can," the man said with a certain pride.

Lugh turned to him eagerly.

"If you can know such things, then you must know about me . . . about who I am . . . why I was sent to you. I have so many questions . . ."

"Of course you do," the tall man agreed pleasantly, moving close to Lugh. "But, you're very tired now."

And, as he spoke, Lugh realized that he was. It had been growing like a weight upon him since he'd arrived, since he'd had that drink. Now everything around him was blurring, and a glow seemed to rise, blossom out from the sunlit trees and meadows about him, join together in one golden haze and envelop him. Even the smiling face of Manannan so near him was dimming, fading into the mist.

"You rest now," Manannan said quietly. "Rest and we'll talk later."

Lugh fought against it. He didn't want to rest. He wanted to ask questions. He wanted answers.

"Manannan, help me!" he pleaded.

The long arm fell about his shoulders again. The face was

only a pale moon above the clouds. The voice was a lulling sound from far away.

"I'll help you, lad. Now rest. Just rest."

A fluttering alarm struggled upward like a wounded bird into his failing consciousness. Had Manannan lied to him? Had it really all been just a trap which had finally closed on him?

He had no will left to fight it. He surrendered and let himself slip into the welcoming darkness.

The figure swooped forward, the immense head coming out of the shadows. The eye clicked open, no slit now, but a line, a narrow beam of energy that struck the captain.

At once he was a torch, a pillar of intense fire that licked out at those around him.

He had not even time to scream. His open mouth disappeared in the fire that crackled over him, shriveled and curled him into a blackened, smouldering slug upon the floor.

The acrid scent of burned flesh and hair was heavy in the air of the closed room, now filled with smoke. But immediately a humming sound arose somewhere beyond the walls, and a light breeze arose, pulling off the smoke through vents in the high ceiling.

The other officers reformed, leaving a wide space around the pile. None of them dared to glance at it, to look away from Balor.

The eye was a slit again, its destructive energy penned. But the voice crackled like the flames, scorching them once more with its words.

"I hope no other of our officers will hesitate to enter a bank of fog in this search. I want that boat found!"

"Commander," another of the captains ventured, "that band of fog that lies always about Manannan's Isle is deadly. We've lost two ships already in the search. If the boy entered it, he is likely dead by now."

"He may be dead, but there can't be any chances taken here. Warn every Fomor garrison to keep alert for him. I must be informed of any development, no matter how vague. And double all sea patrols."

"Even around Manannan's Isle?"

"Even there! That troublesome sorcerer wouldn't dare to

interfere with us. Stay outside the fog if you wish, but keep up the search as long as I command it!"

"Commander, why is this lone boy so important?" a captain asked courageously, daring his leader's wrath.

"It's not necessary for you to know the reasons," came the dark reply. "But all of you should know that failure to find this lone boy may mean the destruction of us all!"

The men shifted uneasily at that. They sensed something in Balor's tones that they had never sensed before. He was afraid.

The massive figure settled back heavily into its shadowed corner of the room. But, even in the darkness, the hard, red glow was visible behind the lowered lid.

IV

A BARGAIN

SUNLIGHT FELL IN a hazy, golden beam to light the grassy floor of Manannan's palace.

Under a giant oak tree near the central ring, Lugh and his host sat eating. They had settled themselves comfortably into the cozy spaces created by the interwoven roots, a wealth of food spread out between them. Lugh was attacking the food with vigor while Manannan made another apology.

"I hope you don't resent my putting you to sleep that way. But I thought after a good rest and some food, you'd feel much more like dealing with things. I trust it's improved your grasp on reality?"

Lugh wondered if it had. He looked about him at the enormous place once again. It seemed as incredible as he'd thought at first. Birds of kinds and colors he'd never seen before flitted through the trees around. A stream played musically through the rocks at his feet. Some of Manannan's people were playing a joyous hide-and-seek game in a nearby meadow. Others strolled the winding paths or tended gardens and grazing cattle herds.

"I'm still not certain I know what's real," Lugh told Manannan honestly. "This place, for instance. I can't believe I'm actually inside!"

"It is a bit overwhelming, isn't it?" Manannan agreed.

"What do you do when it rains? Or, in the winter?"

"Oh, the place simply rearranges itself to accomodate the weather changes," the man casually explained. "It's more-or-less doing that all the time. Sometimes I think the damned place is alive, what with things opening and closing, windows and walls shifting about. But it does keep things pretty much the same in here all the year 'round. Pleasant enough, but terribly dull."

"Dull?" Lugh repeated in astonishment. "Why, it seems like paradise to me! I've spent most of my life either cold or wet . . . and quite often both."

Manannan sighed. "I envy you that. To grow up always challenged by the elements must have been marvelous."

Lugh looked curiously at him.

"Do you mind my saying that you have some very peculiar attitudes for a god?"

"You can say so, yes. It's been said before. But you are wrong in one point. I'm no god. Although it is true that my people have developed certain powers you might consider somewhat . . . ah . . . shall we say magical?"

"Then what are you?"

"You could think of me as a sort of guardian. I was sent here with these others to watch over things, help out here and there." He leaned over closer to Lugh and added confidentially: "I expected it to be quite an adventure, but so far it's been a great disappointment."

A pair of lightly clad young women passed by and smiled warmly at Lugh. He smiled back, watching them walk on, fascinated by the grace of their movements.

"The rest of the people here seem happy enough," he remarked.

"What, them? Of course they are! Happy as ruddy larks, like the rest of my lot back home. And why not? We've learned to control everything around us. Now we're free to take our ease, sing and play and contemplate and chase one another merrily through the meadows. But where's the challenge in that, I ask you? Where's the thrill of real living? That's what I'm looking for. Like that little rescue yesterday.

There was real living! Ah, the weight of that sword, the hot pump of blood through the . . ."

He stopped, realizing Lugh wasn't listening. He was staring in rapt admiration at a group of young women wading in the stream not far away, their long tunics pulled high about their legs. Manannan noted that the boy was definitely flushed.

"I don't think I've ever seen women so beautiful," Lugh said with tremendous enthusiasm.

"Yes. You've mentioned that before," Manannan remarked dryly. "Have you had enough to eat?"

"Oh, I think so," Lugh said absently. "Thanks."

"It's a very good idea to go easily," the host said in a lecturing tone. "One who's lived as simple a life as you have might find our fare a bit too rich."

Lugh realized that Manannan's warning included more than the food. He looked away from the girls, flushing a brighter hue in embarrassment. Then something else in the words struck him more deeply. It recalled to him the grim events which had brought him here and what his purpose was.

"Come on, lad," Manannan said, climbing up. "Let's walk a bit. You've seen very little of my Sidhe!"

Lugh's mind was plunged again in dismal thoughts, but he followed along with his strange rescuer, and as they wandered the lazily winding paths, he found his dark mood lightened by the beauties of the place. Small animals scuttled from their way, and gaily plumaged birds soared overhead. Lush meadowlands rolled out on either side, with cozy nests of trees snuggled in nooks along the wandering streams or warmly furring soft hillsides. Each place looked more comfortable than the last, inviting one to rest there, to be lulled by the bright harp sound of a tumbling brook or the gentle bard's song of the rustling leaves. And it seemed to go on, farther than he could see. So vast, in fact, was the landscape, so bewildering the paths, that Lugh realized he would be surely lost without his guide. It was an absurd thought, to be lost inside a house, inside a mound of earth.

But this was no real place, he felt. There was no time, no space here that he understood. Yet, as alarming as that thought might have been, he felt none, because he felt nothing here but a sense of peace.

And then his sense of harsh reality returned with a sharp jar. For as they topped a rise, a large field came into view. And on that field, several scores of mounted warriors were engaged in battle.

They stopped to watch—Lugh with alarm, Manannan with a cheerful but casual interest.

The men were all dressed alike in silver helmets and breastplates, white flowing cloaks shot through with silver threads. Each carried a slender lance whose point winked with light and whose haft was fitted with silver bands which shook together with a clear, bright jingling sound as the men moved. Each one was mounted on a tall and elegant horse of purest white whose gracefulness did not disguise the power of its rippling body as it ran.

These silver warriors were divided in two companies which dueled with each other. They formed in ranks, charged into one another spears set, not colliding but flowing together, intermingling, then parting, only to turn, reform, and charge again. It was one, endless, smooth, shining sweep of action, and a strangely beautiful thing to watch, for all its violent intent. The men and horses moved together, the streaming manes and tails and luminescent cloaks blending to make their movement like a flow of moonlit, wind-swirled fog. And the sound of them was like a rushing sea-wind, playing its mournful tune across the land.

Odd, too, was that this and the musical tones of the silver bands were the only sounds Lugh heard. No clashing of arms. No cries from horse or man. And he noted that when they finished an attack, no hurt or dead lay upon the earth.

"Who are they?" he asked Manannan, shaking himself from the near trance their fluid motions and sounds had nearly lulled him to.

"They are my warriors," the sea god replied. "I call them the Riders of the Sidhe." He walked down onto the field, Lugh close behind. As he approached, they broke off their battle and quickly reformed in two ranks facing one another, an avenue between. Manannan led Lugh up to it, explaining as they went.

"I didn't want you to see them when you first arrived. They might have alarmed you. They really are a grim lot."

Lugh looked around him at each one as they passed between the ranks. On the tall horses, the warriors towered over them, so still and silent they might have been statues graven in silver. Each stared ahead, features largely masked by the helmet face, only tight mouths and glaring, unblinking eyes of brilliant grey visible.

They were indeed an ominous company, and Lugh felt a cold wash about him as they passed through.

As they reached the far end of the avenue, Manannan turned to them and announced: "All right, you may go back to it now."

At once the riders resumed their mock attacks.

"They spend most of their time at playing war," Manannan remarked.

"Don't they do anything else?" Lugh asked.

"Not really, but there's little else to do. And they were created to be warriors."

"Created?" Lugh asked.

"Oh, yes. They're not real men. They're wraiths. Just the form of men given substance to act in this world. I told you my people had become quite peaceful. They had enough difficulty finding me to send to this little outpost. Finding a company of warriors? That was impossible. So the essence of those more violent spirits of our distant past was summoned from its own realms and given the shape you see."

"Who do they fight?"

"No one. At least, not yet. They're waiting, like my four charges, for their time. Why don't we go on now?"

"You have such powers," Lugh said thoughtfully as they continued on the path. "And you say you have knowledge of me."

"I know about most things that happen in my domains," the man replied modestly. "I gather information in all sorts of ways: from passing birds, sea creatures, a stranded sailor now and again. There's very little that goes on without my hearing about it from some talkative dolphin or gull."

"Then that's how you knew my island had been attacked? That I was coming here?" said Lugh, ignoring the remarkable nature of his host's sources.

"To some extent," Manannan agreed.

"That means you can tell me who it was attacked us and why!"

Manannan considered the boy gravely for a moment, then answered regretfully:

"No, Lugh. I'm sorry. I'm afraid I can't do that."

"What do you mean?" Lugh demanded. "You must be able to tell me! You have knowledge of everything... even the future!"

"Of course I have it," Manannan replied evenly. "I simply won't give you your answers now."

Lugh forgot his awe of this odd being in his anger. He turned on the tall man, nearly shouting.

"You won't? Then, why am I here? Why did you rescue me? Why did Taillta send me to you for help?"

"Easy, lad," his unruffled host told him soothingly. "I didn't tell you that I wouldn't help. But first you're going to have to earn that help from me."

The fire went out of Lugh and he grew uncertain again.

"I don't understand," he said.

"First, you must tell me more about yourself," Manannan said. "Do you really know so little of the world?"

"Until that attack, that little island was my whole world," Lugh answered honestly. "I knew of nothing else."

"Then you didn't know about me?"

"Only in tales told the children about the terrible place beyond the fog. I think that was meant just to frighten us and keep us from wanting to sail too far out to sea."

Manannan smiled. "I'd like to have heard those tales. But, what about other lands? Other people?"

"Then, there are some?" said Lugh with rising interest. "I thought there must be, but no one spoke about it. Taillta always managed to put aside my questions."

"It's still remarkable to me that she was able to keep you happy or contented there."

"I hadn't much time to think about it. What she wasn't telling me about the world she made up for by teaching me everything else she could. I've learned all kinds of skills! I can craft in metal and wood, forge, play the harp, and sing. I've been taught the skills of a warrior and I know the secrets of all types of games. I've become a master of many things in my few years. A master of nearly everything except my own life and my own reason!"

This last was spoken with a certain bitterness as the emptiness of his situation filled him again.

"Even so," Manannan considered, "It must have been hard for Taillta to satisfy you as you grew older."

"It was harder every day. I knew there had to be more and

I meant to go seeking it. I think I would have left the island soon if the attack hadn't come."

"It seems to me that she would have wanted that, Lugh," Manannan told him. "She most likely would have sent you herself... when the time came."

"Would she?" asked Lugh. "Then why did she keep me from knowing about the world?"

Manannan stopped and turned to the anguished boy, placing a firm hand on each of his shoulders. His eyes held Lugh's and he spoke in earnest:

"You listen to me, Lugh! Never hold that against her. She must have loved you. She sacrificed herself to save you! Whatever she did she believed had to be done!"

Lugh pulled angrily away, turning his back on the man.

"How do you know that?" he cried. "You tease me with these things. You hint that you know my secrets, but you won't reveal them."

He swung back on Manannan, tense with rage and frustration, his eyes filled with tears.

"You tell me about Taillta. Well, I'll tell you! I still love her, no matter what the truth is. I will avenge her and the rest. But to do it, I have to have your help. Please! Give me your help!"

Manannan's amiable face hardened. He shook his head sharply.

"Very sorry, lad, but I need something from you," he said stubbornly. "What you've told me only makes that more certain in my mind."

"What do you mean?" asked Lugh. "What can I do for you with all of your powers?"

"Come over this way," the tall man said, gesturing up a pathway.

They walked along it toward the outer wall and a large opening. Beyond, they found themselves on a meadow at the base of the mound. Across the meadow and a line of beach was the sea. Lugh could see gulls wheeling above the shallow waters just off the shore, seeking prey.

Manannan pointed out to sea.

"Out there, just beyond the haze, is a large island known by some as Eire—The Pleasant Land. I think it is very well named. It's a place of great richness and great beauty. But I've heard lately that things have become very unpleasant there." He looked down at Lugh. "I want you to go there and find out why."

Lugh swung his gaze sharply from the sea to his host.

"You want me to go? What could I find out that you couldn't learn yourself?"

"For one thing, I'm afraid my abilities are scarcely more than the normal away from the sea. The only thing I can do there is simply send someone to observe. And you are the perfect observer. Do you understand?"

Lugh didn't think so. He shook his head.

"Think how remarkable you are!" Manannan explained. "You know nothing about Eire, its people, or its problems. You'll experience everything with an open mind. In all of my domains, you are the only one I know who could go there and judge the situation without bias."

"To what end?" Lugh asked.

"To help me decide what course I should take. Before I can interfere in what's happening there or use my powers for anyone, I have to have a totally fair assessment of it all. You can give me that!"

"Are you telling me that unless I do this, you won't help me?" Lugh asked carefully, not wanting to believe it.

"I am," Manannan replied impassively.

"I've lost my family and home, I'm lost and alone in the world, and you're going to use that to force me into helping you?"

"As terrible as it sounds, yes. What I need is far too important, whether you understand or not."

Lugh glared at the man in frustration for a moment. Then he stalked away, across the meadow to the shore, and dropped down there. Manannan followed after him slowly, stopping some way behind him.

Lugh flicked a flat stone into the pulsing surf with an irritated gesture.

"It's a rotten thing to do, you know," he said.

Manannan didn't reply. He stood waiting patiently, unconcerned. He knew what the boy's response would have to be.

Lugh flicked another stone into the waves as he considered.

"I wouldn't know how to begin," he said at last," or where to go, or what to do."

"All that would be taken care of," Manannan assured him

at once. He moved down and crouched beside the boy. "They're very suspicious, very closed there now, but I'll work out a way to get you accepted, get you into some place where you can see what's happening. I think the skills Taillta gave you will help to do that. And I'll provide all the assistance I can."

"And all I need to do there is to observe and report back to you?"

"That's all. Of course you mustn't tell anyone why you're there or even mention me. And your observations must be as complete as possible, based on a fair, impartial study of all sides. But, once you think you clearly understand the situation there, you can return to me."

"Then you'll tell me what I want to know? You'll help me to get my revenge?"

"If that's what you want, I will," Manannan promised.

Lugh saw another possibility. He could leave this isle and seek his answers in other places. But, would Manannan allow that?

"You can go where and when you like. I won't stop you," Manannan replied, reading Lugh's thoughts again. "Your choice must be yours alone. But, listen to me, Lugh. I will tell you this much. What happens in Eire will affect the lives of everyone there and far beyond. And you could play a part in it. Your own life, your own destiny, depends upon the choice you make now."

His destiny. There again was that teasing reminder that Manannan knew so much more. How odd, Lugh thought, that yesterday he'd longed for some destiny beyond a peaceful life on a lonely isle. And now, as he looked out across the glittering plain of water toward the curve of sky, he realized that a whole new life lay out there, waiting for him to discover it. There was a chance for him to see places and meet people he'd never known existed. The expectation of that adventure was as much an influence on him as the need to earn Manannan's help.

He looked at the tall man and nodded, saying firmly:

"All right. I'll go and do this thing for you."

"Now, wait!" Manannan cautioned gravely. "Before you make a bond with me, I want it clear that this won't be an easy thing. I said before that on land my powers are very limited. There are dark and terrible powers at work in Eire which you'll face alone."

"I don't care," Lugh answered boldly. "I've no life of my own. To gain one, I'd face any terror, any pain."

"You may have to," Manannan said grimly.

BOOK II
THE MISSION

V

A CHALLENGE

THE CHILL EVENING rain whipped the hilltop fortress called Tara. Sharp gusts of wind drove it in stinging blasts against the wooden palisades and the central hall. Worn by the constant, punishing storms, the neglected structures sagged forlornly.

Up the hill, along a path now more a stream than a road, a lone figure struggled toward the gateway in the outer wall. It was a hard climb through the clinging mud, against the battering wind. He was forced to clasp his heavy, woolen cloak tightly about him to keep the storm from tearing it away.

The cloaked traveler finally reached the gates and found them open. They swung wearily, with harsh, protesting groans, in the harassing winds. He paused by them, waiting for the challenge of a guard. When no one appeared, he hesitantly went on, through the gates and into the fortress grounds.

The central practice fields, a place for warriors to train and boys to play at hurley, was a morass of puddles and heaped mud. Rivulets of rain had cut deep into a surface that constant use should have kept smooth and packed hard.

The cloaked figure paused again to look about. The yard, the whole fortress, seemed deserted. Not a soul moved anywhere. Only the great, circular hall ahead showed any signs of life. There light showed through gaps in the broken wattle of the walls. Smoke rose from the chimney hole to be whisked away into the night.

The traveler crossed the yard toward the hall, hopping from spot to spot in a vain attempt to avoid the deepest puddles. The large door was closed, and he beat upon the thick wood with both hands, hoping someone inside would hear. Then he waited, pressed tight against the door to escape the water which ran in a sheet from the roof edge.

Finally the door opened, just enough to allow a face to peer out. It was a hostile sort of face, with bushy, flaring eyebrows and mustache, and it regarded the cloaked traveler with suspicion.

"It's a bit late to be going visiting, don't you think?" the man asked irritably.

"I'm a poor wanderer, sir," the sodden figure answered humbly. "I've come a great, hard way, and I'm only seeking some simple shelter and a bit of food."

The doorkeeper laughed loudly at that. It was a grating, unpleasant sound.

"If you've come here for that, it's the worst choice you've ever made!" The laughter died and he added roughly: "Now, get on! There's nothing for you!"

He started to swing the door, but the traveler pushed forward, blocking it open with one arm.

"I'll work for it," he told the servant earnestly.

"You will, will you?" the man replied scornfully. "Let's have a look at you!"

The figure leaned forward into the light. A smooth, youthful face, dripping hair plastered to a high forehead, came into view.

"A boy!" the doorkeeper declared. "I thought as much. And what's your name, boy?"

"I'm called Lugh, sir," he answered courteously.

"Well, young Lugh, just what do you think you could do that would be of any worth to the High-King of Tara?"

"I've had training as a carpenter," the traveler offered.

"We have a carpenter here. Luchtar, son of Luachaid," was the reply.

"I've had training as a smith as well."

"Our smith Colum Cuaillemech does all of our work," was the bored response.

"I can play the harp, sing songs, tell fine tales!"

"We've many others who can do the same," the doorkeeper told him, yawning.

"I'm trained in the warrior's arts."

"Warriors are as common as fluttering crows," the man countered wearily. He began to edge the door closed as the visitor kept on gamely trying.

"I can work in silver, brass and gold."

"So can Credne Cerde."

"I have a healer's skills."

"So does the High-King's physician."

"I can play all sorts of games."

"No."

"I can cook."

"No!"

"Then let me be a cup bearer to the king!"

"NO!" the man shouted through the remaining crack. "King Bres has a man who's master of every skill you've named!"

Before Lugh could act, he slammed the door closed.

"Wait!" Lugh cried desperately. "Tell me if he has one man who is a master of them all!"

There was no response.

Lugh turned and dropped back wearily against the rough timbers, feeling defeated. Was his mission here to end so abruptly before he'd even begun? He'd done what Manannan had told him. What could he do now?

He nearly fell backward as the door behind him popped open again. The bristly face peeped out at him with narrowed eyes.

"Can you really do all those things you named?" he asked skeptically.

"Every one!" Lugh replied with renewed hope.

"Go on, boy! No one could be master of them all."

"I could," Lugh said stoutly, and added challengingly: "Go ask your King Bres if there's another here who could. If there is, I'll not bother you any longer."

"I can't ask him that. I'll look a fool!" the doorkeeper protested.

"I can prove my skills. Any one or all," Lugh assured him, trying to look more confident than he felt.

"I don't believe it."

"It's not for you to believe it or not," Lugh said with authority. "Carry my question to him. Let him decide."

The doorkeeper shrugged. "Well, there's nothing to be lost by asking, I suppose." He pulled the door wider. "Come in here and wring yourself out a bit," he said. But as Lugh moved forward, the man held him a moment with his hand, adding gruffly: "You'd best not be lyin' though, boy. You don't know what you've wandered into here."

He turned around and tramped away from Lugh. The boy moved on into the hall, closing the door behind him. The room now before him seemed at first a welcome contrast with the dismal night outside.

The great hall of Tara was a glowing tapestry of sensations, woven of sounds and smells, of colors and textures that drew their strands around the cold and dripping lad.

In size, it was much smaller than the bright, airy Sidhe of Manannan, but it was still impressive. An outer wall of timbers formed the circle around the central fire-pit. Wooden partitions fixed by bright copper rivets divided the area around the outer walls into separate spaces that opened into the main part of the hall. Between these rooms and the fire's edge, low tables filled the open floor, providing space for hundreds of warriors to dine.

The inner timbers spaced around the fire-pit which supported the thatched roof were thicker than a man and soared up nearly five times a man's height. All the wood was red yew, faced with glowing bronze. The timbers were carved from top to bottom with the sinuous line of the artist's skill, with curiously distorted birds and beasts who intertwined in play to form one complex, continuous design that both bewildered and delighted the eye at once.

In the circling rooms were gathered the nobility of the fortress—chieftains, bards and druids—feasting with their families and friends, enjoying the activities in the central portion of the hall.

The place was alive with music and laughter. Jugglers and acrobats moved amongst the crowd. Near the room's front musicians played, filling the air with a fast, merry tune. Pipes and tiompan and harp created their own tapestry of sound, the drummer tapping out a vigorous rhythm on the skin, pipers and harper spinning their light air about it, high and shining, like silver and gold threads woven into the design.

Around the warrior's tables the men ate and drank, indulging in their most loved sport, talk. Most of them were between the fire and the door. Across the fire there was the open space before the raised platform of the High-King's table.

Here were gathered the most favored of the company. The group of men and women about the long table were a bright spot of rich clothing and ornaments, like a jewelled brooch on a cloak.

It was toward this group that the doorkeeper was making his way, winding through the maze of tables. None of the gathering took notice of his passing—save for one. A weary, raggedly bearded face lifted its dull-eyed stare from the table's top as the servant brushed by. He watched with a vague, blurry curiosity as the doorkeeper approached the royal dais, bowed low, and spoke to someone in the group.

A man seated in the midst of the others leaned forward to listen, then craned his neck around to look toward Lugh. The others in the group did the same. The isolated drinker turned too, wondering what was of such interest.

The object of all these stares smiled back at them as amiably as he could.

The man in the center of the company—Lugh assumed it was King Bres—spoke to the doorkeeper, gestured toward Lugh, then sat back, smiling himself. All of them appeared to be smiling, and that cheered the boy a bit. He waited expectantly as the servant turned and marched briskly back to him.

"All right, lad. Bres will see you," the doorkeeper announced. "Go on up there. But, be careful! Bres is not one to be taking chances with!"

Lugh straightened his rain-soaked cloak the best way he could, pushed back the matted hair from his forehead, and strode down purposefully toward the group. He tried not to look self-conscious under the staring eyes.

As he neared them, he began to take in details of the individuals there. What he saw drained away his bit of cheer.

They were tall and lean, and held themselves with self-conscious haughtiness. Their features were bold, with strongly sculptured noses and chins, but their expressions were coldly aloof, eyes sweeping arrogantly over Lugh. He realized that their smiles held no welcome for him, only pompous amusement at the sight of this bedraggled wanderer.

He stopped before them. The man seated in their midst

shifted forward and Lugh had his first close look at High-King
Bres.

The king was certainly an impressive man, although different from the others. His figure was more massive, the
shoulders broader, the head square and settled sturdily on a
muscular neck. His features were more roughly hewn, his
hair dark and rippling back from his forehead in thick waves.
The physical nature of Bres was very pronounced. Suppressed
energy surged through the taut body. Here was a being who
thrived on movement, a warrior who found inactivity an
irritant.

Lugh assessed this much of the man before meeting his
gaze directly. When he did, it was as if night lightning had
flashed unexpectedly, illuminating a scene clearly for an
instant. And, for that instant, Lugh was certain that he knew
this man, that they shared some inner secret that only the
two of them could understand. Then, like lightning, the
impression flickered out, leaving him to doubt the reality of
the image in the uncertain darkness.

But Bres had seen it too, Lugh could tell that. The man's
smile had frozen and the eyes gone blank in that same instant
of contact. He had covered his confusion by breaking off the
gaze, sweeping his head around to smile at his company
before looking back at Lugh.

"Well, now," he said in a soft, slow, oddly gentle voice,
"you're a bit young for claiming such great skills, aren't you?"

The words were mocking, but the dark eyes were scrutiniz-
ing Lugh with deliberation. Bres was a warrior who had
survived by calculating every element, every risk. Now he
had felt something that he didn't understand and it disturbed
him.

This knowledge came to Lugh in a rush. He wasn't sure
how he could so easily understand the king's character, but
he didn't doubt the truth of it. Bres was, indeed, someone
that he had to beware.

The others were laughing insolently at Lugh after the
king's remark. All they saw was a ragged, dripping vagabond,
a peasant boy whom their king had called in for some
amusement.

"How did you learn these skills of yours?" Bres asked.

"I've learned them in my travels, sir," Lugh told him. "It's
how I live."

"And just where have you traveled, boy?"

"In the lands to the east," he replied promptly. This answer, like the others, had been supplied to him by Manannan. "It was fishermen brought me here."

"Who are your people?"

"That I don't know at all, sir. I've been wandering alone since I can remember."

"By the look of him, he's no Fomor," said a raven-beaked fellow behind the king. "But, by the smell, he's surely not high born!"

His rasping caw of laughter was joined by the women's twittering.

"Well, if he has all the skills he claims, we should call him Illdanach, Master of All Arts!" another of the men exclaimed.

"A Master of All Swine would be more suited to his looks," a third responded, and they all joined in the callous laughter.

Lugh flushed with anger and embarrassment. He had no way to respond to this undeserved ridicule. He'd asked only for some simple hospitality. If Manannan wanted him to learn about these people, he was surely doing so—in the worst way. And he certainly didn't like what he was learning.

He told himself to hold back his mounting rage. He had to keep patience. To do what he had to do, he first had to be accepted here.

At the tables behind him, the bearded drinker had watched this exchange with his own growing fury. Now he leapt to his feet.

"I've listened to this for long enough!" he shouted. "No one should be denied hospitality in the house of the Tuatha de Danann!"

Bres looked toward the figure irritably.

"Old man, what's shaken you out of your drunken slumber?" he demanded.

"A drunkard I may be," the other answered, "but I'll not see you shame this boy when all he asks is a chance to prove himself!"

Lugh looked around at the lone figure. He stood stiffly erect, vibrating with his anger. His spare, weathered face, stubbled with grey beard, was hard. His eyes glittered sharply with defiance.

The voice of Bres took on a more strident note as he responded.

"Nuada, you've no say in this court now!"

"No say!" the old man cried. His right hand rose suddenly from his side, lifted high and fell in one, sweeping stroke. It shattered the thick planks before him, collapsing the table in a splintered heap.

With cries of terror, those around Bres pulled back. Nuada stepped toward them, the hand rising again.

It shone bright silver in the firelight and seemed huge to Lugh. He stared at it in fascination as it lifted to point at Bres threateningly.

"This silver hand is the only say left to me," he said fiercely. "But, by its power, I'll see you give this boy his chance!"

VI

THE BATTLE-RAVEN

BRES WAS UNIMPRESSED by this performance.

"Nuada, your drinking has made you a madman surely," he told the old man as if addressing a troublesome child. "I'll not be threatened by you no matter how much furniture you destroy."

"Wait, Bres. He may be right," said a new voice from the group.

Bres looked around in surprise as a girl moved out from the others to stand beside him.

She seemed very young to Lugh, her features softer, less austere than those of the other women. Her small nose and high cheekbones were dusted with freckles, and a wavy flow of warm, red-brown hair fell freely about her shoulders. But her shining brown eyes swept him with a gaze as unfeeling as the rest, and her words were as scornful and cruel.

"This boy should be made to show his skills to us."

"Oh, come now, Aine," Bres replied. "Why waste time with the whelp? He's clearly lying in his claims."

"He has made a challenge, cousin," she reminded him firmly. "If you send him away without making him prove it, you'll make him seem the winner. You'll make it look as if you were afraid to try him."

"Who would believe that?" he asked derisively. But a faint doubt tightened the lines about his eyes.

"Who in Tara wouldn't like to believe it?" she countered. She knelt by him and spoke with intensity. "Do you want to chance giving them another hero? Another reason to call you scornful names? No. You have to try him, make him look the fool." She laid a hand on his arm and smiled winningly, adding in a cajoling way: "Besides, cousin, no matter how badly he does, we can still have some sport with him."

Bres looked into the innocent, smiling face and laughed.

"So young you are to have such a wicked mind," he said, stroking the soft cheek. "All right, Aine. We'll try the lad. And you can choose the skill he'll demonstrate for us."

"Oh, cousin! What fun!" she said gleefully. She jumped up and turned to Lugh, eyeing him carefully as she considered.

Lugh watched her, his nervousness increasing. What was this pretty but very nasty young woman going to do to make him prove his bragging claims?

"He said he was a harper," she announced at last. "Let him play for us. We've no good harpers left here anymore!"

The harp! Relief flooded Lugh at her words. Of all the ways he might have been tried, this was the one he felt surest about. A sense of confidence began to return to him.

"Fetch the boy a harp. Quickly!" Bres barked at the sharp-nosed man.

A harp was brought to Lugh. It was a finely wrought instrument, and the boy held it for a moment, running his hands over the carved ivory and gold, lightly caressing the strings. He recalled another instrument, not so fine as this one, but his own, left behind in the ruins of his flaming home.

"Now then, boy, try to play it!" Bres demanded impatiently. "Let's have this over with!"

Lugh concentrated his attention on the harp. The room, the situation, his own fears faded away. He knew now was the time when the skills Taillta had given him would be his only aide. He trusted to her teaching and began to play.

His music was like sunlight flooding the room. It swept back the night's shadows and the damp, chill air. The company, so recently laughing at Lugh, suddenly found themselves enchanted. The music cheered and saddened, soothed and aroused all at once. Their arrogance dissolved in human warmth as they were drawn completely within the spell cast by the harp.

All except for Bres.

When he saw what the music was doing to his companions, he reacted sharply.

"Enough of this!" he cried, the cold words splashing like icy water on the slumbering group, snapping them back to life.

"He's not so bad now, is he?" Nuada challenged, grinning with enjoyment at the High-King's obvious discomfiture.

"The boy can play," Bres admitted grudgingly. "But it's only one skill. He claims many."

This time, however, there were no supporting words from those around him. The boy's playing had won the admiration of the company.

"By his skill with the harp alone he has proven his worth," one of the ladies suggested. "He is finer than any harper I've yet heard."

There were murmurs of agreement from the others, but Bres cut them short.

"No! Such skill at playing tells me that he could not have had the time to master others. We must try him at something else."

"What will you try?" the beaked man asked. "We can't have him work metal or do healing here and now."

"Try him at games," said Aine. "He said he was a master of them too, didn't you, boy?"

"I've knowledge of many," Lugh replied, a bit less humbly than before. With his first success, his confidence had grown immeasurably. "I'd say I was a fair hand at most of them."

"Oh, a fair hand, is it?" Bres repeated mockingly. "Then, let's see you try that hand at the chess boards."

A carved board with gleaming pieces of silver and gold was set up before the company. The beak-nosed one began, playing casually at first against the boy, then with more care, and, finally, desperation as Lugh destroyed his attack and won in a score of moves.

More of the king's followers tried. Each one lost. As the victories mounted, so did the audible support from the company for this amazing lad. In the end, forgetting their positions, they cheered with open enthusiasm as opponents met defeat, much to the frustration of Bres.

When no more challengers could be found, Nuada prodded gleefully at his High-King:

"Perhaps you'd play against the lad yourself, if you still doubt his skills. You're said to be the finest in all Eire!"

Bres threw a dark look at the silver-handed one. It was clear to Lugh that he'd take no chance of being bested by this ragged youth. The humiliation of the others had been quite enough. Yet, he wasn't about to give up. More than ever, now, he needed to defeat Lugh and be rid of him.

"The skills we've seen so far are only to entertain. There is another, more valuable skill which he can demonstrate to us here." He looked at Lugh. "You claimed that you were trained as a warrior, didn't you?"

"I did," Lugh responded brightly. He was feeling by this time that there was no test he couldn't pass. "I've been taught well in the arts of warfare."

"And, would you be willing to demonstrate those skills to us?"

"Willingly I would, sir," Lugh agreed emphatically.

"Good," Bres said with satisfaction. "Then we'll have a bit of a contest." He lifted his voice and called out: "Morrigan!"

At this call, a figure rose from behind the group, where Lugh had not seen it before. It moved forward, around the others, into the fire's light.

It was a woman. But any surprise Lugh felt at that was obscured by his first impression of her. For she was a strange figure, unlike any woman he had ever seen.

She was very tall, over a head above Lugh, and very thin. The long, straight body was shrouded by a heavy, black cloak furled around her like great wings. Her head was nearly a skull, the pale skin drawn tightly over sharp cheekbones and jutting chin, the eyes an ice-blue glitter deep within shadowed sockets. The effect of it was further exaggerated by glossy black hair, pulled tightly back from a high forehead, fastened behind and left to flow past the shoulders in a wave that glistened like moonlight on a midnight stream.

"You can't pit Morrigan against this boy!" Nuada protested sharply. "He's not a warrior. And he's unarmed!"

"He may be right again, cousin," Aine agreed.

Lugh thought he noted a touch of concern in her voice, and Bres must have too. He looked sharply around at her.

"Worried about the lad now, are you?" he asked. "This was your suggestion, remember."

"I suggested we test him, yes," she said. "But Morrigan is a bit single-minded in things like this."

Lugh had already noticed that. The tall woman didn't seem to have been softened by his music or impressed by his gaming skills. She was staring at him with the keen intensity of a hawk tracking its prey. A little of Lugh's confidence faded. But she was a woman, and a thin one at that, he told himself. And this was only going to be a demonstration, a friendly contest.

While he was working his confidence back up with these points, Bres was countering the objections.

"Look here! Since I began this little trial, Nuada's been throwing this boy's successes up to me. Well, if he's as good at fighting as at the other things, it'll take someone of Morrigan's ability to test him." He looked at her. "And, you'll be careful, won't you Morrigan?"

Her steady gaze remained fixed on Lugh. The thin mouth parted slightly in a smile, revealing even lines of small, white, pointed teeth.

"I'll try to be," she said in a voice that rattled like tree limbs in a winter wind.

"Then get the boy some weapons," Bres commanded briskly.

"He'll use mine," Nuada volunteered.

The old man came around the tables to Lugh. He threw back his cloak and drew out a long and a short sword. As he did so, Lugh noted with interest that the silver hand moved with the same flexibility as the other.

Nuada handed the weapons over. Leaning closer, he said urgently:

"Listen, boy, be careful! Bres means to see you dead in this."

"I don't think so," Lugh answered easily. "What harm can she do me?" He took the weapons and tested them. They were well-made. He smiled at the old man. "But, I do thank you for your help."

Nuada shook his head resignedly and stepped back. Lugh pulled off his cloak and Morrigan did the same. Beneath hers she wore only a warrior's short tunic, belted by her sword harness. Her bare arms and legs were unnaturally long, thin and hard. All bones and tendons they looked, with great hands and clawed, bony fingers.

She drew out her own sword and a short, double-bladed ax and set herself to fight. Her long, corded neck craned forward, the glittering eyes fixed on him.

"Oh, boy," Bres called to him. "Before you start, there is something I should mention to you. Morrigan has promised to take care, but she does have a taste for blood. When she scents it, she loses all control. She becomes quite...ah... unpleasant then. So, please, try not to bleed, all right?"

Lugh looked from Bres to the woman. She was smiling a bit more widely now, and he saw the tip of her tongue flick lightly over those sharp, white teeth. It occurred to him that Nuada's warning should not have been ignored.

Then Bres gave the signal to begin, and Lugh had no more time to consider. The woman was on him.

Her attack was incredibly swift. She moved with sudden jerking movements, so fast she seemed to be coming from several points at once, driving in with both weapons. She poked and scratched at him and flapped around him continuously, while he moved and parried furiously just to keep her off.

She seemed to have unlimited energy, but the constant effort began to tire him. While he was able to barely hold his own, he knew that he'd slow soon, and then she'd strike through his defenses.

And yet, he also knew he couldn't lose this. It was the crucial trial. If she defeated him too easily or too soon, Bres would be rid of him without delay.

He called upon every bit of knowledge, every trick taught him by Taillta and her veteran warriors. Nothing seemed to slow the woman down. He backed toward the fire, trying at least to limit the direction of her attack. As he did, he realized that her lunges at him were becoming erratic.

He watched her moves carefully and finally understood what was causing the change. As he moved before the fire, the bright light of its flames flickered around him, throwing him into deep shadow while the rays shone into Morrigan's eyes. The flashes seemed to distract her, like a shining bauble attracting a raven's eye. Her thrusts became more blind.

He began to use her weakness, jerking from left to right

constantly so that the flares of light pulled her attention back and forth, keeping her off-balance. It gave him a little breathing space.

Soon her frustration at being so distracted brought her in closer and she took more chances, striking at him more wildly, angrily. He looked for an opening, hoping to disarm her without having to wound her.

Then he saw his chance. She brought her ax around in a wide curve, backed with all her strength. He sidestepped it easily, and the weapon struck a thick roof support, sinking deeply into the hard oak. It stuck there.

She thrust up with the sword in her other hand, but Lugh was ready. He caught her blade between both of his, and with a deft twist wrenched it from her grip. It spun away, glittering, to fall into the fire.

A supportive cry went up from the watchers at Lugh's successful move. But his victory was a short-lived one. The disarmed woman drove forward with her head at the unexpecting boy. He staggered back and fell, striking his head against the rough corner of the hearthstones.

He sat up groggily, his temple hot with pain. He saw Morrigan standing over him, arms raised, legs bent, perched as if to swoop. Her head was forward, the blue glass beads of her eyes fixed on him greedily.

The wound on his head was bleeding, he realized. He could feel the wet ooze of it as he watched the hungry light flare in her eyes, watched the tongue flick out across the fine, sharp teeth.

He tried to get his weapons up in defense, but she struck too swiftly. With a hoarse cry that was both hiss and shriek at once, she threw herself upon him. Her weight drove him back against the hearth. But as he fell, he realized with horror that it was now no human being who was upon him, but a giant raven, bigger than a hawk, black as a moonless sea.

The bird was maddened by bloodlust, fighting to strike at his bleeding wound, raking at his chest with its great claws, beating him about the head with heavy wings that raised a deafening thunder in his ears.

So furious was the attack, so stunning in its speed, that the astonished Lugh was nearly helpless. The swords fell from his hands as he raised one arm to shield his face and the other to try to hold the raven off. He was unable to get up or move away. The bird's beak struck in a blur of speed, jabbing at his eyes, cutting his cheek, tearing his forearm.

A detached corner of his mind registered that this bird was going to kill him here. It would tear out his throat, pluck out his eyes, sit on his carcass and slake its thirst in his blood. And he hadn't the strength to stop it.

Then a hand came into his view. It was a silver hand, and that same, detached portion of his mind regarded it with curiosity. The hand was so close that Lugh could see its fine details: etched nails, the lines of the flexing joints, even the faint marks of engraved hair.

The hand gripped the bird about its thick neck, clenched tight and pulled. The bird was torn away from Lugh, flapping and screeching, its claws and beak still trying to rake the boy.

Lugh sat up to see it dangling above him, held out safely at arm's length in Nuada's silver hand.

"Enough!" the old man shouted. He threw the bird away from him with a slight movement of the hand which sent it across the room to land, like a tattered scrap of black cloth, amidst the tables.

It lay motionless a moment, and then it began to move. In amazement Lugh watched the bird's form convulse, shimmer, and suddenly expand as the raven resumed the shape of Morrigan.

Her face was contorted with the blind fury of a raptor driven from its kill. She started back toward Nuada, but the hand came up toward her.

"Back, Morrigan, or I'll wring that scrawny neck of yours as I would any crow's!"

She hesitated, staring fearfully at the gleaming hand. Then her fury died. She slumped back on a bench, drained of her mad energy, the lanky body folding up.

Nuada turned toward the High-King.

"This boy has proven his skills!" he announced. "Few warriors could have done so well against her."

"She would have beaten him," Bres argued.

"Would you have done better, Bres?" Nuada countered. "He's done enough to prove himself. Even your own people agree."

There were mutterings of assent, and Bres glared about at them. They fell silent, but none would meet his eyes.

"And, if you can't find the generosity to give him what he's earned, I'll give it myself!" the old man added. "I'll take him to my home and see he has the comforts of a guest!"

"You've no right to interfere in this, Nuada," Bres warned darkly.

"Then you keep me from it!" the old man answered him.

For a long moment the two glared stubbornly at one another. Then, realizing where all sympathy would lie in this, Bres sank back sullenly.

"Take the boy and be damned!" he growled.

Nuada went quickly to the still-dazed Lugh. He took the weapons from the boy and helped him up.

"Come on, lad," he said, putting a supporting arm about Lugh's shoulders. "Let's be out of here. Even if I can only find you a cow shed, it'll better any comforts you'll find here!"

As he urged Lugh toward the door, Bres watched them go, all his battle-instinct for survival aroused. There was something very wrong about this boy.

He signalled sharply and the beaked one leaned down to him.

"Keep a close watch on that boy, Negran. Report to me on everything he does."

The man nodded. Behind him the girl Aine, overhearing the order, nodded too.

Outside the hall, the cool wind whipped the fine rain about Lugh and Nuada. It seemed refreshing to Lugh now, stimulating his wrenched, overheated body and bringing him back to full consciousness.

"You come to my quarters, lad," Nuada said. "I'll have that wound tended and give you food and a place to rest. It's not a king's hall, but it's dry and warm."

"But sir, I'd really hoped for more than a bed tonight," Lugh ventured. "I'd stay longer here."

"You want to stay here?" Nuada asked in dismay. He stopped to face Lugh, saying emphatically: "Boy, why? What you've seen here so far isn't the worst of it!"

"I'd like a chance to find that out for myself, sir. I want to stay."

"You are a stubborn one," Nuada said. Then a smile lit the worn face. "I've not seen anyone with your courage for a long time."

Then his smile faded again, and he shook his head, adding doubtfully:

"I don't know. You've surely earned the right to stay if you choose. Still, you shouldn't decide too quickly. Stay with me tonight. Tomorrow I'll have a young nephew of mine show all of Tara to you. Go with him. See it all. Then you can decide."

"All right. I will do that," Lugh promised him.

"Good!" Nuada said, throwing a helping arm over Lugh's shoulders again. "You are a lad with the will to fight still in you. I've no wish to see you destroyed by the plague on us!"

VII

THE FOMOR

THE TWO DOGS rolled together on the ground, a tangle of scrawny limbs and swiftly moving jaws as they tore at one another. Their savage battle barely disturbed the flock of blackbirds which covered the nearby carcass like a fluttering cloak.

As Lugh passed by, he noted that the object of this desperate struggle was the wasted body of another dog. From the starved condition of the combatants, it was clear to him that the loser would be joining it as a prize for other scavengers.

Ahead of him now, at the base of the fortress' hill, he could see the town. Already he was receiving a forewarning of what he would face there. The odor of decay and filth and death lifted to meet him on the morning breeze.

His guide to the town below was Angus Og. For Lugh, there was a pleasurable sense of comfortable reality about this amiable, gangly youth. He seemed little more than a boy himself and treated the newcomer warmly and openly. The two had struck up an immediate friendship. It was something Lugh had missed since losing his island home. He'd begun to doubt that his idea of reality even existed anymore.

But as Angus guided him through the town, as Nuada had promised, he found another reality he didn't want.

The place was a horror, a pit of human misery which

sickened Lugh as he and his companion walked the refuse-choked streets.

The starving seemed to be everywhere. Children stared up with empty eyes from behind swollen stomachs. Old men and women sprawled helpless in doorways and corners, their bony legs like brittle twigs, their faces sunken, spotted with festering sores. He saw them, too weak even to crawl from the stagnant muck or sweep away the swarming insects. He saw dying and dead. In one spot a mass grave, filled with dried, broken ruins, was being filled. He saw a large house where scores of wretched people were stacked. And through all of it he heard the cawing of the blackbirds that soared overhead, and he smelled the incredible stench of a dying place.

Yet it had been living once. A living place. A fine place. As in the fortress, Lugh could see the remains of that. Most of the buildings in the town were well-built, decorated with the artistic flourish of people who loved beauty and life, of people who cared. And these wretched people, they had been beautiful too. He saw the nobility, the beauty in the shattered visages of the starving and in the few healthier people who crept amongst the refuse.

"Angus, what's happened here?" he asked his new comrade.

"It's been stripped of everything, as we have been," Angus answered bitterly. Here, amongst the misery, the young man's cheer had vanished.

"Is all of Eire like this?"

"I've shown you the very worst here," said Angus. My uncle Nuada wanted you to see that. I think he's hoping to frighten you away from here. But there are many other places as bad. Some parts of the country are barren, cattle and crops taken. If you travel there you hear the dying rustling through the grass as they crawl away to hide, ashamed to let anyone see them so weak and starved. Why, I've seen them eating the grass, like their poor, starving hounds, because they've nothing else."

"Why?" asked Lugh. "This looks a rich land. Where is all the wealth?"

"It's been taken. Stolen by scum who drain us dry and then give us insult."

"Do you mean Bres?"

"I mean the bloody Fomor!" Angus spat it out like a morsel

of rotten food. "Pirates they are. Barely men at all. They're our masters. Though Bres has his part in it right enough!"

"What do you mean?" Lugh asked, a bit confused. "Is Bres one of these Fomor?"

"No, worse luck. Bres is one of us. Still, since he became High-King, he's done nothing except to convince our people not to resist the Fomor. He's kept alive the fear that they'll destroy us. So we pay 'tribute', as they call it. I call it slavery myself. The Fomor take what they want, and Bres sits on the hill with his protected company and watches."

"They don't bother him?"

"Oh, no! The Fomor and he need each other to keep us in control. His wealth and that of his own company go untouched. For all his saying he's looking to our good, he cares nothing for the rest of us. Many of the court have abandoned him, but the fearful and the ones wanting his power and the ones who feel bound to him by their oaths of loyalty stay on."

"What about Nuada?" Lugh asked.

"Nuada only goes there for a place to drink his ale and dream," Angus said sadly. "He's given up."

"What about the rest of you?" Lugh asked. "Why do you let this happen?"

"Some of us would fight, but the rest are afraid. They're certain the Fomor would destroy us utterly."

"I don't understand," Lugh said. "You're dying now! What are these Fomor that could make the horror I've seen a better choice?"

As they came around a corner, Lugh collided with someone coming the other way. He looked up and then recoiled at what he saw.

The face he looked into was a nightmare one. There was no nose in the folds of hanging flesh, only twin, gleaming caverns which pulsed rhythmically. Above this, close-set eyes stared from behind thick brows of wiry hair. Below, a mouth sagged, the drooping lip revealing broken teeth.

This thing shoved Lugh aside as it brushed past, followed by five others. Lugh watched them pass, fighting back the urge to run, for things like them had peopled the strange tales he'd heard the warriors tell. They were the fears of childhood crawling out from the shadowed passages of the mind.

All were malformed in grotesque ways, twisted like wind-tormented trees, knobbed or bent. Though powerful in build, many lacked limbs or portions of them. An arm was missing here, a foot there, some hands were replaced by odd, wing-like stubs or claws.

But the faces were the worst, as if created by a sculptor whose hand had created human likenesses and then, impelled by some perversity, twisted and mauled them into mad caricature. The head of one seemed melted into his shoulders, without neck or jaw. Another's eyes bulged from the sides of his head. And one had a second, wizened, lifeless face hanging where an ear should have been.

Lugh stood staring after them as they moved on. When they had rounded a corner out of sight, Angus stepped up to his stricken friend.

"Now you understand a little better," he said. "Those were men of the local garrison of Fomor."

"I've never seen anything like them," said Lugh, still staring after them. "What are they? Where did they come from?"

"They come from an island somewhere in the northern seas," Angus explained as he led the way up the street. "Once they were men just like us, at least that's what the old tales say. They were the masters of all the lands then, and they had the control of forces beyond what our druids understand. But then some curse fell upon them and turned them to these monsters." He smiled without much humor. "Oh, there's many a terrible child's story that explains it, and all different. It's hard to separate truth from poet's fancy. I don't know if any of them are true, myself. It all happened hundreds of years ago, long before our own history began. Some of the High-Bards, now, they might know the truth of it."

"I'd like to talk to one of them," Lugh said earnestly.

"Well, not in Tara will you be doing that!" Angus told him darkly. "All our High-Bards were killed or run out by Bres, like the rest of our finest druids and teachers. He called them traitors. He was afraid that they'd keep up a spirit of rebellion against the Fomor." He laughed derisively. "He told the rest of us it was meant to protect us!"

Lugh wanted to know more, but his companion's explanations were interrupted by the scream of a woman somewhere behind them.

Without hesitation, Lugh turned and ran toward the sound.

"Wait!" Angus called after him, but Lugh went on. He had heard pain and terror in that scream. Someone was in desperate trouble.

He rounded a corner and became immediately lost. He heard another scream and followed it, winding through alleys between the buildings, emerging on a broader avenue in what seemed a better section of the town.

He was facing what was clearly a fishermen's marketplace, for the stalls lining the street were piled with a variety of seafood. Before the stalls were the Fomor he'd passed in the street. Two of them held a struggling, sobbing young woman while the noseless one threatened a battered-looking man.

"Pay us what you owe," the Fomor was growling, prodding the frightened man with a longsword. "Pay now or we'll take the payment from your wife!"

"Give me a chance to sell my fish. I've just brought them in today. I'll pay you soon. Please, don't harm my wife!"

"Don't beg from us!" The Fomor cuffed him with a casual brutalness, then hauled him close, shaking him. "We'll take our payment now. These stinking fish are yours."

He shoved the man away from him and turned toward the young woman, his loose mouth lifted in a rotting smile.

"Let them alone!" Lugh cried out, striding up to them.

The noseless one swung around, bringing his sword up as he snarled at the boy:

"I don't know who you are, but clear off or I'll gut you like you were one of these fish yourself!"

There were six men bristling with weapons, while Lugh was unarmed and alone. But with the momentum provided him by his outrage, he didn't even pause to consider that.

He grabbed the first object—a large, fresh salmon—and swung it hard against the warrior's head.

The heavy fish slapped him solidly across the ear, the wet mass of flesh connecting with a sharp crack. The noseless man's head snapped sideways, and he toppled to the ground.

Lugh reached for another fish as a second Fomor lunged. His sword point went home, but the boy only smiled. The puzzled warrior looked down to see his weapon deeply embedded in a fat cod. This gave Lugh time to kick him squarely in the groin. He went down too.

But the other four Fomor were moving in. Lugh spun about and tipped a large cart in front of them. It was filled with herring which poured onto the ground in an iridescent, slippery flood. The Fomor slid into them, crashing down onto the mass of oily fish.

One escaped the tangle, moving around the pile to come at Lugh. The boy lifted a haddock to defend himself, parrying the attack with swings of the long fish, wishing the thing had a crab's hard shell.

The warrior drove him back against a stall, carving away great chunks of Lugh's only defense at every stroke. Meanwhile, the noseless man was getting up. The other warriors were floundering out of the pulped mass of fish, bruised and covered with grease, quite irritated, and still well-armed.

It came to Lugh suddenly that he was in trouble.

"Help me! Get me a sword!" he called to the couple. "Please, do something!"

He didn't consider it an unreasonable request, but they only stood there, huddled together fearfully.

Then somewhere in the distance a dog began to bark. Another answered it, a third, a fourth, and suddenly the sound of barking dogs was rising all about them.

Lugh paid little mind to it at first, largely absorbed as he was in keeping himself alive. But very quickly he became aware that the Fomorians had paused to listen.

The sound was growing, as if the dogs were all moving in their direction, converging on that spot. Lugh didn't understand what was happening, but it seemed to be disturbing his adversaries a great deal. They first looked worried and then outright frightened, drawing together, ignoring Lugh and the couple.

Suddenly from the alleys and streets around there burst great streams of dogs, largely gaunt mastiffs and massive wolfhounds hardened by starvation, pooling in one snarling pack.

The astonished Lugh wondered if the scent of the fish had brought them. He lifted his now limp and well-notched haddock defensively in case they should attack. But the animals paid no notice to him or the frightened couple. They swarmed about the clustered Fomorians who crouched, weapons ready.

The warriors were panicked. They swung about them wildly at the animals. But the lean animals were fast and experienced in fighting. They avoided the swords and axes, slipping behind or under them to tear at the men's legs.

The warriors stood it only a short while. Then they broke and ran, charging blindly through their attackers, galloping madly away up the avenue, pursued closely by the howling pack.

Lugh listened as the barking and the shrieks of pain died away. Then he felt a hand grip his arm and pull him around.

He was looking into a pair of clear, brown eyes. The girl Aine was beside him, holding him, looking up at him angrily.

"Are you mad to face those warriors alone?" she demanded.

"I couldn't let them harm those people," he told her defensively, taken off-guard by her unexpected appearance.

"So you thought you'd get yourself executed? What help would that have been?"

"But, where did those dogs come from so quickly?" he asked her, a bit bewildered by the swift events.

"They likely smelled the Fomor," she answered vaguely. "Dogs hate them as much as they fear dogs."

She left him and went to the couple who still stood with their arms about each other, staring after their vanished tormentors. Aine placed a reassuring hand on each of them. They looked toward her with the frightened eyes that are born of long abuse.

"They won't be coming back soon," Aine told them. From beneath her cloak she pulled a pouch, pressing it into the man's hand. He looked at it dumbfounded.

"If they do return, give them this," she said. "It's more than they deserve. If they dare to bother you further, tell them the cousin of King Bres is watching over you."

She spoke gently to them, but when she turned back to Lugh her voice was hard.

"And you, remember you're a stranger here. Don't be interfering with things until you're certain you know what we're about!"

Before Lugh could reply she'd trotted off briskly along the street. He started after her but was stopped by Angus who ran up to him, breathless.

"Lugh, here you are!" he gasped out. "I lost you in the streets. I've been searching everywhere. What's happened here?"

"That girl helped me," Lugh began, but when he turned to point her out, he saw that she was already gone.

"What girl?" Angus asked with curiosity.

Lugh explained. Angus listened in fascination to the tale.

"So, she has a power over the dogs, has she?" he mused when Lugh had finished. "Few of the de Dananns have any magical skills so developed." He shook his head. "But why did she use them to save you?"

"What do you mean?" asked Lugh.

"Why, she's one of the High-King's circle, and a cousin to Bres besides! She came here from some dun far to the south not long ago, but she's as heartless and arrogant as any on the hill. Bres has taken quite a liking to her. He knows a spirit like his own. It's not likely she'd be rushing to save a poor stranger who had humiliated him."

Lugh understood what he meant. His own impression of the girl matched what his companion was saying.

Angus eyed him speculatively. "If she saved you, it's for some reason, and I'm thinking Bres is behind it. They want you alive, my friend, most likely to find out what you're about. You'd best be careful. With her powers, she could have the dogs tearing you apart next time."

Lugh told himself that Angus was probably right. But there was still a vague doubt in his mind. The girl certainly hadn't needed to help that wretched couple or give them her protection. Was she really so cruel as she seemed?

He just couldn't be sure, of her or of anything. It was all so complex here, and he knew so little, as she had pointed out. It was becoming clearer to him that his task for Manannan might not be such a simple one.

"Angus, I've got to find out a great deal more about what's happening here," he told his comrade urgently. "I need to know about the de Dananns . . . about the Fomor. Can you help me to find out?"

Angus considered a moment. Then he grinned.

"I think it's time that you met my father," he said.

Water gushed up around the pole as it drove deeply into the soft mud, making a viscous, thucking noise.

Three men put weight on the heavy pole and a score of others shifted for positions where they could place their shoulders solidly against the rock.

It was an immense piece of stone, jutting up the height of two men, sitting complacently, stolidly in the pool-spotted muck at the bottom of the trench.

High above, on the trench's rim, Lugh and Angus watched these men and scores of others as they labored to dig a new motte twice the width and depth of the others circling the fortress' mound. Lugh's friend had called his attention to the men pitted in the impassioned struggle with the boulder.

The workers placed themselves carefully, tensed, and at a call, threw their collective brawn into the battle. Legs sank into the gripping maw of the mud, arms slipped, bones scraped raw on the rough stone, muscles pulled and strained.

And the rock moved not one hair's breadth in distance.

"Hold it! Hold it, you fellows!" a voice bellowed above the worker's din.

At once the men desisted, willingly, some dropping in exhaustion where they were. Lugh's attention was drawn from them to a figure that now crossed the trench floor.

It was a black giant of a man who strode toward them. He towered a head and more above the tallest of them. A great, round chest was the source of the booming-barrel voice. Long arms and legs were muscled like gnarled oaks and as thick as the main branches of them. He was black with the rich mud of the trench, so covered he seemed part of the earth himself.

"You're just not puttin' your hearts into it, lads," he complained sadly.

He sighed heavily and stared at the massive thing, walking around it and viewing it critically from all angles. In doing so, his eye was caught by the sight of a few Fomorians who had stopped not far from Lugh and Angus to watch the work. They were pointing down at the men, laughing amongst themselves, as if the failure of these poor slaves was a delight to them.

"Well, that's done it now!" the giant muttered angrily. "They think we're beaten? Then we'll let them see just what one of the de Dananns can do! Stand away there, boys! Stand away!"

He pushed the men aside, eyed the boulder narrowly and worked his muscles to free them for the task.

"All right, now," he told the stubborn mass, "I'll not be

havin' any more of this from you, stone. I will not! Move on back all the rest of you. It's just the two of us this time!"

The man rubbed his hands together. He stepped up to the boulder, dug his legs in deeply, setting his feet firmly into places felt out in the clutching ooze, carefully positioning his shoulder against the rough stone.

The great stomach hardened, forming a trunk. The legs rooted, holding firm. The back and arms strained tight.

There was a long, motionless moment. The Fomor watched with expectant smiles as the black figure fought the stone, two objects of the earth in mortal combat. Then their smiles changed to astonishment and chagrin. The stone began to move.

Slowly, very slowly, it began to pull up from the mud which gripped at it, sucked at it, reluctant to give up its own. The stone shifted up, rolled over with a loud, defeated sigh, and toppled into the cart pushed up behind it.

The giant straightened, glancing at it with disdain. Then he threw a look up toward the watching Fomorians. The black mask of his face split with a broad grin and his eyes glowed as he bellowed up at them:

"Now, who can say the Dagda has lost his strength, ay?"

The Fomor turned away, their monstrous faces twisted with anger, and strode off quickly. The man in the trench watched them go. Nodding his satisfaction, he swung around to see the triumphant grins on his men. It recalled him to business, and he issued brisk orders.

"Enough now, you lads! No more foolishness. I'll not have those scavenging horrors seeing my men idle. Get back to it!"

As they went back to work, he scanned the rim again. This time he noted Lugh and Angus there. He flashed another enormous smile and called up in greeting.

"Angus! Good to see you, son!"

"Father," Angus called back, "I've got someone here I think you ought to see."

VIII

THE MEN OF DEA

CLEAR WATER SLUICED down over the great head, dragging away the coating of black mud, running it down across the swell of chest. From beneath, a face emerged, broad-featured, thick-nosed, a round chin that broadened upward to a large forehead. The whole landscape of it was seamed like an old mountain slope, worn by time and weather and the grandest of living, both good and bad.

The Dagda shook himself as if he were a great hound, showering the two young men with water, and straightened from the water tub.

"Drink!" he barked sharply, and one of the workers resting nearby tossed him a leather flask. He poured back a large draught, belched heartily, and dropped down on a log, setting his thick legs apart and leaning forward to eye Lugh carefully.

"So, you're wantin' to know more about us here, are you?" he asked after a time. His voice was direct and gruff, almost challenging.

"I do, sir," Lugh replied boldly. "I know nothing about your land or people. I want to understand what's happening here."

The Dagda could see the truth of that in the boy's straightforward look. He nodded with satisfaction and smiled with a sudden congeniality.

"All right, lad. I can see that need in you is a real one. And, from what Angus has told me, the de Dananns owe you a bit for your besting our High-King. Bres is a master at humiliating men, him and his arrogant lot!"

He passed the flask to Lugh, who took a light drink for politeness' sake. It was harsh ale and very strong. The boy choked it down as the Dagda continued.

"I'll tell you what I can. But keep it well in mind that I'm no bard. We've few left here now, truth to say. Many are fled from Tara or are dead, thanks to Bres and the bloody Fomor. Between them they've scattered all our brightness, like a cold, fall wind does the turning leaves. They've left us only bare branches, and any tale I'll give you will be as barren."

"Please, tell me everything you can about yourselves and the Fomor," Lugh urged. "I have to know how things came to be this way."

"Ah, well, our struggle with them has a long history to it," the Dagda said. He took the flask back from Lugh, had another, long draught, and settled himself comfortably.

"It was with our leader Nemed that we first came to this place," he began. "We came from lands to the east, seeking our own place. And we found our Pleasant Land in Eire. We found it . . . but we weren't to have it then. The Fomor were already about, you see, raiding Eire from their island home.

"They tried to squeeze their tribute from us, but we would have none of that. We took our ships and attacked the Fomor island.

"But we had no chance at all. Those of us who lived through it will always remember the terrible powers, like none we'd ever faced before. Nearly all the ships were lost, and Nemed perished with all but thirty of us.

"Hard choices were made by the survivors then. Those without the will to go on returned to our homeland in the east. Those of us with the flame of adventure still burning in us sailed into the unknown western sea.

"We found a land out there. A strange and wonderful land it was, called Tir-na-nog, with four cities—grand Falias and shining Gorias, Finias and rich Murias. Their ruler, Queen Danu, welcomed us in and gave us help.

"We lived there for many years, calling ourselves the Tuatha de Danann—the Children of Danu—after that fine Queen. From her scholars our children learned skills and knowledge of the arts and perfect wisdom. Our druids and physicians learned their magic arts. Our numbers swelled and we grew strong again.

"Still, we knew that land wasn't our own. The image of this shining, pleasant land glowed in our minds, and we knew that it was here we would return one day. When that time came, they sent us back in a concealing mist, before a strong and friendly wind.

"Our bards made songs saying that it was as birds we came,

drifting down from the mist. But I know it was ships that brought us, because it was my own hand which burned them on the shore. We'd bound ourselves, you see, never to leave this place again."

The tale had caught up the Dagda fully now. He stared off into another time, his rough voice growing wistful as he remembered.

"Ah, we were a fine, strong people when we came. The young men and women, filled with life and hope—Ogma who taught writing, and Diancecht who understood the healing arts, and Goibnu the smith, and Mabd and Macha, women of fighting skills no man could match, and Morrigan, that Raven of Battle.

"Beltaine was the day we came on—the first of spring—to settle the place where we would find our peace. But there was someone here before us. Firbolgs they called themselves: The Men of the Bog."

"Firbolgs?" Lugh asked. "Who were they?"

"A tribe of men as wild and as hard as the barren lands where they're living now. They know little but the ways of the earth and animals, but they're the finest fighting men I've tried my sword against. When they saw us coming, they drew all their warriors up to face us, and we went out to meet them.

"We spoke to these men so different from us, and we found that our language was the same! They were our own cousins, descended from those who'd gone back to the east. Years of being enslaved there had turned them hard and cruel. But, like us, they'd kept the dream of Eire alive in them. Finally they'd escaped their masters and returned."

"But what about the Fomor?" Lugh asked. "Where had they gone?"

"They were here. They'd made a peace with the Firbolgs who paid a fair tribute. Our cousins had settled the land and built their homes.

"We told them that we only wanted to do the same. We asked to share the land. They refused us. They were afraid to give us anything, thinking we'd someday take the rest. Well, it wasn't war we wanted, only a place to live. But we'd made our vow to stay, and so we made ready to fight.

"A midsummer day it was when the battle began. A bright, warm, peaceful day. Eleven batallions of the de Dananns went out against the same of them. Four days we fought on the broad plains of Magh Turiedh. Great feats there were done on both sides, and many champions came to their deaths. Then at last we gained the better of them and routed them across the bloody meadows. There were only three hundred of the Firbolgs left unhurt in it when they finally made their peace.

"After that they took their families off into the rugged country to the west and south and left the rest to us. We took possession of it and built our great fortress here at Tara-na-Rie—what was called the Beautiful Ridge. And beautiful it was then, with the green meadows rolling away in every direction, thick with grass, furred by great forests, alive with game and with our herds. At last we had our place to live."

He paused there, looking off into the distance, seeing that golden past. Then the harsh reality of the muddy trench and the starving, exhausted men around him returned to him. His face hardened and anger heated his words.

"Then the Fomor came again!"

"I still don't understand how they got power over you," said Lugh. "Didn't you fight them?"

"We might have fought, if Nuada had still been our king," the Dagda answered.

"Nuada?" Lugh said in surprise. "He was your king?"

"It was my uncle Nuada who led the battle against the Firbolgs," Angus Og supplied. "But he lost his hand in the fight."

"Lost his hand!" Lugh exclaimed. "But, that silver hand I saw . . ."

"Diancecht, our surgeon, and Credene, our smith, labored with the skills given us by Danu to build that silver hand," said the Dagda. "Still, it wasn't enough."

"You see, Lugh, it's an old and foolish belief of our people that no man can rule if he's not whole in body," Angus bitterly explained. "It was decided that Nuada must be replaced."

"My poor brother was broken by the loss," the Dagda said, sadly. "He felt that he had failed us somehow. Since that time he's sat alone, drinking in that hall, feeling defeated and useless. His help to you is the first sign of life from him in years."

"How did Bres become the High-King?" Lugh wondered.

"Oh, he was such a fine champion and such a handsome young man when he was chosen," the Dagda replied sarcastically. "A fit ruler for the likes of us. Everyone loved Bres, especially our ladies. But it wasn't long after that he changed. Now he's never open-handed, always using his power to help the Fomor bleed us, to tax us and leave us to decay."

"I can't believe the people let this happen," Lugh said, "no matter how terrible the Fomor seem."

"Our people were ready to believe the Fomor couldn't be beaten," the Dagda said. "Our years in the four cities made us as soft as slavery made the Firbolgs hard. Our younger people had become lovers of beauty, not warriors. Few kept the tough spirit of my son. They were certain it was the magic of our druids, not our fighting skills and courage, that defeated the Firbolgs. But that magic would be useless against the Fomor powers which had defeated us once before. And with only force of arms, we'd have no chance against such monstrous beings."

"There must be others like you," Lugh told the Dagda. "Other warriors ready to fight."

"There are, but we're not many anymore. Some died in the battle against the Firbolgs. Others are held by ancient oaths of loyalty to support the High-King. Look at Morrigan. There're none so independent of spirit as she. But even with that, even with her love of battle and her blood-madness, she'll follow the High-King. So long as he is on the throne, she'll obey his commands, no matter how much she disagrees."

"And the Fomor are draining us in any way they can," Angus put in. "They've done everything they can to weaken us. They've destroyed our schools, scattered or killed our artists, teachers, bards, druids, physicians—anyone who keeps our culture alive. They've starved and defiled us at every chance. And anyone they think might challenge them is kept working at impossible tasks by Bres."

"I've been digging these unneeded ditches about every fortress in all Eire," the Dagda said. "The labor never ends. They hope that by keeping us worn and hungry they'll destroy our will to fight."

"I think they must fear us more than the Firbolgs," Angus said thoughtfully. "The Fomor treated them mildly. But they're out to crush us totally. And they've nearly succeeded. We've barely enough strength to fight. We try to keep resistance alive, but it's growing harder each day."

"It's because of that I want you to understand the way things are," the Dagda told him earnestly. "Because of your spirit, Nuada would like to see you leave us. For the same reason I'd like to see you with us."

"Yes, Lugh, what do you say?" Angus urged. "You must hate the Fomor. You certainly went after them today! You've seen what they're doing to us. Join with us and help us find some way to fight them."

Lugh's first impulse was to say yes to them. But he held back. He remembered his bond with Manannan, and he remembered the words of the girl Aine. He still didn't know enough to make his judgment. He had to keep his mind open. There were still too many questions left unanswered about the Fomorians and too many things he had to see proven.

Regretfully he shook his head.

"I'm sorry," he told them, "'but I can't join you now."

"What do you mean?" Angus said angrily. "What can be stopping you?"

"I need to know more," Lugh said reasonably. "Don't you see? I know nothing about your struggle but what you've told me. If I'm to make a choice, give up my will to you, fight in your battles, I've got to see the truth of things for myself!"

"What else do you have to know?" Angus demanded. "You've seen the suffering, the starving, the cruelties. What do you . . ."

"Quiet now, Angus!" the Dagda commanded. "Don't press the lad. I understand his feelings in this. He's a stranger here. It's not his fight, and you can't make him pledge himself to us until his own mind is settled. I think it would be best for us to help him discover what he needs to know."

"Thank you for that, sir," Lugh told him with relief. "I could surely use some help. It's these Fomorians I need to know about. I've got to get beyond their monstrous look. I've got to get as close to them as I've been to you, to find out who they are and what they're doing and why."

"You'd be mad to try doing that," said Angus. "You look like one of us. They'd kill you without a thought if you came too close to them. And I can tell you for certain that they'll not sit about and drink and talk with you like we have!"

"There must be some way I can get closer to them," Lugh said.

"There just might be," the Dagda responded thoughtfully. "There's a place in the town where they gather to drink. I might know a way you could go in there unknown. But it would be dangerous."

"It is also necessary. I can't tell you how much," Lugh told him firmly. "Please, tell me what I have to do."

IX

THE CLOWN

LUGH PULLED THE coarse wrapping of wool about his face more tightly as a group of Fomorians pushed past him into the building.

He looked the place over uncertainly, wondering if he could get away with this. He'd seen scores of Fomor enter the large, timber-sided hall. He could hear the loud talk and laughter of a large number inside. His hope was that in such a crowd he'd go unnoticed. The wrapping of his face would help disguise him. Angus had told him that many of the Fomor wrapped their heads or other parts to mask deformities too hideous even for fellow Fomor to stomach. If he could play the part, he might be able to talk with some of them.

There was nothing to gain by hesitating longer. He walked to the doorway of the hall and looked inside.

It was a long, low-ceilinged room, well-lit but filled with oily smoke from the many torches. Fomorian warriors filled the tables, crowded the benches about the outer walls. All were drinking. The combined odor of smoke and ale and the stench of the massed beings rushed to meet Lugh. The sight of this sea of monstrous human parodies reminded him harshly how alone and vulnerable he was.

He froze, suddenly afraid to move, the idea of entering this loathsome place too terrifying for the boy to overcome.

As he hesitated on the threshold, a figure weaving its way

through the tables caught his eye. Some of his terror faded, replaced by a curiosity that turned to amusement as he watched. For even here, in this awful place, Lugh felt that this was one of the most peculiar individuals he'd ever seen.

It was a tall and very awkward man, all arms and legs it seemed. He managed to tangle himself in nearly everything he passed so that he was constantly unwinding his limbs and himself from the posts and tables and other men. He wore an old tunic, striped in once bright colors now faded by age, which flapped around his knees. His shoes seemed far too big and flapped too, so that he made quite a noise as he moved along—rather like a flock of rickety crows, Lugh thought.

He had a dull black sword, unsheathed, stuck through his belt and sticking out naked behind where, in his gyrations, it was always dangerously close to sticking those nearby. His cloak was pulled up over his lean head and, through holes in the hood, his ears poked out absurdly. A long, unkempt beard of wispy, yellow hair fluttered about him like a tattered scarf.

As he moved amongst the tables, he somehow managed to juggle four shiny marble spheres, keeping them whirling in a large circle as he staggered around the warriors.

He stumbled and reeled, tripped and nearly fell again and again, but always kept the balls going, adding more to those in the air until a half-dozen were spinning there. The coarse warriors watched his antics with amusement, waiting for him to fall. Lugh realized that the clownish individual was actually trying to entertain them.

The act ended abruptly. The tall man tumbled over a stool and landed sprawling on his back in a wild pratfall. Still, he managed to catch every falling sphere. The Fomor roared with laughter.

But their smiles disappeared when he arose and moved about them, saying imploringly:

"A little drink for some laughter, my handsome warriors? A bit of food for a poor, hungry man?"

The warriors growled darkly and turned away from him. Some pushed him away, and one, irritated by his begging, sent him sprawling again with a solid kick. He rose painfully and shuffled away, rubbing his backside and trying to smile, but ruefully now. Lugh felt a surge of pity for the simple, awkward clown.

Then the man noticed him, still hesitating on the threshold. To the boy's surprise, the clown's face split in a wide, ludicrous grin and he moved toward Lugh, raising a long-fingered hand in greeting.

"Welcome, welcome!" he said heartily. "Though no one else will likely say so here. But you look in need of it, you do!"

He spoke in a rambling way, but with a real warmth and enthusiasm that enveloped Lugh. Almost at once the boy found himself liking this peculiar fellow, and he didn't object when the clown laid a long crook of arm about his shoulders.

"I've not seen you here before, that I haven't," he said, drawing the boy forward into the room. "But I can see by your eyes you're a young one, and alone too. New to Tara are you, then?"

Lugh only nodded. He didn't trust his voice not to give him away yet.

"Ah, well, it's hard being new to a place. You see, I've seen many people in my wanderings. I know when a lad is lonely in the world and needs a bit of comforting, I do that! Now, they're not much for hospitality here, as you've likely noticed, but there's no one ever said Gilla Decair never made a man welcome, that there is not!"

He told all this to the boy with a broad grin as he led him back through the tables. Lugh noted with relief that none of the others in the room gave them more than a passing glance. Many of them did have masked faces, as he did, and the clothing Angus had supplied him was the same. He decided that he would go along with the clown and see what he could discover.

The tall man maneuvered Lugh through the warriors to a far corner where there was an empty space.

"Sit down, sit down, boy!" he invited Lugh, pushing him down on a bench. "You look like you could use some food and drink."

"I could," Lugh said, in as deep and hoarse a voice as he could manage.

"Well, you're not likely to be offered any here. So I'll offer what little I've got to you myself, yes, yes! I will do that!"

He looked around him searchingly to be certain no one was watching, then plunged his long hands into the depths of that ragged cloak. Before Lugh's astonished eyes, he began to pluck forth items and place them on the tabletop.

There was an incredible wealth of food: fruit and bread, vegetables, cheese, and a great slab of roasted meat. The large items appeared miraculously from the cloak and piled up in a heap.

"And you could use a bit to drink as well, I'd guess," said Gilla. With a flourish, he reached again into the cloak, whisked out a leather jug brimming with ale, and set it by the rest.

"There! Enough for two I think," he said modestly and dropped down by Lugh on the bench.

The boy looked it all over wonderingly.

"Where did this come from?" he asked.

"I picked it up here and there," the clown answered lightly.

"You mean, with all that stumbling about, falling over the tables, you were..."

"...collecting," Gilla finished. "That's what I call it. And it's only what's rightly owed me, that it is! In times past I've always been treated well where I entertain. Always feasted at the chieftain's table. But not here anymore. Oh no! They tolerate me because they like a bit of coarse fun. But I'd get nothing from them, the mean, ill-spawned brethren of boars."

"Why are you saying all this to me?" Lugh asked, alarmed by the man's open attack on the Fomor. "Aren't you afraid I'll tell the others you've been stealing? Aren't you worried about insulting one of them?"

"I would be," Gilla said softly, smiling shrewdly at the boy, "if I was speakin' to one of them."

"What do you mean?" Lugh demanded, trying to sound outraged. "I'm as much a Fomor as..."

"...as my poor, tender backside!" Gilla finished. "Come on, lad. I saw it when you came in. All alone, with those bright young eyes and that easy walk."

Lugh didn't know what to say. He was cornered in a room full of these brutal warriors, revealed by this absurd, grinning clown.

"Lad, lad, rest easy!" Gilla reassured him, seeing the alarm in the boy's eyes. "I'll not give you away. I've only admiration for your courage in coming here, though you must be mad for doing it. I only mean to give you help if you need it. Now, have some drink. Relax and tell me what you're after."

Lugh tried to relax. He took some of the ale and drank a bit.

"I'm only here to find out what I can about the Fomor. I'm a stranger to Eire. It's important for me to learn."

"You're choosing about the most foolish way you could to do that! And there's very little you'll learn here from these men. Drinking and the telling of filthy tales are about their only interests. They're not much the ones for talk. They'd be out roaming the streets for women if there were any left to them."

But Lugh wasn't listening to the clown. He had noticed another man who had entered the room. He didn't look like a Fomorian. His body was free of obvious deformities and his features seemed normal, if coarse and very dark. He was dressed in a richly textured tunic and cloak and moved with authority through the warriors. Two Fomor flanked him like guards, pushing a way for him, and those who looked up looked quickly away, as if afraid to be seen watching him.

They made their way through the room to a back wall not far from Lugh and Gilla. A wicker screen was covering a large opening there, and the guards moved it aside so the man could pass behind it.

"Where does that doorway lead?" Lugh asked Gilla.

The clown glanced around at it and shrugged.

"It's just a separate area for Fomor officers. Most of them aren't so hard to stomach as this lot, and they like to have a place to eat where they don't have to see the rest."

Lugh watched the doorway longer, curious about the man he'd seen. Soon, he noticed a warrior near the door get up from the tables and make his way to it. He looked like the other Fomor, shabbily dressed, his face wrapped like Lugh's with a heavy scarf covering nose and mouth.

He paused by the wicker partition and looked around him with that same kind of wariness that Gilla had shown before taking out his food. Then he slipped through the opening into the separate room.

But the quick glimpse Lugh had gotten of him was enough to stun the boy. When he'd seen the eyes above the masking scarf, he had known without doubt that the Fomor warrior who had gone into that room was the High-King of Tara, Bres himself!

Lugh rose swiftly from the table and moved toward the doorway.

"Wait! Where are you going?" Gilla called after him.

Lugh paid no attention to him. It was all fixed on that separate room. He had to know for certain if it was Bres, and why he would come here in disguise.

He moved through the crowd of men, edging closer to the door. There was a large group gathered near it, watching two Fomor locked together on the floor, trying to get at one another with their knives. The rest were betting on the outcome.

Lugh worked his way casually around them and leaned against the wall by the edge of the wicker partition. He'd hoped for a crack that would allow him to look into the room, but there was none. However, the thinness of the barrier did allow the voices of those beyond to filter out. By concentrating, Lugh could pick up snatches of conversation above the raucous noise of the warriors.

"There are still far too many of them left," said a soft, arrogant voice that he recognized. It left no further doubt. Bres was in that room.

"Time and work will take care of them," a harder voice responded. "It'll burn that rebellious spirit out."

"You've said that many times. It still hasn't happened. The Dagda, his son, and the rest of their lot seem as defiant as ever. And now this new lad has been seen talking to them."

"What, now you're concerned about this boy?" the other asked in disbelief.

"This boy . . . yes! He's challenged me, brought Nuada to life, even bested your own warriors in the street. Now that he's linked himself with the others, who knows what it means! I want to explain what's happening here myself. I want to find out what else can be done. I've already made arrangements to be away 'hunting' as before."

"All right," the other agreed reluctantly. "But I don't really see what else can be suggested."

"Something is happening, Streng. I feel it. Something to do with that boy. If I can get no help, I may have to act myself!"

"I think you're putting a great deal too much on this one lad. But we'll leave at once. I've a cart waiting outside..."

Lugh strained forward, trying to get his ear closer to the partition. In his effort to hear, he forgot those in the room around him. Until, suddenly, a hand fell heavily on his shoulder and he was wrenched about. He found himself looking up into twin, slimy caverns topped by a familiar pair of glittering pig's eyes.

"What are you doing there?" the Fomor demanded. "You're not allowed about the officer's section!"

Lugh hunted desperately for some excuse to make, but he got no chance to find one. The man's eyes narrowed with sudden suspicion and he yanked Lugh closer, peering intently into his eyes.

"Wait a bit!" he cried. "I've seen you before. Without this!"

Before Lugh could act, the Fomor reached up and tore the masking cloth away.

X

A LITTLE BRAWL

"YOU!" THE MAN bellowed. He slammed Lugh back against the wall with one hand and drew his sword with the other.

Gilla rushed up to them, pleading with the noseless one:

"Please, let that boy alone! He's done nothing!"

"Quiet!" the Fomor spat. The hand with the sword swept back, the hilt catching Gilla in a blow that knocked him against a table.

But the clown's move freed Lugh of the weapon's threat for an instant. He seized a pitcher of ale from a nearby table and drove it against the Fomor's head with all his might.

Even so, the blow from the heavy pitcher barely staggered the noseless man. It was just enough for Lugh to break free and leap away from him. He found himself facing others of the warrior pack who jumped up from their tables with howls of rage at his attack.

One of them lunged for the boy, but Lugh spun away. He saw that he'd soon be trapped in the tightly packed rows of tables, so he vaulted to a tabletop, starting at a run down its length, skipping over mugs and pitchers and bowed heads.

"Get that damned boy!" the noseless Fomor snarled.

All about the room, men drew swords and began to move in an attempt to surround or grab the bounding Lugh.

He skipped above them, flying nimbly from table to table. At one point he was nearly caught, but Gilla came to his aid. The clown stunned pursuers from across the room with blazing, accurate throws of his stone spheres, whipped from his cloak and fired in a single move. Then, when some Fomor started after him, he dropped to the floor and began to crawl furiously under one of the long tables.

Above him, Lugh continued his little game. The burly warriors shouldered their way like maddened bulls through their fellows in a single-minded effort to catch him. They pushed aside and knocked down and stepped on toes, raising some sharp responses from the short-tempered beings. Some struck back angrily, and rows broke out throughout the room.

Gilla, still crawling beneath the tables, added to the growing confusion, tripping men as they ran by, popping out now and again to throw another sphere, causing pile-ups and more tangles. Soon there was a merry free-for-all in progress. It drew the enthusiastic participation of most of the warriors, who loved a brawl and didn't know or care what the whole thing was about in the first place.

Meantime, Lugh, finding himself suddenly neglected in the pandemonium, decided to head for the main door. There was an open space there between the door and the end of the tables, and no one appeared to be watching it. He dashed for it, springing from the table's end into the space.

It was only then he realized he'd jumped into a trap.

A figure with a frog's slack-mouthed face loomed up in the doorway, blocking it with his squat frame and a naked sword.

Lugh whirled around to see three more Fomor, the noseless one included, moving in from different points, closing the circle.

"I promised you once that I'd gut you like a fish!" the Fomor captain told him with enormous delight.

He stepped forward, but as he did, a head appeared from under the table behind him and thrust forward between his legs. A body followed the head, lifting up from the floor in a sudden move, like a hinge opening up. The head came up sharply into the warrior's groin and carried him on up, throwing him backwards as the figure came erect. The noseless man crashed down onto the tabletop amidst a struggling knot of Fomor.

The astonished Lugh saw that it was Gilla who had emerged from under the table to assist him, sword in hand.

The clown ran to the boy's side, pulling him back as the man in the doorway lunged. Gilla parried skillfully and shouldered aside the warrior's rush, then turned to meet the attack of the others.

"Behind me, lad!" he commanded Lugh. Then the longsword in his hand cut a swift, agile pattern in the air as he parried the first assaults.

Lugh watched in amazement as his new acquaintance met the attack of all three Fomor. His blade licked out at them like a serpent's tongue, stinging them back. All of the clown's awkwardness was gone in his graceful, almost effortless, defense. The buffoonish grin had vanished, and his eyes glinted with a battle fire.

"Look out!" Lugh shouted, glimpsing the noseless man, finally untangled from the mob, charging in from the side.

"Back!" cried Gilla. He shoved Lugh backward out the door, stepped back himself and, in a sweeping move, caught the attacker by neck and sword belt, swung him about, and launched him into the other three.

They all went down together, blocking other Fomor who were moving up behind.

For a moment Lugh and Gilla were free of opposition. The majority of the warriors were still engaged in their own fights.

"Come on, then!" Gilla told Lugh, and they ran from the hall.

The clown pulled the boy sharply to the right as they reached the street. He rushed him to the corner of the building, threw him headlong over a pile of rubbish and jumped over after him.

Lugh sat up sputtering, his mouth filled with the filth. He began to brush rotting vegetables and bits of bone from him, but Gilla pulled him back sharply.

"Quiet!" he hissed warningly. Then he crawled up to peer over the edge of the pile.

Lugh joined him, staying low. The two watched while their attackers emerged from the hall in a confused mass. The Fomor paused, looking around them. They decided to separate, and rushed off in various directions, disappearing into the maze of streets.

"Well, that seems to finish that," Gilla said with relief. He eyed Lugh admiringly. "You surely know how to make a bit of fun for yourself now, don't you?"

"I'm sorry. Really," Lugh said with regret. "I didn't mean to involve you."

"Well, no matter now. It's safe enough. Let's be away from here."

Gilla started to rise, but Lugh abruptly grabbed his cloak and jerked him down. He dropped back into the garbage with a loud squosh.

"What are you..." he began indignantly. But it was Lugh's turn to hiss a warning.

"Quiet!" he said. He pointed back toward the hall. "Look. See those men there?"

Gilla looked. The stranger Lugh had seen enter the hall was coming out with the disguised Bres, flanked by Fomor guards. The meeting was over and the High-King was leaving for somewhere. And Lugh had to find out where!

"I have to follow those men," he told the clown.

"Follow them, is it?" Gilla answered. "Haven't you had enough of this to satisfy your curiosity a while?"

"No, Gilla," Lugh said intensely. "I've got to see where they go. You don't understand, but this could have to do with my whole life."

"It could have to do with losin' your whole life if you keep on," Gilla scolded. But then his absurd grin reappeared. "Still, if you're determined, it sounds like another bit of fun."

The stranger and his guards walked from the hall to a four-wheeled cart pulled up nearby. They climbed into it and the waiting driver at once started the team of horses off.

"Lad, it looks like you'll need my help if you're to follow them," Gilla said brightly.

"You help? How?"

"It's certain you can't chase them on foot. Come with me,

now. I've got some of the finest transportation you'll find in all of Eire!"

"The finest transportation in all of Eire!" Lugh grumbled. "Ouch! I'd not like to see any of the poorer kind."

He winced again as the cart jolted over another mud hole in the rain-battered road. The tiny vehicle, pulled by one tiny, obese pony, was threading its way through the rough spots under Gilla's guidance.

"It's the roads you should blame, not my poor cart," Gilla replied defensively. "The rains keep them rippled like a rough sea."

"Rippled?" Lugh tried to laugh, but nearly bit his tongue as the vehicle jolted again. "This cart's so small, it nearly disappears into these great, gaping chasms."

"It's a good deal better than walking," the clown reminded him, a little indignantly this time.

"It nearly is walking," Lugh returned sharply. "My feet are dragging on the ground."

"Listen, my young friend! I'd not complain at all if I were you. That I would not!"

He was right, and Lugh felt a flush of shame at his complaining. He would never have been able to keep up with the stranger on foot. Since leaving Tara, they had followed the other cart for leagues at a fast pace, along twisting roads, through countryside totally alien to the boy.

"I'm sorry, Gilla," he said contritely.

"It's all right, lad," Gilla assured him, grinning good-naturedly once again. "It's clear that there's a bit of a strain on you."

"Well, I want you to know I'm pleased you're helping me," Lugh said sincerely. Then he added, more doubtfully: "I'm just not certain why it is that you *are* helping me. I've done little to help you. You can't go back to that hall to entertain again."

"There's little loss in that!" said Gilla. "My welcome had worn very thin there. It was time to move on."

"But, why help me? Do you hate the Fomor?"

"Hate the Fomor? I don't know," Gilla answered flippantly. "I've not given much thought to it at all. But I do like a bit of adventuring now and again. And I've a feeling I'll get all the adventuring I want staying with you."

Lugh shook his head.

"Gilla, you are as mad as I thought you were the first time I saw you."

The clown jerked the cart to a sudden halt, nearly catapulting Lugh off into the mud.

"I'm sorry, Gilla!" Lugh apologized. "I didn't mean to give offense."

"No, no. That's not what stopped me!" the clown said, lifting an arm to point. "Look there."

They were atop a slight rise. Ahead the road stretched away into a wide valley. They had a clear view of a large timber building not much farther on. The cart they followed sat in front of it. And as the two watched, its occupants alighted and went inside.

"Do you know what that place is?" Lugh asked.

"A hostel. The Fomor use it when they're traveling this way."

The clown looked toward the west. The sun was low there, its slanting rays starting to redden in the evening clouds.

"It's late enough," he said. "Likely he'll be staying there the night." He smiled at Lugh. "Which means we'd best find someplace else. A place where we can keep our eye on them."

He reined the pony around and drove the cart off the road, across a meadow toward a distant, tree-covered hill. He worked the vehicle carefully through the dense woods, searching about him for just the proper spot.

"Here, I think," he announced, pulling up.

They were in a small clearing, sheltered from any watchers at the hostel below, but able to see it clearly.

"We'll be sleeping outside, I'm afraid," he told Lugh. "I hope it won't be a hardship for you."

"Not at all," the boy said, jumping down. "I'll sleep on stone or on a tree limb if it's needed."

"By your good fortune in choosing me as companion on this little quest, you'll be a bit more comfortable than that!" Gilla assured him modestly. He tossed him down some bundles from the cart and hopped down after them. "Here, lay these bedclothes out. I'll make a tiny fire and cook some food." He patted his cloak and winked broadly. "I've still got quite a fine supply."

The clown did have a good stock of food, and they dined by a small, well-sheltered fire. Afterward they watched the hostel until the sun was down and it was no more than a light or two twinkling in the featureless black.

"Let's get ourselves to sleep now," Gilla suggested. "The first of the sun will have us up in time to see them leaving."

The weary boy agreed, and the two rolled themselves in the heavy blankets close by the low fire.

Lugh stared up into a clear, moonless sky, where the stars were bright points flickering like countless fireflies amongst the gently waving treetops. He stared and he thought.

When Gilla lifted to poke at the fading fire with a stick, he noted the light glint on Lugh's open eyes.

"Can't sleep, lad?" he asked.

"I was only thinking, Gilla," the boy replied. "Things have rushed along so quickly, I haven't had much chance to think how different it all is. This country, the things I've seen, the people—they're all strange to me. And only a few days ago I was as safe as a baby in his mother's arms. Worse, Gilla! I hadn't even had my birth yet!"

"So now you're thinking how great and frightening this is, are you?" Gilla asked. "I suppose you're wishing you were back in your safe place."

Lugh lifted his head and turned to look at the clown. His expression was quizzical, and he replied with a touch of bewilderment in his voice.

"That's what's so odd to me. I don't wish that at all. I can't think of another place I'd rather be than here. Does that make me as mad as you?"

"It makes you a young man after my own heart, it does," Gilla said, smiling. "Now, get yourself to sleep. The dawn will be coming early enough for us!"

They both settled back, and soon their breathing eased into the sleeper's slow, steady rhythm. The fire burned down, letting the darkness creep in, swallowing the trees, the tethered pony, the tiny cart, and finally the bundled forms of the two.

It was then, when the black had cloaked the clearing, that the figures began to move stealthily from the trees.

Nothing of the shapes was clear. They were like things moving behind heavy drapes, their passing rippling the sea of night like pebbles dropped in a still pond.

A single one came first, slipping down to stop near the two figures at the fire. Then several others moved out from the woods opposite, gliding forward silently as if to join the first.

The lone figure had straightened over the sleeping pair. Something lifted high above it, catching the faint gold light of the stars in a pale line, glinting as would a dewy filament of spider's webbing.

There was a sharp crack and a log rolled over in the fire-pit. The unburned bottom of the wood flared up in the embers, casting a flare of red light about it as the startled Lugh opened his eyes.

Across the fire from him, he saw the girl named Aine. She was standing stiffly, like a deer surprised, staring toward him. At either side of her, their shoulders reaching higher than her waist, stood two of the largest wolfhounds he had ever seen.

Before he could act, she had recovered herself. She stepped forward, lifting a hand to point at him.

"Attack!" came her hard command.

And both the hounds leaped toward Lugh at once.

XI

CITY OF THE FOMOR

LUGH HADN'T TIME to do more than raise his hands defensively. But the great animals sailed over him, and there was a shrill cry and the thud of an impact behind him.

The agile lad rolled and leaped erect in time to see a man stagger back and fall with both hounds upon him, unable to bring the ax he held into play against such a ferocious onslaught.

There was a brief, confused struggle, dimly seen, punctuated by snarling and tearing sounds, then another cry, abruptly cut off in a gurgling cough.

"Off!" Aine ordered once, softly.

And both dogs instantly obeyed. They pulled away and trotted back to take up their positions flanking her.

"What's happenin'?" came Gilla's voice. The clown was

levering himself up now, peering around in the darkness in confusion.

"It's all right," Aine replied in a calm, reassuring voice. "I've saved you."

"Saved us?" the clown repeated in perplexity. He stepped toward her, trying to see her more clearly in the uncertain light. "From what? And who are you anyway?"

At his move toward their mistress, the dogs rumbled ominously in their throats. Gilla took a quick step back, hurriedly and humbly adding, "Meanin' no disrespect at all. No, not at all!"

"That man was planning to kill you," she said simply.

"Man?" said the still-bewildered clown.

Lugh gestured toward the motionless, dark bundle beyond the faint light's circle. Gilla gathered up an armful of sticks and tossed them onto the embers. The small pieces flared at once, casting a fair glow across the body. He and Lugh stepped to it. Gilla leaned down but at once recoiled.

"Gagh! He's a fair mess, he is. Throat's torn right out!" He lifted the heavy ax from beside the body, hefting it in both hands. The fine edges glinted in the ruddy light. "Effective lookin' weapon," he noted.

Lugh had been forcing himself to examine the blood-splattered face closely, feeling it was familiar. Now he gasped in recognition.

"I know this man! He's one of the High-King's company!"

"Negran!" Aine spat out the name as if it were an obscenity. "An informer and assassin for Bres. He's been following you since you arrived at Tara, on the king's orders."

"Not a casual robber then," Gilla dryly observed. "But why kill the boy?"

"He's become too dangerous to Bres," she said. "He has learned things he shouldn't have."

"But I'm not even certain yet what it is I have learned!" Lugh protested. He turned from the body to face her, adding, "And what about you? How is it you came to be here?"

"I've been following and watching you," she told him casually. "I saw him following as well. I thought you might be in danger."

Lugh didn't reply to that. He hadn't really listened to her words too closely. He had gotten his first look at her in the light, and most of his attention had been claimed by what he saw.

She was facing them boldly, her slender figure proudly erect, her unbound hair billowing behind her shoulders like a moonlit cloud. She wore the white linen tunic of a warrior belted at the waist by a harness with a sheathed short sword. Over this was a heavy, dark green cloak. A slim-shafted lance she held grounded at her side, its finely worked silver point a bright flare even in the fitful light that also shone in glinting points amidst the lustrous hair.

The massive hounds crouched on either side, her guardians, their great heads up, teeth bared, eyes glowing, bodies taut and ready to spring.

The young man stared at her in open fascination, especially captivated by the intriguing swells of figure and the smooth, white, marvelous length of leg revealed by the short, clinging garment.

Noting his apparently dumbfounded state, she asked impatiently:

"You did notice that you were in danger, didn't you?"

Like a slap in the face, the sharp words awoke him. Abashed, he colored and said defensively, "Of course I noticed." Then, recalling who she was, he added more heatedly, "But why did you save us? You're one of the king's circle yourself. You've helped me twice now when you shouldn't be helping me at all. I want to know why."

He stepped toward her, but again the hounds growled their suspicions.

"Ah, look here," Gilla interjected hastily, "we could dis-cuss this more comfortably without your . . . ah . . . companions."

She nodded. "That's agreeable enough." She laid a hand lightly on the broad head of each animal, saying gently: "Thank you both. You can be away now."

The dogs vanished soundlessly into the night.

"That's a bit better, it surely is!" Gilla said with much relief. He dropped down by the fire and cast a shrewd look up at Aine. "You've got an unusual command of those beasts. Much more than any de Danann would have, I'd say . . . I would that!"

She hesitated, looking from the clown to the young man who stood watching her intently. Finally she spoke.

"Look here, I may as well tell you now. Yes, I've a great

power over the beasts, as my brother has over things of the sea."

"Your brother?" Lugh asked.

"I am sister to Manannan MacLir," she said casually.

"By each and every power!" Gilla said in awe, staring wide-eyed at her. "You mean the Sea-God Himself? That dread thing that towers beyond the mists? Your brother is a great, horrible, flamin' monster?"

"My brother is a man," she replied irritably, but then added thoughtfully, "although, he is quite a peculiar one." She shrugged that off. "In any case, he sent me to keep a watch over Lugh and aid him with my powers when I could. I took on the identity of a cousin to Bres."

Lugh had been listening to this with growing indignation. Now he burst out:

"Aid me? You were sent to aid me? And who was it said I needed any aid from the likes of you?"

"From what I've seen, you're lucky to have had it," she responded with matching heat.

"And what were you about that night I arrived in Tara?" he demanded. "Manannan wanted me to go unnoticed here, and your help put me on display!" He stepped closer to her.

"If I hadn't put Bres in mind of a test, you'd have been flung out in the rain with no chance at all!" she countered, stepping closer to him.

"It nearly got me killed by that mad raven-woman!" he reminded her, glaring down, their faces only inches apart now.

"I've also saved you twice, as you recalled yourself a moment ago!" she retorted, her eyes bright with her anger as she stood glaring challengingly up at him.

"Wait now! Wait now the both of you!" Gilla shouted, moving in between them. "It appears to me you're working together in this—and quite well, too!"

They still stood stiffly, hostile gazes fixed on one another. But they listened. Gilla put a soothing hand on a shoulder of each.

"Now, I'm a simple clown, and not really knowin' what's happening or what you're about. But I do know that with the Fomor nearby, you'd both do well to waste no warring on each other."

The look they exchanged cooled considerably as they rec-

ognized the truth in that. Much of the belligerency left Lugh.
Still, with a touch of defensiveness, he said:

"Manannan might have told me about her."

"He had no thought of shaming you," she told him in a
more placating tone. "I wasn't meant to interfere except if
there was no other choice."

Gilla looked from one young face to the other. He nodded
with satisfaction.

"That's better then. Much better." He took a hand of each
of them and clasped them tightly together. "Be friends.
Lugh, you can surely use the help, that you can. I'm little
enough." He gave the girl a close, critical look. "Besides, she
seems a pleasant girl, even with being a sea monster's sister."

She smiled at that, and Lugh noted it brought a warm light
into her face, like that of a fair spring afternoon.

"She does that," he agreed.

Gilla moved away from them, looking around at the sky
and then down toward where the hostel lay.

"It'll be light soon," he remarked. "Best get ourselves
ready to depart. Right?"

He looked back to them and then smiled himself. The two
were still standing, hand-in-hand, looking at one another.

For three long days they followed the trail of the Fomor
and Bres on into the north. And every day their way became
more dangerous. For other carts driven by Fomor and parties
of their mounted warriors often appeared on the road, the
numbers increasing as they went. Often the trio was forced
into hiding to avoid meeting them.

After the first two days, the country began to change. It
first rose up in swells of the meadowland, receding at times,
only to roll up in yet higher waves beyond. Then it became
more ragged, the lush grass covering replaced by rock and
straggling trees. The ground thrust up more sharply, the path
wriggling its way through rough stone tumbles so steep the
pony labored at its traces and the three walked to ease its
straining. Finally they crossed a barren heights scrubbed
bare by harsh, salt-tainted winds and began abruptly to drop
again. The land ahead changed, like gnarled clasped hands
opening to smooth cupped palms, a wide valley swooping
gently down toward the glitter of the ocean far below.

They stopped on the valley's upper rim and looked over

the way ahead. Far down the road, where it became only a thin scar in the smooth, green-bearded cheek of the hillside, the tiny speck of their quarry's wagon moved toward the coast. There, on a grey-brown patch that looked like ocean scum floating against the shore, the marks of roads and structures laid out in regular patterns were clearly visible.

"What is that place?" Lugh asked.

"The Fomor's largest seaport in Eire," Gilla told him. "There was a feeling in me we'd be comin' here when we started toward the north. All the Fomor roads lead here in the end. All the wealth they've looted from Eire comes here, though there's little of that left now."

"Can we follow the wagon in there?" Lugh wondered aloud.

"We can. But we'll have to take care," the clown declared with unusual gravity. "Even for the Fomor themselves, there's no place in Eire so violent and so dangerous as this." Then he shrugged and smiled and added airily: "Ah, well. A chance for fun then! Let's be off!" And he started the pony down the road.

When the cart entered the streets of the town, Lugh was seated in the front with Gilla, his features disguised again by the Fomor rags he still wore. Gilla seemed to need no disguise, for even his jaunty waves and ridiculous grin drew no notice from those they passed. Behind them, a thoroughly irritated Aine was buried beneath the clown's furs and blankets, trying to catch glimpses and breaths through a narrow crack.

"It's necessary you hide, girl, believe me," Gilla assured her. "And you're missing nothing by not seeing this place."

Lugh realized at once how true the clown's words were. As the cart rattled slowly along the streets, he stared about with a curiosity that turned to shock and then deep disgust. Even in the worst sections of Tara he had seen nothing to compare with the conditions here.

The town, he decided, had been created by a very exacting hand and was quite unlike the random layout of Tara. The straight, wide streets were surfaced with some kind of smooth stone; they criss-crossed at sharp angles to form precise squares, as neat and regular as the board of a fichta game. The houses had also once reflected that sense of precision. All identical, square and sharp-cornered and built of a curious white stone dressed to perfectly matched blocks, they would have looked like carved bone playing pieces set in their even rows along the streets. The whole effect must have been quite clean and stark—and quite uninteresting.

But that, he thought, had to have been very long ago. Now generations of accumulated debris and filth had marked each structure individually, and the wide streets were often nearly blocked by rubbish piles.

The space between the houses was choked with garbage, packed with it, level upon level, sometimes so high it spilled over the rooftops and threatened to engulf the structures. The stench of putrefaction grew as they went farther in, growing nearly overpowering in the heart of the town where sea breezes were cut off and the odor hung heavily in the stagnant air, sticking in Lugh's throat like a solid thing and nearly gagging him.

But even that wasn't so great a horror to the boy as the residents of the place, who crawled and burrowed amongst the filth like maggots in a rotting carcass.

"There's no other animals in the world I've seen who'd live in their own filth and ruin as these do," Gilla said with evident distaste.

Lugh saw Fomor in a wide range of nightmare disfigurements. Many were too badly deformed even to function as warriors. For the first time he saw women and children too. Litters of misshapen whelps—he couldn't come to think of them in human terms—roamed through the rubbish or filled the dim, stinking recesses of the structures. The women were mostly as deformed as the men, but Lugh did notice a few who seemed free of the terrible curse.

"There are women here who look normal," he remarked to Gilla. "How is that?"

"They're not Fomor women," Gilla said grimly. "They're of the de Danann, taken by the warriors as mates. Even these animals can't stand to couple with many of their own. But normal women still only breed more monsters. That's how strong the taint of the Fomor blood must be!"

"De Danann women!" Lugh muttered as he watched one laboring wearily to control a large, hideous brood that swarmed around her. Then he saw another whose beauty still showed through her worn and battered face as she sat, blank-eyed, staring, while a creature of spindly limbs and clawlike hands, more like a crab than an infant, crawled upon her breast.

Lugh turned away and, in a stunned and sickened voice, said:

"But, Gilla! These poor women! Their lives here..."

"...must be nightmares," Gilla finished. "I know, lad. It's their lot that saddens me most." He turned his head to warn over his shoulder: "And you keep well down, Aine. It's you who'd have the worst of it if we're caught here. Can you see? Dying would be your least unpleasant end!"

The sudden image of Aine in that woman's place, in the hands of Fomor warriors burned in Lugh's mind. He recognized that his greatest fear in this wasn't for himself, but for her. Angrily he asked himself why he hadn't forced her to remain behind.

But there was no reason for his newfound worry. They had already picked their way through the worst of it safely. Now they were coming out of the lower end of the town, and the shore and sea were ahead of them.

One final line of buildings separated the town from the water's edge. Square-shaped and built of the same white blocks as the houses, they were much larger and windowless. Their only openings were wide doorways facing the sea.

Beyond them was the shore, a wide swath of coarse sand. There two long, wide-hulled sailing vessels were drawn up for loading. Scores of Fomor bustled about them, carrying bundles and baskets from the large buildings up gangways into the vessels.

Gilla stopped the cart in a sheltered spot between two of the buildings. The wagon of their quarry had gone on to the water's edge where the officer alighted.

"We'll have to leave the cart here," Gilla announced. "Aine, you can come out."

She immediately sat up, casting back the coverings and taking a great breath of air. It was tainted with the smell of decaying food and fish and the Fomor town, but it was still sea air, and fresher than what she had been breathing.

"At last!" she cried. "Gilla, do you ever clean those blankets?"

"I've been very busy lately," he replied. "Come on."

They left the cart and made their way cautiously down through piles of goods and garbage to the shore. They found a spot near the two vessels where they could safely observe the scene.

"See there, the goods brought from all Eire are stored in those houses 'til the Fomor ships come in," Gilla explained. "Then they're loaded and taken out to sea."

"Taken where?" Lugh wondered.

"I've heard it said there's an island out there," the clown told him. "Though no one save Fomor have ever visited it. No one alive, that is."

"And what're our friends up to, do you suppose?" asked Aine. For their Fomor officer and the disguised Bres were in deep conversation with another Fomor who paused at times to shout orders at those loading goods onto the ships.

"I'm afraid they're arranging for passage," Gilla said regretfully. "When one of those boats goes out, which I judge will be soon, Lugh's men will be upon it!"

In confirmation of Gilla's words, the officer concluded his discussion, clapped the other Fomor on a shoulder and went up the gangway into the ship.

"What can we do?" Lugh asked despairingly.

"Well, unless we can find a boat of our own, my lad, your little adventure will be ending right here!"

XII

THE ISLAND

"THERE MUST BE some way to get a boat!" Lugh said with frustration.

"There may be that," said Gilla thoughtfully, his eye caught by something farther up the shore. "See there."

A row of small fishing boats was pulled up on the beach. Nearby a dozen warriors were huddled close around a large cauldron set upon a fire, its contents sending a white wraith of steam into the air.

Lugh was doubtful. "How can we get one of them with the warriors so close?"

"Simple enough," Gilla said brightly. "You and our young houndmaster make your way down and take one of the boats away while I keep the attention of the Fomor on me." He looked closely at Lugh. "You can work a boat, can't you?"

"It was one of the first skills I mastered," he said modestly.

"And you?" Gilla asked Aine.

"I'll match any man at it!" she declared forcefully.

"But what about you?" asked Lugh. "Just how will you get away?"

"I've my ways. That's not for you to be worrying about."

Lugh shook his head and said vehemently, "No! It's too much of a risk for you."

"Is it? Well, lad, if you've another way, best trot it out, and quickly. For your officer's boat is making ready to sail right now!"

He was right. The crew had climbed aboard and readied the long oars while a shore party was heaving the vessel out into the surf.

"Best accept my plan, Lugh," Gilla urged, watching the ship move slowly out. "Once it's under sail, we'll never catch it!"

For a moment longer, Lugh hesitated. But he knew he had no choice. He surrendered reluctantly.

"All right, Gilla!" he declared. "We'll do it as you wish."

The clown smiled and nodded in satisfaction. "Good lad. Now, when I've attracted their attention fully, you two make for the nearest boat and get it away. Pay no mind to me at all. Ready then? Here I go!"

He rose from their hiding spot and strode openly down toward the group of warriors. Aine and Lugh watched apprehensively, wondering if the hardened Fomor would accept their friend or casually cut his throat.

But the warriors only eyed him with a sullen curiosity as he walked up to them and peered curiously over their shoulders into the large pot.

It was filled with water that was boiling quite furiously. Clay bowls and baskets sitting around it were filled with a variety of fresh seafood—crabs and fish and large clams.

"Makin' a stew, are you?" he said with delight. "And such a fine, big one too! Surely you wouldn't mind sharin' a bit of it with a starvin' traveler?"

"Clear off, fool!" spat a warrior whose flattened head and slanting, golden eyes made him look more cat than man. "There's barely enough for us."

"Ah, but maybe I could earn a bowl," Gilla suggested cheerfully. "A good meal's all the better with a bit of entertainment. Here, let me show you."

And before they could protest, he bent his long form forward and swept up a double handful of the clams.

"Say! Give those back!" ordered a snouted, bristle-whiskered warrior.

"Just watch," Gilla said, grinning, and began to toss up the clams until he had half a score spinning in a circle, his hands a blur as he skillfully juggled them. The Fomor watched, fascinated despite their suspicions.

"Now comes the real trick," Gilla promised. "It's very clever. See if you can guess how it's done."

He continued the juggling, faster than before, but the circle began a steady shrinking. The clams were whisked away, one-by-one, vanishing somehow, until suddenly the last popped from sight. Gilla spread his empty hands and bowed slightly, saying with a triumphant air:

"There it is, my friends. Amazing, ay?"

From their expressions, it was clear that the Fomor found it amazing, and a bit more.

"Give back the clams," one said darkly.

"But the trick . . ." Gilla began.

"Never mind the trick. Give back the bloody food!" growled a humpbacked giant of a warrior, lumbering to his feet.

"You're not a very appreciative audience. That you are not!" Gilla scolded.

"Grab him, lads!" the humpback shouted, lunging for the clown.

But Gilla was ready for that. One long leg swung out, kicking the pot over into them. The boiling water washed over the Fomor as they struggled to rise. They fell back, howling with pain. And Gilla was off.

The Fomor were up and after him at once, some limping and hopping a bit from scalded parts. The clown led them away from the small boats and, as soon as they were gone, Aine and Lugh made their run to the shore and pushed off the nearest vessel.

Lugh picked up an oar, but paused, looking off toward where Gilla was running ahead of the maddened pack of warriors.

"Hurry!" Aine urged, seizing the other oar. "We have to get away!"

"What about Gilla?"

"He said he'd look out for himself," she reminded him. "Now hurry!"

Reluctantly, he did as she said, getting the oar out and into the water. The two of them began to pull away from the shore. Aine was true to her claim, he saw, easily matching him with powerful strokes, and the boat picked up speed rapidly.

But as Lugh pulled, he kept his eyes on the clown, for he saw that Gilla had allowed himself to be chased out on a high point of rocks, thrusting far out into the water.

"He'll be trapped!" said Lugh.

"Keep rowing," Aine replied coldly.

Lugh watched as Gilla reached the end, turning to face the warriors who closed in.

The clown backed away from them, then seemed to stumble. His lanky, awkward form teetered on the edge of a sharp drop in an absurd balancing act, finally toppling into the water some distance below. This raised a roar of laughter from the Fomor. They rushed to the edge to peer down.

With their attention on the water below them, none took note of the small craft gliding steadily away. But Lugh's own attention was riveted on the man thrashing in the sea.

"I don't think he can swim," Lugh said with alarm.

"Keep on rowing," Aine said again, more sternly.

The clown was waving his arms madly, and his desperate contortions seemed to delight the watching Fomor. Their coarse laughter reached the couple in the boat.

"Those animals are going to let him drown! We've got to help him!" Lugh's voice lifted in anguish and he dropped the oar, half-rising.

"Be quiet and keep rowing!" Aine commanded harshly. "Or we'll be caught as well."

He turned on her angrily. "How can you let him drown?"

"It's by his choice, as yours was to follow that ship. Stick to your own mission!"

"You can't be so cold."

She met his anguished gaze steadily. "I'm honoring his choice. He's risked himself for you. Can you betray him by not doing as he asked?"

He knew that she was right. Without reply he grabbed up the oar and began to row with her again.

The Fomor still watched the drowning man, but his struggles were weakening. His head went under once, twice, three times, always bobbing back. But a fourth time, it didn't reappear.

"He's gone!" Lugh said hoarsely, stunned at this loss of the peculiar man who had become his friend. His eyes squeezed shut against the sudden tears that started in them.

"Well, that was simple enough. It surely was!"

The familiar, cheerful voice came from behind him, and Lugh jerked his head around as Gilla's long hands gripped the bow and, with only slight effort, he hauled his lean frame into the boat. He dropped down on the forward seat, grinning and streaming water, and held out something in one hand.

"Would you care for a clam?"

Lugh looked in disbelief from Gilla back to the now distant rocks where the Fomor still watched the spot where the clown had disappeared.

"But, Gilla, you just..." Lugh began.

"Swim like an eel," Gilla interrupted. "It's all in the long arms. Now, let's be getting moving. Those bright lads seem finally to be takin' notice of us!"

They were. One of the warriors glanced around and saw them and then alerted the others. They screamed and gesticulated for its return. Gilla waved gaily in reply. Finally realizing their threats weren't enough, the Fomor charged for the other boats.

"That'll do them little good," said Gilla with sly laughter. "I've a feeling that somehow all the other boats have begun to leak."

Lugh saw that he spoke the truth. The Fomor were running back and forth madly along the row of boats. One slammed his great club of a foot against the side of one and stared out at the escaping trio helplessly.

"Did you do that?" Lugh asked.

"Just our good fortune, I'd say," Gilla told him with a wink.

With the fear of close pursuit gone, the three now concentrated on working the small boat out past the headland where it caught a sea breeze. They pulled the single sail up and soon, under Lugh's guidance, they were headed out from land at a brisk pace.

With the combined skills of the three, the vessel flew over the water, cutting a white trail through the sunlit waves. The larger vessel was in sight, and they set their speed to it, following in its wake, keeping it just in sight on the edge of the curving line of the horizon.

It was a fine, warm day under a sky marked only by a few, fat, lazily drifting clouds. Lugh easily managed the rudder, but he found his gaze was constantly shifting to Aine. She had shed her cloak, and he was intrigued by the way her tunic, wet by spray, moved against her supple body as she helped Gilla with the sail.

Once she caught him watching her. He flushed, but she only smiled slightly in an odd, superior way and went on with her task. After that he tried to concentrate on steering.

With his work done, Gilla relaxed in the bow and produced from the unplumbable depths of his ragged cloak the clams he had whisked away. With a slim dagger he shucked them skillfully and one-by-one slid them, raw, into his mouth. He invited Aine and Lugh to join him in this snack, but both, politely but firmly, declined.

And then Aine noticed something that had appeared on the horizon far ahead.

"Look there," she said, pointing. "What's that?"

Gilla and Lugh peered where she indicated. Not far off the course of the Fomor ship they followed, a speck of light glinted on the rim of the sea.

Gilla shrugged. "Who knows? A flash of sun on a peaking wave?"

"No," said Lugh with a sudden certainty, staring at the flickering blue-white light. "It's something more than that."

As they watched, the rhythmic on-and-off of the light changed to a steady glow, like a day star low in the sky. But as they sailed nearer it began to grow, stretching upward as if it were something lifting from the sea.

Lugh thought of icebergs he'd seen drifting past his island home, glowing in the sun. But this had to be much vaster than those, and taller than his island's cliffs.

Now it was a blazing column of light that stabbed at the eye. A mountain of ice. No, not a mountain, for it was too regular in shape. It was too sheer-sided, too sharp-edged, flat and smooth, more like an immense gem, shaped and polished by a craftsman. Not a thing of nature, but something else.

And, with a sudden jolt of recognition, he knew what it was.

It was the tower of glass.

XIII

THE TOWER OF GLASS

IT WAS THE thing of his dreams.

It thrust up from the sea like a polished crystal spire, the facets of its sides sheer to the top. Confounded by the sight of it, Lugh stared while the boat sailed on in the wake of the Fomor craft, directly toward the gleaming structure.

"Lugh, what's the matter?" Aine asked, noting his stricken look.

"I've seen that tower before!" he answered, his voice barely more than a whisper, as if it were some sacred thing he beheld.

Gilla looked sharply around at him. "Seen it? Where?"

"In my dreams," Lugh said vaguely, uncertain how to explain it.

"Have you been here before?" Gilla asked.

"Not that I remember." Suddenly angry, Lugh shook his head. "I don't know. I don't know, and it's driving me mad." He glared up with new certainty at the tower. "But I do know one thing: if that ship is going there, it's doubly certain that I'm going there too."

"Well, no fears of missin' that pleasure," Gilla said brightly. "Your ship's headed in right now."

"Do either of you know anything of this place yourselves?" Lugh asked his companions.

Aine shook her head.

"I told you, lad, it's only Fomor who come here. No one else has ever returned alive," Gilla reminded him.

"Then we'll have to be the first," Lugh said fiercely.

"Fine, lad," Gilla agreed, "but I don't think we should just sail in and present ourselves, do you? Sanity, if I had any myself, would suggest that we look this place over before plungin' ahead."

The clown's reasoning brought a sense of reality back to Lugh. They broke off their trail in the other vessel's wake to make a wide circle about the tower. They saw that it sat firmly upon a high base that seemed made of stone imbedded in the living rock of a tiny island. The barren, rugged land of it extended out only a little way beyond the base and then dropped off abruptly to the water.

After completing a circuit, Lugh eased the small boat in behind the island, opposite the point the Fomor ship had been making for. There was no sign of life on the ragged coast, and they came in closer, easing around a tiny, crooked finger of rocks into a sheltered spot. There the shore seemed to offer a safe landing.

The day was calm, and they had no trouble working the boat in and tying it up. All three then looked over the island and the tower with painstaking care.

"Have we gotten in unseen, do you think?" Gilla asked uncertainly.

"No way to tell," said Lugh, lifting his eyes to the structure that now loomed right above them.

It was silent. No movement was visible on or in it. As Lugh examined it more closely, more of its structure became clear to him. The polished planes of glass were seen to be, not a single sheet, but many, separate, interlocking diamonds whose sides were the length of several men. They were joined by a slender black line, criss-crossing to form a web across each polished face.

From Lugh's low angle, this surface now reflected the sky and drifting clouds above so perfectly that the tower might have become part of the brilliant scene save for the network of lines. It made the tower seem as if it meant to entrap a segment of the clouds in a gigantic net instead of joining with them to be one.

To Lugh, the tower was at once a thing of awesome beauty and of icy terror. For it was so alien, so starkly separate from the natural world surrounding it that he felt there could be nothing of human warmth in it.

"There's no way into it," Gilla observed.

It was true, Lugh realized. No openings marred the smooth surface or the blank stone foundation.

"That Fomor ship had to go ashore to unload somewhere," Aine offered. "There must be a way in there."

"Let's go and find out," said Lugh.

"And hope no one finds this boat while we're away," she added, fastening her long cloak back around her shoulders.

"My girl, why worry?" Gilla said blithely. "Since they're likely going to catch us and kill us, we won't be needin' it."

She threw him a look of annoyance and then turned to clamber from the boat onto the rocky shore. The others were close behind.

Cautiously they worked their way around the island. It was a rough journey, but they finally found themselves peering past a rocky outcrop into a tiny cove.

There the sea washed almost at the base of the tower's foundations, and there were several immense, square openings into the thick stone wall. Before these openings was a system of wharves, apparently of stone, reaching far out into the waters of the cove. The ship they had followed was tied at one of these wharves, and men were already at work offloading the cargo by means that, to the invaders, seemed quite miraculous. One strange contrivance with a long neck of grey metal supported a complex pulley system that somehow worked without men pulling on the ropes. It lifted cargo from the ship with a great deal of snuffling and shrill screams, as if it were some aged beast in pain. Offloaded cargo was set on a sort of raised pathway that ran from the wharf through one of the doorways, disappearing into the darkness beneath the tower. The cargo began to move at once, all by itself, propelled along the path by some unseen force.

Lugh was not at first able to absorb these wonders. His attention was riveted on other ships drawn up at the wharves, and on the men who moved about them.

For the ships were long and slender and of shining black. And the men about them wore tunics and trousers of a metallic grey!

"Those men destroyed my home!" This burst from Lugh before he thought.

"Quiet!" Gilla hissed, glancing up apprehensively at the glinting wall of glass looming above them. "No tellin' what kind of lookout they've got mounted here."

Lugh was already cursing himself for his rashness. He had promised Manannan not to talk of his own past. More, he realized that this discovery had not been such a shock. Since seeing the tower, he had been expecting the appearance of the soldiers of his dreams as well.

"Gilla," he said, now in a hushed voice, "do you know who those men are?"

"I've no idea, lad. Friends to the Fomor, though. That's clear enough."

"I've never seen ships like those," said Aine.

"I have," Lugh said grimly, remembering. Now, more than ever, he had to find out about this place, these men. "I've got to get into that tower!"

"Tryin' to get in there is madness!" Gilla protested. "You know where your High-King's come. It's sure death to try discoverin' more. Come away now and you'll have tales enough for your grandchildren—and a chance to have 'em!"

"Please, Gilla," Lugh said earnestly. "I've other reasons now I can't explain for having to go in!"

Gilla shook his head. "I don't know, lad," he said doubtfully. "Seems to me that your stayin' alive and seein' through this mission you're on is what you should be thinkin' of."

"Gilla, believe me, finishing that mission may depend on going inside."

Gilla considered that. Then he shrugged and said with resignation, "You may be right, lad. Not even your sea-god can know the way a destiny will work itself out. Maybe this is something you're meant to do." He lifted a long finger to point purposefully at Lugh. "But don't you be thinkin' that you'll leave old Gilla out of this." He looked up at the tower, and that delighted grin flashed into being again. "It might just be a bit of fun seeing the inside of that great icicle, so it might!"

Lugh looked to Aine. "You can stay and watch the boat."

"Who are you to give me orders?" she shot back haughtily. "I'm charged with Manannan to see through this mission, as you are. No dangers in that place could match his wrath if I fail him." She added in an aside to Gilla: "He's got an awful, cruel temper, you know. Not an entirely sane man at all!"

Gilla nodded sympathetically at that. Lugh sighed his resignation.

"All right," he said. "We'll all go in. But how would you suggest?"

"The most direct way," Gilla suggested. "All those men are busy about the ships. Seems to me we could slip through that doorway nearest the rocks without being seen."

The other two agreed. They worked their way around the shore of the cove without much difficulty, the rocks giving them cover.

As they passed close to the strange warships, Lugh saw that they were not so sleekly black as they seemed at a distance. It appeared to the lad that the sides were formed of great sheets of metal and riveted one to another, much as the smiths who had trained him had riveted bronze decorative fittings. These sheets were iron, he guessed, because they were rusting along the seams in spots, trailing streaks of red-brown to the water like great, bleeding wounds. He wondered what kinds of forces could have forged and shaped iron in such huge pieces?

Finally they reached a spot near the closest doorway. Far down the wharves, the men were busy still. The way to the unguarded door seemed clear.

"Well, nothing but to try it," Gilla said. He moved from their cover, slipped to the opening and through. The others quickly followed his lead.

As he came into the tower's base, Lugh paused with his friends to examine the place they'd entered.

The room ahead was like a cavern, extending up into deep shadows and away into distant gloom. It was clearly a vast storehouse for the tower, with material of all types piled in great mountains about them. Lugh recognized some of the piled objects as loot from Eire—tapestries, carved wood, weapons, utensils, gleaming treasures of silver, gold and bronze. Unbelievable wealth was dumped in careless heaps, left there to molder and rust and tarnish away.

To Lugh this raised a curious point. Why had the wealth of the de Dananns been stripped away and brought here for no purpose?

There was no time to consider that now. Other shapes in the depths of the room claimed his interest. They were dimly seen bulks of massive size, alien form, unguessable purpose. Some seemed to be vehicles, with great metal wheels, but of such enormous weight that scores of oxen would be needed to move them.

Most had clearly been stored there unused for a very long time. The dust of many years was thick on them and they were scarred by the red corruption that marked the ships outside. As Lugh examined them, more unanswerable questions flooded his mind.

The three moved cautiously on through the towering piles of objects, keeping a careful watch. But they saw no other of the soldiers. They moved farther into the room and then stopped, listening.

For there, in the room's center, they were aware of a sound that seemed to rise all about them. It was a rumble, as of distant thunder, but continuous. A throbbing. And intertwined with it, a high, thin hum, like the sustained note of a harp string.

"It's as if the tower is alive," Gilla whispered, voicing all their thoughts. "Heart beating. Breathing. And we in its bowels!"

"There's a pretty thought," Aine replied sourly. She looked around. "Where do we go now? I've seen nothing of those men."

"They must have gone into the upper part of the tower," said Lugh. "There have to be ways up into it. Let's find the outer wall and follow it around. There'll be stairs somewhere, won't there?"

Gilla shrugged. "In a place like this, there's no way to be certain of anything."

They found a way through the piles of goods to an outer wall. It was of the strange, stonelike material, smooth and apparently jointless. As they felt their way along, Lugh in the lead, the clown trailed a few paces behind, searching constantly around him, his expression quizzical. Something was bothering him.

Lugh came soon upon a hallway, a high but narrow passage leading from the main room.

"Let's try down here," he suggested.

They moved cautiously down the passage. It was faintly illuminated by glowing yellow squares widely spaced along the ceiling. More magic, Lugh thought.

Some way ahead, the passage seemed to enter another

room, opening into a darkness that gave no hint as to what it contained. Still, there was no sign of anyone.

"This is strange. Very strange," said Gilla in a voice tinged with uncharacteristic worry. "We've come too far too easily. I don't like this passage, the way it feels or smells. Something is wrong."

"Gilla, quit your raving," Lugh told him. "Nothing is wrong."

A sharp rattling sound began behind them.

They whirled about to see a door of iron dropping from the ceiling, clanging to the floor, closing off the entrance to the passageway.

"There you are! I told you!" Gilla said with an odd triumphant note.

"It doesn't mean anything," Lugh protested. "We're still safe!"

A sudden, harsh screeching rose about them and, with a violent initial jerk, the floor began to move.

Lugh realized they were on a moving pathway like the one he had noticed on the wharf. It went from wall to wall, leaving no way to get off. And it was now carrying them rapidly toward the black opening at the passage's far end.

"Don't go through that doorway!" Lugh cried. "Hang on!"

He grabbed at the wall to hold himself back, but the stone surface offered no place to grip. He fell backwards and was pulled feet first along, scrabbling madly at the wall to slow himself. Behind him, Aine was down too, fighting vainly to pull herself back. They succeeded in slowing themselves, but the moving floor still dragged them toward that opening.

The hapless Gilla had no chance at all. He had been taken off his feet by the first jerk and dumped in a heap. He could do nothing to slow himself as the floor whisked him along.

"Gilla!" Lugh cried helplessly.

But the clown, a tangled pile of limbs, could only wave weakly as he was launched through the doorway, vanishing into the darkness.

Lugh and Aine redoubled their own frantic efforts to hang on, but it was useless. The belt dragged them relentlessly on, and Lugh soon followed Gilla through the opening.

There was no floor beyond it.

As he went off the end of the moving walkway, he flailed out. One hand contacted a projecting rail and he gripped it as he fell, swinging down. Inches from his face was a spinning metal wheel over which the moving floor somehow rolled, turning back to run beneath the upper surface. He hung by a brace which held this projecting end of the walkway and the wheel.

He had no chance then to see what was beneath him, for Aine, fighting stubbornly to the very end, was at last forcibly cast over the edge. As she fell, he reached out with his free hand and caught her by one arm, her dead weight yanking on him violently, nearly pulling him loose. But he held on and they both hung there, all their weight on the one hand desperately gripping the rail.

He looked around. There was nothing around or below but a dull grey metal surface that funneled down to a round opening some distance below. It was like the gaping maw of some monstrous beast waiting to swallow them, and its chill, sour-smelling breath rose up to envelop them.

Lugh saw no place to put foot or hand, no chance to climb back up, no place to climb to. And his hand was rapidly loosing its grip on the brace.

There was only one other choice, and he took it. He let go.

XIV

A COLD RECEPTION

THEY CLUNG TOGETHER as they fell into the round opening and then slid down a long, sloping tunnel at a breathtaking speed. The slope grew more gradual as they went, slowing them, until they suddenly whumped out to find themselves deposited on a second moving pathway.

From another opening above them, a gust of cold air tainted by a bitter scent blasted their faces as they emerged, instantly chilling them through. Then they were being carried along, through a large, low-ceilinged room filled with mounds of objects thickly encrusted by white frost, sparkling in a hard glare from more of those lighted squares.

Before they could recover their dazed senses enough to act, the moving pathway ended, dumping them abruptly onto a chill, stone floor.

The two sat up and looked around them, trying to understand where they now were. On closer scrutiny, they were able to recognize some of the things surrounding them. Along one side of the room were rows of cattle, pig and sheep carcasses, hung by their feet on great hooks, split and beheaded and pale with their icy coat. There were no more blasts of the chill air, but the atmosphere was already freezing and that harsh, biting scent so strong Lugh felt it as something burning in his nose and throat as he inhaled.

"What is this place?" he asked, his words emerging enveloped in a thick, white cloud of breath.

"They've captured winter and imprisoned it!" came Gilla's voice.

They looked up to see him astride a pile of straw baskets. He had one open and was casually juggling three oddly shaped pink objects.

"Look here!" he said. "It's all hard as stone. Frozen solid!"

"What are those?" Lugh asked.

"Hearts. Sheep, I think. Take a look!"

He tossed one down to Lugh, who had no interest in seeing it more closely. It fell to the floor at his feet and shattered like a clay pot, scattering splinters of its blood-red interior across the floor, flecks bright against the frost-white.

"Clearly it's here they preserve food for those living in the tower," Aine said. "But, how do they keep it so cold?"

"Magic it is, surely," Gilla told her. "Great magic, too. More even than you or your Manannan control, I'd guess, I would that." He gestured up to another of the openings in the ceiling right above his head. "There's a draft of chill air comin' from there to put to shame any winter blizzard I've ever felt."

"I don't see how you can be so cheerful about it, you ridiculous buffoon," Aine complained, tugging her cape about her more tightly. "We'll be frozen as solid as those carcasses before long."

She was right. Lugh could feel the sharp cold cutting through his thin clothing. Damp from the sea, the edges of his tunic and trousers were already stiffening with ice. And for Aine he knew it must be worse.

"Gilla, we've got to find a way out of here!" he said.

"Well, not the way we came in. That's sure," the clown replied, climbing from the stack. "That tunnel we dropped down was slick as a frozen stream, so it was. No climbing back."

"But they must have a way to get this food out of here," the shivering Aine pointed out. "Let's look!"

They found the way soon, in a solid door set in the center of one outer wall. It was securely locked, its metal handle coated thickly with a shiny layer of ice. Lugh wrestled futilely with it, his hands sticking to the frozen surface. Angrily he stepped back and kicked at it with no more result.

"I suppose we'll be hanging up like those carcasses soon," Aine said wearily. She leaned back against the wall, her body sagging. Her shivering stopped. "Or maybe we'll freeze solid standing up and topple down and shatter like that heart." The image seemed to amuse her. She smiled. "Little bits of us all mixed together on the floor. Think what a job they'll have sorting us out."

Her voice was blurring. She was going limp, sliding down the frost-coated wall.

"Stop that!" Gilla said sharply, grabbing her shoulders and jerking her erect.

His harsh treatment seemed to have some effect on her. She pulled herself up, and her dreamy expression vanished.

"That's better," Gilla said. "Lugh, you come here."

The tone of command that had appeared in his voice made Lugh obey without question.

"Now, move close to Aine," the clown directed. "Yes, that's it. Closer. Get your arms around her, lad, she's not turned brittle yet. And you too, girl. Good!" He pulled Aine's heavy cloak out and tucked it carefully around them. "Hold on to one another tightly," he admonished. To Aine's hostile look, he responded, "If you mean to live, it'll take the heat of you both. There's nothing personal involved. Meantime, I'll look around." He grinned. "This cold doesn't seem to bother me so much!"

He went off into the piles of frozen produce, leaving Aine and Lugh. Their quick recognition that it was indeed much warmer this way was enough to keep them clinging tightly together. Lugh felt better quite rapidly, so much so that he became suddenly immensely aware of the girl's body pressed so tightly against his. He could especially feel the heat of her thighs and breasts where they touched him. A new sensation began, like a wave rippling through him. He noted curiously that it seemed to be moving from the inside out. And, without consciously considering, he began a slow but purposeful exploratory movement with his hands.

"Move those hands any further and you'll lose them," she warned sharply.

He flushed and said awkwardly, "My hands are still cold."

"Then warm them on yourself," she said. But there was no real anger in her voice, and Lugh, looking so closely into those grey eyes, saw a flicker there of amusement, and of something else.

"Are you certain of that?" he said with a new boldness. "We may still be turned to lumps of ice here."

She eyed him thoughtfully, that odd, undefinable look even stronger.

"You may be right," she told him and, on impulse, leaned forward to kiss him full upon his lips.

It was a long, earnest kiss, and the warmth and sweetness of her lips seemed like a draught of warming honey-mead streaming into him, flooding through him, bringing every sense and every muscle to a fluttering, tingling life.

She pulled back and gave him a curious little smile of satisfaction.

"There. There's something you'll not have to feel you missed if we die here."

"There are other things," he said, his boldness growing with this surge of new energy.

Her smile grew teasing. "For such you'd have to survive to find a bit warmer place!"

Several very good replies to that occurred to Lugh. But before he could voice any of them, they were interrupted by an excited call from Gilla.

"Aine! Lugh! Come here quickly! I've found something."

With great reluctance, Lugh moved from the cloak and the two crossed the room to find Gilla behind a mountain of stacked produce. There a long contrivance lifted at a sharp angle from the floor to a door set in the corner of ceiling and wall.

"You've got your blood heated enough, I hope," he said innocently. "Look here. This is another of those moving pathways, I think. It goes up through that doorway. I'm thinkin' if we climb up this thing, we might get through."

"If it's to bring food up from this place, it'll likely dump us in a cooking pot," Aine said darkly.

"At least it'll be warm," Lugh said. "I'll climb up first to look."

He pulled himself onto the path, intending to crawl up to the door. But as his weight came upon it fully, something clicked loudly, a whining sound rose beneath him, and the pathway began to move. Before he could jump off, it swept him up through the doorway, the door swinging up out of the way.

He was pushed out onto a low platform. He rose to find himself looking into a long room with rows of cupboards and shelves on either wall and a high, narrow table running down the center. At this table a dozen men and women, dressed identically in the now-familiar grey uniform, stood preparing food. But, attracted by the sound of Lugh's unexpected arrival, all had now halted in their actions and were staring blankly at him.

With as much aplomb as he could manage, Lugh climbed from the platform. Brushing the frost from himself, he began awkwardly to improvise:

"Ah, sorry. I didn't mean to bother you. I was . . . ah . . . just looking around down there, in the ah . . . cold place. Where it's all frozen. Down below."

They continued to stare blankly.

At that moment, the doorway Lugh had come through swung aside again, and Aine was roughly deposited on the platform. She looked around at the workers in alarm, but he quickly helped her down, explaining to them with a smile:

"My . . . ah . . . helper. She was down in the cold place with me, looking over all the . . . ah . . . cold things."

"That's a marvelous explanation," she murmured scornfully. "That'll fool them."

Again the door swung aside, this time to allow Gilla to be ejected from the opening to land sprawling beside them. The scullery workers looked at him, then back to Lugh and Aine. This time she ventured an explanation:

"Another helper. He goes with us when we . . . when we . . . ah . . . look around at cold things."

"Oh, that's much better," he told her mockingly.

Gilla was on his feet now, and by unspoken agreement the three began to move. There was only a single door, at the opposite end of the long room, past the workers. They headed slowly toward it.

"Well, we've got to be getting on now," Lugh said casually, he hoped. "You can get right on with your work!"

"Happy to have met you," Gilla added warmly. "Sorry it couldn't have been longer."

The eyes followed them as they approached and began to edge down one side of the long table. They were nearly halfway when a very broad and very dark man who had been carving at a joint of mutton with a very long knife suddenly came to life. He turned to block them.

"Say hold on! What madness are you speaking? You're not from the tower. You . . ." he poked the knife toward Lugh, "you look an Eirelander."

"Is that a rat gnawing at your foot?" Gilla inquired politely.

The startled man bent forward to look. Gilla grabbed up the joint of mutton and swept it down on the back of his head. The worker dropped.

Gilla was over him before he hit the floor, Aine and Lugh right behind.

They shouldered aside two others and sprinted for the doorway, getting through it before the workers could recover from their surprise.

Now the trio faced another corridor, white-walled and empty and stretching far away into the distance.

"We've got to hide!" Aine said, quite unnecessarily.

The only likely place for that seemed to be one of the many doors spaced evenly down the corridor's sides. Gilla pulled the others to the first one, yanked it open and shoved them through.

They found themselves meeting the gaze of two hundred pairs of eyes. Grey uniformed men and women filled an immense room, sitting over plates of food at row after row of tables. All had ceased eating when the trio appeared to stare blankly at them.

"Not again!" Lugh groaned.

It was Gilla who made the excuses this time.

"Oh, sorry! Very sorry for interrupting your meal," he said, apparently quite unruffled. "Go right ahead." And he ushered the other two back out, slamming the door on the beginnings of a commotion.

They reentered the corridor just in time to see several of the scullery workers, now mobilized and armed with various lethal utensils, begin a charge upon them. Gilla led a retreat the other way.

The three raced to the end of the corridor and disappeared around a corner. When their pursuers, now joined by some sword-wielding soldiers from the dining hall, rounded it after them, they found their quarry had disappeared.

The corridor had opened into a square, barren chamber. On each of the other sides another corridor entered it, and in each corner a broad stairway went upward.

The pursuers, many quite bewildered about the whole affair, stopped as they entered the room, peering around, at a loss.

"Where'd they get to?" asked one of the scullery workers.

"Could be anywhere from here," a warrior replied. "Who were they, anyway?"

"Said they was lookin' around," another worker growled. "Popped out of the freezer calm as you please. But they're not of our lot, I can tell you that!"

"They could be Eirelanders who got lost," a young warrior suggested.

"No, Captain," the worker told him definitely. "One was in the clothes of an Eirelander, but he looked normal enough. All of 'em did. Even that strange, gawky one. In fact, the girl wasn't near bad-lookin'."

"They could be de Dananns then." The young captain's tones grew more worried. "What can they be doing here?"

"We'll have to find them in any case, Captain," a warrior said. "Shall we alert the Commander?"

"No!" the other said quickly. "He'll be angry if he knows they've penetrated the Tower so easily. Better to catch them first. There are only three, and they don't seem dangerous. Organize search parties for the lower levels. Put guards on the main stairs and the lifts. And be certain the perimeter guards are alerted. But, for all our sakes, keep it quiet!" A tinge of fear gave an added bite to his words. "Remember, the Commander dislikes this kind of mistake!"

The party moved back the way they'd come. Their voices faded.

From the shelter of one of the stairwells, three heads were cautiously thrust forth. Aine, flushed with indignation, was the first to speak.

"Not bad-looking indeed!" she fumed.

"At least you weren't called 'strange,'" Gilla pointed out affably.

"Never mind that," Lugh told them impatiently. "We've got to keep moving."

"Well, we certainly can't go back that way," Gilla said.

"I don't want to go back. I want to go up, to see where these stairs take us."

"Go up? Into the tower?" asked the startled clown. "But they're seekin' us now, they are. And you'll never find those two men in the vastness of this place!"

"I've told you, there's more to it now, Gilla," Lugh urgently explained. "I've got to keep going."

"It's madness, it is!" Gilla said with gravity. Then that foolish grin flashed into being again. "Maybe that's why I like it so much! I'm ready to see more of this marvelous place myself, so I am! Lead on, lad!"

Lugh had given up trying to follow the volatile clown's lightning changes of temper. He simply nodded and looked to Aine. She nodded in reply. Without more words, Lugh turned and led the way up the broad stairway.

They crept up, easing around two sharp turns, coming abruptly to another floor. The stairs went up only a single level. Cautiously, the trio again peered out from the well.

Directly before them was a broad, square column of smooth, white stone, featureless except for a wide door of gleaming silver. Past its sharp corners they could just glimpse a large open space, brightly lit. No one was in sight, so they ventured out, like mice·from their hole, scurrying across to the shelter of the column.

They edged around it, away from the silver door, and Lugh hazarded the first look out into the place beyond.

He looked into a vast atrium, a square column of light running up through the tower's center, so wide a spear's throw might not cross it, so high Lugh couldn't see to the top from his vantage point.

It was enclosed by galleries, tier upon tier of them, all alike. At the outer edge of each a silver railing glinted sharply. Behind each gallery walkway was a wall of glass whose interlocking diamond sections echoed the outside. In each corner, a thick, white column, like the one they hid behind, ran up through all of the levels as if supporting them.

Lugh's eyes followed the pattern up until his view was blocked. He noted that all the immense room glowed evenly with the chill brightness of a winter's landscape from a hard, white light whose source was invisible to him.

Oddly, he felt no sense of wonder at this incredible place. Certainly it matched Manannan's Sidhe in its magnitude. But it was far different from what he had experienced there, where magic was an element of the natural aura which softly enveloped him with warmth and life.

Here, there was no magic at all.

Somehow he knew that here the power came from things rigid and cold, from the machines and materials and skills of a civilization far beyond that known to Lugh. Still, the power was sterile, and not a part of nature save in the ruthless shaping of it to the ends of those who dwelt here.

And, with that thought, an image swooped like a shining raven from the night of his dreams into the sunlight of his consciousness. It was the image of this same white glow and of a dark, monstrous shape moving before it. He knew now that hulking thing was something that must lurk within this tower.

"Hold tight!" he hissed. "This column's just come alive!"

Lugh felt the smooth stone beneath his hands vibrating, heard metallic scraping and rattling from within growing rapidly louder. He braced himself, wondering what strange contraption might descend on them this time.

Then the vibration and noise died abruptly away. There followed a sharp clang and then the sound of voices very near. Lugh and Aine flattened against the pillar while the fearless clown peered around the back of it. In moments the sound of the voices began to fade, and Gilla looked back to them.

"It's warriors," he murmured. "But they've gone down the stairs. Come on!"

He led them around the pillar to the silver door at its back. It now stood open.

"They came out of here," he said. "Must have been six or seven."

"What is it?" said Lugh.

"Maybe a way up into the tower," suggested Aine. "I've seen no other stairs."

They warily approached the opening. It seemed to lead into a small, bare room.

"It's another peculiar trap, you know," Gilla announced with childlike enthusiasm. "This whole place is mad. Can't trust it at all!"

"Those men came from someplace. There must be another door from it," Lugh said. "And we'd best find it before those others start looking for us."

They moved into the tiny room, looking about them. Its walls were a smooth, dull-grey metal. It was large enough to hold perhaps a score of men. But there were no other doors, no signs of openings at all save for a square marked in the center of the ceiling.

Lugh was staring speculatively up at this when, without any warning, the silver door dropped from the ceiling, sealing them into the room with a very final-sounding clang!

XV

RISING TO THE TOP

"SEE THERE?" SAID Gilla delightedly. "And I knew it. I knew it. You can't say I didn't!"

"Your constant joy at all of this is getting just a bit tiresome," Aine told him coldly.

"We've got to get it open again," said Lugh, searching fruitlessly for a handle. But then that peculiar clattering noise began again, and they felt the room begin to vibrate. More, all three were aware of a sensation of pressure on them.

"Something's pushing down on my insides!" Gilla exclaimed, voicing the feeling of the rest.

"We're rising," Aine stated. "This room's lifting up!"

"We've got to stop it. Get out of it quickly," Lugh said with urgency. "When that door opens again, there might be a hundred warriors on the other side."

"Only one chance that I can see," said Gilla, pointing upward. All three looked up to that small square. "That might be a door out." He stooped and held out his cupped hands to Lugh. "Have a look?"

Without argument, Lugh climbed up. The lanky being easily came erect, lifting the lad up close to the ceiling. Lugh pressed upward on the square and it rose. He saw it was a separate place resting in the opening and thrust it aside. There was a dense blackness beyond this hole, and the clattering noise much increased. But, with little other choice open to them, Lugh hesitated only a moment before hauling himself up into it.

Once through, he crouched where he was in the darkness, trying to gain some impression of what surrounded him. The scraping and rattling were very loud here, and echoed as in a cavern. It was dark, but not profoundly so, and after some moments, he began to see. He realized that there was enough space there to hold them all.

"Quickly, climb up here!" he called back down to them.

Gilla passed Aine lightly up, then leaped up to grip the edges of the hole with his long arms and lever himself on through.

"Watch the walls around us!" Lugh warned. "They're sliding quickly down past us. If you touch one, you'll be pulled down into the space between the wall and the roof. It's only as wide as my hand."

Aine looked around her in wonder. The four walls ran straight up around them to be lost in the gloom far above.

"The walls aren't moving down. We're moving up!" she said. "Somehow that little room is rising up a shaft. But, how can it work?"

"How can those pulleys and those moving paths work?" Lugh returned and shrugged. "Anyway, it must take people up and down the tower. If it stops somewhere else, maybe we'll have a chance of getting off."

"By good fortune we seem to have come visitin' at mealtime," Gilla said. "There are few movin' about."

It was true. Lugh had seen no one moving on the galleries around the central atrium. At other times the tower might be swarming with warriors.

He set the square cover back in the hole, leaving it slightly ajar so he might lift it again. Then they waited. The car rose up past one and then another doorway into the shaft, each tightly closed by a similar metal door. After a third door had slid down past the edge of the roof, the clattering died again and the car jerked to a shuddering stop.

Lugh lay down flat on the roof and peeked into the little room as the door opened and two men entered. With a jolt of surprise, he recognized one of them as Bres! The other, Lugh guessed, was the officer named Streng. Both had given over their Fomor dress for the sleek grey uniform of the tower dwellers, and Lugh realized Streng must be one of them. He could see little of him but the tip of a projecting nose and a thinning head of dark hair, but he clearly had none of the Fomor deformities.

"I'm very sorry for the wait, Bres," he was saying apologetically as they stepped into the car, "but this is the only lift which is operating at present, and it's cursedly temperamental."

Lugh saw him touch a hand to a row of ornamental markings beside the door. At once it slid closed, and with another jerk, the room began to move slowly upwards again.

"Things are more wretched here every time I come," Bres complained. "I am unable even to receive hot water in my rooms. I would appreciate it if you would try to do something about that."

"I will try, High-King," the other promised. "However, I am afraid I cannot really promise anything. You see, as you have not lived in the Tower, I'm afraid you don't understand the difficulties we face here. This is a very large and very complex structure, not some primitive hut of sticks and mud." The tones were austere and condescending. It was clear that the man had no liking for the demanding Bres. "The technology of our ancestors which created all this is now many hundreds of years behind us. Systems have become worn and parts are harder to replace. Skills necessary for maintenance have become harder to master with each generation. Still, the main systems which sustain the Tower were built to operate without repair almost indefinitely. We do the best that we can with the rest."

Bres's reply came sharply, as if he resented being spoken to like some backward student:

"Even so, I feel a great deal more comfortable in my own hall than here."

"I was certain a man like you would, High-King," the other replied, the sarcasm barely disguised.

Bres shot the man a hard look, but chose not to reply. The ride continued in silence.

By now, the car had risen many stories in its noisy and somewhat shaky climb up the shaft. Lugh paid no attention to their progress, trying to overhear the men below, until Gilla tapped his shoulder. When Lugh looked up, the clown gestured into the darkness overhead. In that void, something had become visible. It was a faint square of light, dim at first, but becoming brighter as they approached.

It was the top of the shaft.

"Lie flat!" Lugh told them. They went down on the roof beside him and waited as the car crawled on up, carrying them relentlessly toward the flat and very solid-looking ceiling.

They were passing another doorway. It was the last. Lugh realized the car was going all the way up, all the way to the top. It was slowing now...slowing...slowing...but not enough to save them from being crushed.

Aine buried her face. Gilla threw up an arm in a vain gesture of defense. Lugh tensed for the impact.

And they stopped.

With a whomping and chattering, the room beneath them shuddered to a halt just as Gilla's outstretched palm slapped against the cold stone of the top.

"Ah, here we are!" Streng announced to Bres as the door slid up. "If you'll follow me to the waiting area, I'll inform the Commander that you're here."

The two stepped out of the room. Their footsteps died away. The trio atop the room waited breathlessly for the car to move again. But it was still, the doors staying open.

"All right. Here's where we'll get out too," Lugh said.

He lifted the panel and lowered himself through, dropping lightly to the floor of the room. He peered cautiously out the doorway. To his right, the two men were walking away along a gallery like those he had seen from below. Still, there seemed to be no one else about. He signaled the others to come down and helped them into the room.

"Now where?" Aine asked.

"Follow me," said Lugh. He was determined to see who it was that Bres had come here to meet.

He led them out onto the gallery. The two he followed had

already reached its far side and started up a hallway leading off of its corner. Lugh started after them, but stopped as he realized the others weren't with him. Both were at the railing, staring raptly down.

Lugh joined them, saying irritably: "Come on, then. What's wrong with you?" Then he glanced over himself.

He was looking down the atrium from a tremendous height. At least a score of levels were between them and the floor, a tiny square, far below.

"It seems much higher from up here," Gilla said in an exhilarated way. "It makes me feel my head is floatin', so it does."

"It seemed to me it already was," Aine gibed absently as she gripped the rail tighter to lean far out.

Watching her made Lugh feel quite giddy. He'd never been up much over two stories in his life, and the experience was not a welcome one. He couldn't see why the others seemed to be enjoying it. To him it seemed as if the whole structure were teetering and he was certainly about to fall.

He backed away until the inner wall of the gallery touched his back. In a rather hoarse voice he called:

"Look, could we be going now? Please?"

"Oh, right. We're coming!" Aine said, recalled to duty. She slapped Gilla's shoulder. "Come along, clown. And mind your head's on tight!"

They started after Lugh along the gallery. But after a few steps, Gilla and Aine couldn't help noting that Lugh stayed pressed flat against the glass inner wall, creeping along sideways. Not only did it look peculiar, but it slowed their progress a great deal.

"Lugh, why are you moving like that?" Gilla felt obliged to ask.

The lad hesitated. He was ashamed to admit his weakness to his comrades.

"I . . . thought there'd be less chance of our being seen this way," he finally lied.

Aine and the clown exchanged a glance and a brief smile of understanding.

"In that case, I think we'd better do the same, don't you?" Aine suggested.

"Aye, we should," Gilla agreed. They moved to the inner

wall and took up positions on either side of him, Gilla in front.

"We'll stay close," Gilla said. "Let's move along."

Somehow the presence of his companions on either side steadied Lugh. When they went on, he was able to control the feeling of vertigo and stay with them. As soon as they had crossed the gallery and moved from it into the enclosed hallway, the feeling disappeared.

In the time it took them to reach the hallway, however, the two men they had followed had disappeared as well. The hallway was empty, the walls blank. But not far ahead it opened into a room. Toward it the trio made their way carefully, cautiously, silently.

"I'm getting good at this, I am!" Gilla said brightly.

"Shhh!" Lugh warned, fearful of being overheard.

He need not have worried. The room ahead was empty. It was another of those stark, coldly lit rooms, its only furnishings a row of simple benches of grey metal lining one wall. Three doors were in the opposite wall. Small ones were in each corner. An immense double door was in the center.

Lugh approached the central ones and bent close to them, listening intently. From beyond came a faint rumble of voices, one much louder than the rest, but none understandable.

He took one of the door handles but then released it. There was no way to know what waited beyond. His fists clenched in frustration. He wanted to punch the shining metal. He couldn't have come so far, gotten so close, only to be thwarted on the threshold of his goal!

A sharp hiss brought him around. Aine was standing at one of the smaller doors. She had it open.

He and Gilla joined her. Beyond the door was visible a flight of stairs leading up.

"I've been doing some exploring this time," she told them with a triumphant air. "I think this leads into the room beyond. I didn't go up all the way, but I could see bright light, and I heard voices quite clearly."

"Aine! Good work!" Lugh threw his arms about her in a joyous hug. She put up very little resistance.

"No one hugged me when I found a way from the cold place," Gilla complained, assuming a hurt tone.

"I'll do it later," Lugh promised. "But, quickly now! Let's try to find out what's happening in there!"

They all but crawled up the stairway. The way was gloomy, thrown into shadows by the blaze of light above.

The voices were growing in volume as they went. Lugh felt his excitement surging higher at each step. All fears were cast aside now in the expectation of final discovery.

At the top, they found themselves on a wide balcony. Beyond its edge the room dropped away into a large space filled with a brilliant, blue-white light.

Lugh and his comrades moved gingerly to the silver rail along the edge. He peered over, wondering how far this drop was going to be. He found with relief that it was only to a level right below.

Still, it was a large room he looked into, a triangle that clearly took up a corner of the tower, for both the outer walls the balcony faced were made of glass. And Lugh realized that the blue-white light was that of the sky beyond.

From their height, the whole sea seemed to stretch out before him, and such a breathtaking sight might have claimed more of his attention if he hadn't been so intent on the room itself. For in the center of the floor below him stood the two men they had followed. They faced a raised platform filling the outer corner where the glass walls met. And upon that platform, something massive sat.

To eyes unaccustomed to the glare, it was at first little more than a dark mass, featureless, its shape hard to define. But as Lugh's eyes adjusted, he realized that what he looked at was a monstrous being!

XVI

BALOR OF THE EVIL EYE

AGAIN LUGH SAW a hulking black form come toward him out of a white glow, saw it raise a massive arm threateningly.

But that was an image from his dream, and this was real. Another part of a childhood's nighttime terror had come to life.

It seemed to be a giant, seated on a heavy metal throne. Its shape was a parody of a man's, with two arms, two legs, hands, feet, a head, but all in massive proportion. Each leg was thicker than a man, and the head was like a huge, squat cauldron set directly upon the great width of squared shoulders. Each hand looked fully capable of squeezing a man in two.

The body seemed fully enclosed by some kind of armor with the same black hue as the hulls of the metal ships. Even the great head was covered by a helmet. Thus, the being had no visible features, save one, and that one was the most terrible aspect of its appearance. For in the center of what ought to have been the face there was only a single eye.

The metal lid that covered it was down, nearly closing the eye. But through that narrow slit, Lugh could see a ruby-colored light that had to be of incredible intensity.

"By all that's livin', what's that!" Gilla whispered in a choked voice.

"I don't know," Lugh answered honestly. "Listen."

"There are still too many problems with the de Dananns," Bres was arguing. "They still show sparks of rebellion, despite the harsh way we've trampled down their fire. I want you to help me make an end of them now."

The reply came from the terrible form in a rattling, echoing voice that held no trace of human tones:

"I fear you seek a final solution to your own problem. But you will have none from us. You will have to continue to bleed them as you are. If they are weakened to the point the Fomor garrisons in Eire can destroy them, you may do so. But I wonder at this drive to see them exterminated, considering that it is their blood which half fills your veins."

"It is that very blood which causes my hatred of them," the High-King explained. "I mean to prove myself wholly Fomor. Any aspect of that other half must be wiped totally away!"

Other half! To the listening Lugh, this revelation was both startling and very illuminating. Bres was only partly of the de Dananns, and a traitor to that part.

"I commend your loyalty, if it is genuine," the black figure said. It shifted slightly. The movement was incredibly slow, the upper body tilting stiffly to bring the head forward. The red eye rested upon the officer. The voice continued in words as hard as the clang of iron on iron. "But understand me well!

All the scientific skills of our civilization at its highest level of achievement created this Tower. It is the last bastion of our race. I will not risk those living here without good cause. It is up to you to maintain control in Eire without any help from us. Do so!"

These words were clearly meant as a dismissal, but the stubborn High-King had more to say. He stepped boldly forward.

"There is another matter, Commander. About a boy."

The hard voice responded at once, demanding, "Boy? What boy?" There was an almost-human note of curiosity in it this time.

"It is some notion King Bres has," Streng put in. He sounded apologetic at having to disturb the being with something so trivial. "It's hardly worth even bringing it up to..."

The eye shifted just a fraction. The light was suddenly a glowing beam, playing across the High-King.

"Just tell me about this boy!" came the command.

"He is a wanderer named Lugh who appeared mysteriously at Tara!" Bres quickly explained, his face suddenly shining with sweat. "He proved himself a Master of Skills and won a place there. Now he seems to be in league with the Dagda and his son. And he created a riot at the inn where I met Streng. I think the lad is dangerous. He's another reason I wish to act. He may be part of some conspiracy to..."

"A Master of Skills?" the metallic voice broke in sharply. "What kinds of skills?"

"A great many," Bres assured him with increasing urgency as the heat grew more uncomfortable. "He was a swordsman, a games player, a master of the harp..."

"The harp!" This crash of sound cut the man off again. From its side the figure lifted a hand, palm up, fingers outstretched. The fingers curled back into a massive fist.

"That boy must be captured now!" The ringing words vibrated the room with their volume. The fist shook. The hot light bathed the now soaking High-King. "Go back at once. Find that boy without delay. You understand? Without delay! Find him and bring him to me!"

"I will, I will, Commander," Bres promised in a voice pitched high with agony. "But why..."

"It's not for you to know!" the hard reply came. "Now go!"

Under the circumstances, Bres had no inclination to argue

this. He turned and strode away, trying to keep himself from running to the doors.

The figure of the Commander came slowly erect again. The eye narrowed and turned toward Streng, who had been waiting patiently nearby.

"See that High-King Bres returns to Eire at once," the voice ordered. "And have the woman sent to me. I want to see what she thinks of this news."

"Yes, Commander," the man replied. He turned to follow Bres from the room.

But as he departed, he was immediately replaced by another uniformed officer. This one Lugh recognized as the young captain they had seen below.

He approached the motionless giant slowly. His expression was not a happy one.

"Commander," he began in a nervous voice. "I . . . I don't mean to disturb you, but I felt this could not wait longer."

"Well?" asked the iron voice.

"There are some strangers in the Tower," he said in a sudden rush, as if to get it over. "Parties are searching for them now. There are only three. Possibly de Dananns. A man, a girl, and a boy."

"A boy!" the voice cracked with the power of a lightning stroke. "That fool Bres! They followed him here from Eire!"

With relative speed the head came forward, swiveling on the thick neck, throwing the crimson beam about the room. The three watching from the balcony ducked below the rail as it swept above them.

"He is here!" the Commander rumbled. "He saw Bres meet with Streng. He followed them here. I know it must be. I can feel it!" The metallic voice was marked now by a very human note of triumph. The eye swung back to the waiting officer. "He mustn't leave the Tower. Have everyone alerted. Search every level. And send Bres back here!"

"Yes, Commander," the captain said briskly, happy to have escaped the Commander's wrath.

On his departure, the figure again sat back. This time the lid on that terrible eye dropped fully closed, cutting off the line of ruby light.

The trio above waited for several long moments, but there was no further sound or movement from the figure.

"The bloody great thing's gone to sleep!" Gilla whispered. "Time to be goin'!"

Lugh agreed. They moved off of the balcony, back down to the outer room. It was empty. The captain had already gone.

"Once he raises the alarm below, warriors will be swarmin' over this whole tower," Gilla said. "It would seem a good moment to make our departure, so it would."

Lugh hesitated. "But there are so many questions, so many things I don't understand," he told them. "And the woman. Who is she?"

"You've no time to find out now," Aine said urgently. "We've got to get away before we're trapped. It may already be too late."

As desperately as Lugh needed to learn more, he also knew the risk had become too great. He nodded.

"All right. We'll go. Let's make our way back to that lifting room. Maybe we can go down the way we came up."

"That captain may have already taken it down," said Gilla.

"Then we'll have to hide and wait until it comes back. There doesn't seem to be much other choice."

They made their way back to the central gallery. Their good fortune seemed to be holding; the gallery was still empty.

They started at a run for the column with the lifting room, Lugh suppressing his fear of the height by sheer willpower. But they were only halfway across the gallery to it when a party of soldiers rounded it from the other way.

Both groups stopped in surprise. There were four grey-clad men, and they surrounded a woman in a soiled and ragged gown. Lugh knew her at once. It was Taillta.

In his joy he started toward her, crying her name. She recognized him then, and her face lit with her elation.

"Lugh!" she called back, trying to push forward past the guards.

But they pulled her roughly behind them, while one warned darkly: "Get back, now, whoever you are!"

"You let her go!" Lugh shouted and charged forward, all sense of logic gone in his explosion of anger.

The guards, though startled by the attack, were well-trained and hesitated only an instant before seizing their sword hilts to draw. Four blades would have met the lad's attack if the quick-thinking Taillta hadn't leaped forward, throwing herself sideways to crash across the backs of the guards' legs. All of them staggered, and two went down over her heavily as Lugh slammed into them from the front.

Lugh's attack had also taken his friends by surprise. But now they moved in to aid him. Gilla—the only one of the trio adequately armed—drew his sword and ran to engage the two soldiers still on their feet. Aine sprang onto the figures struggling on the floor.

Gilla's opponents were skilled and aggressive in their swordplay. Their weapons were of a silver-grey metal much thinner and lighter to wield than his, yet as strong. For all his own prowess with a blade, he looked as if he could barely keep both attackers away.

They forced him to retreat until his back was to the inner wall, and then they came in from either side. The clown drew his dagger and fought with both hands, lunging constantly from side-to-side to parry their slashes and thrusts.

Meantime, Lugh had become locked in a battle of strength with one of the other soldiers. He was vastly overmatched in it. His opponent was burly and much larger. Lugh had secured a desperate grip on the man's sword hand with both his own in an effort to wrest the weapon away. Now they rolled across the floor, the soldier battering at Lugh with his free hand, each trying to kick the other with their feet.

Aine had joined Taillta in an attack on the fourth soldier. They drove him down onto his back, and the older woman fell across his sword arm, pinning it. Aine then sprang forward, landing with both knees on his groin.

She had hoped to incapacitate or, better, kill him. She hadn't reckoned with his toughness. The pain only galvanized him to a superhuman effort. He rose, throwing both women off, bellowing for good reason like a bull castrated by hot iron.

But as his weapon came up, Taillta threw herself upon him again. The sword flicked toward her as she came in, the slender blade driving up into her side below the ribs.

She grunted sharply with pain, but didn't pause, pushing the weapon out and away from the man's body, leaving him unguarded.

Aine was quick to take advantage of the opening. Whipping her short sword out, she thrust it forward, backed by her body's full power. It struck home, cracking through the man's breastbone, burying itself to the hilt in his chest. Instantly dead, he collapsed backward, his blade pulling free of Taillta.

Lugh and his soldier, still locked together, had now struggled to their feet and were against the outer rail of the gallery. They were bent sideways over the top of it, their upper bodies hanging far out, swaying over the sheer drop.

Lugh was trying his best not to look down as he tried to maintain his grip on the man's sword hand. Still, he was feeling a certain dizziness. It was not lessened by the fact that his opponent was slamming punches into his stomach with his free hand. Lugh was jerked farther up and out by each one.

He felt himself weakening. The eyes so close to his own were pitiless. They saw that he was failing. The tight lips lifted in a grim smile of victory. The fist delivered another jolting blow to Lugh's lower ribs. Lugh felt blackness washing up through him, rolling through his brain like a wave that would drown him. He cursed his weakness and he thought of the battle with Morrigan. Here it was, happening again, only this time no silver hand to save him.

Then he heard the cry of pain from Taillta. He glanced aside to see her stepping back from the sword point, to see the rush of crimson from the wound.

That was enough. He went mad with a white-hot rush of new anger, and the madness gave him strength. In a sudden move, he released the man's sword wrist with one hand and swept the arm down to hook under his legs. The soldier, his arm drawn back for another blow, was too slow to react as Lugh heaved upward. He tried to grab at the lad as he went over, but missed.

He made no sound as he fell, perhaps too surprised by the defeat. The exhausted Lugh hung on the top rail, watching him plunge toward the atrium floor. It was now flooded with tossing grey waves of uniformed figures. The body dropped down into them, striking with a booming thud audible to Lugh. A band of white appeared around where he fell, widening out like ripples around a stone dropped in a pond. It was faces turning upward to where Lugh stood.

He jerked back from the rail and ran to Taillta. Aine was already at her side. But on seeing Lugh, the older woman pulled erect, pressing one hand tightly over her wound.

"I'm all right," she said stolidly. "Help your friend."

Lugh looked up the gallery to where Gilla still held the

other soldiers at bay. At first glance they seemed to have the poor, awkward clown at a tremendous disadvantage. But Lugh, who knew Gilla's act better by now, realized that the clumsiness was a means of distracting the attackers while he deftly parried their assaults. Instead of rushing to his aide, Lugh simply called to him.

"Gilla!"

The clown looked to him. "Oh, finished already?" He sounded a bit disappointed. "Too bad. I was just having some fun." He looked to his opponents. "Sorry, lads, to be ending this so soon. But it's been good sport, it has that!"

"Why you . . ." one snarled, charging in.

He staggered back at once from a lethal thrust through one eye and fell. The other man hesitated, amazed by the ease with which Gilla had struck. Then he gulped as the clown looked at him, smiling amiably.

"Your turn, I think," Gilla said with enormous glee.

The man turned and ran.

Gilla shrugged and let him go, striding quickly to the others. Lugh turned his attention back to his foster mother.

"Taillta, are you certain you're not badly hurt?" he asked anxiously, throwing an arm around her.

"It's just a cut along the ribs," she assured him. Her voice was strong and even. One hand was kept pressed tightly to the wound, but she was in control and evidenced no pain.

She looked closely at him and smiled with great warmth, lifting her other hand to stroke his cheek.

"My Lugh. I never thought I'd be seeing you again." Concern clouded her features. "But, what are you doing here?" She looked over the other two with open curiosity, dwelling longest on the strange-looking clown. "And who are your . . . companions?"

"There's no time to explain," he told her. "We have to go. There are hundreds of warriors below. There must be parties on the way up here now."

"Then our way out of here is blocked," Gilla said.

"No. Maybe not!" said Taillta. "There is a way down from Balor's quarters."

"Balor?" repeated Lugh.

"The Commander. He's a monster so vast that a special lifting device carries him from his ship to his throne room. It's back there." She pointed along the gallery.

"We know well enough," said Gilla. "We just came from there."

"Have you?" She was clearly amazed. "You have been courageous . . . or foolish. Have you seen him?"

"We have," said Lugh.

"Well, I don't know how you survived it, but you'll have to again, for we'll have to go right past him to reach the lift."

"He was asleep," said Aine. "At least, he seemed to be."

"Then maybe there's a chance."

"We've certainly no others left," said Lugh. "Let's be at it."

They started back along the gallery at a trot. Taillta held her own with no trouble, refusing Lugh's offer to support her. No other soldiers appeared to challenge them.

"Why aren't there more warriors on this level?" Lugh asked his foster mother.

"It's all Balor's quarters. No one comes up except on his command. Most of the time he's alone."

"What is he?"

"I don't know. I'm not sure his own people do. But the power from his eye is like no other. It's what blasted our fortress."

"I thought no one had survived. Are others of our people here?"

"They're all dead," she said grimly. "He killed the other survivors trying to make me tell him where you'd gone. She gave a short, humorless laugh. "There's irony for you! Now you come walking in his door!"

"But, Taillta, why? Why does he want me?" Lugh asked her urgently.

She looked at him gravely. Her voice was firm.

"Lugh, that is something you cannot ask me. Please, promise you will not, if you love me."

"If you wish it," he agreed reluctantly, adding, "at least not until we're safe."

They reached the corridor that led to Balor's throne room, and ran up it to the central doors. Lugh put his ear to them and listened. There was only silence from beyond.

"There's a short hallway leading from the outer corner of the room on the left," Taillta explained softly. "To reach it, you'll be crossing the room right before his throne. The door to the lift should be open. If we can make it there, I think I can operate it. I watched them when I was brought up in it. It'll take us right down to their wharves."

"Perfect," said Lugh. "But, if anyone of us doesn't make it, the rest must go on. There's no stopping once we've begun. Right?"

All agreed. They understood the hard logic in his words.

"If we're separated, we can meet at the boat," he went on. "Don't wait long, though. If there's any danger, get out to sea." He looked at his foster mother. "Taillta, you'll go first. You're most important now."

He eased one side of the huge door open a way and peered through the crack. The throne room was empty save for the giant figure. It sat motionless as before, the eye closed. Lugh pushed the door wider and whispered to Taillta:

"Go ahead, then. As quickly and silently as you can. Don't pause for anything!"

She nodded. Then she smiled and kissed him lightly on the cheek. "Good fortune to you," she said, and slid through the opening.

Anxiously he watched her cross the floor. She went swiftly, fearlessly, gliding without a sound to the far corner, disappearing into the entrance to the hallway. The black figure made no move, gave no sound to show it had been disturbed.

"Good! She's made it," Lugh said with relief. "Now you, Aine."

This time she didn't challenge his order. She moved to the door, then paused before slipping through to lean back and give him a kiss herself.

"My wish of good fortune matches hers," she said lightly, and then she had gone.

Like Taillta, she flew silently across the floor without incident. The being called Balor slumbered on.

"Your turn, Gilla," Lugh said. He grinned at the lanky man. "I've decided your clumsiness is only an act. I hope I'm right."

"I'll try not to fall," the clown promised. He leaned toward the lad. "Want my kiss for luck as well?" he asked, puckering his lips.

"Get on with you," said the embarrassed Lugh, shoving him toward the door.

True to his promise, the clown made his silent way across the room, past the figure who might have been a statue cast from iron.

Now it was Lugh's turn.

He slipped through the opening, closing the door behind him. He began to move stealthily across the room. He glanced up at the black giant as he went. No life there.

He was crossing right before it when the voice spoke, the sound of it clanging hollowly, like a metal drum.

"Lugh!" the voice of Balor called to him.

XVII

THE STORM

LUGH FROZE, ROOTED by a fear that pounded madly in his tight chest, dried his mouth, stopped his mind.

He forced himself to look up toward the figure. The eye was still closed. It hadn't moved. But the voice clanged from it again.

"It is you, isn't it, Lugh? I saw the others pass. I let them go. I knew none could be you. I waited for you."

Lugh stood staring at the monstrous form. He battled inwardly to control the fear, more intense than any he had ever known, which threatened to block his reasoning.

"You cannot escape this Tower," Balor said flatly. Very, very slowly the head began to tilt toward him. "Surrender to me now and no harm will come to any of you. I promise that."

"You promise!" Lugh answered scornfully. "Your warriors destroyed my home, my only family." He took a step back, away from the figure, toward the corridor.

"Don't try to run," the voice commanded. "Stay where you are. Don't make me destroy you. You are too important to me."

"Important? Me?" said Lugh, startled by this. "How? What do you know about me?"

The head stopped moving, the closed eye now directed toward Lugh. The iron voice boomed heavily, like a slowly tolling bell.

"I know you can decide the fate of Eire, of all of us."

This was a further shock to Lugh. Did this being know about his mission? He had to escape. He took another step backward.

"Stand still!" the voice threatened. "I warn you, if you move I will have no choice."

The massive lid was still fully down. Lugh was certain the thing couldn't see him. It had to be guessing where he was by the sound.

As silently as possible, the young warrior took another step back.

The lid of the great eye began to lift.

Lugh threw himself sideways as a line of crimson light burst from below the lid. It struck the spot where he'd stood, blasting it with a flare of searing heat.

Lugh scrambled up as the beam began to move, swinging toward him with increasing speed, crackling across the floor in a blazing line of light.

The lad ran for the hallway's entrance, the energy behind him, so close he felt the heat of it against his back. He felt it touch a heel, a lick of raking fire, and dove forward, rolling into the shelter of the hallway as the beam struck the wall outside it. A corner of the entrance was blown away by the explosion. The room shook with the force.

Lugh rose unhurt and went on along the hallway. Behind him the doors to the throne room burst open as scores of soldiers poured in, Bres at their head.

Balor's eye closed and the head swiveled to them.

"The boy is here?" the High-King asked, glancing around.

"He went up the lift hallway!" the Commander roared. "Get after him. Don't let him escape!"

Bres obeyed, leading the soldiers at a run for the hallway.

Lugh meanwhile had reached the far end, and the lift. Its silver door was closed. It was already gone.

He hadn't time to feel any regret at being left behind. The thunder of the warriors' footsteps was approaching quickly.

There was only one other possible way out—a smaller door next to the lift. He tried the handle. It was locked. He was trapped.

He turned to face the solid wall of advancing soldiers now slowing to close with him, weapons ready.

Then a hand grabbed his shoulder from behind. The small door had opened and he was hauled through to have it slammed after him. He found himself in semi-darkness, facing a figure whose wide grin still shone clearly. It was Gilla.

"Stairway!" he said simply. "Come on!" And he led the way up the narrow flight at a run.

"Convinced the ladies to go on," he explained in abbreviated form as they climbed. "Seemed they should get out. Stayed behind, myself. Thought you'd want some company. We'll keep their interest while the others escape."

The door below crashed open.

"Oh, here they come now!" he announced as if guests had arrived for a feast. "Hurry lad!"

Lugh didn't need the urging. He sprang up the stairs three at a time, still barely managing to keep up with the long-legged clown.

At the top another closed door blocked their way. The two threw themselves against it without slowing. It gave way, and they stumbled forward into bright light.

There was only sky above and on all sides.

"The roof!" Gilla exclaimed.

"Clever guess!" Lugh said. "Now where?"

They ran to a corner and looked over. Lugh immediately turned away, his head reeling. It was a sheer drop of smooth, shining glass all the way to the ocean, very far below.

The soldiers streamed from the doorway behind them. They spread out into a line blocking the two into the corner of the roof.

Gilla took a deep breath of the sharp sea air.

"It's a fine view," he said appreciatively. He turned to the line of soldiers, asking: "Don't you all think it's a fine view?"

Bres moved forward from the rest, and it was clear from his grim look that he wasn't interested in the view.

"I don't know who you are, fool, but you made a fatal mistake joining this boy." He looked at Lugh. "And you made yours following me here." He gestured sharply to the soldiers. "Take them."

Several began to close in. Gilla drew his own weapon and pushed Lugh behind him, into the corner of the roof.

They were forced to come at him from the front, and bunched together tightly. Gilla kept them at bay with his lightning reflexes; his blade nipped the hand from one, punctured another's stomach, left a third spurting blood from a severed neck artery.

Less anxious to press forward, the soldiers became tangled awkwardly, their attacks grew ineffective, and Gilla wounded two more before they pulled back, facing him, reluctant to try again.

"Incompetents!" Bres shouted, pushing through them to face Gilla himself. "All of you can't defeat one gawky clown? I'll do it! Get back!"

The soldiers withdrew, most with expressions of relief. Without preliminaries, Bres drove in with a clever feint and a hard cut that had taken off many a veteran's sword arm. But Gilla parried with speed and ease and a power that staggered Bres back.

The soldiers surged forward, but Bres lifted his hand for them to stay.

"No! No help!" He smiled at Gilla with savage delight. "This will be more enjoyable than I thought."

He came in again, more warily, and they exchanged a flurry of hard blows. Crouched behind Gilla in the corner of the roof, Lugh tensed with anger and frustration at his own helplessness. He should have a sword. He should be facing Bres, not the amiable clown!

Bres kept on with his attack, avoiding Gilla's skillful cuts and thrusts, countering with swordplay that kept the clown busy.

"You're very good!" Gilla told him with open admiration, also throwing over his shoulder to Lugh, "He's very good!"

But it was a stalemate. And Bres was too crafty a warrior to waste more time and energy, or risk himself. He broke off the fight and stepped back.

"All right, fool!" he said. "You are good, too. But you can't protect that boy forever!" Lugh squirmed with indignation at that. "It only means you'll die here!"

"I agree with him, that I do!" Gilla said to Lugh. "Except for the 'fool' part. This is only delayin' things a bit." To Bres he called, "Could we talk it over?"

"Quickly," said Bres. "My patience is wearing thin."

Gilla turned to Lugh, watching the soldiers from the corner of his eyes.

"What else can we do but surrender?" Lugh asked in desperation.

"Well, you know, when you've reached the top, there are very few places to go except down," Gilla murmured.

Lugh caught his implication. He glanced toward the edge. That was enough to make him giddy.

"No!" he protested. "We'd be killed."

"Maybe not, if we hit the water."

"What are you discussing?" Bres demanded suspiciously. "You've only one choice left!"

Lugh's mind was spinning. Of all the dangers they might have faced, why this?

"Gilla, I can't do it!" he said despairingly. "I'm too afraid."

"No worry there," Gilla told him cheerfully. "You won't have any choice!"

And, with an airy farewell wave to Bres, the clown dove suddenly sideways against Lugh, carrying them both over the side.

Lugh's fall was a mad jumble of images, real impressions mixed with more of his nightmares. The fall of his dreams was repeated here: the spinning view of sky and sea, the tower of glass seeming to shoot upward, the awful sensation of helplessness.

Then came the plunge into the sea, the walloping impact with something that felt solid but immediately gave way to swallow him, filling his gasping mouth and nose with its harshness, paralyzing him with its sudden chill, dragging him down below the reach of the sun.

He thrashed out wildly, and something gripped him. The rest of the dream played itself out again as hands pulled him up, up, from the frozen darkness toward the wavering light. He broke surface, blowing a great spray of sea water from his mouth, sucking in the air with a great, rasping sigh.

Gilla bobbed beside him, grinning out through a thick mat of hair the water had plastered across his face. This time the rescuing hands had been his.

"We're alive!" Lugh cried out in delight.

"For the moment," said Gilla. "Can you swim?"

Lugh nodded.

"Then get at it. The place where we hid the boat is this way!"

He led Lugh in a swim back in toward shore. They had landed in the water very close to the rocks, and it was only moments before they were clambering up from the water and beginning a scramble across the ragged stone.

Lugh kept glancing up at the tower looming right above them. But it was as frozen and lifeless appearing as before. There were no signs of pursuit.

In their hurry, they all but tumbled down into the little cove where their boat lay. Lugh saw with elation that Aine and Taillta had already reached it. The older woman, however, was lying back in the bow while Aine struggled to free the mooring ropes.

She looked up at them, her own expression lighting up with relief as she recognized who they were.

"Thank the Powers!" she cried, and then she noticed their condition. "But what happened? You're all wet!"

"Warm day," Gilla replied lightly. "Went for a swim. Now hurry! Let's cast off!"

The two men leaped into the boat. Gilla drew his dagger and slashed the ropes while Aine and Lugh pushed off with the long oars.

"A weakness came on Taillta," Aine explained. "I thought we'd surely be caught here."

"Did you have any trouble getting away?" Lugh asked.

"Only a little," she said, gesturing toward the shore.

Lugh looked back. A party of soldiers was rapidly making its way across the rocks to them.

They redoubled their effort, heaving the small boat out from shore just as the first soldiers reached it. One leaped forward to catch the stern, but a sideways swipe of Aine's oar caught him and slammed him down into the water.

"Row! Row!" Gilla ordered, and the two young people fell to work, sending the light craft bounding out over the incoming waves.

The soldiers hesitated on the shore only a moment, then turned back, disappearing quickly over the rocks.

Once safely out into the water, Lugh paused in his rowing to look back toward Taillta. She lay limply in the bow, her face ashen, a large red-brown patch of blood marking her side.

"She was more badly hurt than she told us," said Aine. "She must have a strength that matches her courage."

"Leave her for now!" Gilla said sharply, climbing to take the tiller. "We've got to get out to where the sail will catch. Row lad!"

"But, I've got to help her!" Lugh protested.

"The best way to do that is to get us away from here. Row! Row! This isn't over yet!"

Reluctantly, Lugh stayed to his oar, matching the rhythm of the tireless Aine. Their combined effort sent the boat flying across the sea.

They rounded the island, heading back toward Eire. The vast wharves of the Tower came into their view.

"Look there!" Aine cried in alarm.

Lugh had already seen, and had realized what Gilla's warning had meant.

One of the strange, black ships was putting out to sea!

"Can they catch us in that great whale of a ship?" Lugh asked.

"There's more of that Tower's magic in 'em," Gilla said somberly. "We're in a race for our lives now!"

They began rowing with that strength reserved for those who see their own deaths pursuing them. The black ship, without having raised a single sail, glided smoothly away from the wharves and straight out through the waves into the open sea.

The small boat had gained some distance from the shore, but the pursuing ship was closing that gap with incredible speed, coming on with grim relentlessness.

Once beyond the shelter of the island, the wind caught the little boat. Aine and Lugh hauled up the sail and it snapped full, drawing them ahead of their pursuers in a rush.

The relief was only momentary, however. For the black ship raised a sail too, an immense, billowing spread decorated with an iridescent pattern that glowed in the sunlight like the wings of a soaring sea bird. It filled quickly and the sleek ship was slashing ahead through the waves, closing the gap again.

"They'll catch us soon!" cried Lugh. He could see the soldiers aboard the vessel now. They were moving forward to line both sides of the bow. He caught the glint of sunlight on their drawn weapons.

But for Gilla all sense of urgency seemed to have faded away. Now he leaned casually over the tiller and yawned widely.

"Oh, I don't think they'll catch us," he said easily. "We're on the open sea now."

Lugh looked toward the clown in disbelief.

"Are you mad? Take a look, man! They'll be on top of us in a moment!"

Gilla eased back to make himself more comfortable. He fished in one of his bottomless pockets and pulled out a clam.

"Here's one left!" he said, examining it critically. "I wonder if it's still good?"

Lugh could see the hard glitter in the eyes of the soldiers. He could see them making preparations to cast the grapples.

"Gilla, you are mad!" he shouted at the unconcerned clown. "How can you just sit there?"

"Simple enough. We'll be helped soon enough by that storm there."

Lugh scanned the sky around them, then looked back in irritation at his friend.

"Don't play now, Gilla. The sky's all blue. What storm?"

"Why, that one, lad!" said Gilla, pointing ahead.

This time when Lugh turned toward the bow to look, a blackness was towering in the sea ahead.

A great cloud, like some giant living thing growing from the sea, was swelling, billowing up, cutting off the sun with its denseness. And it was sweeping toward them rapidly, somehow rushing forward against an opposing wind, throwing out bloated, grey-black arms on either side to encircle them, to swallow the tiny specks of the two vessels with a maw as black as a moonless night.

Lugh stared up at the thing looming over them, his mouth open, stricken by the enormity of what was descending upon them.

"Gilla, it won't help us. It will destroy us!" he managed to gasp out.

But Gilla was absorbed in prying open his clam and seemed not to hear.

Lugh moved to Taillta, lying down to shelter her from the storm's onslaught.

"Get down, Aine!" he called to the girl. She seemed not to hear him; she only stared up at the clouds.

The scent of the storm came first, followed by a first puff of wind, damp with the rain it carried. Lugh crouched protectively over Taillta, bracing himself, prepared to be carried under by the capsizing boat or swept away by the blast.

The seas crashed around the boat. Wind shattered on the

rising points of sea. Lugh felt the first drops of rain splatter against his exposed neck.

Then . . . nothing else.

He held his position for a few moments more, waiting. Still nothing. Finally, curious as to why he wasn't yet dead, he lifted his head to look.

He saw the solid blackness surrounding them. The clouds towered above and around the boat like walls, shutting off the sky. Lugh swung his head around. The storm was close on every side. The sound of it was terrific, with powerful gale force winds howling and roiling the clouds, but he felt nothing.

His gaze came around to Aine, placidly watching, and to Gilla, still lounging at the tiller, smiling inanely and humming a bit of a tune. Beyond him, Lugh saw the ship of their pursuers, and there his attention fixed.

Their enemies were not so fortunate.

In the sea, barely a spear's throw from the stern of the little boat, the sleek, miraculous ship was floundering, caught by the full violence of the storm. Those aboard it were fighting desperately to keep the craft afloat, but the vessel which had seemed so vast to Lugh was like a leaf on a rushing stream, borne before the storm's fury, hammered by rain, thrashed by the wind and the curling whips of the waves.

Lugh watched intently, fascinated by the force at work, captivated by the horror of it. His own craft sat in a cradle of serenity, gently rocked by the monstrous clouds' wind as if it were a babe in a mother's arms. He and his friends were safe while, within their sight, men battled vainly for their lives. That they had meant to kill him somehow did not lessen his pity for them in their plight. For they had no chance, and no will of their own could change the manner of their deaths.

At least it was over quickly. The battered craft was toppled, crushed, flung away. The soldiers fell upon the spikes of the angry sea and were gone in moments. The black clouds covered and hid the wreckage, and Lugh's last sight of his pursuers was of the faces of the remaining men, mouths gaping in fear and filling with the cold, salt sea.

A breeze picked up his little boat and thrust it gently forward. The storm fell back ahead of them, rolling away to the sides, almost as if giving passage to them. Blue sky showed ahead, and in moments they sailed out from under the dark canopy into a warm sun.

Relieved, Lugh lifted his face to the light, then back to the storm. Already it had nearly disappeared, the clouds shrinking, falling back into the sea which had spawned them.

"That storm," said Lugh incredulously. "It's as if it saved us deliberately."

"It did that," Gilla agreed. "But then, many strange things can happen on the sea." He winked broadly at Aine.

"He's thinking of my brother," said Aine. "It must have been Manannan. He can be very ruthless and cruel."

"A monster, as I said," Gilla put in, then grinned at Lugh. "So, be happy he's on your side, lad. Be happy!"

The young man and Aine looked then to Taillta's wounds while Gilla held the course back toward Eire. The Tower of Glass seemed to slide back down into the water, and Lugh's last sight of it was of a single, icy glint on the crest of a wave.

Bres and Streng stood before Balor's throne, the being's red gaze resting on them fixedly.

"They have escaped, Commander," Streng reported unhappily.

"Then send more ships," came the hard reply. "He must be caught. It is as I feared. For him to so boldly come here and escape, he must be charmed. He must be! Every Fomor garrison in Eire must be alerted to seek him. And you, Bres, understand that this boy's visit here puts you in the gravest danger. It is your overthrow that will be joined with ours if this one called Lugh isn't caught!"

The great head turned slowly toward the windows, the red gaze coming to rest on the distant haze where Eire lay.

"More is at stake in this than control of that isle. It is all our lives now. All our lives."

BOOK III
THE SILVER HAND

XVIII

THE HAUNTED MOUNTAINS

THE SUN BROKE over the ridge of the mountains, rimming it with light. It lifted higher to flood across the wide meadowlands that stretched to the night's edge falling away toward the west.

The sudden deluge of light caught and revealed something moving on the vastness of the plains. It was a pony cart accompanied by several figures, and they made a tiny, lonely company as they crawled steadily on through the empty lands.

A strange, tall being led the pony, the faded rags of his once-bright clothes flapping about him. A much worn young man and woman followed behind. Amongst the blankets piled in the cart, another, older woman lay pale and still.

As the first rays of the morning sun touched them, the tall one pulled to a stop and raised a hand to shield his eyes.

"Daylight at last!" Gilla the Clown exclaimed thankfully.

He gazed ahead toward the mountain range which thrust up so abruptly from the level plains and filled the whole horizon to the east. With the sun behind them, their western slopes were still filled with deep shadow, in sharp contrast to the brightness of the plains; they seemed like some dark beast brooding over its domains.

"At last you can see clearly where we're bound!" he called to the others. "The Mountains of Mourne!"

"How much farther are they?" asked Lugh, trying to estimate the distance himself.

"We'll be in them by nightfall," Gilla promised him with that buoyancy which no amount of hardship seemed able to defeat.

Aine had climbed into the cart to examine the resting woman by the light. She did so gently but thoroughly, her youthful face aged by her concern.

"She's still the same," she told Lugh. "The wound's not bled more, but she's very weak. And I can't arouse her from sleep anymore."

Lugh shook his head irritably and looked urgently to the clown. "And you're certain we'll find help for Taillta in those mountains?"

"By the whispered rumors I've picked up in my travels, many of Eire's druids and physicians and artisans have taken refuge there," Gilla said. "It's sure that with my own modest skills we'll find help for her and safe haven from the Fomor for all of us as well."

"Look, couldn't we rest, just a bit?" Aine complained wearily, climbing down. "We've been traveling a day and a night without letup. The jolting can't be good for Taillta."

"We have to keep moving," Lugh said firmly. "I feel that if we don't get her to a healer quickly, she'll have no chance. Just thank Gilla that we have the cart to carry her."

On their return to Eire, it had been the courageous—or foolhardy—clown who had boldy re-entered the Fomor seaport to fetch out his pony cart. They had then sped away inland, hoping to stay ahead of the Fomor parties they assumed would be sent after them. Lugh's one goal since had been to find help for his foster mother.

"Now that I can see, I can try missin' some of the biggest holes," Gilla said, urging the pony on again.

The two young people fell in beside him.

"One thing worries me, Gilla," Lugh said thoughtfully. "Once we reach the mountains, how will we find these people?"

"I know generally where to go."

"Generally? Is that enough? I mean, it's a very large place."

"It's enough. Once we're close, I'm thinkin' they'll find us. They're on the lookout for strangers enterin' the mountains, that they are!"

"But since we are strangers, will they accept us?" Aine asked.

"I've an acquaintance with some who've taken refuge there," Gilla explained. "They'll accept me all right." He paused and then added lightly: "Of course, we'll have to live long enough to find them!"

"And what is that supposed to mean?" asked Aine.

"Ah, well, the mountains are said to be haunted!" he answered in a careless way. "A shoeugy place indeed. The tales of the things dwellin' there could drive a man mad with fear! It's for that very reason the de Dananns have chosen to hide there. Few Fomor would have the courage to seek them in that place and risk a meetin' with what's lurking there!"

As usual, the clown passed on these distressing facts with great gusto. Lugh wasn't sure whether to take Gilla seriously or not. But he did keep a keen eye on the mountains as they approached, and he did notice with a certain disquiet that even when the sun rose to light the western slopes, the shadows weren't completely chased away. They only retreated to the hollows and vales to lie in wait for the coming of the night.

As the sun settled redly behind the western plains, the shadows crawled forth again to reclaim the mountainsides. They engulfed as well the little party that made its way laboriously up into them.

Gilla came upon the semblance of a trail winding into the lower hills. It made their travel a bit easier, but the efforts of all three were needed to move the cart forward at times.

Lugh hoped that they would find some haven soon. Beyond Taillta's worsening condition, the rest of them were rapidly growing weaker. They'd had little rest in days, food and water were gone, even the contents of Gilla's amazing cloak were exhausted. It was only the need to find shelter and help for Taillta quickly that kept them pushing onward.

Above them, the Mountains of Mourne rose ominously under the drifting oval of a nearly full moon. Its light glazed the mountain tops and open surfaces of the slopes with a white glow. In contrast, the bewildering series of canyons they made their way along were often plunged into a profound darkness that found the trio linking hands for safety.

The farther they climbed, the greater Lugh's sense of

discomfort grew. He became more and more certain that something was indeed haunting this place.

He couldn't find a clear reason for his concern. He felt that something was around them, something strange and hostile. He searched the moonlit hillsides, the shadowed rocks, the path behind and ahead continuously and saw no signs of life, no shadows moving save their own.

He began to wonder if his imagination was creating the impression in his mind. Until Aine moved close to him and murmured:

"I have the oddest feeling about this place. It's so empty! I've no sense of any animals around us. It's as if something had chased them all away."

"I've no unhappiness about that!" Lugh replied. "My worry was more that something was stalking us."

"But that's just it. Don't you see? There's nothing at all out there. Didn't you notice how silent it was?"

He understood then that this was exactly the thing that had been disturbing him. There was a heavy silence around them, as if they'd been sealed inside a jar. No night birds called. No insects played their songs. No wind whistled in the rocks. The only sounds were their own, and even these were curiously muffled.

"It's nothing to be concernin' yourselves about," Gilla told them in an airy tone. "Just keep on climbin'. I think the slope is opening out ahead."

It was. The moonlight now began to fall upon the ground around them, and they could see that they had left the canyons to mount a smooth hillside. It swept up in an easy grade before them toward a rounded top that showed grey against the darkly brooding backdrop of the higher mountains.

Gilla stopped abruptly, staring ahead.

"What is it?" Lugh asked.

"Look there," Gilla said, pointing ahead.

Lugh saw it too. A cone of yellow light thrust skyward from the crest of the hill.

"There's a fire up there," said Gilla.

His words were immediately followed by a dreadful clamor. It was a ragged tear of sound, a wailing cry from many voices, blending into one pain-filled noise. It came from above, hanging and then echoing away.

"A fire . . . and something else," Gilla amended. He looked to the others, beaming. "Well, shall we go see?"

"Gilla, do we have to?" Lugh asked his friend with immense fatigue. "So much has happened to us these past days. I'm not certain I can deal with anything more. And what about Aine?"

"Nonsense, lad. Your adventures have only made you the stronger. Just assert that will of yours. And Aine can surely deal with anything. She's a god's sister, isn't she?"

He slapped her playfully across the back at this. She cast him a nasty look in reply.

"Look, you want to find shelter and aide for your Taillta," Gilla went on. "So you'll have to trust me now, that you will. You'll have to stay by me and follow me without questions."

Aine shrugged. "If it's some magic, I don't think any of the powers I have will help us, Lugh. It looks as if we'll have to trust the clown."

"Thank you for your confidence!" said Gilla with mock graciousness. The foolish smile beamed again in the darkness. "So, then let's be on, shall we?" He started off with the cart, but as if an afterthought, he threw back over his shoulder to them: "Oh, and remember, whatever happens, show no fear. No fear at all! It could be your end, that it could!"

"He is doing very little to ease my worrying," Lugh remarked glumly to Aine as they fell in behind the clown.

They reached the crest of the hill and climbed above it very slowly, easing up into clear view of the light's source. Lugh was tense from anticipating what they would find now.

But it didn't seem alarming. Only a bonfire in the center of a flat, circular hilltop, surrounded by small objects—at least two score—set at equal distances. The fire cast long shadows out from each object like spokes radiating from a wheel's hub.

The three paused on the crest of the hill to survey this scene.

"You've come at last, have you!" a cracked and dusty voice called from the direction of the fire. "I've been waiting long enough for you. Come closer."

Gilla at once moved forward, leading the pony cart. The other two stayed close beside him. As they neared the circle of objects, Lugh began to see why Gilla had told them to show no fear. For what surrounded the fire, set on short stakes, were human heads.

All were turned inward toward the flames. Their eyes were shut. Long hair, loose in the warrior's style, hung around the ragged stumps of their necks in tangled masses. They must have been freshly severed, Lugh thought, for although no blood dripped from them, the features looked soft and untouched by decay. Indeed, the ruddy, shifting glow of the bonfire endowed them with an eerie semblance of life.

The three stopped once again at the edge of the circle, the backs of several heads right before them. Now Lugh was aware of a figure seated across the fire, looking toward them. It seemed to be a woman, scrawny and very old, her hair a thick, woolly mass of grey about her head. Though she looked toward them, he couldn't see her eyes, only shadowy patches in the thin face.

"Come closer. Closer!" she complained in a harsh rasp. "I want to see you."

"We'll leave the cart here," Gilla murmured. He dropped the pony's lead and stepped forward, Aine beside him.

Only Lugh hesitated, but he recalled the clown's words and the woman lying wounded in the cart. He could let nothing risk his losing Taillta a second time. He followed them through into the circle, stepping between two of the heads and stopping beside Aine and Gilla, close to the fire.

He now had a clear look at the hag through the flames. It told him that no matter how close they came to her, she wouldn't be seeing them. She was blind, blinded in some grotesque way that had taken her eyes and burned away the surrounding flesh so that now her eyes were only gaping sockets, like those of a skull, surrounded by cracked folds of white scar tissue. But the black caverns weren't quite empty. In the left one shimmered the delicate silver tracery of a spider's web spun across the opening. And in the center of the pattern the bloated insect sat, its glossy red body glinting fixedly at them like a pupil set in the ghastly, silken eye.

"I've my own ways of seeing," she grated, startling Lugh with her apparent reading of his thoughts. "It's two score pairs of eyes I have, and two score mouths to welcome you as well!"

She raised a wand of polished wood from her lap at this and swept it around the circle.

As she did, each of the heads came to life.

Their eyes flicked open and rolled wildly around. Their

faces worked in dreadful contortions, and from the open jaws of each there came a screeching, the strident voices joining in a stupefying din, a chorus swelling to reverberate through the surrounding hills.

Lugh's instinct was to recoil, to turn and bolt from the circle. But he looked to Gilla who stood calmly beside him, smiling his foolish smile, apparently quite unmoved. It helped the young man recover his own will to fight the terror down, though it held his insides in a grip of ice. He forced himself to endure the piercing noise without an outward sign of fear. A glance at Aine told him she was doing the same.

At last the caterwauling died away. The jaws set themselves in leers of death. The eyes fixed wide open, all staring up at the trio.

"A clever little trick," Gilla commented pleasantly. "Did it take you very long to train them all?"

The hag's head snapped toward him, the eyeless sockets leveling upon him as if she fixed him with her glare. The web shivered.

"You are a courageous man," she grated. "But you'd do better not to anger me! It is the witch of the Mountains of Mourne I am, and no one enters them without gaining my leave."

"And how is it you keep everyone out, old woman?" Gilla inquired, not sounding particularly impressed.

The rod swung out again, this time pointed higher. As it completed its circle, the sound of footsteps arose all around them in the darkness. They came closer and figures emerged from the black beyond the firelight, marching into the wedge-shaped rays cast between the heads.

They were warriors, brightly cloaked, richly harnessed, glinting longswords clutched ready in their hands. But they were not living men, for none of them had his head.

From all sides they moved in, coming to the edge of the circle, each stopping close beside one of the heads, and completely surrounding the three. Lugh watched them, realizing with a sinking heart that they had managed to get themselves trapped once again.

That fact seemed not to bother the clown at all. He looked with interest around the circle at the nightmare band, saying:

"Ah, is it the other part of them come now? They'll likely

be happy at bein' so close together again. Or, are they matched up properly?"

"Your jesting won't help you, fool," she answered. "These warriors angered me. They tried to battle me. You can join them if you wish. Or you can leave these mountains with your heads."

"We're not going back," he said stolidly.

"You'll not go on either unless you accept my company without complaint," she told him, and commanded sharply, "Sit!"

Gilla did as she asked, crouching by the fire. With a wave of his hand he signaled the others to do the same.

"Now you'll share my food," she said.

She lifted iron spits laid in the fire and handed one across to each of the three. Their ends were fixed with fat chunks of meat. But although they had been lying directly on the flames, they had not cooked. The red, sagging flesh oozed with dark, half-congealed blood that plopped in thick globules onto the bare earth.

"It's raw," Lugh said in unconcealed disgust.

"If you refuse my food, you insult me, and you'd best leave my mountains before my wrath falls upon you!" she threatened.

"Well, we're not leaving, and we're surely not eatin' this muck," Gilla responded boldly, throwing down his spit. "And I'm thinkin' we've had more than enough of this, I am that!"

"You defy me?" she cried, drawing her scrawny body up.

"I mean, it's all really a bit much, isn't it?" Gilla went on reasonably. "You didn't expect to frighten us with it, did you? So, just be good about it. Let it go."

She rose to her feet and lifted her bony arms above her head. Vibrating with rage, she swung the wand violently back and forth around the circle.

"Leave these mountains now," she shrieked in a voice like cracking ice. "Leave now or you will be destroyed! Destroyed! Destroyed!"

Her voice rose higher on each of the final words. The wand swung faster. The warriors seized the heads beside them by the trailing hair and lifted them from the stakes. Together, like one being, they strode forward, the glaring heads uplifted in one hand, the swords brandished in the other.

Lugh and Aine rose and moved back to back, awaiting the

attack. The lad was certain that this time the clown's madness had doomed them.

"If you're going to be unfriendly about it..." Gilla said with resignation and launched himself forward, the power of his long legs propelling him across the fire upon the hag.

She fell back as he grabbed at her, the wand spinning from her hand, falling into the flames.

The fire exploded.

It seemed to blossom, flames curling open like the petals of some giant, incandescent flower. It rolled out from the center in all directions, sweeping over Lugh, Aine, Gilla and the hag, the warriors and their heads, burying them all with its brilliance.

XIX

THE DRUID'S HOUSE

LUGH LIFTED HIMSELF cautiously from the ground and looked around.

The hilltop was now lit only by the moon, and by it he could see no sign of the headless warriors. Beside him, Aine lifted her head and he moved to her, helping her to sit up. Like himself, she seemed to have been stunned by the explosion, but showed no marks of harm from the flames.

"Are you all right?" he asked her.

"I'm fine," she assured him, looking around the hilltop in bewilderment. "But, what happened to everything else? The warriors, the fire..."

"That blast of flames swept them all away," said Lugh, "stakes, heads and all! No sign they were ever here. There's nothing left but us and the pony and cart."

"Where's Gilla?" she asked, the anxiety in her voice revealing her concern for the gangly clown.

"I'm right here!" his voice answered her. Not far away a familiar tall form heaved upright, dragging a second, smaller figure up with it. "And I've still got myself attached to our witch, that I have!"

But the being the clown still gripped tightly by the arms was no longer a ragged, sightless hag. Now it was a white-haired, frail-bodied little man whose large head contrasted with a tiny face whose most striking features were a sharp-ended jut of nose and a pointed chin. Around his narrow shoulders hung a long, multi-hued cloak that shone like a shifting rainbow even in the darkness.

He was still struggling fiercely against the clown's grip, but when Gilla saw who it was he held, his face split in a broad grin and he shook the other lightly, crying with delight:

"Findgoll! Findgoll, it's me! Look at me, man!"

The small man stopped his struggles abruptly and peered searchingly up at his opponent. Then his own expression changed, brightening with surprise and pleasure.

"Gilla Decaire!" he exclaimed. "It's you! I didn't know you in the darkness."

"Aine. Lugh," the clown called to them. "This is a friend of mine. Meet Findgoll, a High-Druid of the Tuatha de Danann."

The little man bowed to the young pair. Then his expression changed to frowning puzzlement as he examined them more closely.

"It's no wonder I took you for Fomor. The lad is in Fomor dress and you all look so ragged. Well worn, too." He turned back to Gilla. "What is it that's brought you here?"

"We're in sore need of help, Findgoll," the clown said sincerely. "My friends and I are hunted by the Fomor, and we've a badly hurt woman in the cart. This was the only place I knew to come for help... if you'll give it."

"My old friend, why of course! Of course!" Findgoll assured him with enthusiasm. "My own arts won't be much help to her, but come with me. My home is very close by. I'll take you there to rest while I fetch our healer."

"Eat up all of that broth now, you children. Get some strength into yourselves," Findgoll insisted with motherly concern.

Lugh gladly did as he was bidden, for the broth was hot

and rich with lamb. He drained the last of it and sat back comfortably on the pile of furs.

It was a circular liss of stone that the druid had brought them to. It was a crude and simple dwelling that Findgoll had apologized for several times. But mean as it was, it seemed a fine and cozy place to the worn lad.

Bright tapestries and furs were hung upon the walls to lessen their stark look and reduce the chill drafts that in rainy Eire seemed always to be creeping in. Thick rush mats were scattered upon the packed earth floor. In a central hearth a fire blazed against the cool of night, providing a bit of cheering light as well. It had been many days since Lugh had felt this sense of comfort, this sense of a home. Not since his own had been destroyed.

And there was something else that brought even greater comfort to him. Tailta would live.

He glanced across the liss to where she lay resting in one of the small rooms that surrounded the central one. She lay upon a soft bed while a man bent over her, cleaning and dressing her wound by the light of several tapers.

He was Diancecht, the greatest healer of the de Dananns, Findgoll had told them before he had rushed to fetch the man. Lugh had watched him skillfully and gently examine Tailta and heard with relief his declaration that her amazing strength would ensure her recovery. Now the young man and his friends waited by the fire and talked quietly as he finished his work.

"You really have been through a great deal, haven't you, poor babes," Findgoll fussed on. He flushed from chagrin with himself. "And here I was, trying to frighten the life from you!"

"Don't you be feelin' badly about that," Gilla consoled heartily. "I told them there was nothing to fear. Nothing to harm us at all! I knew it was the druid illusions we'd be facin'. I should have known that it was you as well. That colorful bit of horror had the mark of your own sly, twisted mind on it."

Findgoll gave a delighted trill of laughter at that.

"It was a fine bit of work, wasn't it? And it would have sent you screaming in terror from these mountains, too, if you'd been Fomor," he assured the clown. "I've used it with great success before. Oh, you should see them scampering away!"

His tone grew more sober as he added, "And it is a good thing for all of us hiding here that such tricks do work, for we've little else to protect us."

"Findgoll is a true master of cunning tricks, he is," Gilla told the young pair, and chuckled at his memories. "Why, in Tara, he caused Bres many a trouble helping the de Dananns. Once, when the king put a tax on the cows' milk, it was Findgoll made three hundred cows of wood with pails for udders and used his magic to make them look real. He put black bog stuff in the pails. When Bres came to see them and have them milked before him, it was the bog stuff they squeezed out. Bres took a great drink, thinkin' it was milk!" The clown hooted with laughter. "Ah, the king wasn't the better for that for a long time. That he was not!"

"Gilla may praise me, but he is a clever one with the tricks himself," the druid responded warmly. "It was by his cleverness that I escaped from Tara when the Fomor came to raid our schools and destroy us. It was many a teacher and artist and bard he saved from them. And many of us hiding safely here owe our lives to him."

Lugh eyed his odd companion with increased interest.

"I hadn't realized he was so great a help to you," he said thoughtfully. "It was my good fortune to meet him, it seems."

"Gilla is a modest one," said Findgoll. "He's never even said why he risked himself for us. He's not one of our people." He smiled. "At least, I don't think so. No one knows much about Gilla."

"There's little to be told," the clown replied lightly. "I'm a simple, rovin' entertainer, searchin' for ways to keep life lively. And if a man does have reasons for what he does meant for only himself, then what business has anyone else to be pryin' into them. Right lad?" He gave Lugh a mischievous wink.

The young man caught his meaning. Though he might have, Gilla had never asked the lad questions about his purpose in Eire or showed any curiosity about Aine's presence. Lugh owed him the same courtesy.

"Prying or not, I'd still like to know more about you," said a new voice. "My poet's instincts tell me there must be some good tales in your adventures."

The speaker was a man who had just entered the liss. He

was a youngish-looking man, tall and slender like most de Dananns, with fine, blond hair plaited loosely at his back. His clothing was simple, his cloak of plain, dark green wool. But at his neck he wore the intricately patterned golden torc of a Filid, the highest rank of bard.

"It's Bobd Derg, isn't it?" Gilla greeted him cordially. "I've not seen you in some years."

"Long ones, Gilla," the man said, crossing to the fire. "Findgoll passed word when he fetched Diancecht that you had come."

As he moved closer, Lugh examined him more closely. He had a narrow face with a wide brow, high cheekbones and strong chin. Large eyes of a light grey-green were set close to a straight, finely drawn nose. These features might have made him handsome once, but now they were exaggerated by an excessive emaciation that had hollowed the cheeks, and thrown the jaw and nose into sharp definition.

He stopped by the fire and stood uneasily, his hands kneading one another, his head and eyes moving jerkily as he glanced from one to the other of the group. He seemed charged with some nervous energy that made him vibrate like a harp string stretched too taut.

"I can see how weary you are. Still, I thought..." he hesitated, then tried again, his tone apologetic. "You see, we get so little news of the rest of Eire here. I hoped..."

"We'll talk with you gladly," Gilla said heartily. "Sit with us." He turned to the young pair. "Lugh, Aine, this is Bobd Derg, one of Eire's finest bards, and a son to the Dagda himself."

The man sat down beside Findgoll. He smiled gratefully and looked around at the sleeping Taillta and the young pair in a quizzical way.

"You're none of you de Dananns, are you?" he inquired. Before Lugh could reply, Aine quickly spoke.

"We're visitors to Eire from far away. We were traveling when the Fomor set upon us. Gilla rescued us and brought us here."

Lugh gave her a puzzled look, wondering why she was spinning out such a tale.

"The Fomor! They're a cruel whip upon all in Eire!" Bobd Derg said. The voice of the bard was intense, clear, each word given its own, ringing emphasis. It was the voice of one who could enthrall hundreds with vivid pictures shaped only by his poetry. Now it was sharp with his hatred.

Lugh's impression of him was of a man whose physical aspects had been wasted away, leaving him frail, almost a wraith, powered only by some inner vitality too intense for the weakened body to control, showing itself in the voice and in the fevered lights that danced wildly in his eyes.

"But you've been traveling," he said, the hatred giving way to anxiousness. "What have you seen of Eire? And Tara, Gilla? Have you been there? How does she fare?"

"Tara is . . . as it has been," Gilla said vaguely.

"Then it must be worse, as I feared." The bard shook his head sadly. "Bad enough that you're reluctant to say. And what about my family? Have you any news of them?"

"They're all well, Bobd," Gilla assured him.

"I saw your father and brother there," Lugh put in. "They seemed healthy, filled with energy and defiance for the Fomor."

If he had hoped to gladden the bard with this news, he failed. Bobd Derg only grew more melancholy.

"They will never learn. The Fomor will lose patience with them one day and they'll both die. The last champions will all die, and then the last fires will go out."

He stared down into the flames before him. They reflected a red glare from the bright, liquid eyes. His voice grew harsher with his bitterness, each word like a separate, heavy blow of a hammer.

"Three long years we've been here. Three long years of cold and wet and hunger and fear. And nothing has happened to change things in that time. No miracles have come. No powers have appeared to aide us." He looked to the old druid. "What about this champion, Findgoll? This champion your prophecy has said will lead us to freedom? What of him? Admit that it was just more of your tricks to give us empty hope while we grow weaker and our chances dwindle away."

"It was not!" the druid replied with unexpected ferocity. "The prophecy was given through the powers of the Four Cities. I believe it. He will come."

"Will he?" said Bobd Derg, smiling wearily. "Well, if he does, he'll find little enough to lead." He leaned toward the druid, his voice taking on a note of desperation. "Don't you see it yet, Findgoll? Don't you see that there is only one chance left to us?"

"To leave Eire?" the druid said, sighing heavily. "Ah, Bobd, your own father would never accept such a choice."

"My father is of the Old Ones. Most of us are not. We were raised in a land of peace and beauty, taught to create, to love life, not to destroy it. We were never warriors. The only remnant of that lies in my father and the old champions. Our battle with the Firbolgs should have proved that, even to them. With all our powers we were nearly defeated."

"We had to come back to Eire," Findgoll insisted. "It was our dream. For all of those years in the Four Cities, it was our only dream."

"The dream of the Sons of Nemed, you mean. I had no memories of this land. My only home was with Danu's people. They've offered us a place with them, and we should have accepted it. We should go back and accept it now!"

"If we return to the Four Cities, we'll never have a place or a life that is our own," the old druid argued doggedly.

"And have we those now? Do you really believe we'll have them? Our freedom and possessions have been stripped from us, our teachers and artists accused of rebellion and exiled or killed, until we are denied even the chance to think for ourselves."

The physician had finished with Taillta and had crossed the liss to stand nearby, listening to this. He was an older man, but large and quite hardy-looking. His face was large featured and craggy, with thick eyebrows bushing out above sharp blue eyes. Grey hair covered the high-domed head in tight waves. Lugh had found him to be a brusque, impatient man, and it was clear from the way he glared at Bobd Derg that he wasn't pleased with what the bard was saying.

"You are too quick to give up," he scolded in a deep voice, stepping forward. "Many of the young de Dananns have the will to fight. Your own brother is one of them."

"The fire of their youth still keeps rebellion alive," the bard answered. "It will burn out too."

"Not if they can be brought together," Diancecht said with force. "Not if they can be led to fight."

"Do you still argue that?" Bobd Derg said with impatience. "Bres will never lead them. He's convinced that placating the

Fomor is our only chance. He's ordered the de Dananns to lie down and we have. So long as he is king, we'll stay down."

At this mention of Bres, Lugh opened his mouth to speak, but Aine laid a hand upon his arm. When he looked at her, he saw her mouth a single word: "Quiet!" He held his tongue, not understanding why.

"That can be changed," Diancecht told Bobd pointedly. "You know there is a way."

"I know what you believe. But it would do us no good anymore. And it would be madness to try. Dangerous madness!"

These words stung the old healer. He pulled himself stiffly erect, his expression growing hard. In formal tones, he addressed himself to the visitors.

"Your friend will recover completely. But it will take time and much rest. She'll sleep for some while, and she'll be weak for many days. Don't disturb her. I'll come back to see her tomorrow. Good night!"

And with that he shot Bobd Derg a final angry look and stalked from the liss.

A faint, weary smile touched the bard's lips.

"Poor Diancecht. Another of the Old Ones, still clinging to the dream."

"I'm one of them too, if you'll recall," Findgoll said sharply, a bit offended himself. "I can't so easily give up our land either. I want to believe we can still challenge the Fomor."

"Findgoll, be realistic," the bard reasoned. "What would we gain? If Bres did decide to lead us in rebellion, if we could gather enough strength to defeat the Fomor garrisons, we'd only face those from the island again. The tales of that first defeat brought nightmares to every de Danann child. Even the hardened champions like my father fear the powers dwelling in that tower."

"Tower?" Lugh repeated excitedly. "A tower of glass?"

Bobd Derg turned a curious gaze on the lad.

"Why, yes. Do you know of it?"

From the corner of his eye, Lugh glimpsed Aine's warning look. Again he held back the truth he wanted to blurt out, replacing it with a vague reply.

"Oh, it's just a story we heard in our travels. Something to do with a tower like a great crystal, and magical black ships, and warriors dressed all alike in grey."

"It's much more than a story," Bobd Derg said grimly. "It's

all very real. It was those warriors and the powers of that
tower which destroyed the fleet of the Sons of Nemed long
ago."

"They are leagued with the Fomor then?" Lugh asked,
unable to completely hide the intense interest in his voice.

"No, lad. Not leagued with them. The Fomor power has its
very heart and mind in that tower. The warriors who dwell
there are the true Fomor themselves!"

XX

LUGH'S DILEMMA

"FOMOR? HOW COULD that be?" asked the wondering Lugh.
In his desire to know he ignored Aine's warning. "They look
like normal men. They're different from those in Eire in
dress, in the way they live..."

"It's true, nonetheless," Bobd Derg assured him. He smiled,
clearly amused by the lad's enthusiasm. "There is a very
ancient tale explaining how that came to be. I managed to
acquire it from the Fomor warriors in my quest for stories.
It's vague and filled with things not known to me, but I could
tell it to you, if you'd like to hear it."

"I would, if it's not a bother," Lugh told him earnestly.

For the first time, Bobd Derg appeared pleased.

"It would be a pleasure. It's been some time since I had an
audience. My skills are in long disuse."

He sat back, assuming a more formal, upright pose. As he
did, a change occurred in him. The sense of his weakness
faded away. His eyes took on a faraway appearance, as if he
looked into the realm of the tales he spun. The tension left
him and his voice took on a new strength as he assumed the
bardic role, acquiring a resonant, melodic tone.

"It was in the time long before our tribe rose in the east,
before our own chronicles record. Then the Fomor were a
vast race of enormous power, ruling many lands.

"It was great knowledge these people had, and they used

it to create forces, weapons, tools to build whole cities of the gleaming towers and harness all nature to their selfish ends.

"And then some violent force—a cataclysm either of their making or of a nature outraged to rebellion—fell upon their race, their cities and their lands, wreaking great destruction.

"Of all their number, only a few survived, isolated in the last of their glass fortresses on an isle remote from other men. But even these few did not escape untouched by the vile, contaminating forces which had annihilated the rest. For something malevolent, something corrupting to the blood and bone of man had tainted many of them. And because of the parents' sin, the children were cursed, too. They were born dreadful mockeries of man in form, and their numbers multiplied with the next generation, growing more grotesque. Finally the Fomor knew they must act quickly or none would escape.

"So it was decreed by them that all those marked by the curse were to be exiled to the island of Eire to live separately. And those last, pure members of the once-vast race and any children born without defect were to keep themselves aloof, tied always to that final bastion of their might, the Tower of Glass."

As Lugh listened, he understood the sense of alienation from nature he had felt in that stark tower. The people there had sealed themselves away from the world, from life, and by their isolation in that changeless, barren place grown as rigid and cold as those carcasses in their own freezing room.

"And these powers, the ones you say destroyed the Sons of Nemed, what is the source of those?" he asked.

This time it was the druid who answered.

"We don't know the sources. We don't understand the powers. Even the mystical skills and knowledge we gained from Danu's people in the Four Cities will not help us understand."

"But they are fearful powers," the bard put in. "And most terrible of all is the energy my father tells me shot from the tower like a bolt of fire and blasted their ships away. It came, he said, from a black giant who stood upon its top, a being the tales say is called Balor of the Evil Eye, leader of the Fomor."

Lugh ached to tell them that he had seen this being, had glimpsed a fraction of its power in use. But Aine yawned loudly at this point. Covering it with a hand in seeming embarrassment, she said sleepily:

"Oh! I'm sorry for my rudeness. But I'm having great trouble in staying awake. We've had a very difficult time getting here."

This broad hint brought Bobd Derg's solicitousness back and he hastened to make apologies.

"It's myself who should be sorry for keeping you from sleep. But we'll talk more. You're welcome, of course, to stay with us so long as your friend needs rest. Though it's poor hospitality we can give here." He got up. "So, I'll say goodnight to you."

He walked to the door, but paused there, looking back to add:

"But if you'll listen to my advice, you'll leave Eire as soon as you can. Our foolish arrogance in seeking our own place has bound us here. But no such dreams bind you. If you're seeking a place, there's no hope of it here."

"Hope is something that you have to make, Bobd Derg," Gilla said quietly.

"Making anything takes strength, Gilla," the bard replied disheartenedly. "We've little left to us."

"He's certainly gloomy," Gilla commented when he had gone. "I remember him as quite a sparkling wit. A prime entertainment, a bright spot at every feast!"

"He is a poet," Findgoll reminded him. "His life was one of beauty and peace. This has been especially hard on him. The hunger, the cold, the lack of hope. It's taken a great toll of many of us." Then he shook off his own depression, saying in a brisker way, "Well, never mind. You have to get some rest. I've chambers ready for each one of you. If you feel a chill, there are extra covers in the basket by the door. So, be off to bed, all of you."

They obeyed without argument. Lugh checked Taillta to be sure she rested comfortably. Then he and the others went to their compartments.

Each of the rooms was formed by a stone partition extending from the outer wall toward the central fire, like spokes in a wheel. The inner opening was shut by a moveable wall of wicker to make a private chamber.

Once the visitors had settled, Findgoll put out the candles and stoked the fire for the night before retiring himself. A short time passed. The fire settled to a steady glow. The sound of slow, rhythmic breathing signaled that some in the liss had gone to sleep. Then it was that the partition of Lugh's room was carefully moved open. The young man crept out and padded silently to where Aine slept. He pulled her wicker screen open and entered.

Moving to the covered form, he knelt by her and laid a hand lightly upon her shoulder.

"Aine," he whispered.

She was sitting up instantly, and he felt the pressure of a point against his chest. She held her dagger at his heart. But she dropped it down on seeing him.

"Oh, it's you. Don't you know awakening me that way is dangerous?"

"I had to talk with you," he said urgently.

"Can't it wait until morning? I'm so sleepy . . ."

"Don't try that on me. I want to talk now!"

She sighed. "All right. But be quiet. There's no need to be awakening the others."

He dropped down onto the floor close beside her. She sat up, pulling her covers up around her.

"What I want to know . . ." he began. Then he paused, noticing the sheen of her bare shoulders in the soft firelight. "Say, are you dressed?"

"Of course not. I was sleeping!" she said irritably. "Now, what is it?"

Her sharp question jerked his wandering attention back to his reason for coming.

"All right. I want to know why you kept warning me away from speaking about Bres or our visit to that tower."

"Because it might force us to reveal our mission here," she told him patiently, as if explaining to a child, "and it would serve no purpose."

"No purpose?" Lugh said in disbelief. "What about Bres? He's more than a tyrant. He's one of the Fomor! He means to destroy them! They have to be warned so they can be rid of him."

His voice had risen with his agitation. Aine hissed another warning.

"Quiet down. Listen! It's not your task to tell them. You are on a mission here for my brother, remember? You promised him you would observe, not interfere."

"My mission for Manannan is over. Don't you see? Now that I know that it was the Fomor who destroyed my home, I can't be fair-minded about this any longer. I've chosen my side. My enemies are those of the de Dananns. Bres is my enemy. I have to help them by seeing him destroyed before he destroys them."

"Your mission to Manannan is not finished until you have fulfilled it as you pledged. And remember, there are still questions only he can answer for you. If you feel you're through in Eire, you must go back to Manannan's Isle first!"

"No!" he said vehemently. "I can't just leave Eire and abandon them, knowing what I do. Aine, please try to understand. It's more than our having a common enemy. It's a feeling that somehow I'm connected to these people, that I'm a part of what's happening. I can't leave Bres in power and the de Dananns with no hope."

"And what good will it do for you to tell them about him?" she asked. "You've nothing to prove what you say. They've no reason to believe you—you're a stranger here. And if they did believe you, what could these poor, despairing refugees do, hunted and hidden away here?"

"Then I'll go to Tara and tell them there."

"They've no more reason to believe. And Bres would certainly never let you speak. Every de Danann loyal to him and every Fomor would be against you. You'd only be killed."

"Aine, I have to do something!" he said, his voice tight with his frustration. He dropped his head forward heavily.

She lifted a hand and laid it soothingly upon his shoulder. She could feel his tension in his rigid neck muscles.

"You will, Lugh. All that you can. Return with me and fulfill your mission. Then you can ask for Manannan's help."

He looked up at her again. She saw that the uncertainty was still strong in him. His eyes reflected it.

"It is for the best," she said with strong conviction, desperate to convince him. "You have to believe me. I only want to help you."

"Do you?" he asked, his gaze sharpening with interest.

"Of course!" she told him, smiling softly, winningly. "I know I've seemed harsh with you, but I do like you. I've liked you since you marched so boldly into Tara's hall."

"I've liked you too," he admitted. More hesitantly he added, "I might have told you, but I felt I had no right. You're sister to a god, and I..."

"Oh, I am so sick of being thought of as sister to a god!" she broke in with impatience. "I am as much a human being as you. A woman!"

She slipped her hand behind his head and pulled him to her suddenly, giving him another firm and definite kiss. Then she released him, pulling back.

"There!" she said with a satisfied nod, as if she had proven her point.

She had done much more than that to Lugh. He felt again that curious warmth, that tingling through his limbs, that shortness of breath that had seized him in the freezing room after her first kiss. Now he looked into those luminous eyes, felt the energy rush through him as it had before, giving him that boldness surprising even to him.

This time as she moved back, he took hold of her smooth shoulders with his hands and pulled her to him, renewing the kiss.

She was at first startled by his move, but then she began to respond, allowing him to pull her closer until her upper body was pressed tightly against his, her arms were encircling him, and she was allowing the surge of her own passion to carry her along.

He leaned forward, and she did not resist, falling back upon the pile of furs as he came over her.

The kiss ended and he lifted his head to gaze down at her. She was fully relaxed, a supple form in his arms. Her unbound hair was a glowing fan around her head. Her lips were slightly parted, the eyes nearly closed in the languor of her surrender. Her body was a burning heat against him, the scent of her an intoxicant.

"This is a much warmer place," he murmured. His hand moved slowly down from her neck, sliding across the smooth, warm skin, across her breast, drawing the covering along with it.

Her eyes snapped wide open, filling with alarm. She moved swiftly to grasp his wrist.

"Wait!" she said urgently. "This is going much too fast!"

He rose up, looking quizzically down at her. "Too fast? But, I thought..."

"It's clear enough what you thought," she replied, her voice sharpening with irritation. "I said I *liked* you. That's all!"

"I don't understand," he said in bewildered tones, sitting up. "That kiss. And, in the freezing room..."

"In the freezing room I was only trying to help you stay alive," she informed him brusquely. "Neither of us can afford our personal feelings to be complicating things."

"But the feelings are there," he argued. "I can't ignore them. I don't think you can either."

"You are wrong!" she countered. "Listen to me, Lugh! Everything I do is to make our mission a success. That is my only concern. It should be yours as well."

He opened his mouth to protest again, but she shook her head.

"No! Let's not talk about this any further. It was a mistake. We're both very tired and very... weak now. Go back to your own room and get some rest."

With that curt dismissal, she rolled onto her side away from him, pulling her covers over her.

Lugh stared at her back a long moment, dumbfounded by this sudden rejection. Then, with no other choice, he left her room and crept back to his own.

"Rest, she says," he muttered to himself as he climbed beneath his coverings. "And how does she expect me to do that now?"

He lay on his back, staring up at the light from the fire playing in shifting patterns against the ceiling, but all he saw there were images of her fair glowing skin, blended with some much more intriguing fantasies.

He didn't know that, in her own room, Aine lay sleepless too, staring out at the glowing red embers of the still-burning fire.

The coals pulsed higher under the bellows' puffings. Fire streamed up around a long metal piece, heating it to a brilliant yellow-white. Tongs lifted it to the anvil where the smith used a heavy hammer to shape it to a fine spear point.

It was a woman who worked the metal with such skill and swiftness. Her arms, bared by the short sleeves of the worker's rough tunic, were lean but wiry, tightening to knotted hardness at each blow.

Lugh stood with Aine and Gilla, watching her work attentively. For, along with her skills, she was also quite unusual in appearance. The side of her face to them as she worked the metal was harsh-featured and leathery—very homely, in fact. But as she turned to cool the point, she revealed another side of her face that was strikingly hand-some, fine-featured, the skin soft and very pale.

This woman of contrasts was named Bridget—the Fiery Arrow—Gilla had explained, and her appearance was an echo to her personality. Beyond her skills as a smith, she was a woman of healing and a great poet as well, beloved by all the poets of the de Danann and holding great sway amongst the people.

Lugh shook his head in wonder. Since dawn he had wandered the scattered homes of the hidden village with his compan-ions, still driven to find out more about these people. It had served to make him all the more fascinated by them.

The artisans there still plied their crafts as best they could, and with such skills as Lugh didn't believe possible for men. And so they were not, as the pleasant inhabitants freely explained to him. For the ways of the Four Cities played a part in much of what they did.

He realized that here, in these harsh mountains, was hidden much of the remaining culture and learning of these people, much of what could be called their spirit and mind.

They had stopped again at the smithy to watch the metal workers display their craft. They all seemed to know Gilla and were quite happy to accomodate him and the young pair. Indeed, they seemed anxious for a chance to demonstrate their skills.

Three craftsmen worked there now. With Bridget was the de Danann's greatest smith, Goibnu. He was a thickset, sinewy man, whose broad, good-natured face seemed per-manently blackened by his forge's heat. Cerdene, chief metal worker of the race, was also there. The slender but strongly built man worked delicately at beating out a thin copper bowl with hands of amazing slimness and length.

As Bridget completed her spearhead, she passed it to Goibnu who stood close beside her, watching her work critically. He lifted the still-hot piece without tongs, turning it over in hands calloused to thick leather as he examined it. Then he grunted with satisfaction.

"A good point," he told her. "Near perfect." He grinned, the teeth showing white against the dark skin. "Almost as good as my own."

Lugh stepped closer to examine the point. It was a fine piece of worksmanship, beautiful and lethal at once, much longer and lighter than any he had ever seen, with sharp cutting edges and a slender point.

"It looks to be a very good weapon. But is it strong?" he asked.

"Strong?" Goibnu the Smith replied indignantly. "Why, no metal or bone will blunt this—no helm or shield stop it. There's never been a weapon made as hard or efficient as this. The day we faced the Firbolg tribes, it was myself fashioned a point just like it for every warrior."

Cerdene proudly chimed in at that.

"Don't be forgetting my work. It was I who supplied the brass fittings for those spears, and the sword hilts and shield rims and bosses as well."

"It was grandly we all worked then," Goibnu said with nostalgia. "The forge blazing day and night, sparks rising like a column of gold, the ringing of the hammers making a single, constant note. A glorious challenge we met." He looked down at the point in his hand and his wistful expression turned despairing. "But it looks now like we'll have no more need for such skills. I wonder why we even bother to practice at it here, forging these useless things."

In disgust he flung the point away onto a pile of others already corroding from disuse.

"There might yet come a need for us again," Bridget said in a more hopeful tone. "Another chance..."

"A chance for what?" The smith had now let the gloomy mood claim him totally. He plumped his thick body heavily down upon a trestle, sagging with defeat. "It's too late, Bridget. No one can help us now. Maybe Bobd Derg is right. It's time to give up Eire and go back to Danu."

Witnessing such hopelessness on the part of these skilled, noble people was distressing to young Lugh. It only served to bring back and increase his sense of frustration at not being able to help.

As he and his comrades left the smithy and moved on

through the village, he was more and more conscious of the despair that hung above the refugees' hiding place like a cold mist. He didn't speak of his feelings then, but soon Aine left them to go back to Findgoll's liss and see how Taillta fared. When she had gone, Lugh voiced his feelings to the amiable clown.

"I feel like I'm deserting them. I wish that there was some way I could act. I've felt so far as if I've been drawn along, having no free will. I'd like to do something by my own choice."

"I think I understand your feeling, lad," said Gilla. "But it's true enough what she says. They'd not believe you, and there's little they could do. So, if you've promised to return to this Manannan's Isle for some purpose of your own, why that's what you must do." He paused and added doubtfully, "Though what some so-called sea-god can do, I can't imagine." He shrugged and clapped a hand on Lugh's shoulder, smiling sadly. "When you go, lad, I want you to know that I'll miss you, I will that!"

"I'll come back, Gilla," Lugh promised. "No matter what else happens, I'll come back."

By this time their wandering had taken them beyond the end of the scattered village. Now they faced a rocky hillside rising steeply above them. Gilla drew Lugh's attention to a large opening not far up its side.

"See there? I understand that's the old healer's cave. What do you say if we stop in there while we're lookin' about? I'm wagerin' he's got some marvels of his own."

Lugh hesitated. The physician was a gruff, intimidating man, and the lad was reluctant to disturb him. But the clown's voice was coaxing, filled with a childlike excitement, and Lugh was still enough child himself to be interested in exploring such a mysterious possibility. He agreed to go.

They climbed up a narrow path to the ragged mouth of the cave and stood peering into the cavern beyond.

XXI

THE HEALER'S CAVE

IT WAS A large space with a level floor and smooth walls curving up to form a rough dome overhead. The floor of this cavern was crowded with paraphernalia of peculiar kinds, lit by scores of thick, guttering candles jamming massive iron holders.

Here and there around the floor small fires burned. A variety of cauldrons upon them boiled, sending up vari-colored steams to collect and finally blend in an odorous brown cloud in the top of the dome. The mass whirled and writhed slowly in the stagnant air as if it had its own life.

"Diancecht?" Lugh called, the name echoing within the vast hollow.

There was no reply.

"Now would you look at this grand collection of marvels!" Gilla said delightedly. "Let's take a look about, lad!"

"But, he's not here," Lugh said hesitantly. He wasn't sure, from his impression of the place, that he really cared to go poking about in it after all.

But Gilla wouldn't be denied. "We'll not hurt anything. Come on, lad! Where's your old sense of curiosity?"

"It's gotten a bit worn, Gilla," Lugh replied. Still, he followed the clown into the cave.

They moved through the maze of things slowly, trying to make sense of it. It was a bewildering array. Long tables of rough planks were piled with all manner of objects, mostly bizarre, and Lugh peered at them with mixed curiosity and revulsion.

One area was clearly devoted to the concoction of the healer's medicines. Herbs, roots and leaves hung drying on large racks, scenting the air with an almost overpowering mixture of aromas. Some already ground lay beneath the huge, timeworn pestle in a stone mortar. Fragile glass retorts, bottles and strange contrivances like nothing Lugh had ever seen before were linked in a complex interlace through which bright liquids raced and dripped and rose and fell with some hidden purpose of their own. And in the center of the whole, like some controlling god, a round, copper vat squatted on thick metal legs over an intense fire. It was fully enclosed save for a round opening at the top from which rose a yellow smoke and a spigot near the bottom where a vile green, viscous liquid dripped into a bowl.

Elsewhere, large shelves held a mixed collection of containers in many styles, sizes and materials. They formed a rich texture that might have been pleasing without the surroundings. Lugh peered down into a large pot and pulled back at once. A harsh stench rose from it, and in the liquid filling it there floated a mass of something soft, shiny and unidentifiable, but definitely unpleasant.

A table held a row of animals' heads in various stages of dissection. Eyes, tongues, brains, all kinds of parts were scattered casually around them like parts of some grotesque toy taken apart by a curious child. He peered into another jar there and found it filled with eyeballs that stared back at Lugh as if startled at being disturbed. After that he began peering more cautiously, not wishing more surprises.

One long shelf was lined with human skulls whose black sockets reminded Lugh of his first meeting with the druid. Other bones were heaped upon a table below them. A complete skeleton hung from a post, the bones strung together with thin cord. It rattled dryly when he brushed by it, turning to grin at him with brown teeth.

On another large table whose top was dyed rust from many soakings of blood there lay a whole boar, newly dead. It was slit from groin to neck, and several of its organs were laid out neatly around it. Gleaming knives and other instruments unfamiliar to Lugh were lined along the table's edge.

Unsettled by all the signs of death, Lugh moved to another area where stacked cages held a variety of living animals—hares, badgers, small dogs and other types of game. He wondered what their purpose was until he noted a bandage on the leg of a dog. He examined the rest and found several with marks of wounds in various stages of healing. These wounds, like a knife cut, were always on a limb. On some animals it had healed to a scar, barely discernable in the fur.

On a young mastiff the cut was recently mended. The fur had been shaved away and he could see the wound clearly, a fine line circling the lower leg just above the paw. It had odd marks on either side and he looked closer. He realized that the wound was sewn closed by fine thread, like the joining of two pieces of cloth.

He was about to call Gilla's attention to this when a voice spoke.

"What are you doing here? Come to see the madman's foolishness?"

Diancecht stood in the cavern's entrance. He looked stiff and indignant. His voice was cold with hostility.

"We're not prying," Gilla said cheerfully. "We came to see your work. You weren't here."

"I was seeing to your friend," he told them, moving into the cavern. "I interrupted my own work to do that. So, why don't you go and let me get back to it?"

"Diancecht, don't act the bear with us," Gilla said. "The boy is truly interested in your work. Tell him about it."

The healer looked searchingly at the young man. "Do you really wish to know about my work? It's gruesome enough."

Lugh was already well aware of that and not sure at all he wanted to know more. But Gilla was enthusiastic.

"Of course he does. Come along now. Show us. You've little enough chance for admirers here."

"It has been a long time since anyone showed interest," the healer gruffly agreed. "They're quick enough to run to me with a cut or a cough, but my greatest achievements they care nothing about. And after all I've done to perfect the skills given me in the Four Cities! I've even developed them so far that I can bring a sorely wounded man back from death. From death!"

He was heating to the subject now. He'd accepted the two as an audience and was venting his irritation with his fellows.

"You think it was easy saving your friend? You watched me do a few simple tricks and you breathed easily. But it was from death I saved her, and no one else could have."

"We understand," Lugh said sincerely. "We owe you much."

"They all owe me much, but do you think they appreciate it?" He began to stalk restlessly back and forth. "They sit and moan about their hopelessness while I work, and then they call my finest accomplishment a useless one!"

He gestured sweepingly around the cavern. "Look at this. I've delved into things man has never explored. See this boar? I know the secrets of how it died. I've done the same thing with scores, hundreds of beasts and men. I've gone beyond the surface of how things live seeking my answers."

He led them over to the cages. "And see here. See these animals?" He removed the dog Lugh had been examining, holding it up to display the scarred leg. "The limb on this one was severed. Severed completely! But I put it back on!" His voice rang triumphantly as he waved his hand across the other cages. "I've done the same with all of them, successfully every time!"

He put back the first dog and took out another whose leg was fully healed, letting it walk around.

"See there? No limp, no sign of its having been off at all. It's perfect. Perfect! And I made it so."

"That's interesting," Lugh said. "You cut off their legs so you can put them back on." He threw Gilla a puzzled look. The clown shrugged in reply.

Diancecht noted their doubt.

"You don't understand my purpose, do you? You don't yet see the full significance. Well, come here."

He led them to a large circle of iron set in the floor of the cave.

"Lift that!" he ordered Lugh.

With a certain understandable reluctance, Lugh grasped a large handle and lifted. It came up slowly, pivoting on large hinges. Cold air puffed up into his face as it opened.

He laid it back, revealing a hole neatly cut into the rock. Nothing was at first visible within it but the eddy of white haze as the inner cold air rose to meet the warm above. Then it cleared away and they were looking down into a pool of liquid whose crystal clarity revealed its extreme depth.

Suspended in the liquid on a hammock of fine lines there was a human hand.

It had been cut above the wrist and looked to have been severed recently. The stump was raw, with tendons and vessels clearly visible. The skin was as fresh-looking and red-toned as if it were still on a living man.

"With all my skills and those of Findgoll I have preserved

that hand through the years," the healer told them. "It is as perfect now as the day it was severed."

"But, why have you saved it?" Lugh asked wonderingly.

"Because, young man, that is not just a hand. It is the hand of Nuada, once High-King of the Tuatha de Danann. Now, shut the door again."

As Lugh did so, the healer took up his restless pacing as he went on.

"Since it was severed, I've made its restoration my greatest challenge. The artisans gave Nuada his silver hand, but only restoring the real hand could give him the kingship again. I vowed I would do it. All these years I've worked, experimented. Finally I have succeeded!"

"You can put Nuada's hand back on? Make him whole again?" asked Lugh, recalling the tale of why the kingship had been lost to Nuada.

"I can. And now that I've found it, they all say that it is too late. That it is no use. If I had done it earlier, they say, then there would have been a point. But now it's only dangerous madness." He swung to them. "You heard that weakling Bobd Derg yourself. He even questioned whether I could really do it! Questioned me!"

The force generated by his anger peaked at this, and then, as if expended, was extinguished suddenly. As the energy failed him, he aged in an instant, his body sagging, shrinking down.

"Oh, why go on with this," he said, shaking his head in despair. "Perhaps Bobd Derg is right. Nuada has lost hope, lost the will to fight. Were he restored to kingship, he'd be no more help to us in defying the Fomor than Bres."

Again, Lugh itched to speak the truth, to tell the healer that no man could be so bad as Bres, that he had to be deposed. But all he said was: "If there was any chance Nuada's restoration would help you, wouldn't it be worth attempting?"

"It's not so simple," the healer said. "Bringing Nuada here would be difficult. He is quartered in the fortress. Bres has never trusted him and likes to keep him close. That way he can keep Nuada supplied with drink, immersed in a sea of drunken despair. It'd not be easy to reach him, especially for one of us. None of those here believe it's worth the risk. And as little as I like admitting it, I'm too old. Just too old."

He lifted a small, shining knife from those lined on the table by the boar. He looked at it, stared at it in the grip of his hand. Then he dropped it back.

"Maybe I'm too old for anything," he said, the voice heavy with defeat. "Even I have begun to wonder if I really could succeed were Nuada brought to me."

"No, Diancecht," Lugh said forcefully. "I see what you've done here. I believe in your skills. And I've seen Nuada as well. There's a fire of defiance still alive in him. It would be worth the chance. I know it would. And any chance, no matter how slender, is better than waiting here to die or giving up a dream."

"Do you think so?" said the healer. His face lit with renewed hope, but it faded at once. "Sorry, lad. Perhaps it could be done, but you'll never convince the others of that. There is no one who does believe who could accomplish the task of fetching Nuada here."

Lugh glanced over at the iron lid upon the cavern floor. His expression was very thoughtful and very grave.

"No. I suppose there's not," he said quietly.

He was still lost in thought as he stood upon the hillside above the village, gazing out across the bright western fields. It was a warm spring afternoon, the fragrant breezes washing up the mountainsides to caress him gently and ruffle the thick mane of his fair hair.

"Lugh, there you are!" called Aine, walking up the hillside to join him. "I'd wondered where you'd gone."

He turned to her as she reached his side. She noticed his solemn look.

"What's wrong?" she asked him with concern. "You seem so grave."

"Oh, do I?" he asked, his expression clearing at once. He smiled guilelessly. "I don't mean to. I was only admiring the view from here. It's very nice."

That seemed to reassure her. She smiled back, but with a certain timidness unusual for her.

"I'm glad that's all. I was afraid you might be angry with me. That's why I wanted to talk alone with you. To explain. About last night."

She paused and then went on more awkwardly, as if each word took an effort to force out.

"You see, I don't like . . . losing control of things. That's very hard for me to admit, but it's true. I didn't mean to hurt you. I really do like you. It's just that this is not the time or place. Do you see?"

"Of course I do!" he said agreeably. "I'm not angry with you. We've been through too much together for that!"

Her face brightened. She beamed with relief.

"That's very good to hear," she told him, bouyant now.

"It's a very fine day," he said. "Would you care to walk with me a bit and enjoy it?"

"I would, gladly," she replied, and the two set off across the green hillside.

"You know, this is the first time I've really had a chance to look at Eire, enjoy it at my ease," he remarked as they walked. "I feel like I've been running since I arrived here. I'm just coming to realize what a beautiful land it is."

"Yes, it is," she agreed. "I've seen few lands as beautiful as Eire, or as harsh. Does that sound strange?"

"No. It's what I think makes this a special place."

They reached a craggy knoll where a single yew tree slanted out at a sharp angle as if reaching toward the afternoon sun. There the two stopped and settled into a smooth hollow in the rock below it where they could relax and watch the golden light playing across the meadows far below. It was still and soft and timeless, like a pleasant childhood memory.

"Have you visited many other lands?" he asked idly.

"A few. I've traveled with my brother. He hates staying in one place for long. He's forever seeking new things. I enjoy it too, but at times I miss our homeland. No land in the world is so fine as that. Not even Eire. Each day is as soothing and gentle as this. Flowers always bloom. There is no want, no pain, no hatred . . ."

"Sounds like it could become a bit tiresome," he said laughingly.

She laughed too. "Now you sound like my brother. Even its beauties can't soothe his discontent."

"Aine, you know I've not asked you about your life before," he said more seriously. "I felt it wasn't my right. But there is one thing I'd like to ask you."

"If it's within my power to answer, I will," she promised.

"Well, you said last night you were a human being as much as I. Does that mean you're wholly mortal? You can be harmed?"

"In our own lands we do not age," she explained, "although we can be killed or hurt. Here in Eire, even that is denied. Beyond the powers you know about, I am as vulnerable as you."

"How can Manannan let you take such risks?" he asked in surprise.

She shrugged. "He needs my help, and I love adventure, as he does," she answered simply.

"Still, I'm glad you'll not be needing to take any more risks for me!" he told her with great earnestness.

"Lugh, after we return, after this is ended, perhaps you'll stay in Manannan's Isle," she suggested, adding in a gently enticing way, "We could enjoy it together."

"The time is an uncertain one," he replied quite soberly. But when he saw her grow puzzled at his tone, his mood abruptly changed and he grinned.

"We've this day here and now!" he said. "Let's think of nothing more but enjoying it!" He climbed to his feet. "Why don't we walk some more? It will be evening soon and we'll have to go back."

They set a second, flowered hillside as their goal and started toward it. As they walked they joined hands, as if it were a natural thing to do.

Gilla was being shaken violently. An urgent voice was calling his name in his ear.

Groggily he sat up. Dawn's light filtered into the druid's liss, showing him Aine crouched over him. Her face was drawn with alarm.

"Aine, what's wrong?" he asked, taking her arms.

"It's Lugh!" she cried. "During the night he took food and water and left the village." Her eyes filled with anguished tears. "He's left us. He's gone without telling us why!"

XXII

THE RETURN

THE WHETSTONE SLID up the length of the slender blade with a sharp, metallic hiss. Its user plied the stone with an easy, steady rhythm, in seeming disregard of High-King Bres, who stood speaking nearby.

Bres stalked back and forth along the gallery room above the central hall as he issued his orders. His gaze swept the group of de Danann warriors facing him. Behind him, watching with a seeming impassiveness, stood the Fomor officer named Streng.

"If this boy Lugh should reappear in Tara, there is no excuse for his not being caught!" Bres rapped out. "This is too important to us all. He's to be watched for by every warrior. He's to be caught and brought to me!"

The continued shriek of the whetstone kept drawing his attention to its user who sat atop a plank table, long legs folded beneath her like those of a nesting crane.

"This applies to you and your champions too, Morrigan!" he snapped at her irritably.

He made no impression on her. The careful rhythm of the stone continued. She did not look up. But, in her low rattle of a voice she asked:

"And why is it we must be doing this?"

"Because I command it!" he said, his irritation making him arrogant.

The stone stopped. The sleek, dark head pivoted up toward him on the long neck, and he was fixed with dark eyes bright with the cold, deathly glow of a moon on a winter's night.

Bres knew that look, and knew he had pushed the dangerous being too far. His voice quickly took on a more reasonable tone.

"I mean, I feel that this has to be done. This boy is too dangerous."

"He is only a boy," she said.

"He is much more than that," Bres countered. "You should know the truth of that more than we."

"He has some courage . . ." she began.

Bres interrupted. "He is in league with rebels who would see us at war! He is causing an uproar amongst the Fomor. They believe he is part of a conspiracy to force them to act against us!"

"And why should the Fomor be carin' about that?" asked Niet, a de Danann captain who stood, massive and battle-scarred, beside the raven-woman. "Seems they'd welcome a chance to finish us."

Streng moved forward then, smiling benevolently.

"We have no wish to see you destroyed," he told them with a glib sincerity. "We want no final confrontation." He threw Bres a sharp look at that. "We only want your cooperation."

"And our blood!" the skeptical Niet remarked.

Unruffled, Streng answered this in conciliatory terms.

"We would not be so harsh with you if all your people would cease to defy us. It is your own pride and absurd independence which causes your problems. The Firbolgs cooperated with us and we got along quite well. We would like to prove to you that we truly wish to help you."

"That's why Streng's own warriors will be searching for the boy as well," Bres put in. "We must see this stopped before things get worse." He ran a slow, penetrating gaze over them as he added somberly: "We all know what bringing the Fomor power down upon us would mean."

"Do we?" Morrigan said, clearly intrigued by the notion. She smiled, revealing her sharp teeth, and ran a bony finger along the fresh razor-edge of her longsword. Her bright eyes fixed hungrily on Streng. "I wouldn't mind giving one of them a try, myself."

Streng shifted uneasily and looked to Bres for help, discomfited for the first time. Bres intervened, moving between them and speaking briskly.

"All of you can go now. See to the patrolling of the town and countryside. Report any signs of this boy to me at once!"

Dismissed, the warriors began to file down the stairway from the gallery room and leave the main hall.

Last of all, Morrigan slowly and lithely uncurled her wiry length of legs, stretched, and slipped off the table. She turned to follow the others down the stairs.

"Wait, Morrigan," Bres called.

She stopped, turning back to him, her gaunt face now an expressionless mask, only the keen eyes showing a wary interest.

"Morrigan, I look to you especially as my eyes in this," he told her pointedly. "Keep a watch over Tara, and especially over your old... companion... the Dagda."

Her look grew hostile.

"The Dagda is no traitor," she said, her voice a cold wind crackling the dry leaves of an autumn tree. "He hates the Fomor and will never willingly submit to their control. But he would never do anything to harm the de Dananns."

"So you may believe," he began aggressively. "But it's my..." He paused, considering his words, then went on more moderately, "... my wish that you'll do this, as a truly loyal champion of the king." He smiled graciously.

She jerked stiffly erect and glared at him.

"You've no need to remind me of my bond." Her eyes dropped to the sword still in her hand. "You have my loyalty..." She slammed the weapon into its scabbard, adding pointedly: "... so long as you are king." And, sweeping the black cloak around her lean frame, she stalked proudly down the stairway and out of the lower hall.

"I don't like that one," commented Streng, looking over the gallery railing after her. "When she looks at me, I feel like a hare cornered by a hawk."

"She'd slit you up and suck you dry in an instant, right enough," said Bres with a cruel smile. "But she won't. Her foolish code of loyalty binds her to me, as it does the rest. It makes them so easy to control."

"Don't be so certain that can't change," Streng warned. "This boy could cause you some discomfort if he isn't caught."

"I'm as aware of that as you," Bres assured him, adding more thoughtfully: "And I've my own interest in this boy as well." He walked over to stand close beside Streng at the rail.

He spoke now in a conspiratorial tone. "Tell me, what do you know about him?"

"Nothing," Streng replied truthfully. "Balor feels he is dangerous, but he's not told me why. He's not told anyone. Still, I get an impression he feels the boy has some sort of power."

"Well, he certainly has a charmed life," said Bres, shaking his head. "But there's really not so much he can do here. Who would believe his tale, if he survived to tell it?"

"This Dagda and his son might. They've been seen together. And they'd certainly act if they thought they might dethrone you. My warriors will be keeping a very close watch on them."

"Why not simply seize them and force them to tell you about the boy? They've caused us both enough trouble anyway."

"We can question them, but we don't wish to harm them if we have a choice," Streng told the brutal High-King. "Remember, they've not been openly rebellious as the others were. If we act against them, or if you do, it will only make them greater heroes and raise more defiance in the rest. We don't want that, do we?"

"I think you overestimate the de Dananns' ability to act at all!" Bres said.

"Perhaps. But my companies will follow my orders here. And you'd be best to heed Balor's wishes too and be less belligerent. It was your reckless visit to the Tower that caused your problem now."

"You just handle your business," Bres growled irritably. "I'll take care of my own."

"Really?" Streng said placidly. "Well, while you're about it, I'd suggest you keep an eye on that one." He pointed down into the hall below.

Bres looked down at the lone figure, slumped as usual over a mug of ale in the empty hall.

"What, Nuada?" he asked and laughed derisively. "That sodden old hulk is no threat to us in this."

"He befriended the boy once. Maybe he's part of some conspiracy. Perhaps there's more life in him than you think. He was High-King."

"He never will be again!" Bres responded heatedly. "He's nished!"

"Watch him anyway, Bres," Streng said patiently. "This is oo vital to take any risks at all."

He walked to the stairway, pausing there.

"Oh, and remember, don't let the boy be killed," he eminded Bres. "There are things that Balor would very nuch like to know before he dies."

He went down the stairs and out of the main hall. Bres vatched him go and then moved to an outer door which he ushed open. Outside a timber bridge connected the upper allery to the parapet of the outer wall. He crossed it and tood looking down to the town spread out around the hill's ase. It lay grey and cold and miserable under a pall of ppressive haze.

Bres's expression was a thoughtful one. There were things bout this Lugh that he burned to know too. He told himself t was not really important, that this boy could not be any hreat to him or the power of the Fomor. Yet, as he looked own onto the streets where hundreds of warriors now pa-rolled, he felt a peculiar uneasiness. For he could sense—as f he were somehow in touch with that boy's mind—that ugh was already in Tara.

Bres was right.

Down in those dismal streets, the muffled head of a Fomor vas at that moment peeking cautiously around a corner of an bandoned liss. Beside it, the head of a young de Danann boy lso timidly appeared.

Across a refuse-littered market square there sat a good-ized house of wattled timber with a thatched roof. Under the rey sky it looked rather sodden and forlorn, like a round loaf f bairnbrech bread left to soften in the rain.

"You're certain that's the Dagda's house?" the Fomor asked n a deep, growling sort of voice, very threatening indeed.

The terrified waif nearly cried. "Yes, sir. Yes, sir, it is. Can I e going now? Please? Can I go?"

He started to pull back, but the Fomor seized his thin arm, ranking him back, pointing toward the house.

"Wait, boy! What's all them men doin' there?"

Nearly a score of heavily armed Fomor warriors were

idling about in the square close before the main door of th
liss.

"I don't know, sir," the boy said in a shrill and desperat
voice. "I swear on my parents' graves, sir. I don't know
There's your troops and our own swarming the streets, searcl
ing everywhere. Likely the Dagda's in some trouble wit
them. He always is."

With a derisive snort the Fomor released the boy, pushin
him roughly away.

"All right then, whelp. Be away from here. And far away
mind! Or I'll slit you up a treat, I will!"

The boy scampered away like a wounded deer. The Fomc
watched him go, then unwound the scarf from his face. H
revealed the youthful and unmarked face of Lugh.

The young man regretted frightening the lad like that, bu
he couldn't chance revealing himself to anyone but the Dagd
or Angus Og. Besides, it had been the easiest way to get th
boy to guide him. When Lugh had found him scavengin
amongst some rubbish piles, it had been a simple matter t
press him into service.

The Fomor disguise had been helpful to him again. He ha
been able to re-enter Tara and move through its stree
without being noticed, only needing to avoid direct contac
with any warriors.

It had been a long and very lonely way here from th
Mountains of Mourne. He had felt often the sharp ache c
regret at leaving Gilla, Aine and Taillta behind. He realize
how much he had come to rely upon the company of hi
friends. However, this reminder of his closeness to them onl
made him the more certain he had been right not to involv
them in this escapade. And soon enough—if things wen
right—he would be seeing them again.

Still, he reflected, it would have been nice to have ther
here now. They might have helped him decide what to d
next.

How could he enter the Dagda's liss? He stared meditativel
at the structure for a time. Then he saw the answer. Ther
was only one other accessible opening into the place—th
large smoke hole in the center of the roof!

Cautiously, Lugh worked his way around the marke
square behind the structures surrounding it. He saw n
one. Most of the structures here seemed abandoned. But

as he neared the back of the Dagda's liss, he saw another
Fomor warrior, clearly on guard there, strolling slowly up
and down.

There was a large drying rack for hides beside the
Dagda's liss. Built of long poles supported on a heavier
framework of logs set in the ground, it thrust up higher
than the edge of the roof only a few feet away. There was
his ladder up.

He waited until the warrior was turned away, walking
toward the far side of the house. Then he charged full run
from his hiding place, swarmed up the poles to their top and,
without hesitating, launched himself across the space to land
upon the thatch roof.

He fell with a faint thump onto the grey-weathered straw,
clutching at the binding of the sheaves to keep from falling
back. He lay there flat and still for several moments as the
guard strode back and forth again below. Then he slowly
pulled himself up toward the peak and peered down through
the smoke hole into the room below.

Directly underneath him, a meager fire burned in the fire
pit, sending up a thin trail of smoke. At a plank table pulled
close beside it sat the Dagda and Angus Og, picking in a
desultory fashion at some sorry remnants of food.

Having little other choice of action, Lugh simply lowered
himself through the hole, swung out beyond the fire, and
dropped lightly to the floor beside the astonished men.

"A bloody Fomor spy!" bellowed the Dagda. And, leaping
to his feet, he seized an enormous battle-ax and swept it up
to strike.

"No! Wait!" cried Lugh, throwing up his hands in vain
defense.

"Yes, father! Wait!" said Angus, rising and grabbing the
Dagda's arm to restrain him. "That's no Fomor. It's young
Lugh!"

The Dagda hesitated, peering closely at the young man
who stood watching anxiously.

"Why, it surely is!" he agreed finally, lowering the massive
weapon. "Boy, it's not wise at all to be dropping in on a man
that way in that kind of dress, let me tell you that!"

"I'm sorry," Lugh said contritely, "but there are men
watching your house. It was the only way I could get to you
without being seen."

"It was good you did," the Dagda told him, dropping back onto his stool and propping the ax close by. "Bres and the Fomor are seeking you. They've come and asked us where you were and, when we told them we didn't know, they put that guard on us." He gave Lugh a hard, searching look. "What's it about, lad? The last time we saw you, you were in those same clothes I gave you and headed for that Fomor drinking lair. We thought you were long dead. Just what have you been doing?"

"A great deal," Lugh said, "some of which you may not believe. But I have to convince you to believe, because I need help and you're the only ones who can give it to me!"

The Dagda recognized the earnestness in the young man's expression.

"All right. We'll listen, that we will," he assured Lugh heartily. "Sit with us and have a drink."

He poured full three large cups with ale from a bronze pitcher and pushed one across the table toward Lugh. The young man sat down at the table and gladly took it up, taking a large swig. Even the harsh ale tasted good after his long traveling.

"There have been many times since I saw you last that I thought I was dead myself," he began. "There are many places I've seen that I barely believe are real. But they are. You see, when I went to that drinking hall, I saw a man disguised as a Fomor meet with a Fomor officer. I followed them far north, to the sea, and then to a tower of glass."

"The Tower!" the Dagda broke in, clearly amazed. "You entered it and came away alive?"

"I did," he assured them solemnly. "And the man I followed to that tower was your own High-King, Bres himself!"

The Dagda and his son exchanged a swift, stunned look. Then they moved closer to Lugh, all attention now focused on him. In a voice now a deep growl with his intensity, the champion demanded:

"Tell us, lad. Tell us all of it!"

XXIII

THE REUNION

IN THE MARKET square, the afternoon passed slowly, drearily for the Fomor guards. A chill mist had arisen to sweep its clammy tendrils over them. Some huddled in the doors of abandoned homes around the square. A few sought comfort from a small fire built from wood wreckage scavenged from the area.

Inside the Dagda's liss, Angus Og threw another log from their own lean supply on the central fire in a vain attempt to chase out the invading dampness. Then he moved back toward the table where Lugh and his father sat.

Their young visitor was just finishing his description of the conversation between Balor and Bres in the tower. As he did, the big man sat back and looked to his son, a hot anger deepening the ruddy complexion of his face.

"Bres! A bloody Fomor himself!" he growled. "We should have guessed some such."

"Then you believe Lugh's story?" Angus asked.

"I do. No one could have described the Tower so sharply without being there. And though I never saw Balor so close as Lugh did, I know that's true as well. The images of that black giant and that blazin' ruby eye are burned into my memory like a brand."

Lugh felt warm relief wash through him. He had gone over the details of the tower many times now, wondering a little more each time if he was really convincing them. He knew he'd had to succeed in that. Without the help of the Dagda and Angus, his chances were very slim indeed.

"Well, I never doubted him," Angus said with emphasis. He looked to Lugh. "And Bres knows what you've discovered. That's why they're seeking you."

"He knows. He saw me there. And he knew that I had

seen him meet with that Fomor officer Streng at the drinking hall."

"Streng?" repeated Angus with a note of interest. "He's at the fortress now! If there was any question of the truth of what you've said, that answers it. They must be very worried to be so openly working together to find you."

"You see now why I had to come back," said Lugh. "It's Bres himself who is your worst enemy. The Fomor only want you to submit, to remain weak. Bres is trying to destroy you completely, and soon! He's the one behind the worst treatment of you. He has to be stopped."

"It's a very brave lad you've been to risk so much for us," the Dagda said warmly, clapping a massive hand to Lugh's shoulder. But the big, weathered face sagged with defeat as he glumly added, "Too bad it'll be of such little help."

"Father, what do you mean?" protested Angus. "We can tell the others! Expose Bres and force him out . . ."

"And will the others take this boy's word? This outsider? With no other proof? No, Angus, their bonds of loyalty to Bres are stronger. And think, son, how long will Lugh survive once Bres sees him?"

Lugh broke in. "I know all of that. I wouldn't have risked coming here just to tell you about Bres. I have more. I know a way that Bres can be deposed."

"Have you now, lad?" said the Dagda, his eyes lighting with new curiosity. He leaned toward Lugh. "Tell us."

"I found your own chief physician in the Mountains of Mourne. He can restore Nuada's real hand!"

"That old bone-binder!" the Dagda said, astonished. "Has he finally done it?"

"He has," Lugh assured him. "I've seen proof. But no one is willing to risk fetching Nuada there. That's what I've come to do. And I need your help. Will you do it?" He eyed the two hopefully.

The Dagda considered. "Diancecht always swore he'd do it. He could if anyone can. If Nuada can be restored, the first loyalty of all the de Dananns will go back to him. Then we'll be free to deal with the Fomor as a united people!"

"But, father, would Nuada be any help to us now?" Angus asked. "He's so sad. So hopeless."

"I saw the spark of defiance still in him," said Lugh

determinedly. "I know it is worth the risk. But it is my choice to do this and my risk, not yours."

The Dagda slammed a hand onto the table top.

"Wrong, lad!" he declared forcefully. "If we can't be rid of Bres and restore strength to our people, we're finished anyway. I'm not sitting and waiting for that any longer. I'm with you."

"And I," added Angus. "But we'll have to make a plan to get Nuada away, and we'll have to slip the leash of our Fomor guardians, and find a safe place to do that."

"How?" asked Lugh. He went to a window at the front of the liss, peering out through a crack in the closed shutters. "They're all still out there." He looked up toward the smoke hole. "Of course, there's the way I came in."

Angus looked at it, and then gave the substantial figure of his father a critical survey.

"Not meaning offense," he said, "but we'd stand a better chance of stuffing a bull through there."

"Careful, son," the man warned good-humoredly. "But we can leave here easily enough. The Fomor are in front. We'll just go out the back."

"There's no door in back," Lugh pointed out.

"Then I'll make one!" the Dagda announced. "These walls aren't made of stone." He lifted his ax and rose. "One stroke ought to do it."

He advanced on the back wall of the liss, the immense weapon coming up.

"Wait!" cautioned Lugh. "There's another guard at the back."

"Just one?" asked the Dagda. "Well, then, you'll just have to slip out there and kill him first. Here." He stepped back close beneath the hole and bent forward. His back became a broad and solid platform. "Up! And be quick!"

"Come on, Lugh," Angus invited and hopped lightly onto his father's back, vaulting from there up to the opening and pulling himself through. Lugh followed, climbing out onto the sloping roof beside Angus. They slid down to the edge and peered over. The warrior was still pacing below.

"Pretty, eh?" Angus whispered, for the warrior's face was nearly featureless, his ears and mouth and nose only tiny slits in a totally hairless face. "Looks like a turtle. Let's crack his shell for him. But be sure he gives no cry."

Lugh nodded. When the man walked right below them the two dived upon him. Both struck the Fomor together, driving him to the ground. Lugh clapped a hand over the lipless mouth. Angus pulled his short sword and lifted it over the warrior's back, but paused.

"I can't do any warrior this way," he said ruefully, "even one of them." He reversed the weapon and brought the heavy hilt down on the shiny head. There was a hollow-sounding thock and the man went limp.

"Like thumping a melon," said Angus lightly, getting up. "Come on."

They trotted to the back wall of the liss, and Angus leaned close to it, calling as loudly as he dared: "Father, go ahead!" Then he stepped hurriedly back.

It was a prudent move, for almost at once the edge of the great ax smashed through the wattle wall near the top and, with a sharp crackling, slashed it asunder right down to the ground. Then large hands thrust through the rent. They gripped the two sides of the cut and shoved the wall halves apart, crushing the wattle back. Through the large opening thus created, the Dagda thrust his grinning head.

"Simple!" he declared, pushing the stocky body through with a little effort. "Let's be away quickly, now. You're certain there was only one guard here?"

"Only one," Lugh assured him.

They turned from the house and found themselves facing half a dozen Fomor warriors, weapons drawn.

"Of course, we might have missed one or two," Angus said apologetically.

The Dagda accepted this setback with his usual lack of concern.

"Let me see to this," he announced, pulling the two young men behind him. "I'm in need of a bit of practice."

And he stalked toward the warriors, the ax swinging up again, ready in his hands.

The Fomor exchanged uncertain glances as the hulking figure approached. Then they steeled themselves and moved in. The Dagda waited until they were within his reach and then swung out with a swift cut of the ax backed by the weight of his whole body.

Nothing could stop or even slow the movement of that blade. It slashed through shields, through swords, through bodies, like a scythe through tall grass, taking an arm off here, a head there, spraying a shower of blood behind it, then turning to drive back.

Only two blows were enough to leave nothing but wreckage on the ground and the survivors fleeing.

"Ah, give me a fight, lads!" the Dagda pleaded after them, but in vain. He shook his head sadly. "Too few of them. Just too few."

"Never mind!" Lugh said urgently, fearful others would arrive. "We've got to get away from here quickly."

The Dagda nodded. He and his son followed Lugh away from the liss, down a narrow way between other houses.

They followed a twisting route through the maze of streets and buildings. Lugh had just about convinced himself that they had thrown off all chance of pursuit when a loud flapping sounded right above him. He looked up in surprise as a large, dark form soared over his head, brushing his hair, forcing him to duck.

With a loud, raucous caw, the thing sailed ahead and settled to the ground in a flurry of wings that raised a swirling wind around them. The broad wings furled and they saw a huge blackbird, head up, glinting eyes fixed balefully on them.

But, in an instant, the image shifted. The shape seemed to explode in shimmering light, grow up and out, causing Lugh and the others to shield their eyes. And then it faded, revealing the figure of the Morrigan, her cloak wrapped tightly around her cadaverous form.

"So, Bres has you spying on us too," the Dagda said angrily. "I should have guessed as much."

Her sharp gaze stabbed at him. "I serve the High-King," she said icily, "as you seem not to do." The eyes shifted to Lugh. "Bres was right about your involvement with this boy."

"This boy means to help us!" the Dagda tried to explain. "Listen to what he knows! He . . ."

She cut him off brusquely. "I don't want to hear it. I only want the boy." A long arm slid from the cloak and rose toward them. A claw-like hand pointed at Lugh. "Give him to me now and I'll not tell Bres he was with you."

"No, Morrigan," the Dagda responded heavily. "It's too important a thing for all of us. Your bonds may keep you from helping, but don't be interfering."

"You know that can't be," she said. She took a step forward. The voice rose in its shrill demand. "Give me that boy!"

The Dagda stepped deliberately in front of Lugh, lifting the ax across his chest in a clearly defensive gesture.

"No!" he said in a final way.

"Then I'll be forced to take him!" she shrieked, and flung the cloak back. It revealed a naked sword already in her other hand.

She dropped into a fighting crouch.

"You're a fool," she told them. "You can't escape from me. I'll see you wherever you go."

"She's right," said Angus. "She'll hunt us."

The Dagda moved toward her. "That means I'll have to kill you surely, Morrigan," he said, his voice taking on a sorrowful note. "Don't be doing this. For our old bonds together, leave off or I'll have no other choice."

Lugh saw in the glinting black ice of her eyes a subtle softening—the first sign of human warmth he had seen. Her reply, too, was colored with a faint hue of regret.

"I've no choice in this myself."

She started forward to close with him. The two moved warily in, speed meeting power, and Lugh wondered who might win this strange contest.

But the battle never joined. There came a sudden, dull thump as an object struck the back of Morrigan's head. It jerked forward on the slender neck, the bright eyes glazed, and she sagged, her body toppling to the ground.

Astonished, the three men moved forward. Lugh saw the round, polished sphere of wood that had downed her lying in the wet earth beside her head and, with a thrill of recognition, realized what it meant.

"Gilla!" he lifted his head and called.

From the top of a small shed the familiar lanky figure slid awkwardly to the ground. He grinned inanely.

"Greetings! I thought I should be stopping that little fight. I hope I've not killed her."

"She's alive," said Angus, who had bent over the woman to examine her. "She's a hard one to kill."

"I thank you for that," said the Dagda gratefully. "I had no heart to fight her." He looked more closely at the clown. "But, I know you! You helped my other son and many others escape Tara."

"As I'll help you!" Gilla replied. "For you've become fully fledged rebels yourselves now. Come along. I've a safe place nearby. Morrigan won't be able to watch over us for a while, that she won't."

"I've no great love of hidin' in a grave," the Dagda said cheerlessly.

They were deep in the heart of a stone passage grave, crowded into its central compartment. Great slabs of rock surrounded them. Around the outer edge of the circular space were the hollowed-out spots where the ashes of dead warriors lay. The place had a chill and an earthy smell to it, and their single torch lit flickering patterns of shadow on the low roof and walls, and made the spirals and interlace designs on the rocks seem to writhe and entwine like serpents.

"Come on, then, my Brave Champion," Gilla teased. "It's surely a place no Fomor will dare look, and close to the town. You're not frightened by hiding with the poor, soggy dust of the dead, are you?"

"No!" the Dagda protested, shifting himself with an effort and a grimace of pain. "There's just not enough room for the likes of me, that's all."

"But there's plenty of ale, and that'll ease your pain," Gilla said, pulling an enormous leather skin filled with ale from beneath his baggy cloak and passing it to the big man. "And I did manage to gather a few provisions from our Fomor friends." He reached again into the cloak. "Including some more clams." He brought out a double handful, holding them toward the others. "Have some. I think they're nearly fresh anyway."

None of his companions accepted the offer.

"What are you doing here, Gilla?" Lugh asked.

"Why, savin' you, of course," Gilla replied affably.

"I mean, how was it you found me?"

Gilla shrugged. "Simple enough. You asked Findgoll for directions to Tara, and your thoughts were plain enough after you talked to Diancecht. It was a fair guess, and another that you'd seek out the Dagda here."

"But you weren't meant to come!" Lugh told him irritably.

"Lad, I couldn't let you have such fun alone!" Gilla said, smiling broadly. "Besides, it wasn't only my choice, it was not!"

"What do you mean, not only your choice?" Lugh demanded, afraid he already knew the answer.

"Well, you see, I didn't come alone."

A figure moved into the passage opening, into the fitful light of the single torch, and Lugh's fear was confirmed.

It was Aine.

XXIV

INTO THE FORTRESS

"AINE!" SAID LUGH. "Why did you have to come?"

"Because you're still my charge," she said, moving into the central chamber and dropping down beside him. "I couldn't let you run off on this foolish venture alone. Why did you think you had to do it?"

Her tone seemed to him like that one would use on a wayward child. He resented it.

"Because this needed to be done," he replied heatedly. "It was my own choice. I'm tired of doing what everyone else wants."

"You promised to go back with me," she reminded him.

"And so I will. But only when this is finished."

She sighed. "I was afraid that would be the way of it. Well, shall we be at the planning of it, then?" she added resignedly.

"We?" he repeated. "This isn't to include you. Don't you understand I left you behind on purpose?"

"And don't you understand I didn't stay behind?" she shot back.

"Aine, you've taken enough risks."

"So have you," she said stubbornly. "Besides, I enjoy them."

"I refuse to involve you."

"You haven't any choice!"

The Dagda, watching this exchange with growing irritation, cast a look askance at the clown.

"They love to go on like this," Gilla supplied affably. "They're very close."

Dismissing him as obviously mad, the big man shifted his weight and lightly dropped his ax between the young couple. The ponderous head clanged loudly onto the rock. Both looked up in surprise.

"Children," he said tersely, "there's not the time for this. Everyone in this town will be a-huntin' of us now. We've got to make our plans and move quickly. So, who is this girl and what's her worth to us?"

She glared defiantly at him. "I'm the one whose help you'll need if you mean to reach Nuada."

"But, she's Bres's cousin!" Angus protested. "She can't be trusted to help us!"

"Yes, she can," Lugh admitted grudgingly. "She's been helping me all along. She's no cousin to him."

"Then who are you?" Angus demanded.

"That's nothing to do with you," she curtly answered. "You only need to know you have my help. And you'll be needing it. The fortress is heavily guarded by warriors on watch for you. And agents of Bres are always close to Nuada, too."

"How do you know this?" the Dagda wondered. He pulled his ax away and heaved himself closer to the girl, curious now.

"I've just come from there," she replied in a casual way.

Lugh's reaction to this was not so casual.

"From the fortress!" he cried angrily. "You went back there?"

"I live there, if you'll remember. I'm still Bres's cousin, so far as he knows. The Dagda and Angus can't go there now, and you and Gilla are known to Bres, so I'm the only one of us who can safely get inside the walls." She smiled with that teasing arrogance. "And I'm the only one who can help you get inside."

Gilla nodded emphatically and looked around at the others. "It's likely she's saying the truth in that, yes, she is!"

"Maybe so," said Angus guardedly, giving her a close, appraising look. "If we can trust her."

"We can trust her!" the Dagda suddenly and wholeheartedly decreed. "She's a fighter. I can see it in her eyes." He took up the skin of ale and passed it to her. "Here. Drink with us."

She smiled cooly and took it. Upending it, she let a stream of the ale rush into her mouth, swallowing the harsh stuff as it came, without a pause. After a long draught, which all the men watched with amazement, she tossed the much deflated skin back.

"There," she said evenly. "I've passed your little test. Now, could we get on with the planning?"

As Aine came into the main hall of Tara that night, she paused to look around her. Her bored and haughty demeanor masked the care with which she was examining the scene before her.

Things seemed much as usual. The royal company was engaged in talk or play or enjoying the entertainers as they awaited the serving of the food.

Aine was herself once more a part of that company. She had given over the simple warrior's dress for a long gown of rich, green cloth embroidered with golden thread. Her free billows of hair were confined in loosely plaited braids at either shoulder. They glowed softly like entwined torcs of the finest gold against the dark material.

Bres, noting her entrance, left his dais and crossed the room to her at once. He was smiling broadly and his greeting was warm.

"Aine! I'm so happy you're back," he said, taking her hands. "How is your father?"

"He's doing well," she lied sincerely. "He sends his greetings to you and hopes to see you."

"I'd go to visit him," Bres said apologetically, "but his dun is so far."

Luckily, thought Aine.

They walked through the room toward the dais and the king's table, surrounded by his closest circle. As they progressed, she continued to search the gathering in the hall. She spotted Nuada in his usual place, alone over a mug of ale. But there was something different tonight, and she noted it carefully. There were scores of warriors placed all about the room, at the doors, near the dais, and on the upper gallery. The warriors were not participating in the dinner; they were heavily armed and clearly on guard.

As they mounted the dais and approached Bres's table, another man moved from the gathering there to approach them. He was a new face at the feasts in Tara's hall, but he was unpleasantly familiar to Aine. It was Streng.

"This is my cousin Aine," Bres said to him. "She has just returned to Tara." He looked at her. "Aine, this is Streng, a captain of the Fomor garrisons."

Her first close look at Streng did not improve her feelings about him. He was a short man, barely taller than she, but squarely built and with a thick neck on which his fat oval of a head sat like an egg in a cup. His dark, thinning hair was combed across the top in a vain attempt to cover the balding spot. His face—round-cheeked, smooth and almost chinless—had an infant's quality, reinforced by pale blue, guileless eyes and a tiny mouth that bowed upward in a cloying smile.

But the sense of innocence was sharply countered by the bold gaze that ran lingeringly over her like a pair of hands searching her, caressing her against her will. It made her feel as if she needed to bathe.

"It is a great pleasure to meet you," he said. The voice was another contrast. Slow and careful, touched with arrogance, it conveyed the sense that each word was calculated for its effect.

She wanted to knock that leering, precious smile off his face. Instead she smiled her most winning smile.

"Captain Streng? You are a Fomor?" She tried to sound impressed and flustered. "But, you are so . . . pleasant." She flushed in embarrassment. "I'm sorry. I didn't mean . . ."

"I quite understand," he said good-humoredly. "We aren't all so hideous. Some of us you might quite like!"

The personal tone of this remark irritated Bres and he gave Streng a hard glance. Then he placed a proprietary hand on Aine's arm.

"Come. Sit by me," he said.

He led her to a seat at the long table beside his. But Streng was not about to be outmaneuvered. He moved to the seat on her other side, turning its occupant away with a single, withering look. As the stewards began to serve the meal, he leaned close to her and picked up the conversation in an oily, intimate tone.

"You know, life with us would not be so unpleasant. Look at how we've treated Bres and the other de Dananns who have accepted us. All Eire could be the same, if everyone would cease to defy us."

"Do you really believe that?" she asked with all the innocence that she could manage.

He smiled again, more winningly. The eyes were close to hers, the blue gaze penetrating.

"We're not really so awful. Only our enemies have to fear us. Our friends can have anything they desire."

On her other side, Bres listened with clear distaste, unable to interrupt as he directed the stewards in serving. But now he took a great tray passed to him and plopped it down on the table between Streng and Aine.

"Here," he said to her. "Maybe you'll find *this* stuffed pig more to your taste." And he glared at the Fomor captain who only smiled contemptuously in return.

Aine had a peculiar feeling this was going to be a very long meal. She wondered if she was going to get any chance to act. She glanced around her at the guards and then up to the one pacing the gallery just above her head.

Along the outer rampart walk of Tara-na-Rie another guard paced, cloaked tightly against the mist that had grown heavier. Now it was a curtain that shrouded all the stars and left the moon a white, hazy glow, swollen and very pale, like a long-drowned face beneath the waves. It also covered effectively the four figures that crept up the hillside toward the palisade.

Lugh reached the wall first, flattening himself against the rough timbers. The others joined him one by one.

"Thank the Powers for this mist!" said the Dagda. "The Morrigan won't be seeing us easily tonight."

"Shhhh," Lugh warned, gesturing up. The sound of the guard's footsteps was clearly audible above.

They waited silently until the sound faded.

"Let's move to the side gate," the Dagda whispered urgently then.

They worked their way around the wall, coming to a small gate. The Dagda tried it carefully. It wouldn't budge, even under his powerful urgings.

"Locked up for the night, as we supposed," he said.

He dropped down on the ground nearby and pulled the leather wine skin from beneath his cloak. "It's good I brought this. It's a chilling night and may be a long wait." He took a long draught and settled back against the logs.

"A man of my own thoughts," Gilla said brightly and dropped down too, taking the skin the Dagda proffered.

Angus joined them too, leaving Lugh standing, staring at the door.

"Come on, lad. Rest a bit," Gilla urged.

"But Aine may be in danger," Lugh fretted. "If Bres suspects..."

"She has her own mind in this," said Gilla. "There's nothing we can do. It's up to her now. Here. Take a drink."

Still uneasy, Lugh took the skin of ale and, eyes still fixed upon the door, lifted it to drink.

The golden honey-mead gushed from the pitcher as Bres filled his cup again. Then he lifted it and moved it toward Aine's.

"Would you like more?" he asked her.

"No, thank you. I've never been able to drink very well," she answered demurely.

The feast was ending, people making their farewells to Bres and leaving the hall. She kept her eye on Nuada who still nodded over his own drink.

"I'm very weary from my traveling," she said. "I'll be retiring soon."

Bres leaned toward her, laying a hand on hers.

"I've missed your brightness here at Tara," he said, his darkly handsome face close to hers. "Stay with me a while more."

The man's intense energy enveloped her. She could feel the power in the brown eyes holding hers.

She looked away with an effort. Across the hall, Nuada was now pushing himself unsteadily to his feet. He was leaving. She had to get away now!

She looked back to Bres, smiling a coy smile. Her voice was low, promising.

"I'd like very much to stay with you. But not tonight." She leaned close to murmur in his ear. "I need my rest."

That seemed to convince him. He lifted the anchoring hand laid across hers.

"By all means. I want you rested too. Good night."

"Good night," she said and rose, turning to Streng. The Fomor had vied with Bres for her attention all through the meal. "And good night to you, Captain Streng."

"I am sorry you must leave us," he said regretfully, then smiled that childlike smile that was somehow so obscene. "I hope I'll be seeing more of you. I almost feel as if I have known you before."

A fist clenched around her heart, but no flutter of alarm touched her face as she replied lightly.

"Really? I feel the same. I'm certain I'll be meeting you again."

He nodded, still smiling, and she moved away from the table. As she did, the two men exchanged a hostile look over her vacated seat. She sighed inwardly with relief at her escape. She'd felt like raw meat between two famished wolves.

By now, Nuada was on his way out, winding through the tables with that cautious dignity of the very drunk. She followed at some distance as they left the hall.

The cold mist swept about her as she came out. She pulled her cloak tightly about her and lifted the hood. It was very dark, with only the smothered moon and the struggling light of a few wind-fluttered torches. She kept Nuada barely in sight, following him around the hall to his quarters.

She watched him enter and waited in the shelter of a shed. Long moments passed, but no one else arrived and no guards appeared. Nuada was alone.

It was time.

She whistled softly. From the darkness two forms appeared— great mastiffs of the fortress and Bres's own pets, but tonight answering loyally to the powers of another master.

"Good lads," she said softly, patting the massive, flat heads. "I've a little work for you to do tonight."

Lugh tried the heavy door again, then tried futilely to peek through a crack.

"What's taking her so long?" he fumed, pacing back and forth. He felt something was wrong. Then . . .

"The door!" Gilla hissed.

Lugh dropped down against the log wall with the others, waiting breathlessly. The door creaked open. A head, barely discernible in the darkness and mist, was thrust cautiously out.

"Lugh!" Aine's voice called softly.

"Aine!" he replied thankfully, jumping up and moving

quickly to her. He took an arm, asking urgently, "Are you all right?"

She gave him a disapproving look.

"Of course. Why not? Come in, and hurry."

They slipped in through the door and she closed it behind them. Just inside, crouched against the wall with legs drawn up and arms raised defensively, were two gatekeepers, white-faced with terror. The reason for their fear was obvious. Two very large, snarling dogs stood threateningly before them.

"I told them the dogs would tear them apart if they cried out or moved," she said casually. "That seemed enough."

"It would be for me," the Dagda said earnestly. "Let's tie them up."

"Nuada is in his quarters," she told them while this was done. "He is alone."

"Guards?" asked Angus.

She shook her head. "They don't seem concerned about him. But there are nearly a hundred in the main hall."

"Bres protecting himself!" the Dagda snorted derisively. He stepped back from the trussed guards and nodded with satisfaction. "Good enough. Let's be going."

They worked their way around the great inner court of the fortress without seeing any warriors, save a few moving on the upper ramparts. Beyond the main hall, they came to the quarters of the warriors, a structure divided into many separate compartments reached by doors around the outer wall.

"This one," said Aine, moving to a door.

They followed her. The Dagda tried the door and found it unlocked. He pushed it open and led the way into the room.

A single candle inside fluttered violently in the blast of damp air they carried in with them. The room's lone occupant, sitting slumped at a small table, was startled and looked up to them. Puzzlement filled the sagging features as the drunken mind tried to understand. Then a faint light of recognition dawned.

"The Dagda!" he exclaimed. "Angus! And . . . young Lugh!"

They all moved into the room. Aine stopped just inside, peering out through the partly opened door on watch. The mastiffs sat on either side of her.

"What are you doing here?" Nuada asked thickly.

"We want you, Nuada," said Lugh, advancing to him. "You have to come with us!"

He looked bewildered. The heavy brows knitted in a
frown. "Me? Where? For what?"

"We're going to take you to Diancecht!" Lugh announced
with a triumphant air. "He's going to restore your real hand!"

Lugh had expected some spirited response from Nuada at
this news, but he was disappointed. The old king seemed to
fall further into despair, sagging forward, dropping his head
onto his breast, eyes drooping closed.

"Let me alone," he said in a hoarse, pathetic voice. "There's
no use to that."

Lugh dropped down beside him, putting a hand on the
bent shoulder, speaking more urgently.

"Nuada, don't you understand? He can restore your hand.
You can reclaim your kingship!"

With an immense effort the head came up again. The
bleary eyes fixed on Lugh.

"I've lost the right to that. I'm useless now. Useless to
everyone."

Lugh stared into the lifeless, dull eyes. He hadn't realized
how solid was the wall of drunken despair the old king had
thrown up. Desperate to break through, he looked to the
others for help.

The Dagda stepped forward and spoke with force.

"Look, Nuada, this lad believes in you. I don't know why.
But he's risked his life to help you."

"No one can help," the man murmured sullenly, dropping
his head forward onto the table top.

The Dagda slammed a hand down on the planks and
bounced Nuada's head. The old king sat up and the Dagda
leaned close, saying angrily:

"You drunken, whining sot! This isn't just for you. It's for
all of us! Listen, man! Bres is . . ."

The door was jerked open, pulling Aine forward. A hand
swept around her, yanking her helplessly to the chest of a
man who moved into the opening, a sword in his free hand.

"Bres is here!" the High-King announced.

The dogs both went for him. The sword swept out in a
swift and skillful blow and one animal dropped with a split
skull. The other dodged the blade but caught a boot kick in
its chest and tumbled back, stunned.

The Dagda started forward, but more warriors crowded in
behind the High-King, weapons ready.

"We can take them," the Dagda growled.

"She'll die if you try it," Bres told him. He pulled the struggling Aine tighter to him and lifted the sword to lay the glinting edge across her belly, smooth beneath the clinging material.

"Drop your weapons or I'll gut her now!"

The Dagda looked to Lugh. The young man saw the anguish in the old champion's eyes. He wondered if the man would act. Desperately, he pleaded with his look.

The Dagda understood. With a sigh of regret, he lowered his massive battle-ax to the ground.

XXV

CAPTURED

IN THE BLACK water at the bottom of the well floated the Dagda and Angus Og. They looked up the smooth cylinder of rock to where, far above, High-King Bres stood looking down at them.

"Sorry for the wet, my friends," Bres called down to them with a gloating smile, "but we've just no other place strong enough to hold the Dagda in. You know, I'd really like to thank you for making things so simple for me. I've always wanted to be rid of you. Now you've given me an excuse. You're much too dangerous to leave alive any longer."

"Just give me a chance at you, Bres!" the Dagda raged. He grabbed at the rock walls of the well and tried to pull himself up but fell back.

Bres laughed. "You're much too old and fat for such activity. You'll not climb up from there. I've heard the Firbolgs used this well for sacrifice. I'll dedicate your deaths to them."

He started to turn away, then paused and looked back, adding as an afterthought:

"Oh, and try not to thrash about too much down there. You'll last much longer."

"Bres!" the Dagda's voice thundered, the booming sound echoing up from below.

Bres ignored it, only grinning the more broadly as he turned away and crossed the yard to the main doors of the hall. There, Aine, Nuada and Lugh waited, surrounded by a guard of Fomor under the command of Streng.

"All right," he said to them, "your companions are settled. I think we can go inside."

"What are you going to do to them?" Lugh demanded.

"Me?" said Bres with mock surprise. "I'm not going to do anything. Anything at all. Now, get inside!"

He signaled the guards, and they seized the three, forcing them along into the hall.

Lugh cast a final look around the fortress yard as they went through the doors. His mind was racing. What had happened to Gilla?

None of them had noticed that the clown had not been with them when they entered Nuada's room. He had apparently escaped capture and was presumably at large somewhere in the fortress. But could he stay free? And could he act alone to help them?

Inside the hall, the evening's feast had long since ended. All the gathering had gone, and the vast room was largely deserted.

The Fomor marched them across the room to the king's dais. While Bres and Streng mounted it, the three prisoners were lined up in front. Lugh noticed that, in addition to the half-dozen guards with them, there were perhaps a score more around the room. All were Fomor.

Bres noted the boy's curious gaze.

"I've sent all the de Danann warriors down into the town to search for you," he supplied. "I surely don't need them to overhear this little talk of ours. It involves too many things best kept between us."

"And what about them?" asked Lugh, nodding at his companions. "You don't care if they hear?"

"Well, Nuada is of no importance. His knowing or not will make no difference. He's completely harmless."

The old king shifted slightly. The lolling head rolled loosely back and forth but stayed down.

"And Aine?" said Lugh. "She's your own cousin."

"I believe she already knows my secrets." Bres stepped

down from the dais and walked to Aine. He lifted a hand and lightly cupped her chin, pushing the head up, looking into her defiant eyes.

"You were the girl at the Tower, weren't you, my dear?"

She said nothing.

"You see, my agent Negran had already told me about your helping Lugh. And your leaving Tara at the same time I did was very suspicious. When you returned, I had to watch you. I hoped all the time that I was wrong. I suppose you killed Negran too?"

She glared up, her mouth stubbornly set.

He shook his head. "What a pity," he said with faint regret. "We seemed so much alike. I had almost hoped that . . ." He broke off and shrugged resignedly. "Oh, well. Too bad."

He released her and stepped over to Lugh.

"And now for you, young adventurer." He surveyed Lugh closely, peering questioningly into those angry eyes. "There is still something about you that nags at me. I have to know what it is. I have to find out who you really are."

"Excuse me, Bres," Streng said with concern, stepping from the dais to join the High-King. "I thought you understood I was to take him to Balor."

Bres dismissed this with a negligent wave. "He'll have the boy. But only when I'm through with him."

"Bres . . ." Streng began in an argumentative tone.

Bres rounded on the Fomor. His voice was hard.

"Streng, I am the ruler in Eire. This is my decision!"

Streng fell silent, but his look was hostile. Bres turned his attention back to Lugh.

"I'm sorry my best druids are gone from Tara," he said with a cruel smile. "I'm left without their interesting little methods to make you speak." He glanced at Streng. "Unless you have something to suggest? The Fomor are so practiced at causing pain."

The Fomor captain eyed him sullenly. Then his eye shifted to Aine and his look grew bright and covetous.

"I'll help you. But I want the girl for it."

Bres gave her an indifferent look. "Why not? She's nothing to me." He looked at Lugh as he added: "When you're through with her, you can give her to your men."

A flare of pain burned through Lugh at that. His face tightened with it. Bres noted it with satisfaction.

"Of course, if you would tell me what I wish to know, none of this would be necessary," he told the young man.

"I've nothing to tell you," Lugh said stoutly. "And this girl has nothing to do with me."

"Is that true?" Bres said with clear skepticism. "We'll see. Streng? Do you think you have something to make our friend more . . . pliable?"

"I may have a method that will work," Streng said. "I've something in my quarters that I'll need."

"Then fetch it," Bres ordered. "We can't keep our guests in suspense all night."

In the well, the Dagda and his son were struggling desperately to climb out.

The giant man was trying to use his bulk to bridge the width of the well, his feet pressed against one side and his arms braced against the other. With a massive effort he remained wedged there while Angus climbed upon his shoulders, trying to reach some climbable point further up. But as high as he could reach, the young warrior found only water-smoothed stone, without any handholds.

Then, his own precarious hold slipping, the Dagda collapsed, slamming back down into the cold water, bringing Angus down on top of him.

They sputtered up to the surface and tread water there, looking at one another with hopelessness. It was clear that there was no way to escape.

As they floated there, Angus tried not to think about the black depths below them. He'd heard of the sacrifices made in the well. He kept picturing the pile of white, grinning skulls mired in the slime at the bottom.

"They've certainly got us properly this time!" the Dagda raged, his great strength for once made impotent.

"You don't need to be kickin' me for your anger!" Angus told him sharply.

"I didn't kick you," the Dagda protested.

"Well, something hit my foot!" Angus said, and then stiffened with a startled look.

"I felt it again!" he said.

"So did I!" the Dagda said, concern now showing in his face.

"Father," Angus said with rising fear, "what is it?"

"I've heard some tales," the Dagda began, "about . . ."

But he didn't finish. For his head abruptly vanished beneath the surface.

"Father!" Angus cried and dove at once on the spot.

He struggled down into the depths, the chill rising about him. He stretched down, arms before him, trying to reach his father, but his fingertips touched nothing below.

Finally he came up, gasping for air. The water around him lashed up wildly as if a giant ladle was stirring it. Some struggle was going on far below, and he could feel the waves of water from down there sweeping up to him.

He felt a stark terror rising up uncontrollably in him, a terror of the unknown depths, of whatever lurked below, of his father's fate and of being left there alone.

Then, with a tremendous upward explosion of water, something popped to the surface like a whale breaching, blowing out a great whoosh of spray.

It threw Angus violently back against the wall of the well and he clung there, staring wildly. In the uncertain light it took him a long moment to identify what was now thrashing madly on the surface.

He recognized his father first. He saw the face set in rigid lines of strain. But somehow he seemed much larger, and it took another moment for Angus to realize with horror that his father was wrapped around with coils of something thick and gleaming.

He could see that it was alive, like one muscle tensing, pulling tauter. Then he saw the head lift from the water, saw the flat skull, the tiny eyes, the wide slit of a mouth, and knew it was an eel.

It was larger than any he had ever seen before. Its body was the thickness of a man's neck, and it had to be three times a man's height in length. He realized it was a giant well eel such as the Firbolg said inhabited the sacred wells of Eire. But he had never believed their tales . . . until now.

His father had a grip upon it right below the head, his big hands pressed deeply into the scaly throat, squeezing, the arms tensed to rock hardness as he fought to throttle it.

The beast seemed to be in distress, its free tail segment threshing so wildly about in the narrow space of the well that Angus could barely avoid being struck. He was forced against the side and trapped there to watch this mortal combat helplessly, wondering who would win.

For his father, too, was in distress. Wrapped in the tightening coils, his face was rapidly darkening with the increasing pressure. Slowly, steadily, relentlessly, the two powerful giants were strangling one another, and there was no way Angus could guess which one would finally succeed.

Streng approached the High-King, a large, wooden case cradled in his arms. He stopped, lifting a hinged lid to reveal the contents.

Within the box lay a strange-looking device. In part it seemed to be a bow, very short and made of a dull grey metal. It was affixed at right angles to a curiously shaped handle of metal and wood, set in an intricately worked mechanism that Bres did not comprehend.

Streng lifted it out and passed it to the High-King to examine.

"This is a bow of amazing power," he explained with pride. "Our ancestors produced it long ago. It is one of the few of their weapons that we can still make work, and even it is growing rapidly more scarce. But with its construction it can hurl a bolt like this..." he lifted a short, thick arrow of the grey metal from the box, "...with a force that will drive it through a shield and the man behind it."

"How can it be used to convince our friend to speak?" Bres wondered.

"It is also very accurate," Streng said. "A few bolts placed skillfully around—or in—the subject will usually bring the desired result."

"Very good," said Bres. He gestured to the guards. "Then just tie the young woman to that roof pole."

"What?" cried Lugh. He tried to get to Bres but the other guards seized him, pulling him back.

Streng's face showed he was taken aback as well. "But you promised her to me!"

"I know, Streng. Sorry. But we don't want the boy damaged, do we? As you reminded me, Balor might be unhappy about that. And the boy is clearly very fond of her, as I guessed." He tossed the bow back to Streng. "Here, prepare this."

Reluctantly, Streng did as the High-King demanded. He

took a leather quiver of the bolts from the case and slung it on one shoulder. Then he prepared the weapon by levering the heavy bowstring back and locking it into a hinged device. He selected a bolt, laying it carefully in a groove along the weapon's top, its tail touching the string.

Meantime, Lugh and Nuada were dragged back to clear an open space before the dais while two Fomor bound Aine to one of the heavy roof pillars near the fire-pit.

As the guards stepped back from her, Streng lifted the bow and set the wooden butt end solidly against his shoulder, pointing the arrow toward the bound girl. A forefinger rested lightly against the lever which would fire it.

"I'm ready," he said.

"Well, Lugh," Bres said, "will you tell me now? Who are you?"

Lugh cast a desperate look at Aine. Her chin was lifted, her face set in defiant lines. She gave a small, sharp shake of the head. Lugh set his own face grimly and stared at Bres without reply.

Bres shrugged and ordered, "Shoot!"

The bow snapped with a hollow, metallic sound. The bolt flashed to the target, thudding home in the hard wood of the thick post close beside her head, burying half its length.

"Not close enough," Bres remarked critically. "Prepare another bolt."

Lugh cast his gaze wildly about the room, searching for some sign of hope, some help. But there was nothing. He determined that he couldn't let Aine die. If there was nothing else that he could do, he would barter for Aine's life and tell Bres everything he knew. The only difficulty was that what he knew was likely not enough to satisfy the ruthless High-King. Which meant that they were doomed in any case.

An object dropped on the ground right at his feet.

It landed noiselessly amidst the thick rushes scattered there, and no one noted its fall except for Lugh. He looked down at it. It was round and smooth and white and looked familiar. And then he realized what it was. A clam shell!

He looked up, searching around the room again. This time he saw the tall figure peering over the rail of the gallery above the dais.

Gilla saw that he had gotten Lugh's attention, lifted a hand in a jaunty wave and smiled reassuringly. Lugh felt his heart lift. He didn't know how Gilla could help, but he somehow felt new hope.

"Shoot!" Bres ordered again, and another bolt slammed into the wooden pillar, less than a finger's breadth from Aine's head. She showed no sign of fear; she didn't flinch at the impact. Still, Lugh wasn't sure how long he could stand this. If Gilla meant to act, it would have to be soon, and he would need help.

The young man leaned closer to Nuada who stood slumped, spiritless, beside him, chin on chest, eyes staring at the ground.

"Nuada," he whispered urgently. "Nuada, you've got to help us! Help us fight him! He's a traitor to you. He means to destroy all your people. Fight!"

Bres noticed this. Smiling broadly, he strode toward them.

"Don't waste your final breaths on him. That drunken wreckage. He and all his kind are nearly gone, and their great dream with them. Soon there'll be nothing left but my own power. It'll be my Eire then." He pushed Nuada's head roughly back, looking into the bleary, blankly staring eyes, then let it drop forward again. "He's finished."

He walked away. Nuada stood as before, defeated and motionless. But there was one movement, one slight, unnoticed movement. Slowly, very slowly, the silver hand closed itself into a fist.

Bres walked back to Streng. "I'm bored with this. I want to try it. Here, show me how it works."

While Streng explained the device to Bres, Lugh risked another look up toward Gilla. The clown had now moved to the end of the gallery directly above a pair of Fomor warriors. Lugh realized that he was planning to jump.

Once more the young man found himself questioning the strange clown's sanity. Did he mean to try to rescue them all alone?

"Is this the way it works?" Bres was saying, examining the weapon. "All right. I think I see. Hand me some bolts."

Streng gave him a handful which the High-King slipped into his sword belt. He loaded one into the weapon and lifted it toward Aine.

"Of course, I'm not likely to be very good with it," he said carelessly.

It went off.

The bolt slammed into the pillar, just touching her as it slid by her shoulder at the base of her neck. It had nicked the flesh, drawing blood. It flowed down onto the fine, green material, making a startlingly bright stain as it spread.

Lugh nearly went mad with rage and only restrained himself by a massive effort of will. If there was any chance to escape, he couldn't ruin it with a rash act. He had to trust in Gilla and wait. Aine, stoic as ever, had herself shown no reaction, no sign of pain.

"Well, Man of All Skills, are you going to tell me what I wish to know?" Bres asked, fitting another bolt into the weapon.

"He'll tell you nothing," Aine answered for him with determination, fearful Lugh might be weakening.

Lugh shook his head.

"Then this game is over," Bres said coldly. "The next bolt will not miss." He lifted the bow toward her. "Sorry, 'cousin.' You'd best pray that this one kills you quickly."

At that moment, the doors to the hall burst open and two figures charged in, disheveled and streaming water but fired with anger and brandishing swords in either hand.

It was the Dagda and Angus Og.

Gilla used their appearance to act himself, leaping from the gallery, bringing down the two Fomor below him in a heap.

It caused distraction enough, jerking the attention of every warrior in the hall to these attackers. But it didn't come soon enough to stop Bres from firing the bolt.

"No!" Lugh yelled as the bolt flew unerringly toward the fair, smooth and vulnerable throat of the helpless Aine.

XXVI

BACK TO SAFETY

THE BOLT WAS only a spear-length from its mark when a gleaming hand rose in its path. The bolt struck it with a sharp clink, glancing off its smooth, rounded edge and driving harmlessly into the earthen floor.

Nuada stood now before the girl, the silver hand upraised, a look of blazing hatred bringing the worn old face to life.

Startled, Bres glanced around him to discover what had happened. All the Fomor guards had rushed to engage the three attackers, Streng moving to help those struggling with Gilla. Bres was left to face his prisoners alone.

Nuada went to Aine and seized her ropes with his metal hand to tear them loose. Bres cocked the bow with a savage move and slammed another bolt into the notch, planning to shoot him down.

This time it was Lugh's turn to act. He took three long steps and launched himself at Bres, hitting him in the middle as he tried to bring the weapon up. It was knocked from his hands and spun away as the two sprawled onto the floor.

They rolled apart. Lugh came up, meaning to pounce again, but a well-placed foot in the chest from Bres sent him backward.

The High-King sprang up, drawing his sword, his gaze focusing on Lugh with a grim determination.

"Boy, I don't care who you are. You are going to die right now!"

The Dagda, battling with Angus against a score of Fomor saw the plight of his unarmed friends. There was no time to reach them. Instead he swung back one arm and launched a sword in a long, high arc toward the old High-King.

"Nuada! A sword!" he cried.

Nuada saw it, raised his silver hand and caught the weapon in midair. As the hand closed around its hilt, he was transformed. As if the weapon had some magical power of its own, all trace of weariness and age fell away. He was once more the champion of old.

And, as Bres advanced on the defenseless Lugh, Nuada stepped forward, bringing his weapon down to knock away the High-King's first swing.

Surprised by this intervention, Bres looked to him.

"Now, Bres," Nuada said, his voice vibrant with a new energy, "now try me."

"Why, you old fool," Bres grated. "You made a mistake coming to life. You'll die here with the rest."

He pushed impatiently forward, as if he could simply brush the older man away to get to Lugh. But the sword of Nuada moved to block him.

Bres drove in again and again. Each time Nuada was there, his weapon parrying with speed and power.

Bres now began measuring his opponent's skill with greater respect. He couldn't believe that this sodden hulk of a man could be so suddenly dangerous. Frustrated, the High-King began a more heated attack.

Nuada's years of inactivity and drink began to tell. The older man was growing weary. His veteran's skill and aroused courage kept him stoutly fending Bres off, but he was having increasing difficulty.

The young man looked desperately about. The others were putting up a splendid fight, but they were heavily outnumbered. And it was only a matter of time before the battle attracted more warriors. This rescue attempt, valiant as it was, seemed doomed to failure.

"Hold, Bres!" Aine's voice commanded sharply, cutting through the noise of combat.

The High-King glanced aside at her, then froze. In the confusion, she had been forgotten. Now she stood not far from him, pointing the loaded bow at him very purposefully.

"You gave me an opportunity to observe the use of this very closely," she said with heavy irony. "I'm quite sure I can fire it. Now, drop your sword!"

He hesitated, his eyes darting around at the other warriors.

"Now, Bres!" she ordered coldly. "Or you're going to find your backbone cut in two!"

He believed her. "All right!" he said quickly and let his weapon drop.

"Now order the Fomor to stop the fight," she said.

He raised his voice and called to the others, "All of you, cease fighting! Cease fighting!"

The clatter of the weapons died. The Fomor looked around toward Bres with curiosity. So did Lugh's comrades, surprised by this sudden surrender.

"And now what?" Bres inquired.

"I'd like to finish you, Bres," Nuada said, raising his sword threateningly. "After all these years . . ."

"Kill me, and none of you will leave this fortress alive," Bres promised in hard tones.

"He's right, Nuada," Lugh said urgently. "Killing Bres won't free your people. It will only see us killed and their last hope gone. Leave him. We'll return. I promise you."

The old king considered this as he glared at Bres. But then he nodded.

"You're right. Let's be away from here."

"Good!" said Aine. "Now, Bres, I think this nasty device of yours will insure that we can at least leave the hall in safety. Move very, very slowly over to the dais and face me."

Bres moved without argument, standing with his back to the wooden planks of the raised platform.

"Good. I can keep you in clear view until we reach the doors. Just stand very still, and hope all of your Fomor do the same."

With Lugh and Nuada beside her, Aine backed away from him slowly. The others joined them as they moved toward the doors, Aine keeping the weapon trained unwaveringly on Bres.

"You're mad if you come back here," Bres called after them. "You're all doomed. And you, Lugh! Someday we'll meet when you've no one to protect you!"

"When we do, I'll have a sword of my own!" Lugh promised.

They reached the doors without event. As they started through, Aine paused on the threshold and smiled evilly.

"One last thing, Bres. Now *you* pray that *I* can aim!"

"What?" said the stricken king. "No!"

She fired.

His eyes squeezed shut as he tensed for the impact. But when the thunk of the bolt came, he felt no pain. He looked for the bolt. It had gone home in the planking just below his groin, pinning him to the wood by the hem of his tunic.

Relief giving way to rage, he looked up to see Aine and the others disappearing into the night.

"Get them!" he roared, yanking the bolt free. "Sound the alarm! Don't let them leave the fortress!"

Outside, the little party was already running for the main gates at Gilla's urging.

"What if the gates are locked?" Lugh asked.

"Trust me in that," said Gilla. "Just run!"

They ran. Halfway across the courtyard to the gates the alarm went up, the clanging of the bronze gong that called the household companies to alert. Behind them and then on either side shouts were heard, followed by the sounds of running men and rattling arms. Lugh glanced around him. Figures were visible in the darkness of the yard, growing clearer as guards converged from several points on the fleeing party.

But ahead, the gates were now visible too. With a final burst of speed, they reached them before any of the warriors and found the massive timber portals standing ajar just the width of a man. Lugh noted four guards stretched out neatly on the ground beside them.

"Resting," Gilla supplied affably and began pushing his companions through the opening.

Last of all, Gilla himself squeezed through, just ahead of the arriving pursuers. The Dagda threw his bulk against the heavy gate, slamming it back into their faces. The first warriors were thrown back into those rushing up behind, and they were all knocked down in a tangle. While they were struggling to rise, the Dagda seized a carved wooden ogham twice his length and girth and wrenched it from the ground with a single heave of the massive shoulders and arms. He swung it around and wedged it tightly against the doors, effectively trapping the warriors inside the fortress.

"You're a most useful person, that you are!" Gilla told the big man, clearly most impressed.

"You're one yourself!" the Dagda replied heartily. "Saving us was a marvel."

"I only threw a rope to you," Gilla said modestly. "But the way you crushed that well beast was amazing, it was that!"

"As your sword work is!" the Dagda graciously countered. "I've seen few to match your skills."

"Nothing to match yours," Gilla returned. "I especially liked that angled down-stroke. Pretty, it was!"

"Could we exchange compliments at some other time?" Lugh requested impatiently. Warriors were now beginning to beat on the inside of the doors.

"The lad is right," Gilla conceded. "Shall we get on?"

"But not toward the town," the Dagda suggested. "There'll be warriors swarming up from there to answer that alarm. This way."

He led them off, down along a side of the great dun, into the countryside.

They found a temporary hiding place at a hill north of Tara, sheltered in a small cluster of abandoned homes surrounded by a low wall of piled stones. They waited there, watching to see what Bres would do.

The mist had lifted its veil of modesty, leaving exposed a naked dead-white moon to light the countryside. Scores of yellow torches were visible around the dun, shifting constantly, at that distance like fireflies swarming thickly upon a flowery knoll. The forces of Streng and Bres were scouring the hill and the town below. But none had moved their search toward the real hiding place of the group.

"Safe enough," Gilla declared with satisfaction after observing for a time. "They've no idea where we've gone, nor where we'll be goin' next. It's only for us to go."

"What about food?" asked Angus. "And drink?"

"Especially drink," the Dagda added.

"I've enough for us," Gilla assured them with a knowing wink at Lugh and a pat on the miraculous cloak. "I've stocked myself up."

"And where is it we're going?" the Dagda asked.

"To the Mountains of Mourne," said Lugh. "It's there that Diancecht is hiding with the other exiles."

"We're exiles too, now," the Dagda said. "Well, shall we be starting?"

"That's up to the High-King, I think," Lugh answered, looking toward Nuada. All other eyes turned toward him as well.

Nuada looked around him at their expectant faces. His own expression was grave, thoughtful. His gaze dropped to the sword that he still held. He hefted it. Then he shook his head slowly.

"No, Lugh. Not High-King," he said in a low voice. Then his head lifted again and they saw the smile tugging at his mouth, lighting his eyes. "Not yet!" he added with new decisiveness. "But we'll give Diancecht his chance!"

Dawn found the travelers far north of Tara, crossing the countryside and avoiding all roads. It was not easy going through the thick woods and rocky meadowlands, and Gilla complained aloud.

"I'm missin' my little pony and cart now, that I am!"

"You know it would only have slowed us," Aine told him.

"But a few horses would have been nice," the Dagda said wistfully. He gave Gilla a speculative look. "You wouldn't have some tucked into that cloak of yours, would you?"

"I hadn't time to steal any," Gilla said, grinning.

"Bres's men will surely have them," Angus reminded them, without humor. "They could still catch us easily."

"We're safe enough," said Lugh. "How could they guess which way we've gone?"

"They've no need to," the Dagda said with sudden heaviness. "We've forgotten one thing."

He gestured upward. High above, a large, black shape sailed, broad wings outstretched.

"The Morrigan," Lugh said, his heart sinking.

And the raven-woman had seen them. As they watched, she banked into a broad, lazy spiral that brought her swooping down lower at each turn. The shimmering glow of her transformation began on her final glide in toward the earth, and it was on human feet that she settled onto the ground before them, letting the fluttering cloak fall around her.

She had landed at a safe distance and looked around her warily. She was not going to be taken by surprise this time.

She looked them over with the intense, black eyes. Then she spoke, the voice an ominous, dry crackle.

"The riders of the High-King are awaiting only my directions to pursue you. You cannot escape them."

"If that's so, why aren't you about telling them?" the Dagda asked suspiciously. "Why come to us?"

She hesitated, her eyes shifting from one to another of them again.

"You aren't certain, are you, Morrigan?" the Dagda said. "You're not certain you're doing the right thing."

"I'm acting by my bond. I serve the king," she said stubbornly. But there was a tinge of doubt coloring her words.

"Morrigan, we want to serve him too," the Dagda reasoned. "But a true king. Bres is none. He's the traitor to us. He's not even wholly de Danann. Fomor blood runs in him."

"Prove that to me," she said.

"We can't. But we can do something else. Listen, Morrigan. We can restore Nuada's hand! We can put him back in the kingship. We can release you and all of us from all bond to Bres. We will be free and we can unite against the Fomor."

She said nothing, but her eyes were narrowed thoughtfully. She was wavering.

"Morrigan, we're making no attack on Bres. You'll not betray your bond to let us go. If we succeed, you'll gain salvation for our people. If we fail, things will be no different. Only you can keep us from trying now."

As if to herself, she said in a soft rattle, "Free! To be free of him . . ." Her hand rested lightly on her sword hilt. Then she grew stern again.

"All right. I will not betray you," she told the Dagda, "for my old trust and love of you. And if you are right, I'll drink the blood of Bres myself. But, if you fail, the Powers help us both if we ever meet again!"

Then, in a sudden burst of light, she was gone.

As the group looked up, eyes recovering from the startling glare, they saw a black form, great wings laboring to pull it higher, already soaring away back toward the south.

"She is a strange being," Lugh said, looking after her.

"She is that," the Dagda agreed. He looked at Lugh, an odd, sad smile on his broad, battered face. "She was also once my wife."

In his cavern, Diancecht labored over his mortar and pestle, grinding out more roots to make a healing salve for a baby's rash and grumbling to himself. He was so absorbed in his dreary self-pity that he was not aware of the party entering until a voice spoke.

"Diancecht, it's time for you to put all your skills to work again!"

He looked around, unable at first to discern who his

visitors were against the sunlight flooding the cavern's mouth behind them. But he thought he knew the voice.

"Is that the Dagda?" he asked in disbelief.

"It is," the man replied. "And we've brought you something."

He and his companions moved forward and the old healer saw them clearly. He recognized all of them, but his attention was taken by the man who stood beside Lugh, smiling at him.

"I understand you made some claim to this lad," said Nuada to the flabbergasted physician. "I decided to come and see you make it good. You were always such a braggart in the old days."

XXVII

NUADA'S HAND

"GENTLY! VERY GENTLY with that!" Diancecht cautioned.

From the clear, chill pool beneath the cavern floor, the hand of Nuada was being carefully lifted. Clouds of frigid vapor rose around the physician and Findgoll as they arose, gripping the sides of the netting that held the precious object. The hand rose clear of the hole, dripping the bright liquid in shining streaks back into the pool.

"Now, to that table," Diancecht directed. He and the little druid sidestepped cautiously to a table sheeted with what seemed bright silver. It pulsed with a kind of inner light and threw a fine, white radiance, like a bright sun luminous in a mist, into the vast, dim cavern.

Beside this table sat another covered with layers of white linen. On this lay Nuada, motionless but awake and watching the actions of Healer and Druid with great interest. He was covered with another covering of white to his chin. His arm and its silver hand were exposed, stretched out to one side so it lay on the glowing silver sheet. The metal hand seemed dull in contrast to the polished surface beneath it.

Now, beside the cold, mechanical hand, the two men

gingerly placed the real one in its fine net. The physician delicately pulled the mesh away from the hand, leaving it clear.

"We must move quickly now," he said to Findgoll. "Out of the liquid it will begin to decay quickly. If we don't succeed in restoring its blood supply soon, it will never function."

He looked at Nuada.

"There is a risk, my King," he said formally. "I want you to understand that."

"I do, my old friend," the reclining man told him earnestly. "But our people are in greater risk now, and this may be our last chance to save them. It's time to prove to them, and to ourselves, that we are not finished yet. First you must prove it, and then will come my turn."

He turned his head to look aside at the metal hand. He smiled. "You know, this hand has done me good service. I think I may actually miss it." He looked at Diancecht. "All right, physician. I am all yours now. You may begin when you wish."

"Just lie back then," Diancecht said. "Close your eyes." He nodded to Findgoll who moved to stand at the old High-King's head.

The little druid placed the slender fingers of his fine hands lightly on Nuada's temples. He began a slow, crooning chant. After a few moments, the body of Nuada began visibly to relax. The breathing gradually slowed to a shallow, even rhythm.

"He is asleep," Findgoll quietly announced at last.

Diancecht had by now laid out a wide variety of small, delicately fashioned instruments, ranging them precisely along the edge of the glowing tabletop. The soft, unnatural light from it somehow bathed everything upon it in an equal wash of light that left no shadows. It seemed to glow through the severed hand, giving it a rosy blush of life, revealing its structure of bones and tendons and veins as darker lines.

Findgoll came back around to the physician's side. He looked down at the hand and then up at Diancecht's face, his normally mild expression marked by his concern. He saw the tension in Diancecht too, pulling deep furrows in the long face, drawing fine beads of sweat across the high forehead, narrowing the clear eyes behind the shaggy thrust of frowning brows.

The druid laid a soothing hand on his comrade's arm. His voice exuded an assurance that he really didn't feel himself. "You can do it, Diancecht."

The old healer steeled himself and drew his lean body up. His voice took on its normal gruff, uncompromising tones.

"Of course, Findgoll," he said gruffly. "Don't prattle on so. Here, help me with this silver hand!"

And, as the druid carefully positioned the hand and arm of Nuada, Diancecht chose a short, razor-edged blade and skillfully guided it to the flesh of the man's wrist.

Outside the cavern, the little band of adventurers who had brought Nuada there waited anxiously.

The delicate task of the physician went on through the afternoon and into the night. As the time passed, word began to spread through the hidden settlement about who had come and what momentous event was taking place. Soon, the inhabitants began to come up to the cavern to greet the arrivals and join their vigil. Goibnu, Bridget and others came, happy to see their old comrades again, anxious to hear the tale of Nuada's rescue.

By the time the sun pulled itself above the eastern mountains and spilled its first cup of light into the sheltered valley, the entire population of the settlement had gathered at the mouth of the healer's cave. Even the darkly brooding Bobd Derg had come to meet his father and brother and join the company, although he never ceased to pace constantly, muttering his gloomy predictions of disaster.

Now, in the clammy dawn, those clustered around scores of comforting fires were settled into a silent company. They waited, their faces carefully neutral, not speaking for fear their fragile hopes might flit away like startled butterflies. They watched until, at last, a figure became visible in the cave's dim recesses.

It moved forward to the cave's lip, into the light, and they could see that it was Findgoll. He stopped there and stretched himself. He moved stiffly, wearily. He blinked often in the light of the sun as his eyes adjusted. Then he looked down at the crowd below him.

"It's finished," he announced in a voice of fatigued relief. "The hand is restored."

Lugh let out a whoop of joy and the rest of the gathering joined in, releasing the pent-up tensions of the night. But

Findgoll raised his hands for silence, and when they had quieted again, he spoke in cautious tones.

"The hand has been reattached, but it has not yet been determined whether it has been done successfully. Nuada is awakening now. He wishes those who brought him here, and all the rest of you, present when the final test is made. So, follow me."

He turned back and led the way into the cavern. The scores outside followed him, crowding through the entrance into the vast area beyond.

Inside the cavern, the silver-topped table had lost its glowing light, and was now reduced to only a dull sheen. The physician's normal fires and torches were all that lit the room. On his own table, Nuada now sat propped up, awake again, while Diancecht stood beside him.

With a brusque command, the physician stopped the crowd just within the entrance. He allowed only the party of those who had rescued Nuada to come forward and stand close around the old king.

"I don't see the need to make a public spectacle of this," Diancecht said disapprovingly. "You should avoid any unnecessary strain."

"No, Diancecht," Nuada countered soothingly. "I need them there. Their courage and belief brought me this far. It will help me make that final step."

All of them were staring at the hand. It lay upon the coverlets beside the reclining man, bound from knuckles to elbow in a fine, white cloth. They were staring most closely at the exposed fingers—fingers so long dead and frozen away—now pink with the living man's blood again. But could it function? Had Diancecht succeeded? That was the final test it must pass.

Nuada's face furrowed with concentration. He stared at the fingers, willing them to move.

Nothing happened.

The watchers exchanged sidelong looks of despair. Had all their efforts been for nothing after all? Lugh's heart plummeted.

But Nuada had not given up. He was still trying, straining now with his efforts. And then, slowly . . . slowly, the fingers began to move.

It was first a barely visible twitch. Then there was real movement as the fingers began to curl upward together.

A sigh, like a first breath of spring wind, lifted from the company. They watched the fingers continue to lift, jerkily and then more smoothly, curling into a fist. Nuada clenched it, with a touch of agony at the unaccustomed pain, but with a smile of satisfaction too. He relaxed the hand, let the fingers fall back, then curled them again and again, each time more quickly, more easily. The smile grew wider. It was the first truly happy, truly confident smile that Lugh had ever seen him wear. He was ecstatic, like a child playing with a new toy, pumping the fingers open and closed.

"It works!" he cried joyfully. "By Danu, it works!"

"Don't thank Danu," Diancecht said without modesty. "Thank me!" He moved forward, laying a restraining hand gently, gently on Nuada's, stopping the movement. "But don't tax it too much yet. Let it rest. Let the joining heal. In a few days you will be fully healed. You'll truly be a whole man once again."

"Then we will go back to Tara and face that traitor Bres!" Nuada exclaimed. He pulled himself higher and called to all those gathered. "Any who wish to may join us. We will all go and end his tyranny at last!"

"And bring down the power of the Fomor upon us," Bobd Derg said gloomily. "It is madness still."

"It was you who said not long ago that Nuada would never be made whole, wasn't it?" the Dagda reminded him in a scolding voice. "And even if we are destroyed, at least it will be as free men, fighting for our lands. Better that then the degradation upon us now!"

"The de Dananns cannot fight," Bobd Derg insisted doggedly. "We are not warriors. We are craftsmen, artists, men of peace."

"No!" Nuada shouted back. "We are lovers of life, but we have earned nothing of life if we aren't willing to fight for it." He smiled at Lugh. "We have to do it for ourselves or we are nothing. This boy has taught me that." He looked back to his gathered fellows. "My spirit is alive. Is yours? Do we fight?"

"Aye, we do," said Goibnu, and the others there joined in a loud cheer of assent that echoed triumphantly in the cavern.

Bobd Derg said no more, but deep misgiving still filled his brooding look.

"Then we'll go together," Nuada declared. He looked again

to Lugh. "And you, lad, will march at our front, as one of our champions. That you've won the right to do."

Lugh exchanged a glance with Aine. He understood clearly the message in her eyes. He nodded his agreement to her. To the companions around him he said: "I'm very honored by that. But I've a bond of my own I must be fulfilling first. I put it off as long as I may. I'll be leaving tomorrow."

"Leaving?" Angus said, surprised. "What for?"

"I've an appointment that I must keep. It has to do with my whole destiny."

"If it's your bond, you must go," the Dagda said. "And it's not for us to be questioning it. But you'll be missed."

"I'll return," said Lugh. "I promise that. With luck, I'll meet you at Tara when you return there to face Bres."

"I hope so, lad," Nuada said with great intensity. "We owe you a great deal. You've restored my life to me along with my hand. You've given us all new hope. Whatever happens to you now, we'll not forget that!"

"He's right, Lugh," the Dagda agreed heartily. He stepped close and clapped a huge hand to the young man's shoulder. "You're one of us now, whatever else you are. Good fortune to you."

Abashed by this warmth, Lugh looked about him, to find the others of that gathering were beaming in open friendship. He felt a closeness to them, as though he really was a part of them, as if they were a family to him.

But he saw Aine, and was reminded that his life was not yet his own. It was time to make it so.

Diancecht shooed the company out of the cavern then, to let Nuada rest. Lugh parted from the de Dananns and made his way back to Findgoll's liss, accompanied only by Aine and Gilla.

"We may as well prepare to leave at the next dawn," he said resignedly. "Taillta is nearly recovered." He looked around at the clown. "But, what about you? What will you do?"

Gilla smiled in his unaffected way. "Why, don't you know? I'll go with you! With Taillta still needing rest, you'll need a pony cart like mine to carry her. And I'd not leave you now! Your company is too exciting!"

Lugh smiled. "I thought the excitement here would be more to your taste. But I'm very glad you're coming. I'll welcome a friend with me." He looked at Aine. "If it's all right for him to come."

She shrugged. "He's earned his welcome." She looked the clown over and added in joking speculation. "I'd like to see Gilla and my brother meet. Two such strange beings together would be an entertainment."

Gilla laughed, but Lugh remained quiet, his expression growing more somber. Now that he was truly going back, he felt a vague tremor of concern. This finding out his own identity, his place in life, had been put aside in his need to act. Now that it was done, the need to learn the answers to his questions began to take on vast importance once again.

He realized that he was anxious to go, to face Manannan and finally be free of all uncertainties.

That night, after all preparations had been made, he stood again with Aine on the hillside where they had talked those few, long days before. The sun was just settling behind the western plains, and the grassy meadows were like a rippling sea of gold.

"I hope I can return to Eire," he said. "But I wonder if I'll ever see it again? Is my life linked to it in some way, or will what I learn take me on some other path?"

"Only Manannan can tell you that," she said.

"I know," he agreed. "I'm ready to go back."

"You told me that the last time we came here," she reminded him. She turned toward him, took one of his hands and clasped it tightly in both of hers. "This time I'm making sure you don't change your mind."

He looked down into that fresh, bold face, that wealth of hair and bright eyes, both touched with the sunset's gold. He forgot his worries about what would come and pulled her to him.

"If you want to make certain I'll not slip away, you'll have to stay close . . . very close," he said.

She met his gaze with a challenging one.

"I'd rather tie a bell to you," she said.

BOOK IV

THE ANSWERER

XXVIII

MANANNAN'S SECRET

ONCE MORE LUGH stood inside the entrance to Manannan's vast Sidhe, looking across the confusing landscape that seemed to be inside and outside at once. It was as if years had passed since his first visit there.

The return trip had been swift. Aine had led them through the Mountains of Mourne to the eastern seacoast. Directly ahead, on the rim of the horizon, lay the mystical isle. At the shore a sleek bronze and silver ship had awaited them and taken them off, gliding away smoothly through the sea, sweeping them through a gentle, silver mist to the soft greenness of Manannan's home.

Again the folk of the sea-god had provided a welcome and accompanied them to the mound. The grim, silent Riders of the Sidhe had escorted them. But there was no Manannan.

"He waits for you in the circle," cooed a lovely, lithe sprite of a woman who floated up to Lugh and caressed his cheek.

Aine gave her a look that sent her away like a snowflake licked by a flame. Then the girl put her own hand on Lugh's arm and spoke reassuringly.

"My brother wished to see you first alone," she explained. "We'll stay behind for now. I'll see to the comforts of our friends."

"But, Aine..." Lugh began, a little uncertainly. He felt a vague discomfort at the idea of this meeting. He had no way of guessing how the peculiar being would react to his handling of the mission.

"I know what you're thinking," the perceptive Aine said gently. "But it will be all right. He is still my brother, remember? He's safe enough. We'll see you soon. Now, go on. I know your desire to know must be nearly unbearable by now."

That was right enough. He could barely catch a deep breath for the fist of anxiety clutching at his heart. Odd, he thought, how before he had put this out of his mind, and now that it was so close, the idea was nearly overwhelming. The tension had grown steadily the nearer they had come. He was certain that by now the jittering he felt through his whole body must be visible to everyone.

Drawing a deep breath and steadying himself, he left his friends and started down the path that led from the entrance on the outer rim to the central mound and its circle of stones. He tried to see if Manannan was already there, but the path dropped down into a lower meadows, and he lost sight of the circle. Then he was climbing back up again, and the mound was right above him.

He climbed it slowly. As he came into sight of the first stones of the circle, he again began to look for Manannan to appear. His heart was beating so stridently, he thought it would burst from his chest at every stroke. He climbed on, his steps heavy, coming up to where the whole circle was in view. Then it was that he glimpsed a figure, its feet hanging over the edge of a large stone.

They were very big feet, he noted. And the legs were very thin. They looked, he realized with worry, very familiar. Too familiar. Suddenly, he realized why.

"Gilla!" he cried, stopping in amazement.

The clown was draped casually across a stone, humming a merry little air and peeling a fat red apple plucked from one of the Sidhe's trees with his knife. Seeing Lugh, he stopped and grinned in his familiar, foolish way.

"Welcome to you!" he said. "It took you long enough to get here, so it did."

Lugh was horrified. "Gilla! What are you doing! Get out of there!" He looked around fearfully. "Quickly! Before Manannan sees you. Please, Gilla. Don't make him angry!"

"Calm yourself, lad. Manannan won't be comin'," Gilla said easily. He sat up, dropping his long legs to the ground, and set the apple and knife on the stone.

Then, with a single, swift move, he seized his long beard and yanked it up and away from his face.

It seemed to Lugh that Gilla's face was torn away with the beard. It peeled off like wet gauze. But it revealed another face beneath.

"Manannan is here!" the man said gleefully.

"You were Gilla?" gasped Lugh, staring in disbelief.

"All of the time!" he said, pulling off the ragged hood and a covering of shaggy hair, leaving exposed his own head of silver. "Not bad, eh? Impressed?"

Lugh plopped down on the ground where he was, astounded by this discovery.

"You were with me all the time?" he asked in bewilderment. Then an angry note entered his voice. "Wait! You were with me and you kept it secret? Aine kept it secret? Why?"

"I couldn't resist a chance to have a bit of excitement for myself!" he admitted quite openly. "And I wanted to give you what help I could, even though my powers are nearly useless in Eire. Of course, that only makes it the greater adventure to me."

Lugh gave the tall man a sour, disgruntled glare. That absurd, gleeful expression that was still Gilla only increased his irritation.

"You're certainly enjoying this fun—making me look a fool!" he said harshly.

Manannan waved his hand. "Lad, I'm not."

"You are!" Lugh insisted. "Sending me into Eire to spy for you and all the time you were there yourself! What was I? Some kind of game? Some object of fun to keep you from being bored?"

When Manannan saw that Lugh was truly upset, he sobered at once. He walked to the young man, knelt by him, and placed a hand on his shoulder. His voice grew earnest, intense.

"Lugh, you were never that. I had to do what I did. Believe me. It all has to do with you, with your life, and with so much more."

Lugh looked into the now serious eyes with suspicion.

"I don't know if I can believe you now."

"Look, just come walk with me," Manannan offered, getting up. "Let me explain. You'll understand. I promise that."

Lugh looked up at him and then shrugged wearily.

"I've come this far."

* * *

The seashore was the same—as a seashore tends to be when left alone. Even the same gulls seemed to be sweeping low over the water as before, so long before. Lugh wondered as they strolled what did seem so changed to him. Then he realized with a start that it was himself.

Before, the land beyond the horizon's haze had been strange to him. He had been an alien, unknowing and alone. Now, his isolated life was gone forever and, whatever happened, he would never again be content with the simple, peaceful life he had once lived. From now on there would always be more horizons to peek over.

He and Manannan waded shoeless in the surf like two small boys, both enjoying the water wash soothingly across feet calloused and sore from the long days of trekking.

"I have to tell you more of myself first," Manannan said. "I told you once before that I was a sort of guardian. Well, I am, but only to the de Dananns. You see, I'm from the Four Cities of Tir-na-nog. It was Queen Danu herself who sent me here to keep watch over her children."

"You're from the Four Cities?" said Lugh. "But why do you keep that a secret?"

"The de Dananns are very proud. Do you remember what Bobd Derg said? They came back to Eire to prove themselves and earn a place of their own by their own powers. They wanted no help from us. Queen Danu agreed to let them come, of course, but she knew they were going to need a little help. She has this way of foreseeing certain future events. Amazing how she does it, really! But she foresaw the de Dananns trouble with the Fomor. She couldn't ignore that. We know the Fomor too well. We've our own reasons to want them defeated."

"Have you?" Lugh asked, much intrigued.

"Oh yes. It was one of the reasons we helped the Dagda and his companions when they first landed on Tir-na-nog, after that first encounter with the Fomor. Our own rivalry goes back to the time the Fomor ruled the world. They hated my people of course. We were too independent, too interested in foolish things like the seasons and birds singing. And they thought we laughed much too much. Our tastes were also quite opposite. Well, you saw that Tower!"

Lugh vividly recalled his impression of the stark glass

building. He could see how its inhabitants and the people of Manannan might not get along.

"Anyway, they tried for years to change us, and then to annihilate us. Finally we retreated to those isles and used our powers over nature to hide them. We knew the civilization of the Fomor had collapsed. We thought they were all gone until the survivors of Nemed chanced upon us."

They reached a little finger of rocks that thrust out to sea and stopped there to rest. Manannan stretched himself out comfortably on the weathered boulders and Lugh sat listening rapt as he continued.

"Of course, my people didn't like seeing the de Dananns come back here to face those pirates alone. But we understood that they had to do it for themselves if they were really going to earn their own place." He smiled cunningly. "But that didn't mean we couldn't help them along a bit. Without their knowing, of course. So I came here to keep an eye on things.

"I helped out where I could, but I couldn't take the lead or interfere with their choices. That was the maddening part—watching Bres using them, watching them submit so meekly to the Fomor." Some anger crept into his tone at that. Then he shrugged resignedly. "But there was nothing I could do, except to wait."

"Wait for what?" asked Lugh.

"Why, for you!" Manannan announced.

"You mean that I'm some part of all that?" Lugh said, his interest now increased considerably by this personal turn in the story.

"Of course you are. Your life with Taillta was at my arrangement. The only error in it was that you were discovered. That meant you were sent to me a bit earlier than I had planned. But Taillta's training of you served you well. You know, I'm very glad we got her out of that tower. Even my powers are useless against it, and I was certain she was dead." He dropped his head back and looked up to the sky, his voice taking on a certain nostalgic air. "Ah, that was a treat, going in there, rescuing her, fighting our way out..."

"Manannan," Lugh said, interrupting, "could you please go on? Why did you and she do this for me?"

"Sorry, lad," said Manannan, sitting up again. "You see, one thing Danu foresaw was that a champion would appear to lead the de Dananns to freedom and destroy the Fomor power." He clapped a hand to the young man's shoulder. "That champion is you!"

Lugh felt like laughing. "Now you are playing with me again. Me, a champion? I don't feel like one. I surely don't look like one."

"Oh, well, the look is mostly in having the proper clothing," Gilla assured him. "It's all really in the attitude. Believe me, Lugh, you are the champion."

Lugh shook his head over this. Then a new realization came to him and he looked to Manannan with rising excitement.

"If it is true, then I must be de Danann myself! Is that what I am?"

Manannan didn't answer at once. He reached into the baggy cloak of Gilla which he still wore and brought out the skin of ale.

"Still a bit of this left," he said, shaking it and then holding it out to Lugh. "Would you like to have a drink first?"

Lugh pushed it irritably away. "I don't want a drink. I just want to know who I am! Please, Manannan, don't torture me any more! Just tell me."

"It may be difficult," Manannan said. "You might like a bit of fortification first." But seeing the lad's agonized look, he nodded and dropped the skin. "All right, lad. I'm sorry. Here it is then. Your father was a de Danann. He was a champion himself named Cian."

It was something Lugh realized he'd felt deeply. He understood that sense of being a part of them.

"But what about my father?" he asked. "What happened to him?"

"Balor killed him," Manannan answered directly. "You see, Balor learned of the prophecy from a powerful druid of the de Dananns he had captured. He also learned that the son of Cian would fulfill that prophecy and destroy the Fomor power. He came to Eire himself and found Cian and your mother. She was already pregnant with you.

"Cian fought him bravely. He managed to nearly defeat the monster. But in the end he was beaten. Balor took your mother back with him to the Tower. That's where you were born."

Lugh listened silently, rapt, trying to convince himself that this was something to do with him, not some tale, some impossible tale he couldn't accept.

"Balor wanted your mother kept alive," Manannan went on, "but you were a different matter. You were far too dangerous. Of course, I learned what was happening. Since I hadn't been able to stop your father's death, I meant to save both of you. I managed to contact your mother and arrange a rescue. But Balor discovered it and tried to stop her. Desperate to save you, she managed to fling you from the Tower. It was my own hands that plucked you from the sea."

The images of Lugh's dreams now returned to him again, more vivid than ever before. He knew that woman's face above him was his mother's. He saw Balor moving forward to destroy him. He relived the plunge to the sea and felt the hands of Manannan lift him. He saw the Tower of Glass looming over him and he knew that everything the sea-god had told him was true.

"And my mother?" he asked. "What happened to her?"

"Balor gave her no other chances to escape after that," Manannan said sorrowfully. "She died very soon of her grief over you and Cian, still imprisoned in that bloody Tower."

Lugh sat staring at Manannan when he had finished, trying to deal with the flood of conflicting emotions.

"Lugh? Are you all right?" Manannan asked anxiously, somewhat alarmed by the dazed expression of the young man. "I know that learning all this at once might be a bit overwhelming..."

"A bit!" Lugh exclaimed sarcastically. "My parents are dead; the de Dananns are expecting me to save them, and a one-eyed metal giant is trying to kill me. Why should I find that overwhelming?"

"Good!" said Manannan breezily, smiling. "I knew that you could handle it." He jumped down from the rocks. "I'm relieved that's over. It was the difficult bit. Shall we go on?"

He trudged off briskly along the shore. Lugh rose and trotted after him, still sorting the thing out in his mind. He had many more questions.

"Balor knew you were alive and never stopped searching for you," Manannan was explaining. "I had to hide you until you could grow up and fulfill the prophecy. I took you to Taillta. She was a daughter of Mac-Erc, one of the last Firbolg High-Kings to defy the Fomor."

"Taillta is a Firbolg?" Lugh asked.

"She and all those who raised and protected you. They had their own reason to hate the Fomor for breaking them and killing Mac-Erc. They knew the prophecy and that one day you might also be the instrument of their revenge."

"But why keep me from knowing my true identity or anything about the outside world?" Lugh wondered.

"Well, for one thing, we were trying to hide you away until you were old enough to act," Manannan explained. "If you had known the truth, you'd have been impossible to keep on that isle. Taillta had enough trouble as it was. You'd have been off at the first opportunity and before you were ready, going to Eire, and likely getting yourself killed.

"More important, it was stated in the prophecy that the champion could only succeed if his choice to act was made freely. Do you see? Knowing who you were and what was happening in Eire from birth would have made a truly free choice out of the question. So you were kept isolated until you'd reached an age of independent reasoning and then sent to Eire as an outsider, making your choice to help only because your mind and instincts told you it was right."

"But, how could there be any doubt that I would help people so desperate?" Lugh asked.

The sea-god put a hand on Lugh's shoulder and said in a fatherly tone: "My boy, as you grow more wise in the workings of the world, I'm afraid you'll discover many who choose to stay uninvolved, no matter how desperate the situation. Come on. This way."

He turned aside from the shore and led the way across a meadow. The Sidhe, in its subtle way, softly enveloped them and Lugh realized suddenly that they were back inside. Ahead of them he saw the central mound, which now seemed to be busy with moving figures.

"Now that you've made your choice," Manannan said, "you are ready to assume the role foreseen. You've already begun to fulfill the prophecy. Now it's time for you to truly become the champion of the de Dananns."

They climbed the slope to the top of the mound. Lugh saw that Taillta and Aine were there now, waiting inside the circle of stones with several of the isle's inhabitants. Around the circle, motionless and grim, the Riders of the Sidhe sat on their white mounts.

Before entering the ring, Manannan stopped Lugh and

murmured: "There's a flamin' great ceremony involved with this, investing you with the mantle of champion and all. It's a lot of foolishness, but Danu insisted. You're certain you want to go through with it?"

"Well, I still don't feel much of a champion," Lugh admitted. "But if I can help the de Dananns, it doesn't seem as if I've much choice."

"All right then, lad," Manannan said, grinning. "Just follow me." He started forward, but then leaned back to add as an afterthought: "Oh, and try not to laugh. This is very serious."

They moved past the Riders and through the stones into the ring. Manannan strode to the center to stand by the small, rounded stone he had called the Lia Fail. A woman of the Sidhe held a garment of shimmering silver cloth. The sea-god slipped out of his worn cloak and allowed her to place this new one about his shoulders. As the bright garment fell about his shoulders, a change began.

From its folds appeared fine lines of blue-white light that crackled across the surface in all directions, interweaving to cover the cloak with a meshwork of pure energy. And Lugh looked on with growing awe as this strange garment of light seemed to transform his friend.

Slowly Manannan pulled his lanky figure fully erect. The light now fully covered him, playing over him, enshrouding him with its shifting interlace of energy. The tall figure seemed to grow even more as the aura about it strengthened, assuming a towering presence now. The head lifted, and Lugh saw the new force altering the amiable features. A new firmness sharpened them, gave them a gravity and strength and boldness. The eyes took on a radiance, as if they were the focus of this energy.

No longer the carefree adventurer, Manannan now stood before them as a being of grandeur and power. The aura of light about him had grown to fill the circle and encompass them all.

He stood proudly before the Stone of Truth, the other objects in his care forming a triangle about him—the cauldron, the sword called The Answerer, the deadly spear bubbling in its vat. Before him stood young Lugh, feeling very self-conscious and a bit afraid, with Aine and Taillta on either side, providing some comforting support. Around them all sat the motionless, gleaming Riders of the Sidhe, making a silver wall.

"Now we are ready," Manannan announced, his voice assuming a low note of great intensity that seemed to boom in the vast space of the Sidhe.

The power around him seemed to multiply, creating a column of energy radiant with light and heat like molten glass. He raised his arms and this column rose up, stretching toward the dome of the structure high above.

As if it were a liquid filling a cup, the stream of light collected in the circular space, forming a pool of luminous white. So smooth and solid it looked to Lugh that it might have been a mirror of polished silver.

As he stared up in it in open wonder, he began to note some movement in the perfect surface. There were vague shapes at first, formless and colorless, shadowlike objects moving in a fog. But they came clearer, taking on color, growing darker, coalescing into a single object. And, suddenly, Lugh realized that he was looking at a face.

The face was enormous, filling the circular dome, and it had a sense of depth, of roundness, as if a real, giant head were suspended there. But there was nothing awful or threatening about it. For the face that looked down upon them was a woman's, the features soft and of great beauty, the expression one of warmth and pleasure.

The young man felt the eyes upon him, and sensed in them an easy intimacy, as if this were some old and valued friend, and very much more.

"We call upon Danu, Queen of the Four Cities of Tir-na-nog, as witness," Manannan intoned, speaking to the watcher. Then his gaze dropped down to the young man. "Lugh, you must now give your decision here, before this gathering. Tell us if you choose to take on the mantle of champion and give your service to the Tuatha de Danann."

"I do," Lugh said solemnly.

"And is this choice made freely and willingly by you?"

"It is."

Manannan looked around him at the gathering. "Then witness that this boy is a boy no longer! He has accepted the duty of a man and earned the right to the title of warrior. He assumes responsibility for the Four Gifts sent by each of the cities of Tir-na-nog to aid the de Danann people."

He moved from the Lia Fail to the flat stone on which the sheathed longsword lay. He lifted the weapon and carried it to Lugh.

Standing before the young man, holding the sword forth in both hands, he continued:

"This sword will be your instrument and your symbol of your duty. It is called "The Answerer," and the answerer you have become in correcting the wrongs done to your race. When the time comes for the other gifts, it will also be for you to see that they are used. Do you accept this responsibility?"

"I do," said Lugh.

Manannan passed the sword to Lugh, and the young man took a firm hold of it. He felt at once a warmth and an energy radiating from it, tingling along his arm, flowing into his body as if the weapon had its own life and was feeding its vitality to him. And with that new power, he recognized the courage and strength within him that had always been his. For the first time, he felt a warrior.

Manannan looked up again to the serene, watching face.

"With the powers entrusted to me by Danu, I proclaim Lugh, Champion of the Sidhe, from here forward to be called Lugh Lamfada—Lugh of the Long Arm. For his arm shall carry the wrath of the Four Cities against the Fomor." He gestured around him at the ring of mounted warriors. "These Riders of the Sidhe will accompany him in his task." He lifted his arms up to include the whole gathering, "And the love and support of all within this Sidhe will be always with him."

He placed a hand firmly on either shoulder of Lugh and addressed him with the deepest gravity.

"Now you can return again to Eire, join the de Dananns at Tara, help them as they begin their battle against Bres and the Fomor!"

At this most solemn point, the tall man glanced upward to the watching face as if to see how closely she was observing him. Then, quickly, he leaned toward Lugh. The somber visage dissolved into a grin and he softly added in the clown's familiar tones:

"And don't you be worryin', lad. You'll not be alone. Your comrades will be right there as well." He winked broadly. "Old Gilla'd not be missin' this little brawl, that he would not!"

XXIX

THE CHALLENGE

THE PARTY HALTED at the edge of Tara. They looked along its empty streets and up toward the dun where the great fortress loomed, silent and ominous and waiting.

It was early dawn, the sky uncommonly clear and of a deep blue, the town and hilltop lit by the sharply slanting rays of a bright summer sun.

The Dagda looked from the fortress to the group gathered around him. Several scores of the exiles from the Mountains of Mourne had chosen to join in this confrontation with Bres. Flanking him at the front of the company were his son and Nuada. Behind them stood Cerdene, Goibnu, Bridget, Findgoll, and even Bobd Derg, who had accompanied the others despite his misgivings.

All were armed with the swords and shields and bright-headed spears fashioned by the skilled de Danann smiths. The gleaming metal caught the flood of light, shattering it like glass and sending the fragments flickering against the buildings around them.

There was no movement in those buildings. The town could have been abandoned. The old veteran warriors gazed about with carefully assessing eyes and listened for any suspicious noise. But there was nothing.

"Where are the people?" Angus asked.

"Cowering inside their homes, most likely," Bobd Derg answered darkly.

"What about the warriors of Bres, and the Fomor companies?"

"They're at the fortress," said another voice.

The company turned toward it and saw the figures of two women and a lanky clown emerge from the shelter of a liss.

"My friends! It's good to be seeing you again!" the Dagda exclaimed happily, striding forward to greet them. He looked curiously at the handsome older woman who, like Aine was in warrior's dress, a sword at her side, a spear and shield in her hands. "But aren't you Lugh's other companion who was so badly hurt?"

"I'm fully healed now," Taillta replied forcefully. "I've waited a very long time for this. I'll not be left out of it!"

The Dagda smiled, impressed by the determination in her bold look.

"As a friend to Lugh, you are welcome!" he told her sincerely. "But, where is he? I'd hoped he'd be with you!"

"He is coming. He'll be here soon. I promise that!" Gilla assured him.

"I hope so," said Nuada. "But we've no time to wait for him. Tell me, Gilla, have you been here long?"

"Aye, long enough to have a bit of a look around. Bres knows you're coming. He's been expecting it since we escaped. The warriors have all been withdrawn to the fortress. The main gates are standing open."

"That surely sounds like an invitation," said the Dagda.

"That's what I thought, I did," Gilla agreed. "Bres wants you to meet him on his terms."

"It could be he means to trap us there and destroy us at once," Findgoll prudently pointed out.

Nuada shook his head. "I dislike giving such an advantage to Bres. If more of the de Danann's were with us, he'd not dare to act."

"Perhaps if the people of Tara knew we had come," Findgoll suggested.

"They know," Aine supplied brightly. "Somebody..." she smiled at Gilla, "...has been passing word that you would come."

"They'll not help us," said Bobd Derg with glum certainty. "They are too afraid."

"Well, help or not, we must go on," Nuada said fiercely. "Or we may as well join with Bobd Derg and sail away forever from Eire. Are you staying with me?"

Firm voices of assent arose in the company.

"Then we'll go and visit our High-King in his den!" said Nuada, starting forward.

Gilla, Aine and Taillta fell in with them as they strode boldly through the streets. Their arms raised a hard and martial clatter in the quiet dawn. Their faces were set in defiance. They would not be turned back from their goal now except by death.

And as they moved forward, the town began to come alive around them. People began peering out as they went by. A few began to slip from their shuttered homes to follow after them. Then more started to come, their courage swelling with their numbers, until they poured from the buildings and the avenues as the company passed, joining the now massive throng. Most came out of curiosity, to see their outlawed friends defy the king. Some came to support them, taking out weapons long hoarded toward such a day, or seizing tools, cooking spits, wooden staves, and other lethal instruments. Some were hopeful, most were afraid, but still they came. And Nuada and his comrades, striding at their head, heard the rising murmur at their back with growing pride.

Above them, the fortress loomed ever larger. Now it was coming to life too. First came the shout of a lookout. Then came the ringing of the alarm gong and the sounds of voices and rattling arms. The forces were mustering inside.

The huge mob of de Dananns climbed the slope to the open gates. Without hesitation, Nuada led them on through into the inner yard. Ahead, before the entrance to the main hall, Bres waited, cool and arrogant, watching their entrance disdainfully. On his left, his own household companies were drawn up, Morrigan and the other loyalist captains at their front. The raven-woman, wrapped in her black cape, watched with seeming impassiveness, but her eyes were bright.

On the right of Bres was massed the Fomor garrison of Tara, led by Streng. They were a motley and a nightmare band, especially since the most horrible abberations amongst them had been ranged along the front. Bres had suspected some of the de Dananns might find the courage to support the Dagda and his friends. He had decided that a graphic reminder of the Fomor awfulness would be enough to cow them.

It certainly had its effect. As the de Dananns followed the Dagda's party through the gates and saw the Fomor, the crowd hesitated, halted; they pooled like water coming against a dam, backing and filling up the inner curve of the wall just within the gates. Only Nuada, the Dagda and the rest of their company advanced to the center of the training field and stopped there in the open, halfway between their own people and Bres.

A silence fell as the two factions eyed one another appraisingly. Finally, Bres spoke.

"So, you have returned. I'd hoped you would be foolish enough to do that. Now all of our people can see how traitors die."

"They may see that, right enough," the Dagda agreed. "But you're the one who's a traitor to us, Bres. Or you're a traitor to whatever in you is de Danann. Your only loyalty is to the Fomor blood that's running in your veins!"

An astonished murmur ran through the assembled de Dananns, including the contingent of the High-King's warriors.

"Lies!" Bres shouted over it. "Of course you would say that to justify your crimes, to shake the loyalty of those who would keep their bonds to me."

"We are here to break those bonds," the Dagda said. "We're going to free all de Dananns from your tyranny and restore the rightful one to kingship. Nuada!"

The old king stepped forward from the rest. He stopped and fixed his gaze challengingly on Bres. All the eyes in the gathering went to him. Morrigan watched him with a special intensity.

"Nuada!" Bres laughed loudly at the idea. "He can never be king again. The laws we have all sworn by make that so. Or do you deny them now?"

"There is no need to, Bres," Nuada said. He lifted the hand, until now kept down within his cloak. He swept it up high so all could see that the living hand had been restored to him.

"My own hand is mine again!" he proclaimed. "I am whole!" He turned and waved it, clenched and unclenched it so that the de Dananns could be certain it was no trick.

A shout of unbridled joy rose from Nuada's people. Bres stared, caught offguard by this unexpected move. He had seen no way that their challenge of him might be made a serious one. But now . . .

He signaled Streng to him, saying urgently under the cover of the cheering: "This could get beyond our control. I think we should destroy Nuada and his party now!"

"No!" Streng told him emphatically. "Balor wants no use of force except as a last resort. If we attack Nuada, we confirm

his kingship and deny yours. You must keep him from making
the challenge good."

"You're a fool to hesitate in using our power," Bres told
him. "But I'll try it, if Balor wishes." He raised his voice and
again shouted over the crowd, "Hold! Hold!"

Slowly the cheering died away. Nuada lowered the hand
and turned back to face his rival.

"The kingship is still mine," Bres said. "That was given me
by law, and by law I hold it."

Findgoll pushed out of the group behind Nuada to answer
that:

"Only in death does Nuada relinquish the kingship. That is
our law."

"There's no reason why those of us loyal to de Danann
principles should listen to a treasonous, little druid," Bres
answered cuttingly. "And even if that ridiculous claim were
true, you seem to overlook the fact that I hold the kingship
now because Nuada passed it to me. I've no intention of
passing it back to him. It stays mine."

"There are many here who think Nuada is the true king,"
Findgoll said. Voices of agreement rose in the crowd at that.

"They are misguided or mad," Bres countered, looking
sharply around. "But the warriors of the High-King are loyal
to me. They will ensure that I keep my rightful place."

"Do you really think so, Bres?" the Dagda asked, smiling
grimly. "Look around. How many of them would turn on you
if Nuada's claim were proven stronger than yours? How many
are already uncertain?"

Bres turned to his companies, searching the faces. He saw
the growing confusion there. Morrigan especially, he noted,
eyed him with a particular interest, her hand gripping her
sword hilt.

Bres cast a look askance at Streng. The Fomor captain
shook his head. The High-King would have to try to regain
control himself.

"Nuada is a useless old man, his mind soaked with ale," he
harshly accused. "These other traitors are using him as a tool
to force us into war. That would destroy us. I've kept us at
peace. I've saved your lives."

"You'll not use that lie on us any longer, Bres," Nuada said.
"You've drained and bullied us long enough."

"Have I? Well, you still have to prove that my claim to the throne is not as strong as Nuada's. And that you cannot do!"

"I can do it, Bres," a voice called from the gates.

All eyes went to it. There, on a horse that glowed white in the morning sun, sat a warrior.

He was dressed in a tunic of the finest linen, its hem embroidered in silver threads. Across his shoulders lay a rich, green cloak fastened with a brooch of shining gold. Another ornament held his streaming mane of pale blonde hair behind his neck. His face was stern, the features bold, cast in sharp planes by the low, slanting light. And at his side was fastened a sword whose scabbard and hilt dazzled the eye with their jewels.

Bres stared narrowly at him, trying to see him clearly in that glow. A disquiet flicked about his mind. That voice had been familiar!

"Who are you?" he demanded.

"My name is Lugh," the warrior simply answered.

The Dagda and his friends exchanged glances of astonishment at this. Gilla and Aine exchanged clandestine smiles.

"Very effective, don't you think?" the disguised sea-god remarked to his sister.

But for Bres, a sharp clamor of alarm had been raised. It was like a nightmare come to life for him. This warrior who now seemed to come out of nowhere to face him was the ragged and soaked wanderer who had appeared at his hall and had haunted him ever since. Indeed, there was some terrible power in him.

Lugh urged his horse forward into the yard. As he passed through the gates, other horses and riders appeared behind him. While the gathering looked on in growing wonder, Lugh led a strange procession into the fortress.

Two by two they rode, a score of mounted warriors, masked by silver helmets, lances held upright and brightly tinkling from their encircling silver bands, gleaming shields on their arms, bright swords at their sides. Silver cloaks flowed in the morning light like a moonlit mist behind them. Their tall horses, of matching grey-white, cantered forward with an easy grace, like trees leaning in a gentle wind, manes and tails an incandescent torrent.

Their company almost seemed to float into the yard behind Lugh. When he pulled up beside his friends, they went on,

turning across the training grounds toward a small rounded
knoll at one side. There they divided and circled it on either
side, joining again to form a single ring around it. The horses
turned outward, making spokes with the knoll as a hub.
There they halted, each standing like the next, lances up,
horses and riders becoming motionless.

Bres watched them warily until they had come to rest.
Then he looked back to Lugh.

"And just what is this unearthly company?" he demanded.

"We are the Riders of the Sidhe," Lugh answered. "We
have come to help the de Dananns and prove who is the
rightful king."

"And by what power do you and these... things presume
to take such authority?" Bres asked scornfully.

"By the power of Danu herself, Queen of the Four Cities of
Tir-na-nog!" Lugh declared.

Another rumble of excited voices rose from the assemblage.

"If that *is* true," Bres said challengingly, "just how do you
plan to make this proof? We'll surely not accept a stranger's
word."

"For that I have brought to you a gift from the Four
Cities," Lugh said, gesturing toward the small knoll and its
ring of silver warriors.

Immediately, the reflected sunlight from each of the bright
spear points flared to an almost blinding intensity. Then, from
one spear point a streak of light arched to the next, and from
there on to the next, hopping around the circle, joining all
the points in a continuous, flowing band of piercing white
light that crackled with energy as in a bolt of lightning
leaping from cloud to cloud.

The brilliant, diamond-light rivaled the golden sun for
brightness, casting its own sharp shadows across the yard.
The people looked away or shielded their eyes as it grew
brighter and enveloped the Riders and the rounded hill
within its ring. It seemed as if it must consume them with its
incredible energy, though no heat radiated from the spot.

"Marvelous effect, don't you think?" the sea-god murmured
to his sister and Taillta.

The crowd, however, was nearing panic and beginning to
push back. But the light grew no brighter. It had already
peaked and it began quickly to fade, as if the spears were
drawing the power back within themselves. It shrank back

down to the single, narrow line of light joining the spear points and then, one by one, each point flicked out like a candle suddenly snuffed.

The immense energy displayed had not disturbed the Riders or their mounts. All was the same, save for one thing. On the bare top of the again-visible knoll, there now sat a smooth, grey, round-topped stone.

"It is the Lia Fail," Lugh proclaimed. "The Stone of Truth, sent from the city of Filias to you. And its own voice will say if the one who sits upon it is the rightful High-King of the Tuatha de Danann."

"This is some kind of trick," Bres cried. "I'll not trust the kingship to the magic of some false stone!"

"No!" Findgoll shouted. He moved further into the open and turned to call to the gathering: "It is the Lia Fail. I have seen it myself in Filias. So have many others here. It is from Danu's people."

There were answering voices of agreement from many in the group, including those of Bres's household companies.

The Morrigan spoke up now, in a low but dominating rattle of a voice that immediately claimed all attention.

"I too know that this is the Lia Fail. Agree to take the test, Bres, or you will forfeit all claim to the kingship now."

Her eyes fixed on him with that raptor's glow. Her bony hand rested significantly upon her sword hilt. Bres looked from her around at his warriors and the increasingly hostile gathering. He looked at Streng. The man was stone-faced, waiting. Bres had no choice in this. He nodded.

"All right. But Nuada is the challenger. Let him go first."

"I will, gladly," the older man answered.

He strode boldly forward to the mound. The Riders of the Sidhe opened a way in their ring and he climbed the slope to stand beside the stone. There he stood a moment, looking at it. He felt a faint tremor of doubt run through him. This was his final test. Could he pass it?

"Go ahead, Nuada," Lugh urged, understanding his hesitation. "The power of Danu will not fail her children. I have that fact on the best authority." He glanced aside at Gilla and Aine, and the girl detected just the hint of a wink from this stern warrior.

The disguised Manannan leaned close to Aine and Taillta once again and whispered, "Now we'll see if this thing really works!"

Aine looked at him in shock. "Don't you know?"

He shrugged. "It's never been used for this. Better wish hard, sister, just to be certain."

She held her breath as she watched Nuada pull himself onto the stone, settling on the top.

Almost at once there began a vibration of the ground, as if from some movement far below. It increased, and a grumbling sound began, growing louder, like approaching thunder, moving upward, focusing its power on the knoll, then on the stone itself. A high, clear note sounded from the Lia Fail with the force of a gale wind blasting across a sharp cliff. It was a powerful sound, a triumphant sound, the victory clarion of the earth itself announcing one whose right was to rule over it, proclaiming a true king.

It died away then into a humming that drifted gently away into the morning sky. It left behind an atmosphere hushed with expectation, charged with energy as before a storm breaks. The eyes of every one—de Danann and Fomor alike—were on Nuada.

He looked around him, the last remnant of his old doubts gone, a High-King again in mind and manner. He lowered himself from the stone and stood proudly before his people. Then his eyes came slowly around to rest challengingly on Bres.

"Now you may take your turn!" he offered coldly.

XXX

THE RISING

BRES HAD SENSED the outcome. While attention was focused on Nuada, he had edged away from the de Danann warriors toward the ranks of the Fomor.

"Now, you fool," he had muttered to Streng, "I think you'll agree we have no choice?"

"No," Streng had glumly agreed. "We must use our force to stop this here and now. If we can."

"You still give too much credit to them," Bres had assured him confidently. "That will be the simplest thing to do."

Then Nuada's challenge brought the attention back to him. His response was shouted defiantly.

"Take your kingship, Nuada. I'm happy I no longer have to live with the pretense." He swept his disdainful gaze across the de Dananns. "Yes, I'm half-Fomor in blood, and all in mind! I disavow all relationship with you. You disgust me. You call yourselves people of the mind, of beauty and of peace, but you use your fine sensibilities to cloak your weakness." He looked back to the now High-King. "You are welcome to them, Nuada. It will do you little good. It is too late for them."

"Leave here, Bres," Nuada commanded, striding back from the mound to the center of the court. "This fortress is yours no longer. Leave Tara and take your Fomor 'brothers' with you."

Bres laughed aloud at that.

"Leave here? Me?" he asked, vastly amused. "You don't understand yet, do you? I'm not leaving here." The amusement was suddenly replaced by deadly chill. "You are! But not alive!"

He pulled his sword. At his move, the Fomor all went on guard as well. Their massed force now bristled with glinting weaponry.

"Did you seriously think you could challenge me?" asked Bres, gloatingly. "I don't need to be the king to control you anymore. I have the Fomor to do that. They'll serve as my power in Eire. And the first service that they will perform for me is to destroy you, Nuada, and the rest of your little band of adventurers."

Morrigan stalked forward, her tones crackling with rage.

"The companies serve Nuada now, Bres. If you move against him, you'll face us as well."

"Of course you will," Bres said carelessly and shrugged. "That only means you want to die with them. You haven't enough warriors left to even give us a good fight."

"There are enough de Dananns here to do much more," said Nuada, waving his arm across the massed population of Tara behind him. "Think, Bres. If you choose to have this out here and now, you'll face more than a few score warriors."

"What, do you mean them?" Bres laughed again. "You are mad, Nuada, to rely on them. They are finished."

"You said the same about me," Nuada reminded him.

"And it's still true. If they defy me, they'll only provide me with the excuse to do what I've always wished to do—destroy them all utterly. Now, let's waste no more time." He turned to Streng and ordered curtly, "Seize our new High-King and his comrades and disperse all this rabble. Kill anyone who opposes you."

The Fomor officer shouted the commands to his forces and the massed Fomor started forward, a relentless force, like a single, terrible beast.

Lugh sat unmoving, waiting. His impulse was to charge in, but he recalled Manannan's last admonishment to him: he could not take the lead! He had pointed the way. The de Dananns must take it by their own choice, as he had, or they would never be truly free.

Nuada drew his sword and held the shining blade aloft.

"Now, my people, you will live in fear or you will fight with me!" he called to the gathering, and then he charged for the Fomor, shouting his battle cry.

Picking up the cry, his comrades followed him, joined at once by the de Danann companies led by the Morrigan. And, finally, raising their own cry of renewed courage in a roar, the people of Tara swarmed forward across the open ground to meet the Fomor horde.

They were largely unarmed and much weakened by their years of long abuse. But their awakened pride and anger drove them forward in an angry wave, crashing against the Fomor whose solid mass was jolted by surprise and shock, washed over and shattered by the ferocity of the onslaught.

At once the courtyard was the scene of a wild melee, a writhing mass of bodies battling at close quarters. The unarmed de Dananns fought with bare hands or with weapons wrenched from their enemies. After the years of savage treatment, they took their revenge. The soft and soggy earth was trampled to a mire of mud tinged rusty with blood, heaped with bodies of dying and dead trampled into the ooze by the feet of those struggling above.

The Fomor fought with cruelty and strength, but for once it was their minds that were touched by fear. And the clear, calm, morning air was filled with the sounds of pain, with the smell of fear and death, with the deafening clash of metal on metal.

Morrigan, her own fury now unleashed, flew upon the Fomor, raking them with her swords, tearing through them in search of Bres, to slake her rage in his hot blood. Nuada, flanked by Angus and the Dagda, cut a wide path into the Fomor, leading their fellows in an expanding wedge that split the Fomor forces like the ax of the Dagda slashing through an opponent. Aine, Taillta and Gilla were in the midst of it as well, the clownish figure gleefully committing mayhem on anyone foolish enough to challenge him while the two women, back to back, equalled his carnage with their own longswords.

As the others plunged into the fray, Lugh led his Riders in as well, slashing into a flank of the Fomor mob, throwing them into even greater confusion. The grim silver warriors were frightening enough, but the now desperately battling Fomor also found them unkillable.

Once into the thickest of the fighting, Lugh slid from his horse to fight on foot, laying about him with his Answerer and hewing a path through the Fomor. Suddenly, the enemy dispersed before him, leaving the way open. He realized he was near the central hall, behind a wall of Fomor, and that ahead of him, standing by the doors, was Bres.

Streng had drawn back a portion of his warriors and regrouped them in a densely packed mass before the doors to hold off the de Danann attack. Behind this barricade he had pulled Bres and was now addressing him in desperate terms.

"We're lost!" cried the now-battered officer. "These people you were so certain would not fight are about to kill us all!"

"Perhaps you're right," Bres reluctantly admitted, shaking blood from his sword. "A withdrawal might be more practical now."

"Withdrawal?" Streng repeated in disbelief, looking around. "Where? They've trapped us here."

"There's another way," Bres said cooly. "Come with me!"

He turned and went through the doors into the hall. Streng signaled a pair of burly warriors to come with him and followed Bres in.

Not far away, Lugh watched them disappear, then moved purposefully along the wall after them, unnoticed by the Fomor trying to fight back the attack against their front.

Inside the hall, Bres strode quickly across the floor, Streng hurrying to catch up with him. The vast room was empty, the sounds of the battle raging outside muffled by the heavy walls.

"We'll go up and across the walkway to the parapet," Bres said. "We can cross the outer wall and be away before they notice."

"What about the others?" Streng asked. "Do we just abandon them?"

"Of course!" Bres curtly replied, as if Streng were insane in suggesting anything else. "They're only Eirelanders. They'll insure our escape."

Streng had to admit the ruthless man was right. Their own survival was most important.

But as they started around the central fire-pit, a familiar voice called after them:

"Hold on, Bres!"

They halted and looked back. Lugh stood alone just inside the doors.

"That cursed boy again," Bres rapped out impatiently. "This time I'm going to finish him!"

He started back toward Lugh, but Streng stopped him by gripping one arm.

"No!" the Fomor said urgently. "We can't delay here or we'll be caught!"

"I suppose you're right again," Bres agreed with immense disappointment. "We'll have to go on."

"You two stop him," Streng ordered the accompanying warriors, pointing to Lugh. Then he and Bres hurried on toward the back of the hall.

"Wait!" Lugh called after the escaping Bres. "Come back and face me!"

He started forward, and the two Fomor moved to block him.

"Out of my way!" Lugh said impatiently, and charged directly into them.

The fight was short, fast and brutal. Anger at being thwarted added power to Lugh's attack. The Fomor were much larger, but clumsy and slow in their defense. The whirlwind force that blasted against them could not be stopped. In moments, one had lost a head and the other a sword—with the arm still attached. The wounded Fomor dropped down, clutching the

raw stump to staunch the pulsing spurt of blood. Lugh
shoved him callously out of the way as he headed after Bres at
a run.

Bres and Streng meanwhile had passed the dais and mounted the stairs to the upper gallery.

"Running away from a boy, Bres?" Lugh shouted after him.
"Have you lost all your courage then?"

Bres whirled toward him. A brief surprise showed in the
man's expression as he realized how quickly Lugh had defeated
the warriors. But no note of concern touched his voice.

"You are surely persistent," he said truthfully. "And very,
very lucky."

"Don't let him delay you!" Streng pleaded. "There's no
time!"

"I'll follow you," Lugh promised. "You know that, don't
you? I'll haunt you for so long as I'm alive."

"He's right, Streng," Bres said. "I've really no other choice
but to kill him now." He smiled with malicious pleasure.
"Besides, I want one satisfaction from all of this."

He stepped back from the parapet toward Lugh. The
younger warrior started across the walkway to meet him.
Their weapons came up on guard.

"You made your final error, boy," Bres said smugly. "This
time, there's no one to protect you."

"This time," Lugh boldly replied, "I have a sword of my
own!"

"Best use it, then!" Bres cried and leaped forward, swinging a great downward cut of his weapon with both hands.

With the advantage of surprise and the speed of his move,
he had expected to finish Lugh with a single blow. But Lugh
moved even more quickly, sweeping the bright Answerer up
to easily block the other weapon and knock it aside.

Bres realized that he was facing a formidable opponent. He
drew back and the two tested one another's skills with a series
of preliminary thrusts and blows and feints. Then the battle
began in earnest.

The heavy weapons struck together in a flurry so rapid they
sounded an almost continuous ring. Back and forth along the
walkway they fought, each battling for an advantage but
failing to gain it.

Down below, the combat in the yard was nearly over. The
de Dananns were working out the last of their fury, ruthlessly

annihilating any resisting Fomor. Nuada and his champions moved through the carnage, trying to bring some order. Gilla, looking around him to see if his comrades had all survived, realized for the first time that Lugh was gone.

He called for him.

"I saw him follow Bres into the hall," the Dagda called back. "I was too busy to go after him."

In the relative quiet that had fallen, a sound from above now drew Aine's attention to the walkway. She cried out to the others, pointing up to the fight raging there.

The two men on the walkway were now using every trick and move they had to get an edge. They fought with their fists as well as their swords, used their bodies to slam one another away, kicked out to give or fend off a blow. At times they grappled, locked close together, battering at one another, rocking against the weakening rails of the walkway as they bounced back and forth, making the whole structure sway.

Both men were bloodied now, streaked with small wounds. Both were worn, but they struck at each other with no less determination. Bres, more powerful, more cunning and more desperate, was a deadly opponent. But Lugh's energy, his reflexes, and his stubborn courage were making him a match.

As the friends of the young warrior watched from below, Bres slipped under Lugh's guard and drove him back against the walkway rail, holding him there, trying to push him over the edge. Aine gave a gasp of fear. The Dagda started toward the doorway to the hall. But Gilla stopped the champion with a grip on his arm.

"No!" he said. "This is Lugh's fight!"

Reluctantly, the Dagda nodded and turned his attention back to the battle above.

Lugh broke the hold of Bres and knocked the older warrior back. Again they faced each other, swords up, both breathing hard, taking wary account of one another before making a new move.

Streng stood on the parapet, sword drawn, watching the fight and wondering what to do. He wished he could abandon the arrogant Bres, but he imagined Balor would not approve of such an action. He had thought of helping Bres dispose of Lugh, but had hesitated, afraid that would not be appreciated by the former High-King.

Now, however, he was aware of the attention fixed on them from below. Something had to be done to end this quickly, he determined, and began looking for an opening to finish Lugh.

It came soon. The two combatants drove in close, weapons locking together and pushed up as the two men collided and grappled. They swung around in their struggle, and so focused was the young warrior on his contest with Bres that he was unaware that he had left his back open to Streng.

The Fomor officer crept forward, off the parapet, along the walkway toward Lugh, his sword lifting for a fatal thrust.

"Lugh! Behind you!" Aine cried in desperate warning.

The young man snapped his head around to look and saw the danger, but too late. He couldn't move quickly enough to escape the blade.

Then Streng was knocked backward by the blow of an enormous battle-ax. The wide head of it had struck below his neck and split his chest, throat-to-navel, tearing out through his spine in an explosion of blood. The force of the blow lifted him and tossed him back onto the parapet as if he were a bundle of dried sticks, and he fell brokenly onto the planking.

"A fine throw!" Gilla called to the Dagda.

"Keepin' things even," the man replied. "I hope it's enough."

Above, the distraction had given Bres a chance to act. When Lugh had tried to turn toward the new danger, the ex-king had jerked the young warrior off balance, sending him staggering up the walkway into the rail. Then Bres had run to the body of Streng and grabbed the handle of the ax in his free hand. Now he yanked at the formidable weapon. But it stayed fast in the body.

Lugh started for his opponent again. Bres launched his sword at the young champion to drive him back. While Lugh paused to knock aside the flying weapon, Bres seized the ax handle in both hands and, with a massive effort, wrenched it free.

The huge weapon was a tremendous and unwieldy weight to all but one of the Dagda's size. But once in motion, it was nearly impossible to defend against. Bres brought it up with both hands and launched it in a wide, sideways swing meant to take off Lugh's head.

The young warrior didn't attempt to stop or turn it. Instead, he ducked under it, letting it whoosh over him as he tried to come in at Bres from the side.

But Bres was fighting with the strength of desperation now. He managed to check the swing of the great weapon and sweep it back, with a speed that surprised his adversary. This time Lugh barely had time to dive away as the blade smashed through the wooden railing, shattering it as it slashed through without slowing.

Lugh hit the planking and rolled toward the parapet end. The momentum of the heavy ax spun Bres around to face him. The ex-king brought the weapon up high with a grunt of effort and sent it in a downward cut at Lugh as he started to get up.

Unable to jump from the weapon's path this time, Lugh lifted The Answerer up in both hands in a desperate move to turn the ax away.

He barely succeeded. The ax was deflected, but the weight of the head forced down the blade, ramming it deeply into the timber flooring and pinning it there.

Lugh yanked on its hilt to pull it free, but without budging it. He looked up to Bres who stood over him, holding the sword down with his weight on the ax. The ex-king grinned at his opponent, then lashed out with a savage kick that caught Lugh solidly in the side of the head, flinging him back.

The young warrior toppled heavily onto the parapet, his back slamming against the outer wall. Dazed, he lay beside the split carcass of Streng. Bres pulled the great ax up once again and swept it high over his head. With a triumphant laugh he started toward Lugh for the final blow.

The groggy youth lay helpless, until his eye fell on the sword of Streng that lay beside the body, drenched in blood. He stretched forward, gripped the hilt, and lifted the weapon in what he assumed would be a vain gesture of defense.

Bres saw the weapon rise, but too late to check himself. As the slender blade drove through his side, he twisted sideways, tearing the weapon from Lugh's grasp. He staggered into the outer wall, the heavy ax plunging over the side and dragging him after it.

Bres released the handle and flailed out wildly for a grip on the timbers as he toppled over. It was a futile move. He fell, landing heavily on the ground below the wall and tumbling further down the steep slope.

Still dazed, Lugh climbed unsteadily to his feet. He moved to the wall and looked over. There, on the slope far below him, the motionless figure of the former High-King lay sprawled, covered in earth and blood, impaled on the now broken sword of Streng.

A cheer went up from the watching crowd as they saw Lugh victorious. Aine, followed by Gilla, rushed into the hall and up to meet him as he wearily came back across the walkway, retrieving The Answerer on his way. Her usual restraint forgotten in her relief, Aine threw her arms about him and kissed him soundly and unabashedly. Gilla watched, grinning his approval. The kiss did a great deal toward revitalizing Lugh. He threw an arm about both of them and, together, they went down through the hall to the main doors.

There they were met by the exultant de Dananns, led by their restored High-King.

Nuada greeted Lugh warmly as he came out, speaking loudly to be heard above the happy tumult.

"You did it, lad," he said. "You've freed us of Bres."

"You all did it," Lugh said, gesturing around at the de Dananns. "Don't ever forget. It was your choice."

The Dagda pushed through the throng to them. He clutched his battle-ax again in his hands, but his broad face was dark with some concern.

"What is it?" Lugh asked, puzzled.

"It's Bres," the Dagda told them. "I just went out to fetch my ax and bring that traitor's head back here to Lugh." He gazed around him at his comrades and his eyes showed his disbelief. "He was gone!"

"But, how could he be gone?" the amazed young warrior asked. "He must have been dead!"

The Dagda shook his head. "Don't be so certain," he said heavily. "I know him well. He is not such an easy one to kill."

"Search the countryside," Nuada ordered his companies. "If he is alive, I'd not like to see him get away from us!"

XXXI

A BEGINNING

THE VAST HEAD swiveled slowly around, bringing the red gaze from the distant haze of Eire back to the Tower room.

The doors had opened to admit a man who shuffled painfully forward. He crossed the floor to stand before the dark figure, one hand pressed to the wound in his bound side, meeting the ruby eye with a dark, malignant stare.

"I am surprised to see you still alive, Bres," the metallic voice said.

"The de Dananns themselves taught me the healing arts when I was a boy," he answered. "I learned them from that old fool Diancecht. I've survived many wounds as deadly as this."

"So, you survived. But still, you failed," Balor accused.

"It was your warriors who failed," Bres countered boldly. "Those monstrosities that cannot even be called beasts, the ones you said could control Eire, couldn't even put down a rebellion by a starving rabble. If you mean to stop this before it spreads, you will have to give me more help, Balor."

"The Prophecy!" the black giant rumbled. The eye swung back again to the windows and the land that lay on the curve of the horizon. The voice took on a human note of wonder as the being softly added, as if to himself: "I wonder if it can be stopped now."

In Tara's hall, the festivities were at their height. There was a truly joyful feel and sound to the night that had long been missing.

Some faces, however, were missing. The members of the court who had supported Bres had wisely decided to remove themselves from sight, before the vengeful fellow citizens made their removal a bit more permanent.

But there were bright faces enough to fill the gaps. The

exiled artists and scholars and druids were there. Tara's finest bards and harpers had returned, singing new ballads of their victory. The restored High-King and his loyal champions were back where they belonged, at the table on the great hall's dais. With them sat Taillta, enjoying the food and drink and talk. With her years of hardship ended, the marks of care which had so aged her had vanished. She seemed a young woman again, filled with life, easily captivating the warriors around her.

Gilla Decaire was also enjoying himself immensely, performing his clownish tricks to a laughing audience who showered him with gifts of food and drink so lavishly that even his amazing cloak was finally stuffed.

From the gallery, Aine and Lugh watched his antics with a special happiness. Then, both feeling a need for solitude, they left the hall, crossing the walkway to the outer parapet. They stopped there to look down at the town, glowing in the rays of the late afternoon sun.

It was a soft, quiet evening, and further sounds of merriment, of music and laughter, drifted up to them from the houses below. It warmed Lugh, as he had once been warmed by the loving Firbolgs who had raised him. And he realized that he had found a home again.

"It's quite marvelous what the de Dananns have done these past few days," Aine said. "Cleaning, rebuilding... why, all of Tara has come back to life!"

"As all Eire will do, once the Fomor have been chased from it completely," Lugh added.

She noted the determination in his voice.

"And you will be a part of that, won't you?" she asked softly.

He looked at her. His face was very stern. His tones were low and sure and very much those of a veteran warrior.

"I must be. You know that. These are my people now."

"Of course," she agreed readily, but he didn't see the faint regret that showed for a moment in her eyes.

"And what about you?" he asked, trying not to sound concerned. "Your task is ended here. Will you go back to your isle?"

She looked up at him, her shining eyes holding his thoughtfully while he waited, trying to maintain his gravity.

Finally, she shook her head.

"I don't think I'll go back. Manannan will surely stay, and so will I." She smiled. "Besides, I've gotten used to sharing sunsets with you." She paused, looking searchingly at him, then added hopefully: "As long as you don't mind, of course."

His face lit with pleasure and once more he was only the boy Lugh. "I'd mind anything else!" He put his hands on her shoulders lightly. "And maybe someday there will be time for just the two of us."

She moved in close to him and they turned, arms around one another, to watch the setting sun. It sank down past the black horizon as if a lid were closing slowly over a blazing, crimson eye.

ABOUT THE AUTHOR

Kenneth C. Flint is a graduate of the University of Nebraska with a Masters Degree in English Literature. For several years he taught in the Department of Humanities at the University of Nebraska at Omaha. Presently he is Chairman of English for the Plattsmouth Community Schools (a system in a suburban community of Omaha).

In addition to teaching, he has worked as a free-lance writer. He has produced articles and short stories for various markets and has written screenplays for some Omaha-based film companies.

Mr. Flint became interested in Celtic mythology in graduate school, where he saw a great source of material in this long neglected area of western literature. Since then he has spent much time researching in England and Ireland and developing works of fantasy that would interest modern readers.

He is the author of one previous novel, A STORM UPON ULSTER. His next novel, CHAMPIONS OF THE SIDHE, will be published by Bantam in the winter of '84/'85.

SPECIAL MONEY SAVING OFFER

Now you can have an up-to-date listing of Bantam's hundreds of titles plus take advantage of our unique and exciting bonus book offer. A special offer which gives you the opportunity to purchase a Bantam book for only 50¢. Here's how!

By ordering any five books at the regular price per order, you can also choose any other single book listed (up to a $4.95 value) for just 50¢. Some restrictions do apply, but for further details why not send for Bantam's listing of titles today!

Just send us your name and address plus 50¢ to defray the postage and handling costs.

FANTASY AND SCIENCE FICTION FAVORITES

Bantam brings you the recognized classics as well as the current favorites in fantasy and science fiction. Here you will find the most recent titles by the most respected authors in the genre.

☐	25260	THE BOOK OF KELLS R. A. MacAvoy	$3.50
☐	25122	THE CHRISTENING QUEST	$2.95
		Elizabeth Scarborough	
☐	24370	RAPHAEL R. A. MacAvoy	$2.75
☐	24169	WINTERMIND Parke Godwin, Marvin Kaye	$2.75
☐	23944	THE DEEP John Crowley	$2.95
☐	23853	THE SHATTERED STARS Richard McEnroe	$2.95
☐	23575	DAMIANO R. A. MacAvoy	$2.75
☐	25403	TEA WITH THE BLACK DRAGON R. A. MacAvoy	$2.95
☐	23365	THE SHUTTLE PEOPLE George Bishop	$2.95
☐	24441	THE HAREM OF AMAN AKBAR	$2.95
		Elizabeth Scarborough	
☐	20780	STARWORLD Harry Harrison	$2.50
☐	22939	THE UNICORN CREED Elizabeth Scarborough	$3.50
☐	23120	THE MACHINERIES OF JOY Ray Bradbury	$2.75
☐	22666	THE GREY MANE OF MORNING Joy Chant	$3.50
☐	25097	LORD VALENTINE'S CASTLE Robert Silverberg	$3.95
☐	20870	JEM Frederik Pohl	$2.95
☐	23460	DRAGONSONG Anne McCaffrey	$2.95
☐	24862	THE ADVENTURES OF TERRA TARKINGTON	$2.95
		Sharon Webb	
☐	23666	EARTHCHILD Sharon Webb	$2.50
☐	24102	DAMIANO'S LUTE R. A. MacAvoy	$2.75
☐	24417	THE GATES OF HEAVEN Paul Preuss	$2.50

<u>Prices and availability subject to change without notice.</u>

Buy them at your local bookstore or use this handy coupon for ordering: